W

MW00513087

WIDE OPEN

Nicola Barker

THE ECCO PRESS

Copyright © 1998 by Nicola Barker
All rights reserved

THE ECCO PRESS
100 West Broad Street
Hopewell, New Jersey 08525

Library of Congress Cataloging-in-Publication Data

Barker, Nicola, 1966–
    Wide Open / Nicola Barker. — 1st ed.
        p.   cm.
    ISBN 0-88001-632-9
    I. Title.
PR6052.A64876W54   1998
823'.914—dc21   98-14083
                                                            CIP

9 8 7 6 5 4 3 2 1

FIRST EDITION 1998

I dreamed I saw you dead in a place by the water.
A ravaged place.
All flat and empty and wide open.

1

Each day Ronny saw the same man waving. The man stood in the middle of a bridge, at its very centre point, but always looking outwards, facing away from London, never towards it. Ronny drove under that bridge in a borrowed car, a Volvo (the big bumpers reassured him), and into London along the A2 for three consecutive weeks. Every day, no matter what the time – he was working shifts, and by no means regular ones – the man stood on the bridge, waving.

He didn't wave randomly. He picked out a car as a smudge on the horizon and then focused on that car alone, until it had passed from sight, until it had driven right under him. Until it had gone. Then he'd choose another car and the whole process would start over.

Ronny noticed that the man preferred white cars and yellow cars, that he never waved at red cars. Ronny's car was green. He was waved at sometimes, but infrequently. He didn't wave back.

Some days it rained. It was the tail end of summer. It was the beginning of winter. It was autumn, formally, but Ronny hated gradations. It wasn't summer. Summer had gone. It wasn't winter. Winter was frosty, traditionally, and it was nowhere near cold enough for frost yet. It was simply a wet time. The whole earth was sodden and weighted and clotted and terrible. It was raining. Always raining. But the man stood on the bridge and he waved, nonetheless.

On the last day, the final day of his three-week working stint, Ronny looked out for the man but saw that he was not waving. He was there, sure enough, but he was crouched over, hanging, it seemed, across the bar of the bridge. What was he thinking of? What was he doing? Ronny scowled and tried to keep his eyes on the road.

He didn't want to stare, but his eyes kept shifting from the road to the bridge, from the road to the bridge. He indicated and then swung into the inside lane. He slowed down, inadvertently. A truck honked and jolted him out of his eye-high reverie.

He passed under the bridge and then out the other side. He checked his rear-view mirror. He couldn't see anything. Why should he? He was on the wrong side now. He slowed down even further. Three cars overtook him. His foot touched the brake.

What was he doing? He didn't want to stop but he found himself stopping. He pulled into the hard shoulder. He turned off the engine, unfastened his seatbelt, stepped out of the car, slammed the door shut behind him but didn't pause to lock it. Instead he started off towards the bridge at a lively pace. His keys bumped and jangled against his thigh in his pocket.

He reached the embankment, drew breath for a moment and then began to climb. It was steep. The soil was damp. His shoes – white shoes – were muddied. He cursed.

Eventually he made it to the top. He clambered over the fence, crossed the road, and was finally able to see the waver up close. He felt an unexpected surge of gratification, as though this visual intimacy was something he'd longed for, only he hadn't quite realized it.

At first glance the waver seemed fairly unexceptional. He had a beard and longish, tangled brown hair. He was pale. His clothes were shabby. He'd been crying.

Ronny drew closer. He stamped the mud off his shoes. 'Is anything the matter?'

The man was bent double, was curled up like a dirty bandage, but he grew and grew like Jack's beanstalk when Ronny spoke to him. He seemed to unfold, to unwind to his full height, which was considerable. Tall, Ronny thought, and thin. Ronny was thin too, but he felt much smaller.

'Is something wrong?'

2

The man was standing now, and Ronny saw that he had not in fact been squatting before but sitting, on a small battered-looking cardboard box. He had his left hand cupped, and in his curved palm he held something.

'What is that?'

The man answered, his voice nearly extinguished by the roar of the traffic below, 'Come and see.'

Ronny drew closer still. He stared into the man's hand. He inhaled sharply. The man's fingers were shiny with scar tissue, but only on their tips, where they shone as smooth as wax, as pale as lard. Nestled in the centre of these strange fingers was a dirty palm. In the palm was a wasp.

'A wasp,' Ronny said softly. 'What's wrong with it?'

'It was in a puddle. I should have left it but I saw it was still moving so I picked it up. I believed I could save it.'

Ronny stared at the wasp more fixedly. It was still alive. It moved, but only slightly. It seemed to be arching itself, the dainty waist between its black thorax and striped abdomen virtually snapping in two.

'It's been writhing,' the man said, his voice – Ronny felt – ridiculously emotional.

'It's been in so much *pain*.'

Ronny adjusted the blue woollen hat he was wearing. He pulled it low over his eyebrows. He cleared his throat, cautiously. 'I don't think wasps feel pain,' he said, anticipating a strong reaction.

The man glanced up, clearly indignant, his eyes, Ronny noticed, a wild cess-pit green, his cheeks drawn and hollow. 'How can you *know* that?'

'I don't. I'm just guessing.'

'Well you're wrong. Look properly for a second and then try and tell me that it feels nothing.'

Ronny tried his best to look properly. The wasp stirred, only slightly, but it seemed to be shuddering. Its movements were small yet jagged and loose and horrible.

'It'll die in a minute,' Ronny muttered, vaguely disquieted, withdrawing again and wishing he could ask the man why it

3

was that he waved, but he didn't because he fancied – quite correctly – that his timing might be off-kilter. The man continued to focus on the wasp .

Ronny inspected his watch. It was getting late.

'I'll be off then.'

The man was very quiet, seemed barely to breathe he was so intent on his vigil. Eventually he said, 'I think he's finally going.'

Ronny nodded and turned to leave. This was a private moment. He had no wish to intrude. He took several steps and then . . .

'My *God*!'

He spun around, his heart racing. 'What?'

'The wasp!'

Ronny smiled weakly at his own faint-heartedness, but he stepped up again with no visible signs of resentment.

'See?'

The man showed Ronny his hand. Ronny looked. The wasp was still. It was dead.

'It's dead.'

The man grunted, unimpressed. 'I know it's dead. But did you see the sting?'

'The sting?'

The man pointed. 'When it died it curled up, incredibly tightly, and then the sting came shooting out from the back there, the whole sting was revealed in that final moment.'

Ronny felt absurd but he bent forward anyway. Sure enough, he saw the sting.

'I see it.'

'There's a wonderful logic to it sliding out like that,' the man said, almost smiling. Ronny tilted his head. 'What do you mean?'

'He's at rest. He's surrendered. He's finally given up his weapon.'

Ronny considered this for a while and then said, 'No. I don't see it that way at all.'

The man looked up. 'You don't? So how do you see it?'

'Well . . .' Ronny scratched his neck. 'He's a warrior. His weapon is drawn even in death. *Especially* in death. That's the whole point of a wasp. He's the kamikaze pilot of the insect world.'

The man smiled at this, he stared at Ronny intently, at his neat edges, his apparent cleanliness, his bright, pale face. Eventually he said, 'That's very funny.'

Ronny rubbed his nose, modestly.

'But all the same . . .' the man continued, 'it's not actually true. Only bees die when they sting. Wasps work differently. They're tougher. He's given up his weapon. That's plainly how it is.'

Ronny didn't agree but he merely shrugged. He found it hard to commit himself to disagreements.

The man was silent for a while. Ronny studied him. He seemed very young but his face was not a very young face. It was lined, vertically, and not in the places normal faces creased and wrinkled. It was as though he'd only just woken up from a hard sleep but his face hadn't shaken it, hadn't hurled off its sheets and its blankets yet to get on with the business of living.

He seemed ludicrously pliant and tractable, but singular. He seemed . . . Ronny shuddered at the thought . . . he seemed wide, wide open. But you couldn't survive that way. Not in this world. Not for long. Ronny knew it.

In fact he prided himself on being shut right up. Like an oyster. Like a tomb. Like a beach-hut in winter; all bolted, all boarded. Like the bright lips of an old wound. Resolutely sealed.

'Well, I think I'll be going,' he said finally, swallowing down his unease and then feeling it bob back up in his throat like a ballcock.

The man glanced at Ronny, but only quickly, as though he could barely stand to drag his eyes away from the dead wasp. 'Today's been worthwhile after all,' he muttered. 'You know? Just to get to see the wasp and the sting and everything.'

Ronny thought the man must be deranged but he nodded anyway.

'Do you need another look before I bury him?'

'Need?' Ronny smiled. 'No, I don't think so.'

The man sighed. 'He feels so hollow and light now that the life has gone. Before he had a kind of weight. Some gravity. But not any more.'

Ronny turned to go.

The man spoke again, a parting shot, it seemed, because as he spoke he also turned. 'I'm Ronny.'

Ronny froze.

'Ronny?'

The other Ronny stopped turning.

'What?'

Ronny pointed to himself.

'*I'm* Ronny too.'

They both paused.

'Uh . . . actually,' Ronny said, 'I'm Ronald. How about you?'

The other Ronny shrugged, 'I don't know.'

'We're *The Two Ronnies*.'

The other Ronny didn't get it. 'What?'

'Like in the comedy show.'

'What comedy show?'

'You don't remember *The Two Ronnies*? The little one with glasses and the bigger, fatter one?'

The other Ronny shook his head. 'No.'

'Oh. I thought everybody knew about them.'

The other Ronny pointed at the wasp and said, 'I think I'd better bury him.' He started walking towards the edge of the bridge. He walked strangely. Ronny thought that this was because there was something wrong with his legs but then he realized that his shoes were several sizes too large. They were white shoes.

'Excuse me . . .'

The other Ronny stopped walking. 'What?'

'We're wearing the same shoes.'

The other Ronny peered down at his shoes. 'These aren't my shoes.'

'Not yours? Then whose are they?'

'I don't know. I must've picked them up somewhere.'

Ronny drew closer to the other Ronny. 'You know, it's a rare thing to see someone in white shoes. And those shoes are special. They're the kind I wear for work.'

The other Ronny frowned and looked down at his shoes a second time. 'Maybe they are your shoes.'

Ronny squinted at this, baffled. 'Pardon?'

'I got them in Lost Property. Maybe you lost them and I picked them up. I'm called Ronny. So are you. Maybe the person on the desk got us confused.'

'Lost Property?'

'On the Underground. The tube. At Baker Street.'

Ronny let this sink in for a few seconds and then he said softly, 'My brother works there.'

The other Ronny was clearly impressed. 'Really? In the office?'

'Yes.'

'What's he look like?'

'Uh . . . reddish hair. Blue eyes. Quite short.'

The other Ronny grinned. 'I know him.'

'You're kidding!'

'Nope. That's Nathan. I know him. I go in there all the time. Ever since I was a kid I've been going in there.'

'What for?

'I keep losing stuff.'

'When was the last time you saw him?'

The other Ronny bit his lip. 'Nathan? Uh . . . a month.'

'How did he look?'

'I think he looked fine.'

Ronny was clearly delighted, but he spoke with an element of restraint. 'Well that's good then.'

'So . . .' the other Ronny seemed genuinely interested, 'when was the last time you saw him?'

'Ten years ago.'

The other Ronny mulled this over for a while and then said, 'I've got a whole family somewhere that I've never even met. Brothers and sisters. All lost.'

Ronny didn't want to appear competitive so he laboriously adjusted his collar in an attempt to distance himself. 'That's a great pity,' he said finally, 'luckily I have no sisters.'

The other Ronny looked serious. 'Yes, that is a relief.'

'It is?'

Ronny was bemused. The other Ronny gazed up at the sky. It had begun to rain again. He turned his attention back to Ronny. 'There's this famous story about a man who meets someone purely by accident but the more they find out about each other the more they realize that they have things in common until finally they realize that they are the same person. I don't know who wrote the story.'

Ronny took a deep breath. 'It wasn't a story. It was a play. It's by Ionesco. And what happens is that the two men realize that they have the same life but that they are in fact different people.'

'Oh. Right.'

The other Ronny suppressed a grimace. He was clearly dissatisfied with this piece of clarification.

'Which makes the whole thing even more absurd.' Ronny added, as an afterthought, 'anyway . . .' He pulled off his hat, 'we don't look alike.'

Without his hat Ronny resembled a king prawn, fully processed; legs gone, shell gone, ready for serving, soft and pink and pale and smooth. Pure and unadorned.

His was a gentle face, a complex mixture of blankness and fullness. He was plain as a boiled sweet, but his eyes were deep, complex and dark-ringed, and his lashless lids were swollen. His irises were the mellow, golden brown of raw cane sugar.

'You've got no hair.'

'No.'

'Are you ill?'

'Alopecia.'

It began raining harder. Ronny put his hat back on again. The other Ronny hunched up his shoulders to keep the rain from dripping down his neck. 'Did you get here by car?'

Ronny nodded. 'Green Volvo. I parked on the hard shoulder.'

'That's illegal.'

'Yes.'

'Unless you broke down.'

'No. The car's fine. I stopped because I thought you might be intending to jump.'

'Me?' The other Ronny looked flabbergasted. 'From this bridge?'

Ronny felt embarrassed. To hide it he said quickly, 'I'm on my way to work. I'm in Tottenham for a while.'

The other Ronny didn't seem to register.

'So . . .' Ronny struggled, 'uh . . . what's in the box then?'

'The box?' The other Ronny looked down. 'This box?'

'Yes.'

The box was approximately a foot and a half square and firmly sealed with strong brown tape.

The other Ronny paused and then smiled. 'My soul.'

'Your soul?' Ronny didn't like this kind of talk. He didn't like talk of souls.

Ronny smiled even wider. 'I'm kidding.'

Then he added softly, without prompting and without feeling, 'I used to live on Claremont Road. In a squat. Now it's gone. They built a link road over it. So I decided to give myself up to the road. To many roads. And now I'm on the motorway. I'm trying to find out what I can get back from it. I've been waving from here for three weeks.'

Ronny was pleased to have had his first question answered at last. By way of recompense he said, 'I live on the Isle of Sheppey. By the sea. Not the sea, really, the channel.'

The other Ronny nodded. 'Yes, Sheppey.'

'You know it?' Ronny strained to think of reasons why a person would go to Sheppey.

'Did you pass through to catch the ferry?'

'No.'

'Are you a keen birdwatcher?'

'No.'

He paused for a moment. 'Were you in prison there?'

The other Ronny smiled and said, 'I know someone who lives there.'

Ronny checked his watch. 'I'd better be off.'

He proffered the other Ronny his hand to shake. He wanted to seal this interlude, formally. He was pleased with it but he wanted it contained.

The other Ronny couldn't shake his hand.

'I can't shake your hand,' he said gently, 'I'm still holding the wasp.'

'So you're left-handed,' Ronny said, 'like me.'

'No. I'm right-handed, it's just that I do everything with my left hand.'

'Why?'

'It's one of my projects.'

Ronny was perplexed. He transformed his attempted shake into a little wave. 'Well, it was nice to meet you.'

'Yes.'

He headed over towards the embankment. He didn't turn around again. If he had, he would have seen the other Ronny go and bury his wasp in the soil at the edge of the bridge and then construct, one-handed and with considerable difficulty, a small marker out of a lolly stick and a piece of dried grass. Next he would have seen him walk back to the centre of the bridge and wash his hands in a puddle.

When he'd completed his tasks, however, instead of returning to his original post, the other Ronny moved to the opposite side of the bridge, the side facing into London, and stood and gazed down the hard shoulder. He saw Ronny climb into his green Volvo, indicate, pull off.

He felt an impulse to wave but defeated it. Instead he touched the wrist of his right hand with his left hand as if expecting to find something there, but the wrist was bare. He smiled gently, peered over his shoulder towards the cardboard box, cleared his throat and then shoved his cold wet fingers deep into his pockets.

2

Laura had imagined herself to be in love with Nathan for the first three years of her five-year tenure in Lost Property. Truly in love. A dizzy, silly, confusing, confounding love. Love like a wave (foam tipped), a wall (straight up and down, solid, well-built), like a wheel (no beginning, no end), like a whale.

A giant love, in other words. A great big whopper of a love. Love. Secret and hairy and cinnamon-flavoured. A hot, sharp-shooting sherbert love. A mishy-mushy, hishy-hushy, splishy-sploshy kind of love.

But the love had been unreciprocated and now she couldn't understand how she had felt it or what it had consisted of, how it had looked or tasted or smelled.

It had been lost, her love, it had been pushed into a file, into a drawer, under a table, into an old suitcase. It had fallen between the folds of a badly closed umbrella. Her love had become another piece of lost property, floating around the office, no one seeing it or caring about it, no one to claim it.

They went out for a drink together, twice, after work. Nathan liked her, clearly, but not in that way. Not enough. Then she found out that he was seeing someone else. A social worker called Margery. She thought Margery such an antiquated name. She thought Margery must be sixty years old with blue hair and a beard. But Margery actually looked like Glenda Jackson. Striking, short-haired and with teeth that needed containing, that needed a brace.

Nathan never mentioned Margery at work. Thank God. And so Laura, rejected Laura, stupid Laura, blonde-haired, green-eyed, snub-nosed little Laura had to force herself to be nice to him. And in the moist dankness of that niceness a worm of

11

hatred unravelled itself. It slid about. It sniffed, blindly, in Nathan's direction. It was soft and vile and slightly, very slightly, ever so, ever so slightly *whiffy*.

The worm turned. The love withered. And left behind in its stead were only suds and offal and litter and a nasty, dirty bath ring which encircled Laura's heart and made all her deepest, sweetest sensations of yesteryear seem like something empty and ugly and pathetic.

Her love was a glob of phlegm on life's high street. It was slippery and slimy and not especially useful. Her love was cancelled. It was all washed out. It was over. Over. Over.

Laura wanted to scorn Nathan, to reject and rebuff, but she was a sensible woman and she knew that he didn't even have the first idea about all the things she'd been feeling, so what was the point?

Instead she made an effort to be nice. A huge effort. If she offered to make her workmates tea she'd ask Nathan first whether he fancied a cup. She always wrote his name at the beginning of the postcards she sent to the office from holidays abroad. She always remembered the date of his birthday. 12 November. Scorpio. She always did a collection. She always saved the hazelnut whirl for him when someone brought chocolates to work. That was his favourite chocolate. In fact, she made all the silly, goofy gestures she'd never made before, when she'd really, truly loved him.

And Nathan always took the hazelnut whirl with good grace. It was his least favourite chocolate but Laura seemed to get pleasure from giving it to him. So he took it.

Did he know how she'd loved him? He didn't think about it. His mind was elsewhere. Sometimes he felt a vague sense of unease when she was near him, when she smiled at him – too brightly – or when she came over especially just to say goodnight.

On these occasions he felt like she was overcompensating – which she was – and although he didn't know what she was overcompensating for, he imagined that it was for something secret and sad and untoward.

He was right. That's just how it was. Three years of dreams. Three years of watching and waiting, of apprehending and misapprehending. All that time wasted. All that time.

He was a softie. Sometimes he cried over the forgotten things. The special things that he kept in the special places. The bangles with loving inscriptions, the tufts of hair in golden lockets, the small dinners in plastic bags. Meals for one, and the one had forgotten them.

Sometimes he came into work early to walk around and feel the forgotten things, to try and remember them. At night he listed forgotten things in his dreams. He lovingly dwelt on the eight hundred and forty-seven black umbrellas, the fifteen hundred and sixty-two single gloves, the books, the pairs of glasses, the knick-knacks, the scarves, the hats. Unclaimed. Everything. All forgotten.

Laura caught him once, after hours, in the storeroom, huddled in a corner, poring over something. She drew close and then softly spoke his name.

'Nathan?'

He sprang up, knocking pictures to the floor, a pile of photographs – polaroids mainly, but some others too, black and white photos. She knelt down to help him retrieve them.

'Isn't it funny,' she asked gently, 'the things people leave behind?'

And in her hands she saw photographs of a little boy with brown eyes and a mop of hair, naked. And there was something wrong with the photos.

'It is strange,' Nathan muttered, his face reddening. 'It is strange.'

And so it was.

'Hello?'

Laura looked up, trying to make eye-contact with the next customer in a long line. It was Friday, a busy day, usually. She focused on a tall man with a beard and dark hair. He was holding a large cardboard box and a white form that he'd just filled in.

'Who's next?'

She waved at him. The man hesitated and then came over. He put the box down on the floor beside him. 'The thing is,' he said, 'I was hoping to speak to . . .'

He pointed towards Nathan who was in the furthest cubicle, collecting the fee and giving receipts.

'You have to see me first.'

Laura put out her hand to take the man's form. He had terrible writing. She stared at it for a while.

'You've lost a watch?'

He nodded.

'When did you lose it?'

The man felt his right wrist with his left hand. 'Uh . . . very recently.'

'Okay. Fine. Hold on a second.'

Laura stood up and went over to the computer. She keyed in the relevant details. Nothing.

She returned to the counter. 'I'm sorry. There's nothing on file at the moment. But don't lose heart. It might be a few days before it's finally handed in. Can you give me any extra details about the watch?'

The man shook his head.

'Make?'

He shook his head.

'How old was it?'

'Old.'

'Was it valuable?'

'I don't think so.'

'Well perhaps you could draw an illustration of the face so that if it's handed in we might have some means of recognizing it.'

The man tried to oblige her. With his left hand he drew a traditional clock face with all the numbers. Laura couldn't stop herself from smiling.

'You've got a lovely smile,' the man said.

She floundered. He looked straight into her eyes. 'I like the way that you said don't lose heart before. I loved that. '

14

Then he paused. 'I'm sorry,' he scratched his cheek, 'I didn't mean to embarrass you.'

'I'm not embarrassed.'

But she was. There was something about his salad-green eyes that disgusted her. Something not right. An emptiness. He was like an old sandwich with curling edges, left on a plate at a pointless leaving party which nobody wished to attend.

She handed him back his form and spoke rather abruptly. 'It's a two pound fee. You pay at the counter.'

'Thank you.' The man nodded, took the form, bent down to retrieve his box, then staggered over towards Nathan's cubicle. He had a funny walk, Laura observed. Her next customer arrived and passed over his slip. She took it, but her eyes were focused, with some disquiet, on Nathan and on the man.

Nathan had been thinking about his lunch. His stomach had been growling. He checked his watch. Someone handed him a slip.

'That'll be two pounds, please.'

He looked up. His jaw went slack.

'It's me,' the other Ronny said, 'like a bad coin. Back again.'

Nathan snapped up his jaw and struggled to contain his surprise. 'You shouldn't have come back,' he said quietly, 'not so soon. Things are too complicated.'

'Why?' the other Ronny looked confounded, 'Why are things complicated?'

Nathan cleared his throat. 'I'll have to tell Margery.'

'Margery who?'

Nathan passed his hand in front of his eyes. 'Don't kid around with me, James.'

'No. Not James. I'm Ronny. Remember? Call me Ronny.'

Nathan shifted on his stool. 'Don't be stupid . . .' he was virtually whispering now, 'we've already had this conversation.'

The other Ronny smiled. His teeth were immaculate. 'I'm Ronny,' he said softly. 'You gave me his shoes.'

'What?' Nathan looked mortified.

'His shoes. You gave them to me. Three weeks ago.'

Nathan put his hand to his face. His cheeks were hot. He

looked around, vaguely panicked. He caught Laura's eye. His blush went deeper.

'They weren't his shoes. You have no reason to think that they were. Anyway, I told you quite clearly last time you came here that if you returned then I would have to call Margery. I made a promise.'

The other Ronny nodded. He obviously remembered. 'You did tell me that last time, but then you went straight ahead and gave me his shoes. His white shoes.'

There was no hint of malice in the other Ronny's voice. Nathan made his hands into fists on his lap. He knew that there was never malice. Not ever. He took a deep breath. 'I covered up for you before. Not again. And they weren't his shoes. They're your shoes.'

'He told me they were his shoes. He said he wore them for work. He's shorter than me but his feet are larger than mine. I have very small feet.'

Nathan inspected the other Ronny's form.

'You want a watch?'

'Yes. I believe I lost one.'

'Here . . .'

Nathan began to unfasten the strap to his own watch. The other Ronny stared, unblinking. 'He said he hadn't seen you in over ten years. He's got alopecia.'

Nathan unfastened the watch and held it out in the palm of his hand. It was a gold watch, an old watch.

'He was driving a green Volvo.'

'Take the watch.'

Nathan proffered the watch. The other Ronny took it.

'It's gold.'

'Yes.'

'It must be worth a lot.'

'It's mine. I want you to have it.'

Nathan glanced up and over towards Laura. She was momentarily occupied.

'You'd better go.'

'You don't believe me, do you?' The other Ronny was frowning. 'You don't believe I actually met him.'

Nathan shook his head. 'No.'

'Maybe I dreamed it.'

Nathan shrugged. 'Maybe.'

'Thanks for the watch.'

The other Ronny smiled again. He took a step backwards. He'd deposited his cardboard box on Nathan's counter. Nathan scrutinized the box.

'What is this?'

'Nothing. Look after it for me. Try not to open it.'

Nathan stood up and touched the box. 'What's inside?'

'Everything.'

Nathan scowled. 'Don't be stupid.'

The other Ronny turned to leave. Nathan couldn't stop himself.

'Where will you go?' he asked.

The other Ronny scratched his nose. 'Manchester.'

'Why Manchester?'

He just shrugged.

Nathan took a deep breath, then expelled it nervously. He wished he hadn't asked. Now he'd be obliged to tell Margery where the other Ronny was, if he was going to be honest. And he wanted to be.

'Thanks.'

The other Ronny limped out. Nathan snatched up his form, screwed it into a ball and pushed it into his jacket pocket. Then he picked up the box – it was heavy – deserted his post, walked into the men's toilets, dumped it down next to the latrines, walked a few steps, rested both his palms on the sink, stared at himself in the mirror and retched. He retched again but nothing came out. Just air. Just gas.

A retch, he thought, is like a dry fuck.

Oh Christ. Oh *Christ*. Where did that come from?

3

'The water's flat and brown. The sand's made of shells. It's been raped by those whelk farmers. The sea, I mean. Raped by those fucking seafood fishermen.'

Lily pointed towards the sea. The man she spoke to was fat and smelled of fish, but he had a good tan and a big prick. He was on his way to the beach.

Lily sat astride her mountain bike. She was seventeen. She was conducting her own little war, but she didn't know what she was fighting about, not yet, at least. She had widely spaced eyes. At school they'd called her Miss Piggy, because of her strange eyes and because her parents ran a farm. They kept wild boar. Although, as Lily often observed, wild boar actually had eyes that were quite extraordinarily close together.

Lily had wide eyes and a flat nose and a gap between her front teeth. It was as though her face had hardly bothered fitting together. But the skin had been persistent. It had stretched and stretched until it finally joined up, until it met in the middle. It had touched bases. It was one of those faces.

Lily pointed. 'That's the Swale. It's a nature reserve.'

'I know.'

The man looked uncomfortable. He made as if to surreptitiously cover over his genitals with his hands. Lily noticed. 'You've nothing there that I haven't seen countless times before.'

He grimaced.

She rubbed her arms. 'Fuck, it's cold. You must be freezing.'

'I'm just going in for a quick dip.'

'Like I was saying,' Lily continued, ignoring his response, 'that's the Swale, and that there's the Blockhouse. Right over there, beyond where you can see is the Ferry Inn and the church. Harty church.'

'I know.'

Lily scowled. 'Would you stop saying "I know" all the time?'

'But I do know. I'm renting one of the prefabs. I'm living in Sheppey now.'

'Yeah, well, what you don't know, apparently,' Lily said, smiling, 'is that I can report you to the police for walking down this road naked.'

The man, under considerable duress, tried his best to hold his own. 'That's my prefab,' he said bullishly, 'I mean I'm renting it. So this here is the front of my house. And that . . .' he pointed, 'is the nudist beach.'

'But this,' Lily indicated with a flourish, 'this is the sign that says you must put on clothes to go beyond that point. See?'

'But there's no one about.'

'I'm about. And someone else lives in that prefab. Your neighbour. He's short and bald and he's always well covered. He would probably also be disgusted if he saw you this way.'

'I'm not disgusting, I'm just naked. And this is a nudist beach.'

'*That* is a nudist beach. *This* is the public highway.'

The man said nothing. Lily appraised him, coolly. 'I've lived around here a long while. See those over there?'

She pointed at a cluster of houses; small, purpose-built chalets. He nodded. 'That's where you people go.'

'Pardon?'

'The Hamlet. It's fenced off, see? That's where all the temporary people go. Nobody permanent has anything to do with them. We think they're weird.'

He glanced over at the chalets as though he hadn't truly noticed them before. 'Perhaps they think you're weird.'

'What?'

Lily crossed her arms.

'I'm going to the beach now. It's too cold to stand around talking.'

'Fine.'

The man – he was called Luke Hamsun, he was forty-seven and a professional photographer – walked past Lily and on to the beach. Lily turned and watched his retreating torso, then she threw down her bike and went to peer inside his prefab.

Luke had found the idea of a shell beach appealing, initially. It brought to mind the image of Venus rising from her oyster. This whole place is practically deserted, he thought bitterly, and yet fate brings me bang into contact with Prissy Miss Moon Features.

He wondered what Lily's name was. He wondered whether she'd prove photogenic.

No people. He recited this like a mantra. No people. That's why I'm here. No drink. No fags. No people. No sex. No stress. No people. Just emptiness. That's all.

The sea was brown. It wasn't even the sea, really. It was the channel. This place is truly the back of beyond, Luke thought smugly. It was grey and bleak and very flat. It was like the moon, in fact. But did they have seas on the moon? He remembered hearing something similar in a way-distant geography lesson but he couldn't decide if the seas in question were wet seas or dry seas.

How could you have a dry sea? And if the sea on the moon was wet, wouldn't the water float off because there was no gravity on the moon to hold things down?

He walked along the beach. The shells were actually quite hard on his feet. His feet were tender, underneath, and so was he. He held in his paunch. Nothing moved. He supposed that the muscles on his gut had stopped working. He breathed out. No, they had been working after all. He coughed. His belly hurt.

The brown water lapped at his feet. It was icy.

Oooohhhhh! Much colder than he'd imagined. He was naïve like that. This instance was entirely typical. He moved back a step. The sky was massive. Flat land, flat sea, and a great big, dirty, mud-puddle of a sky.

It looked like it was going to rain. He shivered. He peered over his shoulder to see if the girl had gone. It seemed like she had.

As Luke strolled back to his prefab he confidently sidelined any thoughts of his own physical timidity (shouldn't the sea feel warmer in cold weather? He'd certainly always thought so. He'd been misled, clearly) and instead he bolstered himself by imagining the cosmos; black, enormous, dotted intermittently with diamond-chip stars, and then a sea, floating. A giant sea with waves and foam and everything. Just, kind of, floating.

He imagined himself, Luke Hamsun, on the moon, moon-walking. He'd been sent to the moon to recapture the sea, to tighten it up, to winch it down.

Over his shoulder Luke pictured heavy ropes which were weightless because nothing weighed on the moon, and in his hands a dozen giant tent pegs. He was supernaturally power-ful. He was Flash Gordon. He had no back problem. No gut-ache. His sciatica was a phantasm. He would never keel over and die. He was no longer forty-seven.

And in some respects this was actually true. At least it could have been true in a different world. It just so happened that Luke Hamsun was an earthling, and as such, he was obliged to endure the drag of gravity. He was grounded.

But he endured phlegmatically, cheerfully almost. He didn't complain. He saved his breath. In fact he hoarded it. He held it.

Lily, meanwhile, had made herself comfortable on Luke's sofa and was inspecting one of his portfolios.

'Oh good,' she said calmly, when he strolled back inside, turning a photo around so that he could see it properly, 'now you've returned you can set me straight on this. Is that a pick-axe up her arse or . . .'

'How did you get in here?'

Lily lifted the photo and reappraised it. 'If you've got no trousers then you've got no pockets. If you've got no pockets then you've got no keys.'

Luke felt enraged, violated, defiled, but when he finally spoke it was with great softness. 'Put those down and get out of here.'

Lily, rather surprisingly, responded to the softness. She closed the portfolio.

'You're a bit of a pervert then, on the quiet?'

'You're a silly little sneak.'

'A what?'

Lily stood up, smirking. Luke felt embarrassed by his naked-
ness and picked up a coat from a chair by the door. He put it on.
He looked ridiculous now, naked, wearing only a coat. The coat
was incriminating.

'So that's why you've come here,' she said, pouting deli-
ciously, 'to take some more of these dirty pictures?'

'They aren't dirty pictures.'

She'd struck a nerve. She knew it. She always knew. She
laughed. 'So what's that then?'

Against the wall, yet to be hung, stood a picture of a naked
female cupping her breasts like they were two neat apples, but
the breasts had been yanked up high as though she planned to
pillow her chin on them. It looked uncomfortable.

'It's a nude.'

'A *nude*. Oh. I get it.'

Lily continued to eye the picture.

'Ouch!' she said.

'Get out.'

'Certainly.'

She sauntered towards the door.

'If you break into my house again I'll call the police.'

Lily just giggled. 'I didn't break into anything. It was wide
open.'

'Get out.'

'I'm getting out.'

The sea lapped coldly outside the prefab's door. Three giant
steps and she was in it. Fully dressed. Feet, knees, hips, breasts.
She waved her arms at him.

'I'm freeeee!' she screamed.

He hated her then. She was free.

In fact she had screamed *I'm freezing!* but a small wave had
hit her.

She had no grand scheme. Not yet. Nothing like that.

4

No one else would do these jobs. It was like being a spaceman, but with all of the discomfort and none of the glory. In the trade they called them *skins*. There was a theatrical side. Ronny did that sometimes but he hated being around children.

Then there was the industrial side. Councils hired him to spray weedkiller, to clean stuff up, to juggle with noxious chemicals. Someone had to do it. So Ronny obliged. He was that someone. A consummate professional.

Others found the precautionary clothing bothersome and claustrophobic. Several people had sued after contracting breathing difficulties and skin infections from handling dangerous substances. Ronny knew that this was because they took off their helmets when it got too hot. They didn't take precautions. He always took them. That was his trademark, his hallmark. That was his stamp of quality.

Anyway, it was part of the kick. No air. To be enclosed. The chafing, the sweating. The chronic discomfort. That was all part of it.

He wore white shoes. Special shoes. In fact the entire get-up was white, even the helmet. Ronny peered down at his shoes. He thought about the man on the bridge, wide open, and in the same instant he thought of Monica.

Monica.

She had been his confidante. His correspondent. His best friend. His *only* friend. He'd liked it that way.

Monica had an opinion on everything. She had an interest in biology. Physical things. She was an adventuress. She hated to be enclosed, which was why, finally, she ended up in Sumatra, in the rain forests. She was working out there with a journalist.

They were interested in DNA; all that complex genetic stuff which, quite honestly, meant precious little to Ronny.

Monica could never simplify the nature of her work in conversation without becoming impish and flirtatious. If Ronny couldn't understand what it was that she was doing she'd crystallize it by saying, 'I'm interested in what it is that makes a man a man, Ronny. I'm interested in *apes*.'

So they were searching for a missing ape in the forests of Sumatra. A missing link. A great ape. A fantastic ape. A pale giant. He walked on his hind legs and to all intents and purposes he resembled a man but his feet turned inwards. And unlike his human relations he had no big toes.

Monica had never seen him. She'd seen Ronny though, but only fleetingly, a long time ago. He'd made a great impression. He'd become indelible. He'd left his footprint in the mud of Monica's brain. She couldn't shake him.

Oran-pendic. That was the ape's name. Mr Unpronounceable. In his dictionary Ronny saw that *orang* – or something quite like it – was Malay for man. Like in orang-utan which roughly speaking translated as 'man of the forest'.

Oranpendic was not in his dictionary. He didn't exist. Not yet, anyway. When Monica found him he would exist but not before. When Monica found him Ronny too would see him, not physically – nothing nearly so dramatic – but slotted in among all his other words and definitions. On paper. In print. In bold.

But for now the oranpendic was their own special creature. Not a fact or a definition. Nothing absolute. Merely a fragment.

Ronny looked up pendic for the exercise but could find only pend which meant to hang (as in 'pendant'). He guessed the word had something to do with per-pend-icular. Upright. Vertical. But frankly he found both this description and the original name unsatisfactory.

Oranpendic.

Monica didn't give a shit. It didn't matter. She was more interested in the hunt. She'd been called a hoaxer. Well, not Monica so much as the journalist, Louis, who was the truly infamous half of the duo.

24

She'd heard him on the radio and then she'd saved up all her money working as a lab assistant at a school in Swindon to fly out and join him. She was impulsive like that. Some called it gullible. Either way, she was never afraid. Nothing daunted her.

Initially the journalist had been discomfited by Monica's presence. He'd felt invaded. Monica could have that effect sometimes. But then he grew accustomed to her and they began the hunt proper.

Ronny had seen several articles about the hoax. Naturally people doubted the existence of the oranpendic. But the journalist claimed to have seen him, briefly, and his account of this fantastical discovery was fairly convincing.

Monica had a theory about faces. She said honesty was something you could see in a person's face. Someone's sincerity, their integrity, was as apparent to Monica on the first meeting as their hair colour or the shape of their nose. This was her preoccupation. Her instinct.

In fact she had two main instincts. The first was for honesty, and the second told her that the oranpendic was alive but that he was afraid. The threat of discovery terrified him. So he kept hidden.

She wrote to Ronny.

He's afraid, Ronny. I know that much. He lives and walks in fear. Some days, if I wake early, I go out alone just after dawn. Everything is glazed. The air is full of moisture. It's as thick, as dense as a woollen scarf pressing down on to my lips and up into my nostrils.

At these times I dream I'll see him. But he's pale like the mist and he's so afraid that it's as if he's only a ghost. I always have the camera – not Louis's big professional thing, I have my own, a cheap one that I've never yet used, just in case – but I sometimes imagine that if I tried to photograph him, the fear, the focus, the technology, would obliterate him. And all that would remain – in the camera, in the world – would be vapour. A mist and a smell.

Fear has its own special aroma. Like soil. Like cider vinegar. Did I lose you yet, Ronny? Did I? Could I?

Here's the truth. If I saw him I would not photograph him. It

25

would be so rude, don't you think? I've never told Louis I feel this way. He'd scoff. I mean that's why he's here, after all. He has more to lose than I do. He's been publicly and uniformly ridiculed and slandered, so that's fair enough.

But if I saw the oranpendic I would not photograph him. I would kneel and I would hold out my hand. I would not stare. I'd look off sideways, like a friendly cat. That's what I'd do. I'd adopt a submissive posture.

Oh God Ronny I wish you were here. I'm sorry you lost your hair. I am. Did I ever say that before? I can't remember. Do you miss me? My own hair is long now. I tie it back. Otherwise it catches on twigs and on branches. It's stupid and impractical but I'm growing it as a tribute. I'm growing it for you.

You feel very close at this moment. Is that stupid? Are you near me? Are you out there, hiding in the jungle, watching, waiting but I just can't see you? Is it me who's dense or is it the forest? Is it me?

Shut your eyes Ronny, and imagine me here. Close your eyes. Close them. Do you see me? My hair is longer. My nails are dirty. Do you see me? I am kneeling. I am holding out my hand.

Take it.

M.

Ronny continued to stare at his shoes. White shoes. Then he stirred himself and picked up his bottle of weedkiller. He had walked five miles that day. He'd sprayed every crack in every bit of pavement. No weeds would come after he'd been. There would be no green after he'd been. No lush diversity in the pavement's monotony. He'd seen to that.

It was hot inside his helmet. But Ronny walked and he sprayed. Like a tomcat, scenting all those docile miles with the stink of poison. He didn't think of the poison though, only of Monica. His own breath soaked his face. The forests were hot and airless. Like this, he supposed. He was close to her. She was right. He was very close. And she was certainly a rare bird.

5

He drove home later than he'd anticipated and hit the rush hour. In his keenness to evade it he'd skipped changing, so wore his white skin-suit, in full, but without the helmet. From the neck downwards he resembled an alien. Or an astronaut. He even wore his plastic gloves, which generated a curious friction on the steering wheel as he turned corners.

Pulling up to a roundabout in Lee Green, Ronny noticed something exceptional. A man was standing on the island in the centre of the roundabout. He was tall with a beard, his arm was extended, his left arm, and in his hand he held something that shone in the glare of many headlights. Something gold.

The traffic was heavy. Ronny waited his turn to join the flow. He stared at the man. Someone flashed their lights behind him. He took his chance. He pulled into the traffic. He did one circuit. He did two. On the third circuit he indicated left and slid into a parking space outside the World of Leather showroom. He sat for a while and gazed at the showroom through his windscreen. Then he climbed out of his car and walked back over to the road. He stopped at the kerb, put his hands to his lips and yelled.

'RONNY!'

The other Ronny gave no indication of having heard him so he whistled and called again.

'RONNY!'

The other Ronny turned, cocked his head to one side but did not move. Ronny waited for a gap in the traffic and then jogged over. The other Ronny continued to hold out the glittering object. It was a watch.

Ronny raised his voice over the honk of the traffic. 'What are you doing here?'

The other Ronny showed him the watch.

'I'm holding out this watch.'

'Why?'

'I'm offering myself. I'm offering my time. To this island.'

After a pause he added, 'I like that suit. You look like the Michelin Man.'

'It's protective clothing.'

Ronny stared at the watch. It seemed familiar. The other Ronny caught him looking.

'Recognize it?'

Ronny swallowed, suddenly unnerved. 'Should I?'

'I don't know. It's just that I think it might be yours.'

Ronny took a step backwards. 'I don't own a watch.'

'Yes you do. You're wearing one.'

Ronny blinked. 'I mean I don't own that watch.'

'It has an inscription on the back . . .'

The other Ronny turned the watch over. Engraved in the gold were the words: 'To Big Ron, with love, your Elaine.'

Ronny began shaking. His suit quivered and it made a strange synthetic sound, a noise like a gust of wind hitting the canvas jib of a small sailing boat, a sound like the beat of a swan's wings in flight. It was clearly audible but the other Ronny seemed not to notice.

'I wish I could whistle like you do,' the other Ronny said, 'but I can't whistle at all. I never learned.'

'Whistle?' Ronny scowled, and then recollected. 'Oh . . .' As a kind of strangled appendix he added, 'In fact it's my father's watch,' and then, with startling synchronicity, his nose began running.

He rubbed at it with the back of his glove, but the glove was plastic and soaked up nothing. Instead it smeared moisture across his cheek for the chill evening air to tip-toe over.

The other Ronny continued to inspect the watch. 'It looks expensive. Will he be wanting it back?'

'No.' Ronny shook his head and then sniffed violently. The

28

other Ronny glanced up. 'Is something wrong?'

'Nothing.'

He focused in on Ronny's face. His gaze was like the pure sweep of a bowling green; it was flat and it was plain and it went on and on. Ronny was alarmed. He began blinking rapidly. A nervous tic.

The other Ronny looked crestfallen. 'I've brought back some bad feelings. I'm sorry.'

He curled his hand around the watch so that Ronny was no longer obliged to look at it. Ronny said nothing but he kept on blinking. If he stopped blinking he'd start crying and that wouldn't do. He'd never cried.

But he remembered the watch. Very clearly. And mixed in with the memory was the scratch of rough hessian and the pungent taint of cider vinegar. Something acrid.

'Is he dead?'

'Who?'

'Big Ron.'

'Yes.' Ronny nodded.

'The way you spoke earlier made it sound like he was still living.'

'He is living,' Ronny struggled. 'I mean, in my head.'

Again he put his gloved hand to his face.

'Actually,' the other Ronny intervened, 'you have a rash. On your cheek. You should stop touching it.'

Ronny took his hand from his cheek and swore softly. 'My gloves might have chemicals on them.'

'You should've taken them off then.'

'They're attached to the suit. I was in a hurry to return the car. It isn't mine.'

The other Ronny craned his neck to peer over at the car.

'Green Volvo,' he mused, unhelpfully.

'Yes.' Ronny spun around and jogged to the edge of the island. His nose was still running. His eye began stinging. He'd been clumsy. He hated himself for it.

The other Ronny watched impassively as he jinked through the traffic.

Back at the car, Ronny unzipped his suit and unrolled the top half down to his waist. It was a complex manoeuvre that took several minutes, during which time the pain in his cheek intensified.

He scrabbled around in the sidepocket on the driver's side of the car and located a bottle of water which he unscrewed, sniffed and then poured on to his hand and dabbed over his cheek. He repeated this process several times and then inspected his face in the side mirror. His cheek, nose and left eye were slightly puckered and swollen. He applied some more water.

'Do you want the watch back?'

The other Ronny had deserted his island and was now standing behind him, holding out the watch.

Ronny prickled, like he was full of static. 'Not at all. You're welcome to it.'

'How's your cheek?'

'It'll be fine.'

'You must be cold. Here . . .'

The other Ronny took off the old brown cardigan he was wearing and proffered it.

'Actually I have a change of clothes in the boot.'

As he spoke Ronny noticed the other Ronny's arms. They were skeletal. He put his hand to his mouth. He felt an unexpected combination of deep alarm and lurching nausea.

'What?'

The other Ronny inspected his cardigan with some confusion as though Ronny's distress had been generated by it and not by him.

'Your arms,' Ronny managed, through his fingers.

The other Ronny looked down at his arms, grimaced, and then put his cardigan back on again.

'I can't keep the watch,' he said quietly, 'I would feel beholden.'

Ronny was shivering. He went and grabbed his clothes from the boot of the car and began dragging them on. He felt sick. His mouth was drowning in a sweet saliva. Was it poison or was it pity? He couldn't tell.

'Pawn the watch,' he said thickly, 'and get something proper to eat.'

The other Ronny didn't appreciate this suggestion. 'I would never consider selling it,' he said and then turned to go, patently wounded.

Ronny panicked, he didn't know why. 'Where are you going?'

'To my island.'

'How long will you stay there?'

'I have no idea.'

He left him.

Ronny bundled his white suit into the back of the Volvo and then sat down in the driving seat. He adjusted the rear-view mirror, initially to inspect his cheek and then to try and catch sight of the other Ronny.

The other Ronny was back on his island. Ronny sat watching him for a while. He wanted to go. But something stopped him. An unfamiliar impulse. He was late. He wanted to go, he wanted to, but he couldn't.

He dabbed at his eye with the cuff of his sleeve. He felt terrible. His stomach was rollercoastering.

'Jim!'

Like a voice in his head. Ronny started and glanced up in alarm. As if by sorcery, the other Ronny had rematerialized next to him.

'Pardon?'

'A gift. From me. In exchange for the watch.'

'I don't get it.'

'A new name. Jim. It came to me in a flash.'

Ronny laughed nervously. 'I don't need a new name.'

The other Ronny was visibly galled. 'Big Ron is dead,' he said, matter-of-factly, 'so why not bury him?'

Ronny was surprised. He was confounded. But above all he had the strong feeling that it was ill-mannered to reject a gift so freely given.

'Jim's a nice name,' he said gently, 'but I don't ever hide from things.'

'You've got nothing to hide from,' the other Ronny insisted, as though he really understood everything. 'You have an honest face. I have an instinct for honesty. In faces.'

Ronny was taken by surprise. He was quiet for a while. The other Ronny misconstrued his silence. He decided that it might be best to return to his island. He took a few steps back. He never pushed things. He was a piece of chaff. A dandelion seed. He floated and landed, floated and landed.

He took several more steps. The wind was behind him. A gust of it touched him and defined his outline against the streetlights and the headlights.

Ronny took it all in and felt his gullet fracture. This man was a streak of piss, a twig, a little foal. He was one small knot in an endless scrag of string.

'If you want to do me a favour . . .' his mouth said – his eyes showing the shock of it – 'I mean if you want to repay me for the watch then you could drive me home. My eye's sore and I feel nauseous. I'm in a hurry to get the car back. You said you knew someone in Sheppey . . .'

'You.'

Ronny frowned. 'What?'

'You're the person I know in Sheppey.'

'But we only just met.'

The other Ronny cleared his throat. 'Same people,' he said, 'different lives.'

Ronny smiled, but thinly. 'I certainly hope that isn't true.'

He meant it. He believed that each person could only lead one life. He sensed that nothing in him could be different from how it was. He was a closed book. His pages were permanently meshed together.

'I live in a beach house,' he said eventually. 'I have extra blankets.'

The other Ronny stood and considered his offer.

'I have no driver's licence,' he said finally.

'Me neither.' Ronny tried to appear indifferent, but suddenly this mattered to him so *badly*.

'It's a Volvo,' he said cheerfully, 'and they have big bumpers.'

32

The other Ronny still seemed uncertain.

'There's the beach,' Ronny said, scrabbling for incentives, 'and a natural wildlife reserve with owls and hunting birds . . .'

Still the other Ronny hesitated.

'And rabbits . . . I mean unusual rabbits. Jet black ones. Wild. It's a strange place, flat and empty like the surface of the moon.'

'And the sea . . .?' the other Ronny said, teetering.

'Yes.'

The other Ronny scratched his right arm with his left hand. 'Fine,' he announced, 'but here's the hitch . . .'

Ronny nodded, ready for any eventuality.

'You'll have to change gear. I don't use my right hand.'

'OK.'

Ronny never yearned for anything. Not any more. Although at one stage in his life he'd discovered a worrying talent for persuasion. Persuasion had become a weakness with him. A sickness. Once he'd set his sights on something he seemed to yearn for it with an almost obscene fervour. Often things he hadn't even known he'd wanted. Those were the worst.

He'd convinced himself that those times were pretty much behind him. This was a blip.

'And the second thing . . .' the other Ronny was eerily emphatic, 'you're Jim or I don't come.'

'Jim.'

'That's my gift.'

'You call me Jim.'

'No. You call yourself Jim and you mean it.'

'Jim.'

Ronny felt a wave of euphoria, like he was lodged in a tiny dinghy and he'd just pushed himself adrift. He was floating. He could leave things behind him. Then it cut off. The euphoria. Just like that. He clambered over to the passenger side.

The other Ronny climbed in. He slammed the door shut, he felt for the pedals and then for the knob to adjust the position of his seat. He found it. He pushed himself back, but only slightly. He turned the ignition. The engine whinnied and then rumbled.

'Get the gears, Jim.'

He carefully adjusted his rear-view mirror.

Jim said nothing. He wiped his eye, sniffed once, and then calmly stuck the gears into reverse.

6

Nathan told Margery before she'd even had the chance to sit down.

'I saw James this morning.'

Margery hadn't had an easy day. One of her clients was in court pleading guilty to a charge of fratricide. Another client, a child, had been taken into care after trying to burn down his grandmother's house. And then she'd spent the remainder of her afternoon unsuccessfully trying to communicate with a young girl who'd become voluntarily mute after witnessing her sister's death in a road traffic accident. It was grim.

'James who?'

'Jim. Jimmy.'

They were in Nathan's flat in Stamford Hill. Above a bakery. Margery lived in Bethnal Green. Next to Tesco's.

'Jim?' She turned to look at him. 'So why didn't you call me?'

Nathan scratched his head. 'When I threatened to he ran off. There seemed no point once he'd gone.'

Margery had lit a cigarette. Nathan didn't smoke. She inhaled and then pulled a smidgen of loose tobacco from the tip of her tongue.

'So you simply didn't bother ringing at all.'

'I'm sorry.'

Margery grimaced. 'To hell with being sorry, Nathan. Did he say where he was going? Did he say where he'd been?'

'No.'

'Then what was he after?'

'He wanted a watch.'

Margery inspected Nathan's wrist.

'And you gave him yours.'

'Yes.'

'And he didn't say where he was living?'

Nathan paused. 'When I asked he said that he was going to Manchester.'

'Manchester?' Margery was bemused. 'Why Manchester?'

'I don't know. Perhaps it was just a whim.'

Margery threw herself down on to the sofa next to Nathan. 'I wish to God you hadn't given him your watch, Nathan.'

'I know. I *know*.'

Nathan felt ashamed but he didn't want a lecture.

'I'm not being nasty,' Margery continued, 'but it's a real *weakness* on your part.'

'I realize that now. And I'm sorry. I just felt . . . I felt pity for him. He was very thin. I thought he might sell it in exchange for food or something.'

'*Please*.'

Margery stubbed out her cigarette with a ferocious thrust. It hadn't made her feel any better. Her lips were burning, for some reason.

Quite unexpectedly, Nathan began crying. He didn't sob or sniff but tears flowed silently down both of his cheeks. Margery scowled. She was unmoved by tears. She'd seen too many over the years. Tears were a part of her job, after all, a part of her life. Tears were an excuse. A mechanism for delay. She felt in her pocket for a tissue. She had none. She felt in Nathan's pocket. She drew out a ball of paper. She unfolded it.

'You were going to show me this, I suppose?'

'What?' Nathan turned and saw the square of paper. He wiped his eyes. 'What is it?'

'He's signed this request form *Ronny*. Did you see?'

Nathan shook his head. 'I didn't see. I didn't read it.'

'And under Address he's written . . .'

The handwriting was so poor that she couldn't decipher it. 'Shelby . . . Shel . . . Well certainly not Manchester.'

Nathan was feeling raw and puny and defensive. 'He told me Manchester. I have no reason to lie about that.'

Margery rubbed her eyes with her hand. A smear of mascara

settled on her forehead above her left eyebrow. Nathan stared at it.

'You know . . .'

She was exhausted and demoralized. 'It's at moments like this that I begin to wonder . . . I mean by rights I have an obligation to contact the authorities.'

Nathan took the slip of paper. He could see that the word written under Home Address was 'Sheppey'. Margery watched him. 'Can you read it?'

'Uh . . .' he swallowed, 'uh . . . no.'

She sighed. 'I just wish you hadn't given him your watch. If something happens to him and they find your watch . . .'

Nathan felt his wrist. 'I hated that watch,' he said.

Margery relaxed her head on to the back of the sofa. 'I'm too tired for this,' she mumbled.

Nathan nodded. 'I'm tired too, but I felt I should tell you.'

Margery ignored him.

'And he did say Manchester,' Nathan repeated, regretting that he had confided in her now and abandoning all previous ideas about honesty being the best policy. He pushed himself up. 'I'll make a start on dinner.'

He went into the kitchen.

Margery pulled her aching legs on to the sofa. She closed her eyes. Her body relaxed but her mind wheeled on in full throttle. She was implicated. She hated that feeling. It was a compromise and she hated compromises. She was hardened. She knew it. And it was a nasty thing to know about yourself.

Her father had been a doctor. Her mother had been a midwife. Two strong service traditions. Caring was just another mechanical gambit she'd learned about in tandem with tying her laces. It was an inconvenience, sometimes. When Daddy had to make a house call on Christmas day. When his dinner went cold. And it was probably only some stupid old woman who was stuck on her own and had no one to talk to. But he took it for granted. They all did.

Margery was disgusted by weakness but equally disgusted by her own disgust. She'd been married, a man she met at university. He'd studied engineering. He was ambitious. It hadn't lasted. It had lacked something. Compassion? Should a marriage be compassionate? Divorce. Then she'd floundered. And finally she'd met Nathan.

It was on the job. A routine investigation into allegations of misconduct at a children's home in the London borough of Brent. There she met James, who was Jimmy, who was Ronny. He was a lost boy. Like in *Peter Pan*. A little lost boy. Nobody loved him. Nobody wanted him. But he was looking for love and in all the wrong places. He was vulnerable.

He'd had this habit of losing things. He didn't have much, but what he had he lost. On the way to school he'd drop his books. He'd leave his lunch on the Tube. He'd take off his coat and he wouldn't pick it up. As if he was a snake and just shedding skins.

Then he'd begun making claims. He'd go and make a claim and he'd hope to get something back that wasn't his. Something interesting that had a life, a meaning, elsewhere. Something distinct. Something whole.

And it was in this place that he met Nathan. And Nathan had once had a brother he'd abandoned who was roughly the same age as James, as Jimmy. So he gave him things. The brother's things. It was a private deal between them. But it was wrong. It was wrong.

Margery had imagined that James was on the game. What else could she think? His steady accumulation of possessions had to point somewhere. So it was a relief when she'd finally met Nathan. He was as harmless as a newly hatched chick. And she liked him. He was steady and gentle and he cared about minutiae. He was lovable.

They went out for a drink together. It was unprofessional, admittedly, but she didn't regret it. She merely told Nathan that he shouldn't see James again. He shouldn't give him anything. That was all. There was no mystery. He'd said, 'I hadn't realized . . . I mean I didn't realize there was anything . . . uh . . . untoward . . . I didn't. God. I didn't think that for a second.'

'It's a real shame,' Margery said kindly, trying to reassure him, 'but the world is such a sick place. You do something in all innocence and the world manages to make it cheap in some way. That's just how it is, I'm afraid.'

Then James went missing. Initially the police expressed a tolerable level of interest. A list of names were fed into a computer. They called on Margery. *Flat hat, blue suit, big boots.* Did she know about Nathan? Did she know about Nathan's history? More specifically, did she know about Nathan's father? He was a convicted paedophile. Did she understand what that meant? Nathan's dad was sexually deviant. He fucked small children. All the time. Big Ron. Big bad Ron. He huffed and he puffed and he blew their fragile houses down. And his own little piggies? He tucked them up tight at night, so tight that they couldn't move their tiny arms, and then he peered and he leered and he panted through their weak straw walls. It was all spelled out. Every letter. And every letter spelled a single word. And the word was horrible.

Horrible. Horrible. *Horrible.*

She wanted to withdraw. But no. Nathan had red hair and blue eyes and skin so pale it was almost transparent. He was almost transparent. So soft and so gentle. He was see-through.

And by then she was in too deep, dammit.

Nathan had prepared a chicken-in-a-bag meal that you boiled for ten minutes. It tasted like chalk, but fibrous. She never told him that she knew. She simply waited for signs of it. She studied him like you'd study a tomato plant in a greenhouse. Was it getting enough water? Were there greenfly? Was there mildew? She kept on waiting for something to go wrong. Like he was a bomb just a tick-tick-ticking.

Nathan watched Margery eating. She didn't complain. She munched dutifully.

'I'm sorry,' he said, 'it tastes awful.'

He was as soft as a strawberry cream.

'It does taste awful,' she said quietly, eating on regardless, then picking up the ketchup from a tray resting on top of a brown cardboard box which had been propped, without her noticing, next to the sofa. The box. All close and closed and tightly bound. Nathan gave it the quickest of glances, every so often. Some things, he resolved, no, many things, many, many things were often better just left that way.

7

'Now here's the thing,' Ronny said, appraising Luke and detecting a powerful smell of fish, 'he's changed his name and now he's called Jim.'

Luke turned to Jim, surprised and clearly determined not to believe the testimony of a total stranger. 'You changed your name since this morning?'

Jim nodded. He already seemed thoroughly reconciled to this superficial alteration. The new name had settled on him during the previous hour as softly and as completely as a thin layer of soot over the rim of a chimney.

Luke frowned, somewhat disgruntled. 'But what was wrong with Ronny?'

Ronny interjected. 'It was his dad's name and he didn't like his dad.'

'Anyway,' Jim said, carefully steering the conversation away from his father, 'my friend here is called Ronny, and if we're both Ronnies it makes things too complicated.'

Luke was tickled by this. His broad face broke into a grin. 'So in fact,' he said, chuckling, 'you're *The Two Ronnies*.'

Ronny shook his head. 'No. We're not the two anythings. That's the whole point of it. He's Jim.'

Luke stopped smiling. Jim took his chance and handed him the car keys. 'I really appreciate you lending me the car. It's been a real life-saver.'

While he spoke, Luke squinted at Jim's cheek. 'You have a slight rash . . .' he indicated, 'just there.'

'He knows,' Ronny said. Jim nodded. 'I think it may even be going down a bit now.'

'Actually,' Luke glanced wistfully over Ronny's shoulder,

although all that lay behind him was darkness and the roar of the tide, 'I met one of our neighbours today. A girl with a flat face. She looked slightly . . .'

'Dirty,' Jim filled in.

Luke laughed, as though this hadn't previously occurred to him. 'That's true. She was dirty. Her neck especially. Do you know her?'

Jim shook his head. 'I've seen her around but we've never spoken.'

'Well she was snooping around my prefab and then she jumped into the sea. With all her clothes on and everything. Crazy, really. I didn't warm to her at all.' Luke paused. 'In fact she actually objected to me walking the short distance from here to the nudist beach with no clothes on. It's not even as if there was anyone about . . .'

'She was about,' Ronny said, but not provocatively. He was rubbing his ear and seemed uninvolved now that the naming issue had been resolved. Luke just grunted.

'Anyway . . .' Jim said, his voice trailing off into the sound of the waves.

'Yes . . .' Luke responded brightly and jangled the keys in his hand, 'any time.'

'Great.'

Jim walked off, expecting Ronny to follow. But Ronny didn't follow.

'Did you see the black rabbits yet?' he asked.

'Black rabbits?'

Luke was temporarily bewildered.

'Jim said that there were black rabbits here. Wild ones.'

'Uh . . .' Luke considered this for a moment. 'I've never . . .' he frowned, 'although now you come to mention it . . .'

He disappeared into his prefab in search of something. Ronny held the door ajar with his foot. He saw the picture of the woman with the chin-high breasts which Luke had now hung squarely, unapologetically, above his sofa. Ronny touched one of his own nipples with his left hand. He had a fantastic capacity for empathy.

'*Ouch.*'

'Pardon?' Luke reappeared, looking testy.

'Nothing. It's just . . .' Ronny pointed, 'her breasts are very high. That isn't natural, is it?'

'Natural?'

Luke didn't understand the implications of this word. He was holding a pamphlet. It was a free handout from the Nature Conservancy Council about the Swale reserve. He cleared his throat. 'Breasts are fatty tissue. That particular model has quite large ones which means that there's some . . .' he searched for the right word, 'slack,' he said, finally, although he couldn't help thinking that it sounded ungallant. Graceless, even. And it was such a *real*, no, not real . . . it was such a *resonant* image, after all.

Ronny was already inspecting the pamphlet.

'Take it,' Luke said, 'I think it mentions something about rabbits in there although I wouldn't swear to it.'

'Thanks.'

Ronny took the pamphlet and turned to go. Luke half-closed the door and then said quickly, 'It didn't hurt, you know.'

'What didn't?'

Luke thumbed over his shoulder. 'The breasts. She's my ex-wife. It didn't hurt. It was actually her idea in the first place.'

'Oh,' Ronny nodded, still clutching his pamphlet, 'well, that's good, then.'

'Yes.'

Luke closed the door. He resolved not to show Ronny his portfolio. He was alone in this wilderness. This moonscape. Although Jim, at least, seemed relatively open-minded. Or was that just . . . uh . . . he searched for the word. Then he found it. Reticence. Maybe Jim was just reticent.

Jim. His neighbour. *Jim*. Bit of a blank spot, really.

Jim's prefab was bare and functional. One bedroom. Small. A shower, a toilet, a sink. The living room and a tiny kitchen. White walls. Linoleum flooring throughout. Red in colour. A portable TV. Terrible reception. No lampshades. Bare bulbs.

Chilly. Ronny was impressed. It was already dark when they arrived but he quickly got the gist of it.

They'd had to wait for ten minutes before entering the island. The Kingferry bridge had been raised for a tanker to pass through. Ronny had clambered out of the car and walked to the river bank to watch. The bridge was a great, concrete, multi-storey car park, but roofless. A monstrosity. A giant. When he climbed back into the car his face was alight. He hadn't bargained on it being a real island.

'You could swim it easily,' Jim said, as they crossed over the river, 'but it's pretty deep in the middle.'

And now they were by the sea. Jim pulled his curtains wide. Outside Ronny saw blackness broken by foam-tipped waves. It was fantastic.

He pointed. 'You're almost on the beach.'

'Yes. In fact, we are on the beach.'

'Just five foot of it and then the sea.'

'That's right.'

Jim was making something to eat, heating a tin of beans and mini chipolatas.

'Are you hungry?'

'Always.'

Jim tipped half of the panful into a bowl. The other half he poured on to a plate for himself. He cut some bread. He passed Ronny a piece.

'No bread,' Ronny said, sitting himself down at the kitchen table. 'I only ever eat enough . . .' he paused, choosing his words carefully, 'to remain active.'

Jim handed Ronny a fork. 'That's a strange habit.'

'Yes,' Ronny agreed, 'but it's these little things that keep me going. These habits.'

He ate with his left hand. He held his fork in his fist with no finesse.

'And you only use your left hand,' Jim said, watching Ronny carefully as though he was some kind of scientific experiment.

'Yes. It slows me down.'

'You feel the need to slow down?'

'I did.' Ronny thought for a moment. 'What I mean to say is that it helps me concentrate. I used to have a very short attention span. Then I started these little challenges. It all came to me on the spur of the moment. I'd always had a natural instinct to do things right-handed, but I began to stop myself. I controlled that instinct. I curbed it.'

He smiled. 'At first it makes you irritable, because the body and the brain hate doing things the hard way. But it's simply a question of working through that initial hostility, and once you've worked it through, you feel this intense kind of joy. Really intense.'

Jim tore a piece of bread in half. At length he said, 'You must have been extremely miserable at some point. I mean before all this.'

'I was,' Ronny grinned, 'but not any more.'

He then ate four mouthfuls of his meal and pushed his plate aside.

Jim focused on the plate. 'It's very . . .' he considered for a moment, 'well, frustrating. It's frustrating to see you push your plate away when you're obviously still hungry.'

Ronny shook his head. 'I'm not hungry.' He rested his elbows on the table. 'You're much bossier than you think, Jim,' he added cheerfully.

Jim was taken aback. He'd been considering Ronny and his unhappiness. He hadn't considered himself as a part of any equation. 'Me? Bossy?'

He saw the guiding light in his life as a palpable indifference. A supreme, a superb, a spectacular indifference. Ronny shrugged. 'If you ate less you might feel better about things. The way I see it, the less you eat, the less energy you have to expend on unnecessary stuff. If you were hungry you probably wouldn't be the slightest bit interested in what I did or didn't do.'

Jim wasn't impressed by Ronny's reasoning, but for the sake of argument he pushed his own plate away for a moment and said, 'Everyone has a few stupid habits. I'm sure I have plenty, but I try not to dwell on them, and I certainly wouldn't want them to influence my life any more than they do already.'

'So what are yours?'

Ronny was smiling as though he imagined Jim's habits would be nothing to write home about.

'Well . . .' Jim disliked talking about himself but he resolved to do so, just this once, to make his point, 'when I was a kid my dad used to break things if I formed an attachment to them. To teach me a lesson about dependence. And in a way it set me free, although I really hated him for it at the time. But now . . .' Jim twisted his fork in his hand, 'now, if ever I form an attachment to something, to anything, I feel the need to break it myself.'

Ronny was clearly impressed. He looked around him, at the furniture, at the walls.

'What kinds of things?'

'All sorts of stuff. Cups. Clothes. Watches.'

'And you still do it?'

Jim nodded. 'Sometimes.'

'Why?'

'I have no idea. I don't bother analysing.'

'But you should.'

Jim shook his head.

'No, really, you should. It's interesting.' Ronny frowned for a moment and then continued. 'By rights you should've grown up to really treasure things. In fact, by rights you should've become a real hoarder. Don't you think?'

Jim was happy to accept this theory, but he wouldn't think about it.

'Look . . .' Ronny took something from his pocket and unfolded it, 'I got this from your neighbour.'

'What is it?'

'A pamphlet. It mentions the black rabbits.'

Jim began eating again. 'And so?'

'For a second back there I thought you'd gone and made it up.'

Jim stopped chewing. 'Why would I have done that?'

'To get me here.'

Jim's stomach convulsed. 'But why?'

Ronny shook his head. 'I don't know. I felt uneasy. Just for a split second, which was stupid.'

'You said I had an honest face,' Jim sounded pathetic, to himself. 'You said it was an instinct.'

'It is an instinct. That's just my point. I was right about your face. This simply confirms it.'

Ronny tossed the pamphlet down on to the table, then stood up and went to the doorway to stare out at the sea. 'Look, a tanker!' he exclaimed. 'Do you see the lights?'

Jim didn't respond. He put down his fork. He'd lost his appetite. He felt very strange, all of a sudden, like this was a dream he was living, like this was a tired, old dream, and he didn't like the *feel* of it. Not one bit.

For a second he wished himself inanimate. It was a knack he'd always had; the capacity to disengage himself from any situation, to empty his body and to go elsewhere. And for a fraction of a second he got his wish. He was no longer inside, but outside, and from outside he saw two men in a bare prefab by the brown sea. It should have been a simple image, thoroughly uncontentious. But it suddenly transformed, it was peeled like a banana, and while the outside had been fine, had been firm, the inside was soft and brown and bruised. The inside was marred and scarred and tarnished. Jim felt a profound, jarring sense of unease. Everything was curbed and complicated and twisted and blocked. Could this be right? Even from the outside, from the cold, cold outside, it all seemed so *pleasureless*.

He blinked and then looked around him, bewildered. He was back, he was back, but who was this man? What was this place? He put up a hand to his cheek, to his nose. He felt his own face. What am I playing at?

For a brief moment Jim questioned his own motivation and then, just as abruptly, he stopped questioning.

'Ronny', he said quietly, 'what happened to all your stuff?'

'My stuff?'

'The box. The box you had.'

'Ah!' Ronny murmured, 'I gave it away. I lost it.'

Jim shuddered. He didn't know why. Suddenly, though, he was wide awake. His nose was tingling. It was getting cold. Cold outside. *Cold*. Cold inside.

8

As far as Lily knew, her father, Ian, had been in Southampton for eight weeks taking care of her grandmother, who had suffered from a minor stroke three months before and was now fresh out of hospital and finding her feet back at home.

Lily's mother, Sara, was taking care of the farm in his absence. Luckily, the farm pretty much looked after itself, because Sara was in a state of flux. She was forty-two and had shed over four stone during the previous year. A yeast allergy. When she'd avoided bread and buns and all those other yeasty temptations – the pizzas, the doughnuts, the occasional half pint of stout – the weight quite literally fell away. She'd been prone to extended attacks of thrush before, and now that had cleared up too, which was definitely an added bonus.

She was a new woman.

They had forty boar altogether. Which wasn't many, actually. But the market for them had become increasingly lucrative over recent years. They were organic. They were shot at the trough. One minute they were gorging, the next they were dead. Quick as anything. The other boars took the shootings phlegmatically, each one just as keen to shove in their shoulder and take another's place.

And in that respect, Lily felt, they were just like people.

Lily enjoyed the boars. She preferred them to pigs. They were hairier and even less genteel. They were bloody enormous. They were giant bastards. But they could be fastidious. They could smarm and twinkle if the mood took them.

Pigs, though, she'd observed, and with some relish, had very human arses. Like certain breeds of apes. Big, round bottoms. And they tiptoed on their trotters like supermodels in Vivienne

49

Westwood platforms. But oh so natural. Boars were less human and they were less sympathetic, but they were so much more of everything else. They were buzzy and rough and *wild*.

Sara didn't like Lily. Lily was not likeable. It was a difficult admission for a parent to make, but Lily was a bad lot. She was rough and she had no soft edges. She'd led a sheltered life. She'd been born premature and had lain helpless and bleating in an incubator for many months before they could even begin to consider taking her home.

And there were several further complications; with her kidneys, parts of her stomach, her womb. Things hadn't entirely finished forming. Nothing was right. She was incomplete. So *fragile*.

And the bleeding. Her blood would not clot. Not properly. Even now, mid-conversation, her nose might start running, her teeth might inadvertently nick her lower lip, her nail might catch her cheek, her arm. Blood would trickle and drip, then gush, then flood. It wouldn't stop. There were never any limits with Lily. There was never any sense of restraint or delicacy.

She was an old tap, a creaky faucet, she was an overflow pipe that persistently overflowed. She would ooze, perpetually. She seemed almost to enjoy it. She was a nuclear-accident baby. She was improperly sealed. She was all loose inside. She was slack. Thin. Pale. Blue-tinged. She was puny.

At first they'd thought they'd lose her. They'd prepared themselves. They'd almost bargained on it. They were on tenterhooks, year after year, just waiting for the life to be extinguished in a flash or a spasm or a jerk or a haemorrhage.

But Lily didn't die. Her own particular brand of puniness was of the all-elbow variety. All-powerful. It burgeoned. It brayed and it whinnied. It charged and trampled. It essentially ran amok.

Her body remained weak but her mind hardened. She got stronger and stronger and crosser and crosser and wilder and wilder. She needed no one. And yet they'd made so many accommodations! They'd changed from an arable farm to a pig farm and finally to boar. Boar were less trouble. Less time-consuming. They'd stiffened themselves for some kind of terrible impact, but the impact never came. It never came. And so things began to fray. Slowly, imperceptibly. Down on the farm.

Sara, staring but never seeing, looking but never focusing, tried to search out probable justifications for Lily's obnoxiousness, but she could find none. She searched her own heart. She wished Lily would do the same. But Lily wouldn't. She didn't. Not ever. And yet Lily had her own moral set-up, her own fears and beliefs, which were complex, abundant, comprehensive. They were simply well hidden. Like potatoes. Several feet under.

She worshipped a deity. It was her secret. The deity had a special name. It was called The Head. It survived in spirit but had been born and had died on one long, still night in 1982. An August night. So it made perfect sense that August should become the month that Lily set apart to celebrate The Head with some special rituals of her own making. She wasn't unduly creative, usually, but in August she made an exception. In August she cut a neat incision on her arm with a piece of wire from the boar pens. Special wire. Then she killed one of the hens and blamed it on a fox.

Fox must've done it.

With the blood from the hen, and with her own blood, she soaked the earth behind the yew tree where she pretended that The Head had been buried. But The Head had not been buried there. It had been taken away by her father and incinerated, in all probability. Although they'd never discussed it.

The Head. A freak. Lily was five and had witnessed its birth. A reliable sow from the old herd had been mated with a boar. The farm's first boar. They'd built a special enclosure just for him. It had been an experiment. Her father had wanted the best of both worlds. He'd called it 'toe-dipping'. And sure enough, the sow had delivered eight healthy young, but then The Head had come, last of all, and it had taken the mother with it. Like Shivva. God of destruction.

Lily didn't get a good look at it, initially. Her father had tried to hide it. He'd tossed it aside and kicked straw over it, like he

51

did with all the stillborn babies whenever Lily was in atten-dance. But then he'd been obliged to run into the house to call a vet when the mother began struggling, so Lily had taken her chance to inspect the freak as it lay caked and smothered in its musty tomb of hay and grass.

When she pulled its cover aside, so tentatively, what had she seen? She'd seen a head – extended, elongated – and the remainder of a body; like a tiny, moist mitten. The body of a baby rat. Or a gerbil. No tail though. But it had lived! She knew it lived. Its mouth moved. Its eyes were as round and as trust-ing as a puppy's. Its skin was pale and soft and glossy like blancmange. She wanted to touch it but her father returned, yelled at her and then sent her indoors.

The next day she could find no sign of it. The Head had gone. And she knew in her gut that he had done it in. Her own father. But The Head did not go, ultimately, because it infiltrated Lily's dreams. It inked up her mind like an octopus. And it felt, strangely, as though there had been a space, a special gap in her imagination which was only just big enough to be inhabited by this particular creature. As though the creature had known that she lacked something. As if it had *known* that she needed it to feel complete. It satiated her. It became a deity. And so Lily cel-ebrated it, and in celebrating it, she celebrated, however lop-sidedly, her own sweet self.

Naturally, also, she blamed herself. And her father. She should have saved it. The Head. If only she could have touched it. If only, if only. It had needed understanding but it had received none. While the mother pig lay dying, Lily had watched coldly as the babies all struggled to suckle. They were not pigs and they were not boars. They were little, hairy hybrids. Striped. Distinctive. Cute, certainly, but neither one thing nor the other. Lily despised them. The Head did not con-sider suckling. He was looking for understanding, not food. He was set apart. The world would have different standards for him. For him things were much more complex. For Lily, also.

Nature was a hard taskmaster, Lily realized. That night she witnessed nature, nurture and then – the final blow – nothing.

Lily alone grieved for The Head. She'd learned that nobody loved freaks. Not Dad, not Mum. No one loved freaks. Only she loved them. That was her role. And when The Head told her in a dream that she too was a freak, on the inside, and that the only reason Daddy didn't kill her was because he hadn't noticed what a freak she was yet, and that Mummy hadn't caught on either, Lily saw no reason to disbelieve him.

But what if they did see? What was to stop them from covering her with straw? From getting rid of her? And acting afterwards like none of it had ever happened? What was to stop them?

Lily grew furtive. She grew *stealthy*.

She'd seen Jim. She'd noticed that he had no eyebrows, no eyelashes. He always wore a hat. Hiding something, she'd supposed. No hair. She imagined that he was ill, with leukaemia. He looked sick. Too pale. Always alone. Bent over like an old man, his body withered. She watched him. Nothing escaped her. She gathered information because it might come in handy, one day. You could never tell.

Sara was in the kitchen leaning against the Aga drinking hot Vimto when Lily arrived home, soaking wet. She demanded to know what was up. Her daughter should have been at college all afternoon, not dawdling on the beach. Lily couldn't face a confrontation.

'Here's what happened,' she said, licking the salt from her fingers. 'I met this man down by Shellness Hamlet. Totally naked. He's renting one of the prefabs.'

'You mean the bald one?'

'No. The bald one doesn't use the beach. He keeps to himself. This guy was fat and smelled of fish. Anyhow, I told him he shouldn't be allowed to walk on a public highway totally starkers.'

Sara frowned. 'What did he say?'

'Nothing. He didn't get my point. He was heading down to the sea for a dip. But then I noticed that he'd gone and left his prefab door wide open. I was cycling past, so I couldn't help seeing that all over the floor were these pictures of naked ladies. And I don't mean just naked, I mean weird. Things stuck up their arses and everything. *Animals.*'

'My God.'

'Exactly. So I confronted him about it and he said it was none of my business. I didn't like the look of him. I mean, he was naked. I thought he might turn nasty so I jumped into the sea to avoid him.'

Even Sara found this last bit difficult to comprehend.

'You jumped into the sea? Why didn't you just ride home?'

'I dunno. I was angry, I suppose. He's a sicko. This is a small place. There's the nudist beach, which attracts the worst kind of people anyway. And now there's this man. Attracted by the nudity. You know? Like this is a sewer. Our home.'

Sara shook her head. 'It's not good, certainly.'

'It's terrible.'

'I don't want you going down there again.'

'Oh no,' Lily smiled at this, her eyes icy, 'no one stops me from going where I want to go and doing what I want to do. No bloody pervert, anyway.'

Sara felt vexed by Lily's moral certainty. 'Go and get changed. You'll catch your death.'

Lily had dripped a puddle on to the kitchen flags. She held up her hands. Her knuckles were purple with cold.

'I'm not saying that there's anything wrong with the human body in its natural state,' she said piously. 'I'm not suggesting that for a moment. But what I am saying, though, is that one thing leads to another.'

She sounded just like her father.

'I'm not saying there's anything wrong with the human body in its natural state,' Sara said staunchly, 'but what I am saying is that enough's enough. My daughter is seventeen. She has a right to travel on a public highway without encountering this kind of thing.'

Luke was fully dressed. It was hard to believe that he would even consider walking a public highway stark naked.

'Maybe you should step inside for a moment.'

He pulled the prefab's door wide. Sara saw the picture of the woman with the high breasts. The woman, she noted, was not particularly attractive, which was good, somehow. Even so, she stood her ground. 'No. I can't stay.'

Lily was right. He did smell of fish.

Luke scratched his head. What should he do? Trouble was the last thing he'd expected here. He'd come for the emptiness. He'd come for an end to people and their associated burdens and stresses.

'Lily arrived home soaking wet,' Sara continued.

Luke nodded. 'She jumped into the sea. I was very surprised.'

Sara shifted her weight from one leg to the other. Luke seemed harmless. But it was the harmless ones, she told herself, who were the real danger. Was that logical?

'The thing is . . .' she cleared her throat, 'most of the people who live around here were upset about the nudist beach. It was a concession to the Hamlet.' Sara pointed, uselessly, because it was pitch dark now. 'I mean, the fenced-off chalets. And in general the rest of us don't have that much to do with them. They tend to come and go. Summer weekends mainly. They aren't what I'd call the community proper.'

'And the prefabs?'

'Pardon?'

'This handful of prefabs. Are we the community proper?'

Sara frowned. Luke was thinking how gorgeous she was. If Sara had suspected, a feather could have felled her.

'I don't know,' she said slowly, 'for some reason we tend to see them as separate.'

She thought for a moment. 'I suppose that's illogical, really.'

'It is illogical.'

'There's the boatmaker at the end of the line. Two along. He's permanent. And then there's the artists down to the left. But they winter in Ibiza.'

Sara felt like she wanted to sneeze. Powerfully. But her nose was clear.

'And next to me,' Luke added, 'is Jim.'

Jim.

'You mean the sick one?'

'He isn't sick. It's alopecia. It's a condition. You lose all your body hair.'

'Oh.'

'He's a nice guy. He keeps my cigarettes for me.'

'Pardon?'

'I gave up smoking, but I've entrusted him with a packet just in case. I'm actually purifying. That's why I'm here. I'm downloading.'

Purifying? Downloading?

Sara stared at the picture again. Luke smiled. 'My ex-wife.'

'Really?'

She blushed. Luke noticed. He found it rather touching.

'The only thing I don't understand,' Sara said, after a short pause, 'is why her sandals are unfastened.'

Luke gazed at Sara with a sense of real wonder. And then he said, so softly that she could hardly hear him, in a whisper, 'Is it you?'

Sara blinked rapidly. 'Is who me?'

He continued to gaze at her, like his face was illuminated from the inside by a high-watt bulb. The glow of it made her step backwards, although she felt in no way intimidated.

'We've never met before,' she murmured. 'I'm me. I'm Sara.'

And then, as if to contradict everything, a wild laugh flew out of her, so quickly, so unexpectedly, that it had filled each and every corner of the room before her own slow hand could move to mask her lips.

9

Jim found Ronny on the beach. Ronny was surrounded by several large piles of shells. It was six a.m.

'What are you doing?'

Ronny was engrossed. He spoke slowly. 'You know, one minute I was just sitting here, watching the sea, and the next I was sorting out these shells.'

'Sorting them? What for?'

'Into families. Into colours.'

Jim sat down. He took one shell from one of the piles and one from another. He held them next to each other. 'I see no difference.'

Ronny inspected Jim's two shells. 'Then you aren't looking.'

Jim put the shells back down. 'So what will you do with them once they're all sorted?'

'I don't know.'

'Perhaps you could create something.'

'Like what?'

'People cover wine bottles in them. Or they make shell frogs or shell dolls in shell dresses.'

Jim watched as Ronny picked up the two shells he had just put down.

Ronny displayed them to him. 'You put these back on the wrong piles. Couldn't you tell?'

Jim focused on the shells again. Ronny held them in his left palm. Jim noted, once more, that Ronny's fingers were strangely waxy at their tips, but also that his wrist had been lacerated. Scars as thick as pale maggots, long scars, nosed out from the dark shelter of his cardigan.

'Maybe there is a difference,' he said, in a spirit of compromise, although if there was then it was so slight that he could hardly detect it. Ronny nodded, gratified.

The squeal of seagulls alerted Jim to the arrival of a woman and a man on a distant section of the beach. They were disrobing. Jim observed them, unobtrusively, from the corner of his eye. Ronny continued to sort the shells, oblivious. The couple undressed completely and then ran into the sea. The cold made the woman yell and the man laugh. Ronny looked up.

'Are they naked?'

'That's the nudist beach. There's a sign over there to say exactly where the nudist zone begins and ends.'

'Ah,' Ronny peered over. 'I was wondering what that said.'

'Why?' Jim picked up a random shell and placed it gently on to one of Ronny's piles. 'Can't you read?'

'I can read,' Ronny said, carefully removing the shell and placing it on to another pile. 'It's just that I prefer to read only certain types of lettering.'

'Certain types?'

'I met someone once who worked in printing and graphics. She told me how there were certain kinds of letters that made you feel happy.' He looked into Jim's face. 'You think that's reasonable?'

'I don't know. I'm not an expert on lettering.'

'Well, there's a particular kind of lettering that's apparently very friendly. And because of the shape of the letters – their roundness, their whole design – they can't help but make you feel cheerful when you read them. They use them a lot in adverts to make people feel good about certain products.'

'I never knew that.'

Jim was fanning at the beach with his hand, shifting shells aside and revealing the sand below.

'How about,' Ronny said, 'you clear a space about as big as a table and then I lay out my shells on it.'

'Like a picture?'

'No,' Ronny spoke gently, but very seriously, 'not like a picture, like a table.'

Jim sensed something contract. His face. His mouth. His

chest. He felt a dart of panic. Was it a sickness? Then he realized that he was not in pain. It was not uncomfortable. It was simply a smile. A smile. He was smiling. It was nothing to worry about.

It was a real smile and it had started off from somewhere deep down inside him, somewhere numb next to his breast-bone. He tentatively touched the spot where the smile came from with his index finger as he shifted forward, clumsily, to clear a patch on the beach. It was all very sudden and rather peculiar. He looked around him, squinting, like he was all at sea in familiar territory.

10

Nathan had received three letters and he hadn't responded to any of them. The first came from the authorities, the second from a lawyer, and the third was from a young woman whose name he did not recognize. Connie. An old-fashioned name. It made him think of lavender and starch and thimbles. But her writing was bold, and her demands – which she clearly thought reasonable – struck Nathan as entirely unfeasible. So that was that.

Each time Nathan received one of these letters, he took it to work and secreted it into a special file, a private file that nobody else ever accessed. He didn't stop and think about why he had done this. Why did he take something so personal from his own private arena and carry it, so brazenly, into such a public one?

Possibly he did it to avoid a confrontation with Margery. In some respects, where information was concerned, where the past was concerned, she was his enemy, she was his inquisitor, his conscience. He had allowed her to enter his home, his life, his bed. But he would not offer her a window into his past. His past was a graveyard that he did not visit. His past was a cemetery full of dirt. Nothing lived there.

The letters found a home in Nathan's Lost Property Kingdom. In his quiet folder they found an appropriate, a gentle and unobtrusive resting place. They snuggled comfortably up against pictures and scraps and other fragments. They had been opened, digested, closed again. They had offered up their information. They had made requests – unfulfilled – but that was not their responsibility. Like butterflies, they had spread their wings – all gaudy glory – and then they had softly closed them. That had to be enough.

The letters referred to a lost friend, a lost soul. They concerned a stranger whom Nathan had once known. But they had no bearing, now, on anything. That part of his life was gone, was lost. It was so private that it was not even private any more. And that should have been an end to it. But like a child with a scab Nathan felt compelled to pick, to poke, to ponder. He nudged at the scab but he refused to contemplate the wound just under. He came back to the file; once, twice, many times. He couldn't drop it.

And then he did drop it. He was discovered, one night, after hours, paging through this private document. It had slipped, it had fallen. Its contents were exhumed. They looked curious in bright light. The letters, the photographs; polaroids, mainly.

'Isn't it funny,' Laura had said, squatting down to help Nathan gather up his past, scooping up his secrets, his life, 'the things people leave behind?'

Nathan had nodded. He'd muttered something. But he'd been flustered. He had given himself away. He sensed it. And he simply hadn't felt right with Laura after that. In fact he felt wide open. A moth with its wings pinned, under the microscope. A girl with her legs spread, no knickers.

And Margery would have said, 'Has it ever occurred to you that you might actually have *wanted* to be discovered? Have you even considered that possibility, Nathan?'

Margery would have said that. So he didn't mention it to Margery. He didn't mention the letters. And when the girl arrived, out of the blue, he didn't mention her either. She called herself Connie.

'You know what Connie's short for?' she'd asked, following him upstairs, and then not waiting for his reply. 'It's short for Constance. But I'm not in the slightest bit constant by nature.'

'Except in this matter, it seems,' Nathan said, prickling with resentment.

'Yes,' she took a deep breath and then looked around her at Nathan's living room, 'but I didn't really feel like I had much choice.'

Nathan was relieved that Margery had gone after breakfast.

Sometimes, on Saturdays, they spent the morning in bed together.

'Have a seat.'

He pointed at the sofa.

'Thank you.'

She sat down. He saw her eyes take in every detail. She looked like an angel, literally, with short, strawberry blonde, kinky hair and a child's face. Skin like a macaroon. She was tiny. Barely five foot. Little hands, little feet. Breasts you could fit into an egg-cup.

But Nathan had no interest in angels. And he mistrusted small people. Especially women. They were usually aggressive, like terriers, yapping for attention. Yet when Connie spoke she did not yap. She leaned forward and slipped her two hands between her knees. 'So you got my letter after all?'

'Yes.'

'But you didn't answer it.'

'I had nothing to answer for.'

Connie frowned at this. 'Answer for? Why do you say that?'

Nathan sat down, stiffly.

'Look,' he said, after an edgy silence, 'Ronny was my brother. But I haven't spoken to him in a long while. Ten years or more. I just can't help you.'

Connie didn't blink. In a flash she said, 'Well, I suppose if you did know where he was then you'd be breaking the law. You'd be concealing a felon.'

'Exactly.'

Nathan paused. 'And the only reason I knew he'd run away from prison was because the police contacted me. Just after. But it's not even as if I could conceal him. He's dead to me. It's as though he's dead,' Nathan smiled grimly, 'and how could I conceal a dead person?'

Connie's head jilted. 'People have managed it. In the past.'

Nathan thought this comment throwaway – which it was – but also morbid and inappropriate. He grimaced. Connie digested his expression. She was feeding off him, he could tell. He hated that sensation. He resented it, sorely. Without thinking, he covered his mouth with his fingers so that she could not see it. Then he realized what he was doing and uncovered it again. He had nothing to hide.

Connie wanted to get to grips with Nathan. She needed a handle. There was something so tender about him, something gentle, and yet he behaved so abrasively. Eventually she said, 'I don't know what Ronny did. I only have his letters.'

Nathan cleared his throat. 'I have no interest in any letters. I have no interest in Ronny. Or in this.'

Connie sighed, then said softly, 'He must have done something so terrible . . .'

Nathan scratched his neck. Connie noticed a heat rash near his collar.

'Water under the bridge,' he said.

After an interval Connie said brightly, 'I'm an optician, incidentally.'

Nathan stopped scratching. 'What was that?'

'I said I'm an optician.'

Nathan smiled thinly. 'How does that relate to anything?'

She was a crazy angel. A crazy angel-optician.

Connie laughed. 'You don't know anything about me. Why the fuck should you want to help a complete stranger?'

Nathan stared at her intently. He hadn't expected her to swear. She'd surprised him.

'But you think I might consider helping an optician?'

In a flash he was flirting. It was out of character.

'I don't know. Perhaps. It's been hell for me, too,' she said, apropos of nothing, not smiling any more, but suddenly tragic. Nathan was taken aback. Tragedy, at this juncture, was the last thing he'd expected. His spine straightened. She was slick.

And because she was slick she saw how her change in tone had affected him. Nathan withdrew again, into himself. She felt a deep frustration. She didn't want to manipulate. She simply wanted to come clean. 'The way I see it, Nathan,' she said curtly, 'we're in pretty much the same position. You don't want to encounter your brother again and I have no particular desire to see him. I simply have an obligation to fulfil.'

Nathan nodded, but his voice was tight. 'You said in your letter that your father had died.'

Connie winced. She was still raw.

'Five months ago.'

'And he had some kind of a relationship with my brother?'

'He was involved in a committee, a government committee that was drawing up a report on prison reform. He was a barrister, originally. He did all this charitable stuff after he retired. Anyhow, he met a wide selection of prisoners during the enquiry and he must have met your brother at some point, because they became acquainted. They became friends.'

'Why did he do that?'

Nathan was talking to himself. Connie didn't understand. 'Why did he do what?'

'Why did he befriend Ronny? Ronny doesn't understand . . .' Nathan corrected himself. 'I mean he didn't understand. About friendship. I still get hate letters. From total strangers. I've not seen him for almost ten years. I've moved house twice. But still they find me.'

'That's scary.'

'Yes it is.'

Connie had stopped glowing. When she'd come in she'd been glowing. But not now. She looked tired. Washed out.

'The point is,' she said, 'my father saw fit to leave Ronny a bequest in his will. Money, basically. A nice amount.'

'A *nice* amount.' Nathan parroted, aimlessly.

Connie's eyes tightened. 'Do you want to know how he died?'

She was suddenly vengeful, like she needed to prove something. Her tragedic legitimacy, her righteousness. Nathan said nothing.

'He was waiting on the platform at Gravesend station for my mother. She'd been to Cheltenham races for the day with her lover. He was standing too close to the edge. Someone opened their carriage door before the train had slowed down. It hit him like a hammer. It killed him.'

'I'm sorry.'

'We were very close.'

Connie rubbed her hands together, like her fingers were cold or her knuckles stiff.

'But not close enough . . .' she faltered. 'I wasn't close enough to know anything about Ronny. Nor did my mother for that matter. And it actually felt kind of creepy. Especially when we found out that he was in prison, and then, shortly after, that he'd absconded. It felt sort of . . .'

Her eyes scanned the carpet near her feet, as though she might see the word she sought enmeshed in its fibres. Instead she saw only an empty wineglass, an ashtray, a tea stain and, poking out from under the sofa, a slip of paper. She focused on this as she completed her sentence. 'It felt almost threatening.'

For the first time during the interview Nathan felt pity for the girl. He imagined that before this trouble her life had been smooth and shiny as new Tupperware. It was no wonder she was shaken. He cleared his throat. 'If I were you I'd forget about the money. Ronny was never particularly materialistic.'

Connie remained unmollified. 'Unfortunately it's a legal matter, not a private one. A large portion of the money Dad bequeathed was tied up in my practice, which has left me in a slightly tricky position . . .'

Nathan could see how this might be the case. 'As a kid Ronny always broke things,' he said, appearing to marvel in the memory of it. 'I mean, he never grew attached to anything. He had no interest in money.'

'He broke things?' Connie's voice was an echo, she wasn't listening, she was trying to figure out what the slip of paper said. She saw an R and an O, an N and an N.

For some reason Nathan felt a touch of anxiety. 'Not aggressively. It was never an aggressive act. Nothing like that.'

'Actually, I'd really like you to see something.'

Connie put her hand into a leather satchel she'd been carrying and withdrew a bundle of letters. She removed a ribbon that tied them together. She offered them to Nathan.

'What are they?' He stared at them fearfully, as if they might spit or bite or combust. As though they stank.

'Ronny's letters.'

'I already said that I have no interest in Ronny's letters.'

Yet for an instant Connie appeared not to understand him and leaned forward further, proffering the letters until, as seemed inevitable, they slipped from her grasp and cascaded down on to the carpet, forming a small paper puddle at her feet. She swore and knelt down to gather them up again.

Nathan felt a curious sensation of *déjà vu*. He didn't move. He remained seated. He wanted nothing to do with these papers. They contained more secrets, more facts, and he'd had enough of secrets and facts in the past. A gutful. Connie picked up the letters and then surreptitiously included among their number the tantalizing slip of paper. She glanced over at him as she did so. Nathan seemed in another world. He was unfocused. He didn't appear to notice. She stuffed the letters back into her bag and then smiled, the very image of angel-innocence.

'That wasn't Ronny's hand,' Nathan offered, eventually.

'Pardon?' Her smile froze.

'I said that wasn't Ronny's writing on those letters.'

'Oh,' she exhaled her relief, 'I know.'

'But you said they were his.'

'I meant that they were written to him.'

'By your father?'

'No. I don't really understand how it was that Dad ended up with them. The letters were actually from Ronny's friend, Monica.'

Connie scanned Nathan's face when she used Monica's name for any sign of recognition. She detected none. His face was soft and sweet, whiskery and gingery. She put her hand into the pocket of the jacket she wore. She drew out a business card. It said: CONSTANCE SUMACH, OPTICIAN. Underneath was an address in Gravesend.

'Here.'

She stood up and offered Nathan the card, but he didn't reach out his hand to take it so she laid it down on the nearest flat surface; a cardboard box which was propped like an apprentice side-table next to the sofa. Then she took hold of her bag.

Nathan stood up too. He wasn't a tall man but by comparison Connie seemed tiny. A porcelain figure. A little Dresden shepherdess. And yet she was bold, he realized. He respected that quality. He accompanied her, without speaking, downstairs and out of his flat.

'Are you working?' she asked, just before taking her leave of him, 'only I called round during the day last week and you were out.'

Nathan nodded. 'I work for the London Underground.'

'Really?' She seemed interested.

'I'm in Lost Property.'

Connie grinned. 'That seems fitting.'

Nathan had idly noticed that Connie was glowing again. She was brightly painted. She glimmered.

'Fitting?' he said. 'How?'

'I don't know. I suppose it's slightly . . . uh . . .'

She knew what she wanted to say but she held it in. She backed off. She waved, suddenly jaunty. Nathan watched her as she walked down the road, searched for her keys, drew them from her bag and opened the door to a Renault Clio. Metallic blue. She'd been parked on a single yellow line and yet she'd not picked up a ticket.

She was very lucky. Not just a pretty face, either, Nathan told himself. She had the sharp eyes of an optician. She had a magpie's eyes. Nathan smiled sourly to himself, because, although it was of very little consequence, so did he.

And that *was* ironic.

11

Lily couldn't resist.

'WOTCHA!'

Ronny looked up. He stared at her. She was pumpkin-faced. She was an essential, a delectable product of this godforsaken place. She'd just skidded to a halt on her bike and had sprayed a fine mist of grit all over him. She'd hit the corner of his shell display. He wasn't angry.

'What are you doing?' she asked, smirking.

'I'm laying out these shells.'

'Why?'

'Because I am.'

'What kind of an answer is that?'

Ronny rocked back on to his heels.

'You're the girl who jumped into the sea,' he said, smiling. This gentle spar took Lily by surprise.

'How'd you know?'

'I guessed.'

'How'd you guess?'

Ronny smiled some more.

'Why are you smiling?'

'Because you have a dirty neck.'

'What?' Lily was offended. She felt her neck with her hand. Ronny watched this cheerfully and seemed not to notice the offence he'd given. He said, 'I spoke to the fat man who smells of fish. He said you jumped into the sea. He didn't know why. Jim said you were dirty. He was right.'

Lily was all the more affronted. She glowered. She'd momentarily lost her pip. Ronny scratched his beard. 'I thought maybe you were cleaning off.'

'Cleaning *off*? You bastard! Who the fuck *are* you?'

'Ronny.'

Lily didn't listen. Dirty. How dare he! She touched her neck again.

'It's a fucking tan,' she said angrily, 'I tan dirty.'

Ronny shrugged.

'You don't believe me?!'

Lily was raging. Tears brimmed on her lower lids like two iridescent soufflés. She took several deep breaths. Ronny eventually apprehended her distress, but not quickly enough, she felt.

'What's wrong?'

'What's wrong? A total fucking stranger tells me I'm dirty and then asks me what's wrong?'

Ronny yanked at his beard. 'Did I say you were dirty? If I remember rightly it was Jim who said you were dirty and then the fish man, Luke, who agreed with him. I don't think I said you were dirty. But if I did then it was rude of me and I'm sorry.'

'Jim who? I don't know any Jim.'

'Wow!' Ronny smiled.

'Wow *what*?'

'It's just . . .' Ronny shook his head, 'I'm surprised that you think being dirty is such a bad thing. I mean it's no bad thing. There are certainly worse things.'

Lily slit her eyes. 'My parents breed pigs,' she said, 'I know all about *dirt*.'

'I've heard that pigs are very clean animals,' Ronny said, all sincere contrariness.

'Well, I wouldn't know about you,' Lily spat, 'but I don't call making a habit out of eating your own shit clean.'

'Some people drink their own urine,' Ronny contributed, unfazed, 'because they think it's good for the skin.'

'Sod off,' Lily bawled, and attempted to ride away in a razzle of sand and gravel. Her wheel lost its grip though, and she didn't move quite as quickly as she'd anticipated.

'Nice bike,' Ronny said. 'I like it. Very smart.'

She heard his compliments as she struggled in the sand.

They struck like darts. She was completely bullseyed. He was the most interesting man she'd ever met. And ridiculously handsome. Oh fuck fuck fuck how she hated him.

Luke had Jim cornered.

'I need a fag,' he said, 'just one. Just a little puff.'

'Why?'

Jim resented him even asking. He didn't *care*. Even so, he had a loose obligation. 'Has it ever happened to you?' Luke patted at his wide stomach while he spoke because it kept on aching. Was it wind? Was it excitement?

'Has what ever happened to me?'

'That real kick in the guts kind of feeling? That love thing?'

Jim shook his head. 'Never.'

'It's really never happened to you? Wham-bam in the belly?'

'I don't think so.'

Luke was obviously disappointed. 'Why not?'

'Uh . . .' Jim had been preparing a flask of tea and an egg sandwich for Ronny. Luke eyed it covetously. Jim was holding a kitchen knife. He wanted to cut the sandwich in two but Luke clearly demanded his whole attention. 'I don't respond to other people in that immediate way,' he said softly, 'not on the whole.'

'Like a real smack in the balls,' Luke said, relishing it. Jim shrugged and cleared his throat, bemused and slightly embarrassed.

Luke had wandered over to Jim's, not just to beg a cigarette, but also for a spate of mannish confirmation, for some friendly reassurance. Jim's reticence was making him feel oafish. Too butch. Too ballsy.

'I'm very pleased for you, anyway,' Jim said eventually, blushing slightly. Agonized.

'I mean there was the physical attraction,' Luke said, withdrawing a little, 'but it was the intellectual thing mainly. She just looked at that picture and then she said, "Why is she wearing her sandals in that way?" It was so strange.'

Jim nodded. He'd already heard this part. He didn't under-

70

stand what it was that he was supposed to contribute, if anything. Luke was actually becoming something of an encumbrance. Jim did not want to be his friend. He didn't make friends. If he'd ever troubled to have a life gameplan then friendship would never have been a part of it.

Luke was waiting, though, his face puckered with anticipation.

'Well yes, it does seem strange,' Jim managed finally, fumbling, stumbling, feeling around in the dark.

'Because no one had ever said that before,' Luke continued, warming up again, 'but when I initially conceived the image for that photo and when I actually took it I was thinking *shoes*. I don't know why. I was thinking *sandals*. And then I got Beverly – my ex-wife, she's the model – to unfasten the sandals. And so whenever I see that picture I think *sandals*, but whenever anyone else sees the picture they think *breasts*. High breasts.'

Jim nodded.

'You thought that too?'

'Yes.'

'But Sara thought *sandals*. It was . . . kinetic. Is that a word?'

Jim touched his chin which was soft as chamois leather. 'I think so. Perhaps you both have a similar way of looking at things.'

'That's precisely what I thought.' Luke was beaming. 'You've hit the nail on the head there.'

Jim was pleased he'd hit something but now he wished Luke would go. Luke sensed as much. 'I shouldn't have intruded. It's just that I was so . . .'

'Understandably.'

'Yes. Excited. And you're right. I don't need a puff. This is all natural energy. It's positive energy. It's just that . . .' he frowned, 'as a photographer, how you see the world is the most fundamental thing. And you yearn for other people to see things in the same way you do.'

Jim was nodding dumbly at this when Lily burst in, unannounced, a random firecracker. 'OK,' she said, panting, her hair, hands, everything all atangle, 'so who's Jim?'

'She never knocks,' Luke said, turning to Jim, his face suddenly creasing with displeasure, 'and I only came to this godforsaken hole in the first place to escape that kind of thing.'

Jim said nothing. He didn't want Lily in his home. He didn't want any kind of interaction with her. Even his acquaintance with Luke had been stretching it, though Luke's car had proven invaluable.

'The fact of the matter is this,' Lily announced, genuinely undaunted by her lack of a response, 'you are a fat dick who stinks of fish,' she pointed at Luke. 'And you,' she pointed at Jim, 'you are a skinny baldie runt of a man. And I don't care if you've got some kind of fatal disease. I don't care. Fuck off!'

She stormed out.

'Would you believe it?'

Luke shook his head in amazement. Jim was still holding his breadknife.

'No.'

He turned and cut into the sandwich. The yolk had gone cold, and the blade was much sharper than he'd anticipated.

12

Remember Big Ron?

He didn't want to remember, he didn't want to.

Remember Big Ron?

Who came home from his long trip away when Nathan was only eight years old.

Remember?

Hell wasn't black after all. It was an endless, hollow, grey colour and it felt slippery. Nathan could find no fingerholds. Even though his hands were still small. He was eight years old and there was nothing to cling on to.

Just Big Ron.

Remember him?

Then Little Ronny was born.

What a *relief*.

Big Ron and all his friends. Feel of brickwork. Half smile. Smell of camphor. Wet sheet.

It's a mould, the letter said, a mould. You wipe it off the wall but it comes back because there's damp in the wall. It comes back. You bleach the wall, you scrub it, but the mould comes back. And the mould's in you. You cunt. You fucking evil cunt. And your brother. Do you know what you've done? Do you know?

Remember Big Ron?

Empty. Twist. Wind. Grave. Lonely. Sharp. Stiff. Spoiled. Breath, no-breath. Ruined. Empty. Hollow, hollow, hollow, hollow.

Oh thank God little Ronny came. Oh thank God, thank God.

But he's only little.
Only.
Little.
And even that didn't stop him.

Nathan's thoughts were a giant, angry sea tap-tap-tapping on a small dyke wall. He tried to hold the sea at bay.

He tried to run it off. He ran, sometimes, through the park, along the road, down by the canal. He ground his teeth on buses. He bit his nails to the quick. He held his breath. He tried to be a gentle man.

But the sea kept on tapping.

After Connie's visit, a blood vessel burst in his eye. He gazed at it in the mirror. It resembled a river. A tiny, bloody Amazon.

Nobody saw. Nobody ever saw. Because Nathan was grown up now. The past was such a long time ago. And Big Ron was dead dead dead. He was *dead*.

13

'I was very surprised by your bathroom cabinet,' Ronny said, wiping egg from his mouth with the back of his hand.

'What were you doing in my bathroom cabinet?' Jim asked, an edge in his voice.

'I was hunting for a razor,' Ronny said, 'and there's an edge in your voice.'

'I don't have a razor.'

Jim was clearing the hearth. It was full of ash.

'But do you have an edge?'

Jim stopped clearing and almost smiled. 'An edge? Doesn't everybody? Don't you?'

Ronny grinned. 'Sometimes.'

'I have an edge,' Jim confided, 'but what I don't have is a temper.'

Ronny sat down on the sofa. He was holding a small pair of nail scissors.

'I'm going to cut off my beard.'

Jim said nothing. Ronny began snipping. 'The way you said it!' he chuckled, *sotto voce*.

'Said what?'

'I don't have a temper. *Have*. Like a temper was something you were really searching for.'

Jim straightened up. Ronny continued. 'Like in a children's story. He was looking for his temper. He looked in the fireplace. He looked in the bread bin. He looked in the bathroom cabinet . . .'

'No. *You* looked in the bathroom cabinet.'

Ronny snorted, but then continued mining the same vein, unrepentantly, 'So Ronny looked for Jim's temper. He thought he'd found it in the bathroom cabinet but in fact all he'd found was an edge,' he looked up, 'and loads of pills. What are they for?'

'Indigestion,' Jim said.

'Really?'

'No.' Jim smiled.

'Hair is extremely flammable,' Ronny muttered, cutting with vigour.

'We need kindling and driftwood if you want a fire later,' Jim said, standing up with the ash-can in one hand and a brush in his other. 'Do you want to come out and collect some?'

'Sure.'

Ronny chucked a handful of his hair into the empty fireplace and then followed Jim outside with all the casual ease and familiarity of an old basset hound.

They walked along the beach. It was mid-afternoon.

'So why did you lose your hair?' Ronny asked.

'I had a habit,' Jim said, bending over to pick up a stick, 'of pulling out single strands.'

'Why?'

'It was a nervous habit. A bad habit. I didn't even know I was doing it. After a while I made a little bald patch.'

'Where?'

'At the back, underneath. You couldn't see it. But one day it began falling out spontaneously. I'd find handfuls of it on my pillow in the morning. Then I was prescribed certain drugs, hormones, which made it worse. Eventually it all went. Even my lashes.'

Ronny kicked at a large log. 'How about this?'

'Not if it's damp.'

Ronny picked up the log. He grinned. 'I thought I might find your temper under it.'

Jim scratched his nose. 'I don't think I'd keep my temper under a log.'

He walked on.

'How come those chalets are all fenced off?' Ronny asked, catching up, readjusting the log under his right arm and then nodding towards the hamlet.

'It's a private community. They think the locals are all freaks. Anti-social. Inbred. So they put the fence up to distinguish themselves. And we tend to think they're weird because they put up the fence and because they come here principally on summer weekends to use the nudist beach.'

'Could I squat one?'

'The chalets? I shouldn't think so. But a couple of the prefabs near mine are empty.'

They had walked far enough along the beach to reach Ronny's shell display which had remained untouched since its completion that morning. Jim paused in front of it, Ronny too.

'What do you think?' he asked, smiling.

'Very . . . uh . . . nice,' Jim said finally, having struggled valiantly for a better word.

'You know,' Ronny looked calmly at his work, 'I think I could mess around with shells forever. It's very calming. Perhaps I'll make this display bigger. I could fill the whole beach with it.'

Jim stared at the shell display. 'What about the sea?'

'What about it?'

'And the bathers?'

'I wouldn't care about them.'

'And how would you eat?'

'I'd fish and I'd pilfer.'

Ronny chuckled at Jim's serious expression, because he hadn't actually meant a word of it. Jim wasn't smiling though. He found it difficult to imagine someone being willing to settle for so little. He said as much.

'Wouldn't you get bored?'

'I don't get bored. That's one of my virtues. I never get bored. I have this great ability to focus.'

Jim scratched his neck. 'I'm unsure whether being unable to get bored *is* necessarily a good thing.'

'Of course it is.'

'OK.' Jim conceded so quickly it was almost comical. Ronny shrugged, not really caring. He pointed towards his shell display. 'Can you read it?'

'Read it? No.'

'Honestly?'

'No.'

Ronny had made a small romantic gesture. Like a girl laboriously scratching a boy's initials on to a school desk. Jim stared blankly at his own name spelled out in sweet pastels.

'And there was a razor,' Ronny said, focusing in on the shells himself, 'in the cabinet. At the back.'

Jim's expression remained frozen.

Sure enough, she'd returned to Luke when the afternoon was getting dolled up in extravagant pinks and violets for the evening. Luke was one of those men to whom such things habitually occurred. His life had been full of women, calling by, dropping in, vacating. So the prospect of another meeting with Sara had left him feeling wonderfully bold, delightfully sassy, and, well, he had to admit it, the smallest, the tiniest, the most infinitesimal fraction *guilty*.

The truth was that he'd been fully intending to clear out: his body, his mind. He'd wanted to rid his existence of people. His last wife (his second wife) had yearned to cram his life full of them, full of herself, principally: her wants, her needs, her desires. But Luke had actually felt himself congested enough already. Crammed up in a too-small space with his booze, his fags, his belly and all his countless other vices.

He'd enjoyed a substantial life, a substantial career, substantial work, he felt, but real substance, true substance, he suddenly believed, depended on a kind of purity. A meanness, a thinness, a vigour. He wanted these things. He'd earned money. He'd been flash and greasy and commercial. And it had filled him up, certainly. But now he felt a need to recreate himself in the image of a world that was sparse and bare and elemental. Reaching the zenith, he told himself, depended not on doing more, but on doing less.

Luke was so unperturbed, so casual, so easy, in fact, following his chat with Jim, that instead of returning straight home in anticipation of Sara's probable arrival, he strolled off along the beach in search of Ronny's elusive black rabbits. He even took his camera with him. Maybe this would be the start of something? He couldn't be a landscape man, not straight off, that was asking too much, but he could be a dot on a landscape man. Any dot would do. A rabbit, a bird, a rat, even.

Sara, for her part, was thoroughly fearful and flustered. It was by no means unusual for her to act on impulse, but her impulses were invariably uniform, dull and doggedly predictable. Fish on Friday. Cheese scones. Skimmed milk. Germolene. She had thought long and hard about what to wear. In the mirror her own face stared back at her, weather-beaten. A buffeted face. Brown, although not with a posh tan or a holiday tan, but with an outside tan – the kind of tan workmen had, and bin-men. She had bright blue eyes and black hair. But her hair was wiry and it wouldn't *go*, not anywhere, it hung around her face, sulkily. It stuck up.

In her cupboard there was precious little to choose from. After a time she decided on something frivolous. Anything wintery was too serious, too full of weight and intent. So outside she threw on her best, long summer dress – even though the summer was over – and inside she wore the special bra and pants that she saved for medical examinations. All new. All bright white. Utterly unimpeachable.

She sneaked out of the house through the back door. Lily was in. She was upstairs in the bathroom. She'd complained that there was never any hot water when she wanted it, so Sara had quietly switched on the immersion. Twice Lily had stood before her, both times draped in a large brown towel.

'Do you think I'm dirty?'

'Of course not.'

'Am I the kind of girl whose friends write about her to magazines?'

'Pardon?'

'Why are you wearing your best summer dress?'

'I'm not. And stop scratching your neck. That's just tan.'

'I know! I told him it was fucking tan!'

'Told who?'

Lily ran upstairs to check in the mirror again.

She returned later and hung around in Sara's bedroom.

'Is that lipstick?'

Sara's eyes widened. 'Lip balm. They felt chapped.'

'What I want to know is this,' Lily mooched, not having listened, 'how come the bald one knew I was dirty when I've never even spoken to him before? It must've been the fishy one who said it first.'

'You aren't dirty.'

Sara slipped perfume and some face powder into her handbag. 'Haven't you bathed yet?'

'No.'

'Isn't the water hot enough?'

'Of course it's hot enough . . .'

Lily's eyes tightened and her jaw jutted out from the smooth coastline of her face. 'Christ almighty. Is it any wonder that I have no self esteem?'

'I wasn't . . .'

But like a pretty pleated skirt at a country dance, Lily flounced right on out.

14

Connie pressed her nose to the sheets of paper. They smelled of tobacco and floor polish. Not traditionally exotic aromas, but in this, her own particular context, she found them bewitching. She was sitting at a desk in the guest bedroom of her mother's house. The room was a forget-me-not blue with a navy trim halfway up the walls and bright white above. Pine desk, pine bed, high-polished pine floors. Everything spotless. She wore a pair of reading glasses which sat far down on her small nose and slipped if she blinked.

Something bit me in the night and now I'm sick. I have nets over my bunk and these stunted ochre-coloured candles which I burn while I sleep in an attempt to keep the mosquitos at bay. But there are bites on my belly, two of them, either side of my navel, like rusty little anthills. The local man – he's no doctor and he speaks no English – expressed no interest in the lumps. Instead he blamed the rain. It's the rainy season, he said, and made the sign of rain falling.

Yet Louis reckons that they could be something more sinister. So I lie in my bed to please him, and although outside it's stupidly damp, inside it's still relentlessly hot, hot, hot. The smell of the candles enters everything. Their scent is similar to cardamom only more acrid. Their aroma stinks up my clothes and my sheets and my hair. I taste it under my nails. I find a brown dust in my nostrils. I have a pathetic cough.

You should hear me, Ronny, with my pathetic cough.

The smell gets behind your eyes and feels so intense, like a bee buzzing in the ridge of your nose, also it tangs bitterly on the back of my tongue. I try constantly to swig it down with glasses of boiled water, but the vinegarish taste just clings and cloys. So what good after all were my countless precautions? I caught this tiresome sickness anyway, and it doesn't even amount to what Louis would call A Proper Ailment. It has no dignity. It isn't grandly tropical like I'd hoped. It isn't a fever or a temperature or anything like that. It is simply a heaviness.

I can feel every bone. Even my individual ribs, which as I breathe are like hard iron hoops tightening around my chest. My knees feel terrible. It's true! Like a gorilla's heavy knuckles, dragging, dragging. I tried to rub them with my hands at first, but my actual knuckles soon grew numb and weighty and ineffectual.

Pity me, Ronny!

Naturally, for all his apparent concern, Louis refused point blank to call out the proper doctor again. Again? He had come once already a month ago when a blister on my heel went septic and my whole foot turned a whitish blue colour. That often happens here. The local people use forest herbs to prevent infections, even the chimps do the same, Louis says, but neither he nor I are botanists.

Anyway, I bound it up. I ignored it. It didn't hurt. And then one day the skin came loose. The layers had separated and resembled a flaky, filo pastry. But harboured underneath this fragile crust were a hundred writhing orange worms. A bright, vibrant, zesty tangerine. A crazy synthetic colour. Orange bodies tipped with jet-black pin-heads.

I went mad. When the doctor came he burned them out. He was disgusted that neither Louis nor I had taken any kind of first aid course back at home. He was a sour, grey-haired, safari-suited New Zealander who clearly thought us both fools. And his fee was exorbitant. Louis literally spewed. He was livid.

So I was glad of the local man, when he came to my shack, inspected my hands, my neck, my ankles and then stuck his tongue deep into his cheek with a correspondingly speculative shrug of his shoulders. One of the trappers – we call him Monty, Christ knows why – told Louis afterwards that the heavy bones are a sign that the soul is light and longs to fly away. Like a butterfly, he said, or like a wild jungle parrot in a keep net.

But nobody keeps me, Ronny.

I have a window. No glass in it. And through the window I can see the forest and the sky as I recline on my bunk. The dense forest and the high grey sky. The air oozes with different sounds. As I lie here, heavy-boned and hopeless, I can detect the calls of twelve distinct birds. The monkeys chatter and squeal relentlessly. I hear the chuck and hiss of a stream. The trees, the leaves, the warm wind. I hear them.

And most of all I hear the rain. The soft earth sucks up its sudden tears so readily with its ardent red-hard lips. I hear nature's lovemaking – the perpetual tickle and thrill of it all – from this my sick-sick bed. But where do I fit? Hidden in my shack. A nut in its husk? Perhaps, I tell myself, I am the earth's pale tongue. Or a small, dull bud. Or a heavy chrysalis. An insect? A turning, yearning, bleached, blanched milk-white aphid.

I lie and I lie and I wonder what I am.

Ronny?

M.

Connie threw down the letter, knocked her glasses off and on to the desk, pushed her chair back and stood up. On the high-polished floor to her left was a powder-blue rug, fluffy and small. She sprang on to it, settled her weight and then kicked off. She had done this before, countless times.

She flew from the desk to the opposite wall, from the wall she flew to the bed and back again. She kept her balance exquisitely, and then, just as suddenly, she absolutely lost it. The rug tucked and gathered. It tipped. She felt the wooden boards jar and crack against her palms and her knees. 'Ow!' she whispered, as a matter of form, and then she lay down flat on her stomach and pushed her cheek hard against the floor's cold, wooden boards. She listened to their creaking as the blood pumped in her ears. She closed her eyes.

It was in this strange position that her mother discovered her.

Lately, Lily had begun remembering things which she knew for a fact she'd done herself, as if somebody else had done them. Small acts of cruelty. Unjustifiable lies. Tiny injuries. Arguments. Plain observations. Whims.

Her brain – keen for mischief, for diversity – had started experimenting with notions of context, and meaning, and responsibility. Lily found herself experiencing certain intimate, everyday occurrences second-hand. She would remember actual events, but only as hearsay, as stories, or as interesting fragments of other people's conversation.

Had she ever doubted her own judgement, questioned her own motivations or struggled against her worse inclinations, this development might have given Lily pause. But she never doubted herself. She was bold and wild and sure. This was how she survived.

Anyhow, that sheer ravine which suddenly seemed to exist between memory and action could be tantalizing when experienced, she felt, and sometimes liberating. Like a drug. Scary. Addictive. And, yes, there was the occasional bad trip, too. Inevitably.

'It must've been the fishy one who called me dirty,' Lily muttered, sulkily, pulling her brown bath towel tighter around her skinny midriff as she stared, shivering slightly, into Sara's hen coop. 'I never even spoke to the bald one before. I never even went near him.'

In her hand, Lily held a sharp blade. Her fingers were cold and clumsy. The hens clucked, to the rear of the coop, suddenly nervous, all in a cluster.

15

Sara walked the longest possible route for her own cautious reasons and ended up in the nature reserve, where you either went forwards or backwards but couldn't easily meander. She wanted to meander though. She'd lost her nerve. To the right of the raised bank and footpath that she tripped along billy-goat-gruffly in her summer sandals – lay the salt flats and the sea; to the left, the freshwater river, and beyond that, just fields.

'I am a farmer's wife,' she kept incanting, 'and I farm boar.'

If she went on saying it then she could almost stop herself from hoping.

'I farm boar.'

The summer dress had been a mistake. Of course. She was no sophisticate and it was spitting.

'Fool's rain,' she told herself, because while it seemed harmless, only a fool would consider venturing out into it unprotected.

'I am a farmer's wife.'

It rained harder. It grew darker.

'I am ridiculous.'

Up ahead, to her left, stood a birdwatchers' hide; mawkish and hutchy on its tall stilts. She wiped the rain from her cheeks and ran over to it. The wood was harsh and splintery under her wet hand. As she began to climb, cool sea air billowed out her skirt and slipped up the back of her dress with all the smart, fine scratch of a beak and a claw. She clambered up the steps, her dress snagging, her sandals clicking.

She'd never been in a hide before. She imagined that it would be black inside and that it would smell of dark things, of treacle and pitch. She presumed that all the peep holes and hatches would be closed, so prepared herself for the shock of darkness. The door handle was wet and turned loosely. She pushed at the door with her knee and clambered inside. The rain followed her. She shut the door and then leaned her back up against it, puffing out her cheeks in the sudden, hollow silence with a sense of genuine relief.

It did not smell sweet and treacly like she'd imagined. It smelled of fish. One hatch was slightly ajar. Its pegs had come free and its latch had slipped by an inch or so. Her eyes focused on this bright gap greedily, on the pearly raindrops that sprang through it and into the hide as if escaping from an infinite frying white heat outside.

But here it was black and warm. Sara stretched a tentative foot sideways to see if she could locate a bench. Her leg touched something woody. She bent over and felt for it, blindly. Her fingers grasped it. She found its corner and then exhaled sharply as her middle finger pushed into a splinter.

She cursed and sat down, at first miscalculating and almost missing the bench. But it was slim and backless so she straddled it like a rocking horse. She sucked her finger. Her tongue explored the nail and pad of her finger gingerly until it located the scratchy woodchip. The chip snicked her tongue's tip and somehow thrilled her.

Her eyes were closed. Or were they? They were closed. But it made no difference. She imagined herself inside an oak casket. She'd gone and stowed herself away. She was wet and the rain on her lips was salty. She licked it. The fishy air. It was low and saucy. It smelled of sex. Of sealife. Damp and crude and tainted. Catfood. Pilchards. In oil, in oil.

Oh yes.

Under her left thigh lay a small bolt which held the top of the bench to its leg. It felt loose. She rocked herself. It wobbled. She shifted slightly and repositioned herself over it. It scratched and it niggled so delightfully. It found no focus. It had a clumsy accuracy. The best kind, she thought, and pulled up her wet skirts to feel her soaking thighs, her damp knees. The bench rocked. A little a little a little.

She felt her knee-bone, the fragile bits at the side, the gulf at the rear. She arched backwards and touched her calves, her ankles, her tinkling sandal buckles which she pulled open, yanking them off and tossing them sideways. Water dripped from her hair, on to her arms, down, down her throat. She was all at sea. She imagined Luke. Was that his name? He was a horse, a pit-pony, barrel-chested, round and solid, hard and musky. Strong hooves. Wide back. Glossy.

She rested her palms right behind her, clung on to the bench with her fingers. And she rocked and she rode, her toes pointing backwards, her hair pulling loose, her ankles aching, the letter D in flesh. Her breasts and her belly the curve, her stiff arms that letter's lovely backbone. Punctuated, utterly, by that delicious bolt. But this was just a tiny part of a long, long sentence. A conversation. It wouldn't end. It couldn't. Not right there and not right then and not right now. Oh . . .

Where would it go? And *ow*! Uh . . . how?

Mermaid, she panted, taking all things into account on this wonderful ramble into a scramble of nouns and sounds and resonance and consonants . . . asp . . . kedgeree . . . the arc of a boar's tusk . . . oh yes, oh yes . . . salt, straw, honey . . . pockets, bacon rind, a little bruise . . . a giant ocean, grapefruit, whiskers . . . uh . . . ink, foam, clay, liquorice, see-saw, she-sore, sea shore . . .

She wanted more. She wanted so . . . go . . . flow . . . much more. She wanted that bench to break. She wanted to break its back before she broke her own. So she rocked it, she lunged, she pushed and she swivelled. Her arms were unhinging at their elbows, her feet were twisted, her chest all rent and rasping. Her neck and head were yanked and tilting.

It came, it was coming! She could feel that bolt loosening, a shifting, a shunting.

One! she said, her own voice stunning her like the sting of a wet rope, Two and Three and Four! She counted and counted. Sometimes she lost the thread but then the numbers came back to her like swearwords.

Oh fuck! On thirty-six her hips went dead. On thirty-eight

that bench just buckled with the sweetesthardestloudest creaking. Crack! She went down with it. This was the hottest and the wettest vandalism. She gasped out laughing. Ashamed and glistening.

The floor was dusty. Her face, inky-rosy. She rolled off. Her limbs were shaking. Her dress was tangled. She tugged some skirt out from under. She put a hand to her medical underwear. She felt herself, holding her breath, suddenly cautious, as though testing the ripeness of an avocado. Oh shit, she whispered, All torn! She staggered to the door. She yanked it open.

'Excuse me . . .'

A voice, from deep in the dark behind her, so muffled, so muffled that it could have been something wildly unbidden hidden inside her own head.

'I think,' Luke stuttered, clutching her abandoned sandals to his wide chest, his face as white and ghastly on emerging from the hide's darkness as what little remained of the bleak afternoon light, 'I think, Sara, I honestly believe you've gone and *killed* me.'

Her face was black with mascara as she watched his knees give way.

16

The doctor was a family friend, naturally. And Connie knew, and Kitty her mother knew, that Connie knew, that Kitty had been fucking him, on and off, for the previous ten years. Kitty was magnificently post-menopausal, with great white curls, snazzy lips and eyes as soft, grey and glossy as a rabbit's ears. And tall. Almost five nine. She rendered Connie dwarf-like by comparison.

Her mother hovered, decorously, on the perimeter of the blue room, smelling of White Linen and a heavy French hand cream, recently applied. She'd been completing the washing-up from supper when she'd heard the crash. Connie wouldn't believe that she'd sprained her wrist. She kept touching it to check if it hurt. And it did, but only slightly.

'You may well be concussed,' the doctor said.

'But I didn't hit my head when I tripped . . .' she was automatic, 'only my knees and my palms.'

'But you have a bruise, darling,' her mother volunteered, 'on your cheek.'

Connie was dazzled at this notion. She had merely pressed her cheek to the floor and listened to her own blood pumping. She had thought she understood her own strength, her own silliness. But apparently not. The doctor had already bandaged up her wrist, made a sling and put some kind of elasticated material on top for support.

'It was a tiny fall,' she repeated, feeling a charlatan. She'd only told her mother she'd tripped to save fuss, not to cause it.

'When I found her,' Kitty said anxiously, twisting her wedding ring around on her finger, 'flat out like that, I was utterly petrified.'

'How about,' the doctor said softly, 'I have a quiet word with Connie here while you fetch her something warm and sweet to drink?'

Kitty pursed her lips and laced her fingers together, softly resisting, but then she nodded and quietly left them.

Connie resented being alone with him. As a child she'd called him Doctor Donald. Now she called him Donald. He had metallic hair and a dimple in his chin that any girl could fall into. He was a big man and perpetually peaking, she felt; always on top form. He was ruddy and Brylcreemed and reeked of suede and clean tweed. Considerably younger, she couldn't help noting, than her father had been.

He was so polite. The situation, the affair, had been so polite. No feathers ruffled, as far as she remembered. Merely her own.

'Your mother is anxious,' he said gently, 'about the will and the special bequest.'

'That's her business,' Connie said abruptly, stretching out her legs under the covers, 'and my business. Nobody else's.'

She imagined that her knees were two volcanoes. In Sumatra there were over a hundred volcanoes. Or so Monica had written. Over a hundred volcanoes. Eighteen active.

'The simple fact of the matter is that nobody actually cares,' Donald said, staring at her intently, thoroughly logical, 'so there's really no need for any of this.'

She brought up her legs defensively. 'Any of what?'

'Any of this . . . commotion.'

'In truth . . .' Connie pondered what she was about to say for a moment, 'it isn't even my mother's business, strictly speaking. It's mine. My business. My loan.'

'Have you been sleeping?'

'Why?' He'd caught her off her guard.

'Did you take the pills I prescribed?'

She nodded. 'Yes. I took them.'

She hadn't slept. She hadn't taken the tablets either. It had been five long months. Waking and dreaming were merging so wonderfully now. And what could be the harm in that?

'So you're still determined to sell?'

Connie nodded. 'Certainly. The money for the premises, the flat above, the stock, everything else should just about make up the required amount.'

Donald was perched uneasily on the desk's small pine chair. He adjusted his weight slightly and it creaked. It was a girl's chair, she thought, and he was no girl.

'What saddens me is that your father clearly wanted you to make a go of this business. He wanted you to be secure.'

'No,' Connie shook her head, 'he didn't want me to be secure. He wanted me to commit myself. Which is something altogether different.'

'I don't see that.'

She was irritating him. He still saw her as a small child. She was a mere toddler. Her knees wobbled, her feet faltered. In his eyes she would always be, at the very best, a dewdrop on life's river bank. She could never cause a splash, the most she could hope for would be to glimmer slightly and then to evaporate. That's what he'd always wanted.

But Connie saw it differently. She had another slant, which she sensed was her father's slant too. The slant was inherited, it was legitimate, she felt, and as such it had to be embraced, it had to be hugged and treasured and cosseted. When she had called herself inconstant to Nathan, that morning, she had not meant it lightly. It was absolutely true.

She was a small blonde flea and she jumped from place to place, from man to man, from job to job. And yes, sometimes she'd found her feet, but only briefly, and on one of these occasions she'd remained static long enough to qualify as an optician. Got the certificate. Got the frames and the lenses and the premises. Did all that stuff. And Daddy loaned her. No conditions. But when he wrote her the cheque he'd said, 'I have a strong suspicion you'll pay me back.'

What had he meant, exactly? Even at the time she'd wondered. And yet now she *was* paying him back. But she didn't happen to know how or why. At first she'd thought it was the other way around, that he was paying *her* back. Now, however, she sensed that doubt itself was his legacy. His gift.

Donald was staring at her. 'What on earth could your father have been thinking of?'

She shrugged. 'Me. Probably.'

'And your mother? What about her feelings?'

Connie felt absolutely no desire whatsoever to discuss any of this with Doctor Donald. Why should she? She sighed languorously. 'My knees feel so *heavy*,' she said.

The Head had instructed Lily not to wash. For the month of August. August was gorgeously equable weather-wise, so she'd perspire less, he said. Nobody would even notice. And hitherto she'd done just as he'd asked. Until now.

Lily gazed at the bath water. She felt slightly dizzy but couldn't think why. She wondered idly what would happen if she disregarded The Head's wishes. Her stomach nagged her. It was a feeling akin to hunger. A pinchy, poky anxiety. She gnawed at her tongue. Then she abandoned her reserve, yelped and sprang in.

Once submerged she forgot all about The Head. Instead she watched her small breasts bobbing in the water. She tried to line up her nipples with her toes. She closed her eyes and focused hard, like a fighter pilot squinting through his viewfinder. Left a little. Right a little. Pow!

Out of the corner of her eye she sensed a movement. She blinked. She sat up and peered around her. Hot water lapped against her ribs. She looked down between her knees and saw a tiny line of gravel on the bath's enamel base. She felt vaguely perplexed. But then she sniffed, casually, and picked up a bar of soap.

Five minutes and the water had cooled perceptibly. She rinsed herself off and then clambered out. She looked around for her towel. The brown towel. It was not on the floor. She turned in a circle, still looking. She inspected the towel rack. There was a pink hand towel, nothing else. She grabbed hold of the hand towel and tried to cover herself.

She wanted the brown towel. Still looking, she walked to the door. She pushed it wide and watched steam escape into the crooked hallway. She walked down and along. On the landing at the top of the stairs she thought she saw the brown towel, all in a heap. Carelessly abandoned. Lily stared at it a while. Could she remember dropping it in that place? It was such a small detail but she scowled because it didn't fit. She wanted it to fit.

She bent down to pick it up anyway. Her hand touched the towel and it felt as light as thistledown. She tried to lift it. It lifted, but not by any significant amount before it fractured in her hand and under its own weight. It was like dust and ashes. It was cobweb, snuff and soft fur.

She gave a little yell. She withdrew and then kicked out with her foot. The towel sprang into the free air at the top of the stairs like a skinny, vital, flat brown creature. A flying squirrel, a feathery, heathery fruitbat. Then it disintegrated. But Lily didn't see this happen. She had sprung backwards and was yodelling because her foot was stinging. She hopped and then whimpered, clutching her injured toes in her hands. There was blood on her foot, and a mark which could have been a scratch, or a nettle sting or, more disgustingly, it could have been a bite.

17

Ronny had been weaving around in the prefab's open doorway, in a state remarkably close to hysteria, for well over an hour. He was ludicrously buoyant, Jim felt, and for the silliest of reasons. 'The rain hitting the sea!' he kept exclaiming, 'Whap! Whap! *Whap!*' From the rear he resembled a little wooden puppet, a stick-doll, which somehow struck Jim as very poignant. He took a deep breath and then tried his utmost to focus on piling up the kindling in the fireplace.

In fact he found the puppet image a surprisingly resonant one, perhaps because for the first time in a long while he felt as though his own strings were being twitched – but not in a terrible way, not in a calculated way – and he was perplexed, jarred, *undone*, even, by the multiplicity of sensations it afforded him.

Usually he lived on one level. He preferred it that way. His colours were one colour, his music a monotone. That's how he liked it. Even so, he couldn't really understand Ronny's apparent fixation on honing things down. To simplify life, certainly, but to achieve this end only through such petty deprivations? He told himself that Ronny had too much time on his hands. Which was true. But Ronny seemed to have no actual notion of time and what it really meant.

'What?'

Ronny had stopped jiggling and was peering sideways, out of the doorway, gesticulating madly into the rain.

Again.

'What?' he said, and then, 'who, me?'

Quick as a flash he bolted.

Jim paused, threw down the kindling and walked to the

doorway himself. A short distance down the beach Ronny joined a man and a woman. The woman seemed to be supporting the man although he was almost half her size again. Ronny procrastinated, just for a moment, and then took hold of the man's other arm and helped to carry him, staggering, towards the prefab.

As they drew closer Jim saw that the man was Luke.

'What's happened?'

Jim assisted them inside. Luke looked terrible. The woman didn't look much better. Ronny was short of breath. 'He thinks he's had a heart attack,' he explained, panting.

They lay Luke down on the sofa. He seemed calm but was pale and incapable of speech.

'Do you have a phone?' the woman asked Ronny. Ronny shook his head. He turned to Jim. 'You should drive him to hospital. That'd be quicker than an ambulance. His Volvo's right outside.'

'Yes,' the woman nodded. Her feet were bare and she wore a light summer dress which was wet and virtually transparent, torn in the skirt and blotched in a couple of places with what looked like mud or lichen.

Jim had no intention of driving Luke to the hospital. He had his own reasons for this which he felt no desire to discuss publicly. Instead he spoke to Ronny: 'No. You should drive.'

'I can't,' Ronny's face glistened with rain. 'I mean I would if it was an automatic, but it isn't.'

Jim turned to the woman. 'Could you drive?'

'No. I don't have a licence. I can't even drive a tractor.' She glanced down at herself. 'Anyway, look at me, what would people think?'

'Does it matter?'

Her eyes were round. She was incredulous. 'How long have you lived in this community? Of course it matters.'

Ronny spoke again, more insistently this time. 'You should drive him, Jim. I wouldn't even know the route.'

Luke grunted from the sofa. His lips were moving. 'What's he saying?' Ronny squatted down next to him and grabbed hold of his wrist. After a great deal of effort Luke raised his head and managed to utter two complete words: 'Recovery . . . position.'

Ronny looked up, scowling. 'Recovery position?'

Jim was flummoxed. 'I don't know any first aid. Would that involve lying him on his side or something?'

He looked to Sara who shrugged helplessly. Ronny turned to Luke again. 'What is the recovery position, Luke?'

Luke waved his hands, weakly, like he was conducting a small rodent orchestra. He clearly had no idea.

Ronny smiled, tickled by something. 'What we should all bear in mind,' he said gently, 'Luke especially, is that dying is not such an extraordinary thing. In fact,' he addressed himself directly to Luke, 'it's actually very ordinary.'

Luke did not react well to this information. He found his voice, somewhere way deep down inside of him, although its note was as weedy as a reed pipe. 'It is . . . bad,' he panted, 'you stupid fuck.'

'Turn him on his side,' Jim spoke to Sara, who was beginning to look frantic, 'his left side, and while you're doing that we'll go next door and find the car keys.'

Sara did just as he'd asked. She was well accustomed to responding without a murmur to curt instructions. Jim walked into the rain and Ronny followed. 'Will you drive him after all?'

Jim didn't answer. Instead he pushed Luke's prefab door open and began scouting around.

'You seem very calm,' Ronny said.

Jim shifted some papers and photos on Luke's table. A strange montage of pictures of a woman inserting the bulb end of a flowering hyacinth into her vagina occupied his attention for a second. They were so irrelevant, so inappropriate that he almost laughed out loud when he saw them, but instead of laughing he pushed them aside, roughly. Several fell to the floor. Ronny picked them up and inspected them.

'I really hope Luke cleared the mud off the bulb end,' he said, 'before he set about taking these.'

Jim found the keys in a cup on the table. He took a deep breath. 'I've got the keys, Ronny,' he spoke quietly, 'but I'd rather not drive him to the hospital.'

'Why not?' Ronny put down the photos.

'They might recognize me there.'

'How come?'

'I stole some drugs a while ago. I don't feel happy about going back.'

Ronny was surprised. 'You stole drugs?'

'I needed them. I had a prescription but it was difficult to renew it. I'll be in trouble if I go back.'

'I don't think they'd recognize you,' Ronny said quickly, 'not in an emergency.'

'They would. This is a small community, and I'm hardly inconspicuous.'

Ronny looked miserable. 'It's just that I already had to use my right arm earlier to carry Luke into the prefab and I felt strange after, kind of sick and fluttery inside. It felt all wrong.'

Jim struggled to sympathize. He struggled. 'Just this once, Ronny. He may be dying.'

Ronny gnawed at his thumbnail. 'But what about her? Why can't she do it?'

'She said she can't drive.'

'I don't believe her. Everyone can drive.'

Jim frowned. 'If we end up having a huge row over it she'll get suspicious.'

'Why should she?'

Jim's face was blank.

'Suspicious about what?' Ronny persisted.

'I'm asking you,' Jim said, his voice so hollow and urgent it was really quite eerie, 'please. *Please.*'

Ronny scowled, snatched up the keys and walked out into the rain.

18

The longer it took for Sara to arrive home, the more enraged Lily became. Where was she anyway? She hadn't told her she was going out. Eventually it grew dark. Lily was freezing. She was still undressed. The pink hand towel was cold and damp. Her legs and midriff felt all itchy and stiff. Her toe throbbed. She shifted. Her arms were indented with the pattern of the woodchip wallpaper. Her bottom was pocked with several small dustballs and hair-clusters which the Hoover hadn't quite reached, but her soft skin had reached them.

She was sitting, knees up, huddled, in a corner of the landing. After the incident . . . The Incident. After The Incident she'd cowered there, more for effect than for anything. What was the point, after all, in making a scene if there was no one present to witness it? She hadn't minded the initial twenty minutes. It had all been quite exciting. But she'd been waiting for almost two hours now, and she was bored and furious. In fact she'd almost forgotten why it was that she had snuck down there in the first place.

The only thing that kept her – crouched and resentfully timorous – in her corner, was the galling apprehension that if she moved all her suffering would be for nothing. And Sara had to be punished. For not being there. For not understanding her secrets. For being old and clumsy and separate. Yes.

Finally she heard a key in the lock. Voices. She listened, holding her breath. Two voices, one of them male. She jumped up and ran to her bedroom – a startled hare – threw on a precautionary dressing-gown, then came on out boxing. They were in the hallway.

'I've been going out of my mind!' she expostulated, making

a grand entrance at the top of the stairs, limping extraordinarily. 'And something terrible bit my toe. Where were you?'

She stopped in her tracks. On the first stair, close to the wall, lay a sharp blade with blood at its tip. She bent down, grabbed it, and held it behind her back. At the foot of the stairs stood Sara and Ronny. Sara looked washed out. She was torn and wrecked. 'Look,' she said hoarsely, ignoring Lily's protestations, 'this is Ronny. He needs to get back to one of the prefabs on the beach. Will you take him? I know it's dark but you could push your bike there and then ride it back again.'

This was all utterly unforeseen. Lily was thrown off-kilter. 'You mean right now?'

'Yes. He doesn't know the way.'

She was disgruntled. And she was about to complain, to hee-haw, to dig in her hooves like a mule, when she noticed that her mother was holding something. 'What is that?' she asked nervously. Sara looked down. 'A towel. It was in the driveway. It must've blown off the line.'

'Oh.'

Lily stared at the brown towel.

'So will you take him?'

But Lily wasn't listening. She was staring at the wall and at the banisters.

'What's wrong?' Sara's eyes followed the route Lily's had just taken. She stepped forward, squinting. 'What is that? What's been happening here?'

Lily recoiled. 'I don't know.'

Sara climbed a couple of the stairs. 'My God,' she stepped back again, 'that's revolting.'

The wall was smeared with blood. A thick blood. Liverish. It was a reddish brown colour and almost dry. The banisters were spotted with it, the skirting boards. It was everywhere.

'What is this? What have you done?'

'Me?' Lily was aggrieved and righteous. 'I haven't done anything.'

But Sara was distracted, suddenly. She was looking down at her own two hands which were red, and the front of her dress, also red. She dropped the towel. 'I thought it was wet from a puddle, not . . .' she mumbled, stunned.

Ronny remained stock still at the foot of the stairs. He had said nothing, hitherto, but he was rubbing his stomach. He looked queasy.

'Oh Christ!' Lily yelled, seeing his expression, her girlish dignity suddenly in tatters. 'All this mess! It's so embarrassing. Why the hell did you have to bring him here?'

'Uh . . .' Ronny interjected, 'I felt sick anyway. It has nothing at all to do with your wallpaper.'

Sara gingerly lifted the bloody towel by its corners. She held it up. Several downy feathers adhered to its sticky, damp fabric. Lily took a cautious step backwards.

'It's absolutely soaking,' Sara said softly, 'heavy. Do you have any idea how this could have happened?'

Lily scowled. 'No.'

'You've not been bleeding or anything?'

'No!'

Lily's eyes were stony with mortification.

'Not even . . . you know?'

'Oh, my God, I hate you!' Lily yelled, sprinting off towards the sanctuary of her bedroom. 'You just want everyone to think I'm some kind of crazy witch or a pervert or a stupid weirdo!'

The door slammed. Ronny sat down on the bottom stair. Sara pushed past him. 'I'd better wash my hands and put this in to soak.'

Lily tossed the knife into a drawer and then listened, furtively. Their voices were muffled but audible. And while she listened she pressed her hands to her cheeks to feel how hot they were and then tried to cool them – first with her fists, then with the back of a plastic hairbrush, and finally with the cool innards of her A Level Business Studies text book. She was a skinny statuette. She was Tome-Head.

'I'm really sorry about this,' Sara said, 'it's just so strange. If you wait in the sitting room until Lily's calmed down, I'll quickly try and clear up the worst of it.'

'I'm fine here,' Ronny said, watching her disappear into the kitchen, remaining seated, picking off a couple of feathers from his cardigan's sleeve and then raising his voice over the sound of water running. 'It smells kind of like iron, don't you think? The blood? Like metal.'

'Yes.' Sara's voice was distant and then close again. 'I'd hate you to think we made a habit of doing this kind of thing.'

Ronny was silent for a moment and then he said thoughtfully, 'Your daughter seems very angry about something.'

'Lily? You think so?'

'Lily. That's pretty.'

'Yes. I've always liked it.'

Lily growled into her text book. She hated her fucking name.

Sara was holding a bucket and a cloth. 'It's mainly just her age. You know? Hormones.'

Lily growled again. Oh how she would make Sara suffer for this! She was seventeen, for heaven's sake. *Seventeen*!

'When I was thirteen,' Ronny said, 'I remember that things seemed very confusing.' He didn't add that they still felt that way.

'She's actually seventeen,' Sara said, wringing out the cloth and applying it to the banister.

'Really?'

'Yes,' Sara grunted slightly as she rubbed, 'Lily's a late developer. She's always been slightly taller than average but very gawky. It's taken her a while to mature physically . . . I mean as quickly as other girls of the same age.'

Lily squealed. She threw down her book, pulled on a T-shirt, some jeans, yanked on her trainers, flinching, slightly, when her sore toe clashed with the fabric interior, then ran into the hallway. 'Let's go! Let's go!' she yelled, facing her humiliation head on, butting it aside, taking the stairs two at a time, pushing past Sara and her bucket of soapy water, grabbing Ronny by the arm and *dragging* him, dragging him towards the front door.

'Come *on*!'

The fire was blazing. Jim was preparing a Fray Bentos chicken pie. It was steaming in the kitchen. He sat on the sofa, a pen in his hand, a pad of paper on his lap. He wore no hat. Light from the bulb above glanced off his bright pate. He was fleshy, like a sea anemone. He was bare.

Jim swapped the pen into his right hand. *Dear Nathan*, he wrote, in shaky print, and then he stared at these words for a long, long time. Eventually he glanced up, into the fire.

Red flames. Red hair. Hot. Hot. *Hot*. It took him right back. He remembered his brother and the last time he ever saw him, in his father's house. Nathan. All tough, and bullish and twenty-four, with a regular job and a bedsit and everything.

'You can sleep on the sofa,' he'd said, his eyes dense and glossed with earnestness, 'and you can stay just as long as you like. That's a promise.'

Little Ronnie, who was now Jim, sat on his bed, his arms around his knees, barely there, really. Eventually he whispered, 'It's too late.'

'It's never too late,' Nathan smiled, 'never. You're fifteen. Fifteen! You can do anything you want with your life.'

'I don't dare think about it,' Little Ronnie mumbled, 'there's just too much stuff . . .'

He gazed around at his dank, grey room, his few books, his posters, his chemistry set, his bed, the notches in the wall from the bedposts, and the scratches in the plaster he'd made himself with a compass. Little pictures and lines and notes and messages in baby code. His scratches. This was everything, wasn't it? These were all his possibilities.

'I've got the car. It'll be two trips, that's all. Two stupid trips.'

'But there's all these *arrangements*, Nathan. Things I can't get out of.'

'I want you to come with me.' Nathan was insistent.

'I can't.'

'I'm begging you to come. I'm *begging* you.'

Little Ronnie looked up into his brother's kind eyes. 'Force me.'

'No.' Nathan would not be drawn. He was better than that, he was bigger than his father, he was decent. 'I can't force you. It's your own decision. You're not a child any more.'

'It's just . . .'

Little Ronnie was tugging at his hair. His thin hair, which was worn and patchy like an old animal pelt.

'Don't be afraid of him,' Nathan exclaimed, 'he's just a stupid, stinking old man.'

'I'm not afraid.'

Oh God, he was.

'Then what is it?'

'I can't make the decision.'

Help me, help me, help me, Little Ronnie was thinking. Help me.

Nathan grew impatient. He was offering the world.

'Is your suitcase still packed and tucked away under your bed?' He suddenly spoke like an ally. Because this was their past, their pact, their sweet secret he'd rejuvenated.

'No.' Little Ronnie shook his head.

Nathan squatted down and glanced under. 'I see it.'

He put out a hand to grab it.

'Not the suitcase!'

Little Ronnie tried to stop his older brother, but Nathan pulled out the case anyway, and Ronnie bent to his will like a strand of corn, a straw.

'Always packed,' Nathan said, 'like when we were kids, remember? And I promised I'd take you away the very first time?'

He was only eight years old when Big Ron returned from his long trip away. But even then he'd longed to escape. He'd planned to.

Nathan opened the case, expecting to find the little shirts and little shoes, the baby clothes that he'd packed himself when Little Jim was still a toddler and he'd yearned so much to save him. But he recoiled at what he saw instead, and then his expression dulled and his eyes glazed over like the eyes of a fish too long out of water.

In the case lay a collection of polaroids, some self-assembled newsletters, a camera, some rope, a knife, a hot water bottle, a roll of thick brown sticky tape, other stuff. He slammed the case shut. Something inviolate had been violated.

103

'What's going on?' he asked. His voice was heavy-vowelled. He was sticky-throated. Little Ronnie scratched at his cheeks like a limp, long-limbed baby monkey. He said nothing. Nathan fastened the locks on the case and picked it up. He wouldn't leave it. No bloody way.

'Are you coming?'

He was rough now. Little Ronnie shook his head. It was too late. It had always been too late. Even breathing implicated him. Even blinking.

'This is the very last time,' Nathan said, his voice creaking, 'that I'm going to ask.'

Little Ronnie huddled up.

Nathan felt his heart judder inside his rocky chest like a pebble on the thick-set surface of an icy pond. He wouldn't crack. He couldn't. He inhaled. Deep, deep. He exhaled. He turned. He went. And that was the end of everything. Because when Nathan left his father's house, all decency left with him.

19

He was sick four times. The first time, up against the back wheel of the green Volvo.

'Yuk.'

Lily watched him.

'Is it food poisoning?'

'Nope.'

'Then what?'

'Misery.'

'*Shiiiiit*!'

Ronny straightened up and began walking down the farm's long drive. It was dark and the moon was high.

'Why don't you take the car?' She limped along next to him.

'I don't want to.'

'Why the hell not?'

He glanced at her with something approaching bewilderment. She was so *angry*. After a while he said gently, 'So we've all appreciated the joke now, Lily.'

'What joke?'

She scowled at him.

'That I walk a little strangely.'

Lily stopped short. 'I didn't even notice,' she said, all stiffnecked huff, 'and if you actually want to know, I've injured my foot.'

While she spoke, Ronny was sick again, up against a wire fence. 'I'm sorry about this.' He wiped his mouth.

'It'll merge in. This is a farm. In the country every-fucking-thing merges.'

'Sick doesn't merge,' Ronny muttered hoarsely, 'it's always synthetic-looking, don't you think?'

'Synthetic? How?'

Lily peered at his vomit in the darkness. She was a farmer's daughter with a cast-iron stomach. She saw nothing amiss.

'The colour,' he said, 'the *texture*.'

Then he walked on, disgusted at himself. 'What about eggs then?' Lily asked, catching him up, 'what about jellyfish?'

'Pardon?'

'The whole fucking world's synthetic.'

Ronny stopped walking. 'Hold on a second,' he said, and made Lily stop too. She thought he was going to be sick again but he wasn't. The problem was something exterior this time. His back and his neck were prickling.

'What's up?'

'I don't know.'

He rubbed his neck and glanced around him. To his right lay a ploughed field. To his left a high wire fence. He was tall, though, and everything was flat here. He tried to adjust his sight-line. He looked low, and then lower. He froze. Lily chuckled. 'It's the beetroots. There's a few of them dropped outside the fence. He wants one.'

'He' was a hairy beast; hunched and bear-like and giant and tusky. His eyes shone out, brownly. Wild, wild eyes. He was prehistoric. Ronny took a step backwards. Lily picked up a beet and tossed it over the fence. The boar ambled towards it.

'Get back to bed you silly bugger!' she hollered, then added, 'See all the others?'

What Ronny had believed to be bushes and hillocks he now saw were animals, bristle-backed with a Bronze Age cragginess. Watching, waiting. Hoofy, toothy. 'Meet the harem,' Lily said, 'they don't often come out at night, but it feels quite balmy and they weren't fed today.'

Ronny moved forward and reached out his hand. Lily said nothing until his wrist was through the fence wire, then she said calmly, 'Well, *I* certainly wouldn't.'

He jerked back quickly and his fist caught in the wire. He yanked it through roughly.

'Aren't they friendly?'

Lily snorted and walked on. Eventually Ronny followed her. He caught up at the gate. She held it open for him and then closed it behind them.

'See the bats?' she pointed.

He gazed into the sky. He almost tripped. It was a rough road.

'So how did you meet up with Mum?'

She needed to know.

'Uh . . .' he thought for a moment, 'is it true that she doesn't actually drive?'

'Yes.'

Lily wondered why it was that people invariably evaded her questions. She'd always presumed that the act of requesting information was fundamental to polite intercourse. Ronny was studying her. 'So how did you hurt your foot?' he asked. Lily paused. It was such a fine dark night. She longed for some kind of spice. For significance.

'Bite,' she said, her voice vibrating, her mouth virtually champing on the thick night air like it was candy floss.

'Bite?'

'Yep.'

'What bit you?'

'A thing.'

Ronny smiled. 'A bad thing?'

Lily shrugged. They walked past a cluster of dark caravans and some large, empty barns. 'A freak,' she said, finally, and then, in case he didn't understand her, 'a demon.'

Ronny veered sharply to the side of the road and sat down on its grassy verge. 'There's no such thing,' he said calmly.

'Why are you stopping?' Lily wanted to walk.

'I feel bad. I might be sick again.'

She stood in front of him, twisting her feet about. Ronny collapsed slowly on to his back and looked up into the sky. 'Demons are just something people invented to channel their feelings of anger and pain. Bad feelings. They're like an excuse, that's all.'

'What?'

'Take poltergeists . . .'

'Poltergeists?'

But Ronny chose not to follow this up. Instead he said quietly, 'I was in Shepherd's Bush,' he linked his fingers over his chest, 'just wandering around, and I saw a small crowd of people outside this antique shop.'

Lily also glanced up into the sky, but nothing she saw there impressed her. She looked down at Ronny instead. He was too thin. She scowled. Something told her that this should've been her big moment, but she'd gone and missed out on it. Again.

'Anyhow,' Ronny continued, 'I wondered what it could be that was causing all this excitement . . .'

'So?' She was rolling her eyes, plainly fatigued.

'A freak,' Ronny said, clearly relishing the single syllable.

Lily stopped rolling. 'What do you mean?'

'In the window. In a little glass case. An exhibit.'

Lily quickly sat down next to him. He, in turn, pushed himself up on to his elbows. 'A little beast,' he added.

'What?'

Ronny's breath smelled of acid. His teeth were white, white. Lily steadied herself, preparing for some kind of a wind-up.

'A little beast in a glass case. For sale.'

'A beast?' Lily loved this word.

Ronny lay back down again.

'And so?' she prompted.

Ronny sighed. 'A postcard at the front of the case said: The Cobham Beast. That was his name. That's what they had called him. I imagine that he must've come from a place called Cobham but I've never heard of it.'

'I have,' Lily nearly choked in her excitement.

'Really?' He turned to look at her.

'Yes. I have an aunt who lives there. It isn't very far from here.' She was excited, a part of the story now.

'And what did it look like, this beast?' she asked with some agitation.

'Like nothing I'd ever seen before.'

'How big?'

'Small. Like a rabbit, but upright.'

'And it wasn't a fake?'

'No. Absolutely not. But it had the loveliest, the sweetest face I've ever seen. A trusting face, full of gentleness.'

'Furry?'

'Short fur.'

'Black?'

'No. Brown. But it stood on its hind legs, like a small person, a baby, only it had four legs and two little arms.'

'A beast!'

Lily lay flat on her back and gazed at the stars. Her heart was red outside and all clogged up at its centre like a ripe ball of Edam.

'So what do you think it actually was?' she said, finally.

Ronny shrugged. 'I don't know. Itself.'

She liked this answer.

'But I had no money to buy it . . .' Ronny sighed.

'How much?'

'It didn't say. A lot, I imagine. So I stole it.'

She sat up. 'You're kidding!'

Ronny sat up too.

'No. I don't kid.'

'How?'

'I went back at night with a brick. I smashed it and then grabbed it and then legged it.'

Lily loved him then. It was as though a gorgeous butterfly had landed on her breastbone, its fragile antennae all aquiver.

'So what did you do with it?'

Ronny rubbed his stomach with his left hand. 'Well, I wasn't living anywhere at the time so I scratched my name into the wood on the side of the display case, put it inside a cardboard box and left it with a man I know at the Lost Property Office at Baker Street. I thought it would be safe there. And, what's more important, it wouldn't be on display.'

'You didn't want people to see it?'

'No. Never again.'

'Why not?'

Ronny stood up. 'Because,' he said, offering her his left hand, 'he'd needed understanding and he'd received none. I wanted to protect him. I saw myself in him.'

Lily smiled and took Ronny's hand. He pulled her up and then let go. She had expected his touch to be a real delight, but instead it was cold. Icy, in fact. Like the hand of a dead man.

Once he'd got it home, the box immediately became just another part of the furniture. He placed his beer bottles upon it when he lounged on the sofa watching TV. The phone was temporarily balanced on top of it. A magazine, a paper, a listings guide. Stuff. But he wasn't hiding anything. Not at all. It was right there, wasn't it? Margery had brushed up against it several times and had even gone and laddered her stocking on a protruding staple. Yes. So she'd been fully aware of its sudden materialization, surely?

Surely. Yet Margery didn't think to enquire about the box. She simply let it ride. There are no secrets here, Nathan thought, righteously. No secrets. It just *fitted*. The box.

And inside? Inside?

Nathan had retrieved Connie's card from the top of it. Then he'd paused for a moment, slipped the card into his pocket and kneeled down to touch the box, carefully exploring the texture of the smooth brown tape which sealed it so well and protected its corners. Slippery. He felt it with his finger. His index finger.

Then he found himself doing something stranger still. He leaned forward and applied his tongue, his *tongue* to the tape. He licked it. He withdrew again. Salty. Synthetic. Soapy. He discovered – there was no denying it – that he'd developed a powerful erection. A. Powerful. Erection. *What*? He blinked. He found himself thinking – couldn't stop it, couldn't – how beautiful this closed tight thing was. This sealed thing. This secret. This hidden. This sticky tape. How beautiful this closed tight thing. Was.

No. He gasped. Oh no. He drank four stiff brandies. One, two, three, four. All in a row. Then he steadied himself and didn't look at the box again.

20

Connie was sleeping. But not properly. Intermittently. And she was dreaming. She was dreaming of a journey, of an island, of a place on the edge of everything. Kitty, her mother, tucked the clean blue duvet under Connie's chin. She picked up the empty teacup from the bedside table, straightened the rug, returned the doctor's chair to its niche under the desk. On the desk were some papers, and letters.

Ronny,

Everything's fruity. Fruity and plush and flowery. I am well. I am celebrating. Here's what happened. Louis and I went on a trip with Monty and two of Monty's friends to see the world's largest flower, Rafflesia arnoldii. It's something of a botanical celebrity in these parts and Louis was taking his camera to get a few shots of it in bloom. It blooms in August. In July it ripens and clusters and glistens. In August it blares like a trumpet.

And I would stand next to it, Louis said, to give his shots a sense of proportion. I had no choice in the matter. We desperately need the money he raises from these bread and butter jobs to keep the whole investigative kit and caboodle on track. Anyway, Louis was determined that I should come along. I've been hanging around in the bat cave – but more of that later – so was slightly niggled at the neccessity of spoiling my routine. 'Won't Monty do?' I asked. 'I mean if it's only proportion you're after?'

But no. Louis was emphatic. In fact he even demanded that I bring a hairbrush and some lipstick along for the ride. We would be two bright flowers together, he chuckled. But there would be no competition. I would be the lesser flower. I would be the unripe bloom, the pale imitation, the pansy, the wallflower, the weed.

Well, you know me, Ronny.

We travelled by bus, initially. It was packed at first but then it emptied, until finally just our foursome and the driver remained on board. Whole segments of road had been washed away in the floods. We bumped and gyrated. We shuddered and bucked. I was too hot. It was hell. I opened my knapsack to dredge up an aspirin and pulled my hand out puce. The lipstick had melted. My bag's interior was like the skewed belly of a calf half ravaged by some wild beast. And my arm was a vulture, dip, dip, dipping. Pecking and schmoozing in its ruby guts.

The road was peppered with pot-holes, some so large the bus could hardly have filled them. At one particularly giant one, our driver slowed down and then ground to a halt.

'What is it?'

I clambered to the front. It was no mere hole, but a crater, and way too deep to negotiate. We needed to sidestep it. But in the measly straggle of road that remained lay a snake. A small python. And he was writhing, but not naturally.

'Oh my God, did we hit it?'

Louis, already at the front, merely shrugged. He was thinking about the flower and how the light wouldn't be with us for an infinite duration. The snake arced and fell, arced and fell. Its neck was cock-angled, its jaw slack.

'Did we hit it?' I asked the driver. He only frowned. Louis cleared his throat and suggested, quite calmly, that we drive on over it.

'We could get over easy,' he said, 'if we steer with care. The wheels are widely spaced.'

I couldn't abide the idea. I couldn't tolerate even the slightest possibility of damaging it further. 'Can't we just move it instead?' I asked, 'away from the road with a stick or something?'

Monty laughed.

The snake kept dancing its gruesome dance. I spoke to Louis again. 'We should shoot it. Monty has a gun. Let him kill it.'

'No. It's protected.'

'But he's killed protected creatures before, hasn't he?'

Louis gave me a bad look. He turned to Monty. 'Tell the driver to go over it.'

He put his hand in his wallet and jangled. Money.

'No,' I said, 'let me at least try to move it.'

Louis caught hold of my arm. He had the snake's grip. He would squeeze me and devour me. And just for a photo. The driver started up the engine. Coins rattled a little tattoo in his pocket. I closed my eyes tightly, feeling every bump and judder. And once we were over, I ran to the back of the bus.

Louis didn't twitch a whisker. He had his light detector out. 'The light's all fucked,' he kept saying. And through the dusty back window I saw the snake, on the road, but not dancing, its tail now crushed but still living. Only its middle moving, like a skipping rope. Kind of scything. Either-ended. A terrible, mud-stuck, tyre-tracked U-bend. And my hands were red as blood, like I'd dipped them in his injury, Ronny. Like I'd washed them in him.

We got to the spot. The flower was one great, big love-in. Its white horn, its giant throat, the focus of a thousand insects, marching and buzzing and jumping and swanking. I stood next to the bloom. It dwarfed me. I was its ugly little sister. A rat to its sex-kitten. My throat was still tight, like that python was draped right around it. I would have my revenge. I would, I would. I made a vicious little promise to myself in that flower's dark shadow.

Louis was suddenly very obliging. Did he feel bad? Monty and his chums had disappeared for a while. They had other fish to fry. He asked me to tuck my red hands behind my back. He took a shot. He took several. One at each and every angle. 'You know what?' I said eventually, having timed it, having bided my time, 'maybe it would be nice if you took a snap or two of yourself. You could send them to your wife and to Lucy' (his daughter).

He wanted to oblige me. I said, 'Should I take the picture?' (My own camera still moist and scarlet, so I'd have to use his.) I knew he would refuse me. 'No,' he said, 'there's the tripod and the timer. I'll do it that way.'

He set up under the giant spread of a durian tree. Every delicate adjustment to his camera and the tripod a kind of mute tribute to me. An apology. I said a little prayer. Where did I direct it? I don't know.

'Are you sure,' Louis asked, 'that this is really the best possible angle?'

I nodded. He blinked back his chauvinism. Because it wasn't the best angled shot, by any means. And he came to stand next to the flower. He reached out his arm to me. He wanted us shoulder to shoulder. Like comrades. I obliged him.

We both stared into the lens. Louis counted down, under his breath. Ten, nine, eight, he said, seven, six, five. We weren't even propped and stilted and steadied yet when the fruit came down. The durian fruit. It falls in July and early August. A giant, spiky bomb of a fruit. A menace.

Phut!

It killed his camera. Yes! It killed it stone dead. And that, I told myself, is the law of this fucking jungle.

M.

21

'Ronny was sick four times,' Lily shouted, like she was proud of his achievement. Jim didn't answer. He was skulking in his bedroom, hiding. He couldn't face her. She busied herself around the prefab. She rescued the pie from the pan in the kitchen which was threatening to boil dry and then tried to invite herself to dinner. She craved a slice of something meaty.

Jim listened as Ronny ejected her. He did it so gently. He said her mother would be worried. He said it was getting late. He said he needed to rest a while. He played every stroke with such grace and finesse. Jim envied him. And Lily, in turn, wanted to nibble him all over. Her foot didn't even sting any more. This was a new reality, she told herself. This was a brand new world. She could step right into it. She could shed her old skin.

Ronny finally closed the door on her. He went and found Jim sitting on his bed. He had been upset by something. Ronny could tell. His eyes were red. He wore no hat. He was round-shouldered, diminutive, buff-headed. 'Guess what?' Ronny was jovial.

'What?'

'Kidney stones!'

'Really?' Jim didn't brighten.

'Kidney stones. They can be very painful. And he'd been having these bad rumblings for ages but he'd been too frightened to go and see anyone about it. He thought he was dying. That's why he came here.'

Jim shook his head at Luke's apparent weakness.

'Sara gave me directions but stayed hiding in the car. I took him in. It worked out just fine in the end. I left the Volvo at the farm. You could pick it up tomorrow. Luke can get a cab home when he's ready.'

'So how do you feel?' Jim said.

'Me?' Ronny was cheerful. Resolutely. 'Absolutely great.'

'Really?'

'Yes.'

He glanced over his shoulder. 'I see you've got the fire burning.'

Jim noticed that Ronny's hands were shaking. He quickly stood up. 'Would you like something to eat?'

'Uh . . .' Ronny nodded.

Jim went into the kitchen. He dished up the pie. He could hear the fire crackling in the other room. He picked up the plates and walked through. He stood in front of Ronny and offered him his plate. Ronny put out one hand to take the plate, then his other. Both hands. A battle took place, inside him, on his face. But he could not take the plate. He suddenly grew stiff. He froze. It was as though he was restraining something huge inside him. An uncertainty. A monstrous indecision. A blankness. He was paralysed.

Jim put down the plates.

'Oh God,' he said, 'I shouldn't have made you go. I knew it was wrong. I have a powerful instinct for survival. That's all. It's my downfall. It's horrible.'

Ronny tried to speak. He whispered something. Jim couldn't hear. He drew nearer. He put his ear close to Ronny's lips, then closer still until finally he heard him. Such a little voice.

'I'm lost. I'm lost. I'm lost.'

Jim felt sick. 'No. You're not lost.'

'I'm lost. I'm lost.'

Jim grabbed hold of Ronny's hand. He had never held another person's hand before. His mother's hand, perhaps, when he was very small. He had been held himself, forcibly, but he had never held.

'Help me, Jimmy,' Ronny said.

Jim could see in Ronny's eyes that he was leaving. He was walking away. His pupils were big at first but then they grew smaller and smaller until they were almost only pin-pricks. Little black tadpoles drowning in a dense, swampy green. He was far. He was further. Like his whole soul was vacating.

Jim wanted to speak, but what could he say? What did he have to say? Nothing. Nothing. He tried to reach inside himself for something concrete, but all he could find was Monica and her words. Monica and her world. Because Monica had a strength, a colour, a real solidity, but hidden inside an almost infinite uncertainty.

Jim started speaking. Randomly. Babbling.

'Come back,' he said, 'I have something to tell you. I have a friend,' he said, 'called Monica. She's far away too. Far away. And she's trying to find this missing ape. She calls it the oran-pendic. It lives in Sumatra. In the rain forests. They have volcanoes. And the world's largest flower. She says in the summer the whole place reeks so violently of pepper that your nostrils feel fiery.'

'Pepper?' Ronny's voice, dazed, dead, an echo.

'Pepper. From the plantations . . . but there's tea and timber and coffee too. It's a kind of paradise. Fertile and steaming and opulent and lavish. The very opposite of this empty place.'

'Oran . . . ?'

'Pendic. Which means upright. He's covered in a pale-coloured hair. He has no big toes. She says he walks the forest but he's so alone. He mistrusts. He's full of fear. And she has no real evidence that he exists, just one brief sighting. She's never even seen him but she loves him. She believes in him and that's enough. It's all instinct with Monica. She's so . . .' Words failed him.

Ronny closed his eyes and saw a chasm. He gasped.

'Intense,' Jim said, 'that's it. She's so intense. There's this story she told me,' Jim paused and then started off again, winding himself up like a clockwork mouse, a watch, a musical box, 'about the day she went to take a photo of the world's largest flower. *Rafflesia arnoldii*. She'd been spending all her time in this bat cave and so she didn't want to go at first . . .'

'Bat cave?'

On Ronny's face, a flicker of recognition.

'Yes, yes . . . bat cave . . .' Jim pounced like a spider. The cave. The darkness. He started talking. And before he knew it he was weaving a yarn. He was spinning it and braiding it and twisting it. And Ronny was found and bound and reeled in. Slowly, surely, safely, soundly.

He was hooked.

22

Lily was invincible. She placed one foot in front of the other and that alone proved it. Legs are strange, she thought. Pink and stick-like and joined at the top but they work in a way that is truly extraordinary. She loved herself. She stared down the dark road.

These pale sticks, she told herself, will take me from here to there in no time at all. She wondered what distance consisted of and whether you could abuse it. Then she plotted her route via Ronny's sticky expulsions. She inspected the wide sky for meteors. She whistled.

Near home, soon enough, on the farm's long driveway, close to the fence which ran along the boar pens, she hunted for Ronny's second ejaculation. She was counting down. She was dot-to-dotting. She had nothing better to do.

Three different places, she inspected, and in none of them did she find what she was looking for. Ahead she saw a shadow in the roadway, like a puddle. That'll be it, she told herself, and drew closer. But then she stopped. It was not a liquid but a solid. A small thing. Hunched over. Engrossed. She held her breath. She skirted, tremulously.

But she could tell that he had good ears. He was a wild one. And he walked on little stumps, but not quickly. He shifted his position. He was not afraid of Lily although caution was inscribed deep within his genes. His giant head was domed. And his mouthparts, they were moving. He was licking. He was gobbling.

Lily edged, she pulled as wide as she could but she was hinged, somehow, on to this thing. It held her in. It plotted her perimeter. Needle-toothed. He chewed. He growled as he ate, unintentionally, breathing laboriously through his flat, misshapen nose. And what was he eating?

Oh God, she whispered, You're eating Ronny! What are you doing?

But the creature did not respond. He remained stooped. He kept on scooping. And Lily kept on edging until she was past him. And then she walked and walked, in slow motion, feeling something ghastly at the back of her.

Sara had bathed. Her hair was coiled up in a towel. Her head was buzzy with regretfulness. A kind of sweet-bitter-sweetness.

Lily came in wiping her mouth. Like she'd been kissing. She had mud on her nose and savage eyes. She smelled of bile. Sara tried to smile but there were miles between them. It was easier not to speak. And so much cleaner.

23

Ronny, darling.

We're still not speaking. Louis and me. He's slow to forgive. It takes him a while. Each new situation leaves him spinning. He has to dig in his heels hard, hard, take a deep breath and then struggle to acclimatize.

So I'm back in the cave. The bat cave. You understand these places, don't you, Ronny? These dark places with tough, rough walls. With each notch, each rocky dimple so staunch and reliable? And every single, individual breath and rustle and whisper and footfall I make is answered by the dark's harsh leathery voice. The darkness attends. It never ignores. With its black eyes and soft grip it asks for nothing, it gives nothing.

And here I find a balance. Because if I were a scale I'd be tipping, Ronny. I'd be all lopsided. I'd be tilting. I don't want to tilt. But I was despairing; walking in the forest, surrounded by brightness but not seeing. Understanding how every single natural thing here has its own special place except me. (And Louis, naturally, but he doesn't care less where he fits.)

I don't want to be the exception. I so want to merge. It was eating me up. I saw myself as an excrescence in the forest's vivid walkways. I was pink and bald in the midst of its green. It was painful. I was squinting and gaping and scrabbling for shade. But then I found the cave. The bat cave. It's a giant. Its roof is all bat-fleshy, like suede. Upside down and dangling. These bats, they chatter. They shit. They blister. Their radar bounces. I've been getting the feel of it in my jaw. I know it sounds crazy. Inside the soft parts of my mouth. The radar gets trapped, temporarily, and sparks from cheek to cheek like static electricity.

Why the cave? I don't know why. Perhaps because if they were

hunting for me I'd run to this place. And so might he. The oran-
pendic. He could be here. He could be near. Am I grabbing at
straws? Louis thinks so. But he would. He's so methodical. He's
so unforgiving. He's so marginal. Do you know what I mean?

In the darkness I can dream I see him. This pale ape. This toe-
less man. And he, like me, is flattened up against a wall. Not in
the main cavern but in an anti-chamber. A crevice. We both feel
around blindly, like deep-water fish. Touching, whispering,
bumping, retreating.

One day I thought I felt a snake. Hibernating, on a rocky shelf.
Thigh-high. And the shock! But then I realized that it was a root.
An ancient root from a giant tree that flowered once, far, far above.

Sometimes visitors come. With their torches, their unbearable
voices and their sharp-eyed guides. I watch them from my
crevices. They don't find me in this labyrinth.

And he is here, somewhere, watching me. I feel it. I am hunter
and hunted. I am avoider, avoided. I am complete. Replete.

Men arrive daily to scoop up the bat shit. Louis tells me they
make medicines with it. They use it for fertilizer.

One day Louis came himself to try and find me. He called out
my name and my name rebounded. I was a spider. I was all eyes.
He couldn't see where he was going. He wasn't acclimatized. He
grumbled and stumbled and his hands were hungry on the walls.
I stood close by him but he couldn't tell. I even smiled at him but
my teeth were as black as the darkness that spiked them.

Two weeks in the cave. In before light, out after nightfall. This
is a dark world. Louis gives me bitter glances when I return. He
gives me the coldest cold shoulder but he doesn't speak. He thinks
I know something that he doesn't know. He's growing distrust-
ful. Last night I heard him taking the film from my camera and
then replacing it with another.

My ears have grown so sharp that I can hear my hair and my
nails growing. My skin is a soft dough-white and I absorb every-
thing. I eavesdrop, I intercept. And like an exotic woodpecker on
a sky-high line I wire tap, tap, tap.

Hear me knocking, Ronny.
M.

24

Nathan was rota'd on for the Sunday shift with Laura and Laura's dumb friend Karen. The office wasn't open. They were merely sorting; slotting stuff into cubicles, tagging it and then tapping it on to the database. Filling in and keeping on top of things.

Mid-morning, Laura consulted Nathan over some art books. They were in a plastic bag. They came from a specialist art bookshop in the West End. Some were in English, others were in foreign languages; Spanish, Italian. Laura was still stuck at that desperately helpful stage. She had yet to evolve from private eye to clerical worker. 'Perhaps we should phone the bookshop,' she suggested, 'the receipt says they paid by credit card. Over a hundred and thirty quid, in fact.'

'They'll find them here if they want them.'

Nathan, stiff-necked and dismissive, waited at the keyboard. He wanted some details so that he could type them in and then abandon the edit.

But Laura had pulled one of the books out of the bag and was turning its pages. Here, after all, was a whole world of art and gloss and gorgeous paper which smelled like high quality furniture polish. Spain. The Prado Museum. El Greco's bloodless gristle. His pale pigments and aching holy ligaments. Then blue. Then red. Goya. All that drowning. Those inky eye-rollers. The lolling.

'Look, a dog,' Laura smiled, 'swimming!'

The Italian Renaissance. 'Just smell the paper, Nathan.' Karen had sniffed already. Laura offered him the open book. He swallowed hard and took it. He sniffed at it. It was open on a very particular page. He looked and then he looked again.

'What's wrong?'

Laura moved closer and peered over his shoulder. She loved the musky scent of him. Man. Soap. Hair oil. And although Nathan wanted to, he just couldn't stop staring. Laura glanced at the picture and then at the adjoining script. 'Antonello da Messina,' she said. 'It's called the *Pietà*. 1477.'

Then she read: 'The picture is remarkable in its use of the prominent psychological diagonal which goes from Christ's face to his right hand . . .'

She inspected the picture. It was Christ with an angel. Christ, crucified, down from the cross, still breathing, perhaps, a wound bleeding profusely under his right nipple. Head back, eyes closed, mouth falling open. A little angel at his right shoulder supported him. Her face shining with tears. And they were all alone. Just these two.

'How amazing!' she pronounced, feeling uneasy. Because there was something not quite right about the picture. Something amiss. Christ had a tiny sheet on his lap which barely covered him, and his hand, not the psychological hand (which was curled back, all cramped and uncomfortable) but the left hand which rested on his thigh, had its fingers curled in a particular way . . . it verged on the indecent. It was sex and death and other stuff that Laura didn't much relish contemplating.

'Do you like it?' She spoke.

'No.'

Nathan closed the book.

He went home. He caught the Tube. She knew his route. She left the office just shortly after. She found him on the platform. Deep down underground. The Tube arrived. She climbed on with him. It was virtually empty. They didn't sit.

'You took the book.'

She was not accusing. He breathed harder, restraining something.

'Why did you take it?'

He shook his head. They didn't speak again. But she went all the way home with him.

In his living room he put down his briefcase. 'Will you report me for this?'

Laura shook her head, almost shocked at the suggestion. 'I imagined you were planning to return it,' she said quietly. As though she knew! She had such faith in him. He nodded.

'I just want you to fuck me,' she added, astonishing herself almost as much as Nathan, 'because I'm honestly starting to hate you and I really want to flush it right out of my system once and for all.'

Nathan was appalled. Against the door, fully clothed, gasping, he did exactly as she'd asked.

Later, much later, he spent hours just gazing. He stared in wonder at the thirteenth-century Christ-as-Masturbator. And the angel. A little angel-optician. Tiny, tearful, bobbing at his shoulder. A languid warmth filled him. From his teeth to his prick to his toes. For the first time in his long life he was truly, unspeakably, ineluctably *suffused*.

The car was the only thing Connie wasn't selling. It was completely her own. She drove one-handed, blinking herself awake, eating a greasy brioche from the services. Her mother had begged her not to go. Sunday morning. Her arm was still in its sling but it felt as normal. She yanked the sling off and used the arm without even thinking. In fact she was almost convinced that all the fuss had been merely a conspiracy to stop her from leaving.

Gravesend to Sheppey was no distance. But she took a diversion to Cobham *en route*, where her aunt lived. Her father's sister. She had packed a case. Enough clothes for a week. The letters in their bright ribbon. And also a cheque for the amount of twenty-five thousand pounds. Her mother had signed it *in lieu*.

It was all so dreamy. The motorway. Crumbs on her lap. It had rained at first and then a shaft of light cut through the clouds and nearly blinded her. She drove on into it, squinting.

Her aunt was exquisitely dithery, which was, Connie felt, just as things should be. She drank some tea. She was loitering.

'You look so tired.'

'Do I?'

'Are you sleeping properly?'

'Yes.'

'And where will you go now?'

'To Sheppey.'

'And where will you stay?'

'I don't know. In a hotel.'

'But you have an uncle . . .' her aunt went and found her address book, 'he runs a farm.'

Connie frowned. 'But I've never even met him.'

'So I'll ring them.'

She rang them. Someone was dead. A vacancy. She needed to feel useful, to fill it.

Connie barely registered the conversation. She was idling in neutral. I am free of all ties, she thought, and I have a cheque for twenty-five thousand pounds. I could take my little smart car and head for Sheerness, drive it on to the ferry and then drive it off again at the other side, just randomly.

It wasn't escape. No. She had yearned for the shock of resolution, the force of will, the sense of sacrifice, of application, to complete her obligations to her father. Before this moment it had all been procrastination. A yearning. A waiting. And yet now that she was moving, now that she had that cheque on her person, now that her willpower had finally been located, shaped, funnelled, she felt an overwhelming urge to do something new with it. To channel it elsewhere.

Was that wrong? She could be the girl in the car commercial who just drove and drove. Or she could be like Monica and search for something that was missing. A missing something. But she was too short to be the girl in the commercial and her hair was too curly, and of the many things she had yet to discover that were missing from her life, the main one was still her own self. Was constancy.

When her aunt handed her a piece of paper with an address on it and specific instructions, Connie slipped it into her pocket, fully intending to ignore it. But in her pocket her hand located something she did not remember packing. Her passport.

In that instant she felt certain that if she had troubled to open her passport and inspect her own pale face in the small grey portrait within, she would have discovered two harsh words boldly inscribed across her sweet, round cheeks: DIRTY FRAUD.

And as luck would have it, this struck her as a perfectly fair assessment.

When Jim awoke – his neck aching, his throat sore – he found himself still on the sofa. Ronny was sitting close by, on the floor, wide awake, fiddling with some of the embers in the fireplace. He was holding a charred remnant with a red tip. He was blowing on it and watching the heated end brighten.

Jim focused on him, blearily, slowly regaining his senses. He saw Ronny apply the ember to several surfaces. First, to another piece of wood. Then to the bottom of his white shoe. Finally, he held it in front of his nose and gazed and gazed. Then he moved it an iota and set fire to his fringe.

He was so slow. Jim expected him to jolt, at the very least, and then to jump up with dispatch to quell the flames. But Ronny did not move. He remained where he was, just watching, as though he wasn't in the least bit affected, as if he'd actually intended it.

Jim thought he must be dreaming. But he was not dreaming. So he roused himself, bounded off the sofa, shouted something . . . He grabbed a pillow from behind him and belted Ronny about the head with it. He hit him and hit him until the flames were all gone. Then he picked up the ember from the carpet, where it burned, slightly fractured now, and tossed it back into the fire.

Ronny lay, prostrate, just smiling, with a black hole in his fringe and the stink of burning surrounding him. Jim held on to the cushion. He inspected it. It was blackened but seemed otherwise undamaged. Neither of them spoke. Eventually Ronny sat up. He felt around in his pockets with his left hand. He drew out a pair of nail scissors. He offered them to Jim. Jim threw down the cushion and took hold of them.

'Are you burned?'

'I don't think so.'

'The smell of scorched hair is sickening.'

'Cut it off then. All of it.'

Jim inspected Ronny's scalp.

'The hair's melted, like plastic.'

'Cut it short and then shave it.'

But Jim had misgivings. 'With no hair and a beard you'll look like Lenin.'

'Then get rid of the beard too.'

Jim hesitated. 'If I do that then we'll both end up looking like members of some kind of crazy half-arsed cult.'

'True.'

Ronny chuckled. He clearly relished this notion. Jim shrugged and began snipping.

'I never worked out,' Ronny said, eventually, watching his hair fall in clumps down on to the linoleum, 'why it was you had that razor. Did you ever need to shave?'

'No.' Jim was wary.

'Then why?'

Jim continued cutting. When he spoke it was without emotion. 'It was my father's razor. I was planning to kill myself with it.'

'But you didn't.'

'No.'

'Why not?'

Jim took a deep breath. 'It would've been too easy,' he said softly.

Ronny smiled. 'The way you explain things,' he scratched his chin, 'it's so, 'he paused, 'it's so *sweet.*'

26

The prison was like a set of dirty teeth, and the land around it was like a bad mouth, and the sky above it was like the grey face of the person who owned the teeth and the mouth and didn't care a damn about either of them. Inside, however, people were surprisingly helpful. Connie used her father's name –like it was a badge, a medal – and that at least seemed to count for something.

Eventually she met a man who claimed some vague – if unspecified – level of significance and so she asked him about Ronny. But he was new, he said, and while he had a file (which he flaunted) he claimed that there were certain things which, in all good conscience, he could not tell her.

She asked if Ronny had shared his cell, if he'd left any belongings behind him, and whether she could – at the very least – take a peek at the cell itself. Yes, the man said, although he wasn't certain he thought that Ronny may have shared his cell for a short while, and yes, a meeting with his old cell-mate wasn't inconceivable – if he proved agreeable – but unfortunately the man in question was elsewhere, had a child sick in hospital so was on a temporary transfer. But he was due back, eventually. Soon even, maybe. Connie scribbled down her forwarding address, in Sheppey, and the unfamiliar digits of her new phone number. She was grabbing at straws. She knew it.

On the understanding that it wouldn't help her one iota, they took her to the cell. It was bare and smelled of fresh paint. She didn't feel Ronny there. On her way out they mentioned Nathan. They said, 'Ronny's brother has everything. The books, the clothes, the other stuff. All that was remaining.'

Then finally, when she'd almost given up hope, they threw

out a bone. A scrap. A parting gift. 'I find your concern strange,' the man said, 'given that the dates don't match up.'

'The dates?' Connie was lost. 'Which dates?'

'Ronny was long gone by the time your father visited us.'

'So . . .' she paused, 'you're suggesting that they never even met?'

'No. I'm suggesting that they didn't meet here. Perhaps they met after. Or maybe even before.'

The man gave her a straight look. And that was that.

Connie sat in her car for a long while afterwards. She was foiled. She was blank. She was dead-ended, already. She reached over on to the back seat and picked up Monica's letters. She looked at them. She felt their weight. She sniffed them. New paint. Floor polish. Then she asked herself a question. Is it Monica I'm really tracking down here or is it Ronny? Because Monica was right there. She was ink and fuss and rage and lust. She was life. And Ronny? Who was he? What did he amount to?

The truth of the matter was that she'd never had much of an interest in the present. It was her chief foible. She despised the present. What she craved now – what she'd always craved – was not the present, not the past, but the absent. Not the possible but the impossible. It verged on the perverse, this craving. It was almost pathological.

And so, by this token, it was not Monica who fascinated her, but Ronny. It was Ronny. It was not the voice that spoke but the ear receiving. It was Ronny. And it was her father. And it was her own sweet and dumb and stupid self. All absent. All vacant. All gone.

Connie rested her forehead on the steering wheel and she howled. Hot tears, dry lips, red cheeks. The business. She allowed herself three whole minutes. That was all. Then she wiped her face with her hands, quite brutally, and started up the engine.

Lily prowled around the green Volvo while Sara fed the boar. She had a bucket of beets which she kept on refilling. They had a ton of them, under tarpaulin. She kept glancing over at Lily.

'If only you could drive,' Lily was griping, 'then we could take the car back to the prefabs.'

'But I can't drive.'

'I know, stupid.'

Sara winced. 'You could give me a hand if you felt like it.'

Lily kicked the Volvo's front tyre.

'No.'

She peered over. The boars were lining up, close to the electric fence. The larger male butted away any female who drew too close. The females – broad hessian parcels with cocked ears – squealed unceremoniously. There's a whole lot of feeling, Lily thought, in a good squeal.

'I think a fox is around.' Sara spoke.

'Really?' Lily inspected her trainers.

'I found one of my best hens dead this morning.'

'Really?' Lily repeated, smiling to herself.

'Yes.'

Sara pushed some hair behind her ear. Lily sniffed. 'You should count yourself lucky that it took only one.'

'Only one, but a good layer.' Sara turned back to the boar. 'And this lot have been digging . . .'

'Where?'

'Towards the back. Part of the fence was down near the gate. I still don't know how they managed it.'

'Instinct . . .' Lily squinted, then added, 'Car coming.'

Sara put down her bucket and gazed off into the distance. A blue car. She felt an intense surge of delight at the prospect of a distraction. Not for herself, but for Lily. She had her own particular diversions meticulously planned already.

27

Jim intended to subtly alter the pattern of his life. It was clear to him – and few things were ever clear to him – that Ronny needed significance. Because he barely existed. He wasn't located. Not anywhere in particular. He was all things to all people. He was malleable. And that was how he had survived, and that was the disease that devoured him.

Jim was willing, if Ronny wanted, to give himself over. To give himself up for Ronny. Because what did he have to lose? It was surely no sacrifice. His name, his gold watch, his shoes, his brother, his home? None of these things amounted to anything. They held no real value. Except to Ronny.

And who could it hurt? Temporarily?

Jim watched Ronny from the edge of the beach. He guarded him. He had eaten no breakfast, as a bolster to Ronny, and he had cut Ronny's hair with his right hand. He had drawn Ronny's attention to it. It had taken him hours.

Later, in the mirror, staring at their two reflections, Ronny had said, 'You know, Jim, we are very nearly the same person.'

Jim had laughed. Then Ronny pulled open the bathroom cabinet. 'If you do things my way,' he said, inspecting the bottles of pills, the packets of tablets, 'you won't need these any more.'

'Fine.' Jim nodded.

'But I mean it.'

'And so do I.'

Although in truth he did not mean it. Not yet.

'Then let's get rid of them.'

Ronny went and fetched a plastic bag and tipped the bottles and the boxes straight into it. He tied up the handles – using his left hand and his teeth – then took the bag off with him. Later, after no lunch – Ronny's idea – Jim suggested he go down to the beach to sort out some shells. Ronny was obliging. 'Only this time,' Jim said, 'you could decorate the wall at the back of the prefab. You could make something permanent.'

Ronny frowned and said he'd give it some thought.

So Jim stood, like a heron, in the reedy fringes of the beach, just watching. Ronny – wearing a baseball cap, his thin face chiselled and clean like a chip of marble – began sorting the shells, then arranging them, then laying them out in some private semblance of order.

He used only his left hand. He seemed cheerful, his equilibrium apparently completely regained. And Jim watched him. He guarded him, like he was a special pedigree poodle, an exotic canary – its wings carefully clipped – or the most lovely and precious little pearl.

He was starving.

While Connie sat at the kitchen table cradling a mug of tea, Lily lounged up against the Aga, occasionally putting her hand on to the cover of the hot plate to see how many seconds she could hold it there. Connie felt a genuine sense of relief that she wasn't actually related by blood to this skinny, wasted, round-faced creature. Sara, meanwhile, with admirable diligence, tried to calculate the nature of Connie's family connection.

'So,' she said, 'your father is Lily's great aunt's husband's brother?'

'Yes, he was. But he died.'

'Which makes you something removed.'

Connie smiled at this. She felt like something removed.

Lily, in turn, removed herself from the Aga and sat down next to her. 'You drive then?'

She peered at Connie intently, as though this driving characteristic might well prove to be the most interesting thing about her.

'Yes,' Connie nodded.

Sara interrupted. 'We farm boar, actually,' she said.

'Really? I don't think I've ever seen a boar before. Do they have husks?'

'Tusks.'

Lily snorted.

'The males, yes.' Sara nodded.

'Are they aggressive?'

'Do bears shit in the woods?' Lily revealed her dimples.

'They're wild,' Sara scowled, 'but very . . .'

'Indigenous,' Lily interjected, 'although you wouldn't think it with all the bother we get.'

Sara cleared her throat. 'People can be wary. Other farmers especially. We've been keeping boar for a good few years now, but the myth that they escape all the time and wreak havoc . . .'

'So what!' Lily expostulated. 'It's our land. We can do what the hell we like on it.'

Connie was intrigued. Sara and Lily spoke directly across her, as if she were invisible. Yet she sensed that this was not the sort of conversation they'd usually have. It was as though she acted like some kind of filter. 'Could I see them?' she asked.

They both turned to look at her. Sara put down the teapot. 'Pardon?'

'The boar. Could I see them?'

'When you've finished your tea,' Lily said, 'I could take you on a tour of the area. There's a nature reserve and a beach . . .'

Connie picked up her mug, took a sip, put it down again. She felt inexplicably genial. 'Yes,' she said quietly, 'I think I might really enjoy that.'

When Nathan arrived, the gallery was closing. He had at best only fifteen minutes, a guard warned him. Nathan ran up the stairs and into the new Sainsbury Wing. It seemed huge, the ceiling so high. Everything hushed and hollow and reverential. He began walking, quickly, from painting to painting. Ravenous. The gold leaf, the flat faces, the beautiful colour. He gorged on the angels, the devils, the other stuff. He appraised each picture. He paused, he passed on.

Is it Christ? He was muttering. But he saw nothing that

moved him. Nothing that connected. There was Christ on the cross. The tears, the torment, the suffering. There was Christ down from the cross, surrounded by mourners. A dumb time, a numb time. There was Christ preaching. Open face, open palms. The goldest halo. But nothing.

Is it the artist? He found several other paintings by Antonello. Each so serene and beautiful. One, a self-portrait of the artist himself – with black hair, heavy stubble, blue eyes and a red felt cap. That was all. And another Antonello Christ, but actually on the cross this time, and tiny, and damaged, and nothing spectacular. A picture of Saint Jerome in his study. An exercise in perspective, and wonderful . . .

He checked his watch. Time up. His heart was pumping.

Sara had disappeared on a mission to borrow some netting from a nearby farm. The pens needed securing. Or so she'd declared. Once she was gone, Lily ransacked the house in search of Luke's keys but she could not find them. She turned everything upside down, she tipped, she ripped, she swore, she expostulated, but she refused, *refused* to believe that Sara had hidden them to foil her. She wouldn't believe it.

Connie went for a wander around the boar pens, supremely oblivious to Lily's frustrations. There were five different fenced-off sections, each holding eight or ten boar. A single male and his mates. One of the sections contained some smaller boar of varying sizes which she presumed to be adolescents. They were brown and muddy and rather endearing. The big ones, however, were very large, awesome, in a barky, hoary way, and quite intimidating.

Eventually Lily joined her. She seemed disgruntled.

'Did you find what you were looking for?' Connie asked.

'No.' Lily shook her head.

'Shall we go for our walk now?'

'I suppose.'

Lily started off. Connie followed.

'So how are boar different from pigs?'

'The meat's less fatty.'

'They seem fairly excitable.'

Lily made a little gun out of her right hand. 'Click, click, bang! They're shot at the trough.'

'Really?' Connie felt vaguely stricken at the notion.

'But they're so fucking powerful that even if you shoot them right in the chest, they run and run, like an engine, like a machine. They're tough as . . . uh . . .' she searched for an appropriate metaphor, 'shit,' she said finally.

'They certainly look happy.'

Connie found herself smiling. The boars' ferocity made her feel buoyant. And Lily's.

'They are happy. Totally independent. Totally self-sufficient. I mean, we feed them every so often, but not each day because that would make them complacent. They're wild. Complacency's like a disease to wild things.'

'You think so?'

'I know so.'

Lily strode on. Connie struggled to keep her pace.

'I was told you kept pigs.'

'We did, years ago, but then we found out about the boar and Dad began interbreeding.'

'With sows you mean?'

'Yep. Same chromosomes. Thirty-six. Strange, huh? It means that you can breed pig and boar without too much difficulty. You get a kind of weird, hairy hybrid . . .' she shuddered and then continued, 'but after a spell he decided that it wasn't quite right. Boars have a greatness, a purity. And that shouldn't be tampered with. It should be treasured.'

They had walked well beyond the pens now.

'And they're much easier to keep than pigs. They even give birth without any fuss. Pigs weren't as uncomplicated . . .' Lily scowled at the memory. Connie nodded. 'So are we going to the beach?'

Lily ignored her. 'And they got terrible sunburn,' she said, 'the pigs. Traditional British breeds were very hairy originally but people don't like pork with hair in the crackling so now they've been specially adapted. They have much longer backs, which provides more convenient cuts of meat, but it's unnatural and causes problems. And their hairlessness means they burn in the sun.'

'I didn't know that.'

Lily shrugged. 'Boar are less work, but you've got to be careful to keep them securely.'

'So they do escape sometimes?'

'Once in a blue moon. It's no big deal.'

Lily stopped walking. 'That way is the nature reserve, but if we head straight on we reach the beach.'

'What kind of beach?'

'Shell. It's OK. There's a nudist section which is good for a laugh.'

Connie nodded. 'That'll be handy. I haven't brought a costume.'

Lily stared at her. 'You're planning to go swimming?'

'Sure. Why not?'

Lily merely snorted and strode on.

Sara found the camera in the hide, on the floor, just as Luke had described it to her. It wasn't a particularly expensive one, but it was his favourite. His best. She picked it up by the strap and then hung it around her neck. He was lucky that it hadn't been stolen.

She went and sat outside, at the top of the stairs. With the hide's dark jaw to the back of her she felt like a mollusc, a beach creature, with its shell tucked neatly behind it. A refuge.

She held the camera up to her eye and found herself staring into the gut of yet another crustacean. She had a particular way of seeing things. She did not notice the view, the exterior, instead she saw the black box, the glass, the interior. And inside this clean little belly she suddenly saw all of life. But everything much smaller and neater.

28

Jim saw her – way off at first – from the far end of the beach. But even at that distance he could see her savage mouth working, tearing, jabbering, as she strode out, swinging her long arms, kicking up sand with her skinny legs. She repelled him. She was unpredictable, stunted, somehow, and raging. He wanted her to leave them alone. Ronny especially. She would drain him dry if she could. He hated this idea. Lily suckling and guzzling.

He watched her. She was expostulating with her hands. She was with a friend. The friend was disrobing.

'But you don't have a towel,' Lily was saying.

'It's windy. I'll dry off soon enough.'

'What if someone comes along?'

'Should that be a problem?'

Connie wore pale linen trousers and a turquoise shirt. She pulled off her trousers. Her knees were both bruised, but she didn't care.

'Will you come in with me?'

'Fuck off!'

'Go on!'

Lily pointed. 'I know those two over there. I'm not stripping in front of them.'

'Fine.'

Connie unbuttoned her shirt. Underneath she wore no bra and a g-string. 'You could swim in your underwear,' she wheedled. Lily scowled at Connie's non-existent bikini line without replying.

'What's wrong?'

'Nothing,' she said, 'and if you don't mind I've actually got some other things to do.'

She stalked off, stiff-backed and bristling. Connie smiled after her.

Jim nodded slightly at Lily's greeting but he didn't speak. Lily pointed. 'Would you believe that?'

'What?'

He stared over at Connie without much attention. She was paler than the shells. Very pale. But distant.

'She's a relative. If my dad saw her he'd shit himself.'

'Your dad?'

'He's anti-nudity.'

Jim remained silent.

'What are you doing?' she asked eventually.

'Nothing.' He scratched his neck. 'Perhaps you should go and move her clothes.'

'Pardon?'

'The tide's coming in.'

Jim indicated. Connie's trousers and shirt were too close to the water. Lily smiled, 'Fuck her,' and bounded off down the beach towards Ronny.

Ronny had surrounded himself with shells. He'd created a circular tableau, and he was at the centre of it. It was several feet in diameter. Lily paused on the edge of it. She stared at him for a while. 'What did you do to yourself?'

He looked up, 'Uh . . .?'

'Your hair.'

'Oh. I caught fire.'

'When?'

'Since I last saw you.'

'What were you doing?'

'Burning.'

'Burning?' Lily was mystified. 'And what are you doing now?'

He grinned. 'Isolating myself.'

'What?'

'With shells.'

'Isolating yourself?'

Ronny put his finger up to his lips. Lily squinted.

He returned to his work. Lily threw herself down on to the sand and chewed her nails while studying Ronny intently. She had no notion whatsoever of a companionable silence. Not even an inkling.

The sea was cold. It reached just above Connie's knees. She debated whether she would swim. The undertow was quite powerful. An unexpectedly large wave hit her. She gasped. Some seaweed caught around her ankle. As she bent over to remove it, she turned and glanced back across the beach. In the distance she saw Lily sitting next to a person in a hat. Someone else stood just beyond them. A man. His hand was raised. But before she could focus in on him properly, another wave hit her. She fell back into it with a small yelp and started swimming.

'Come away from there.'

Luke's voice reached her from the bedroom. Sara wore nothing but a towel and a camera. She tested that the prefab's door was locked and pulled the curtains to.

'I'm certain I heard her voice.'

She returned to the bedroom.

Luke lay on his bed like a tanned sea lion. A beach-master. The bed was old and squeaky. It dipped under his weight. He could feel its springs teasing his spine through the mattress. He still wore his little, plastic hospital wristband. Like a baby, Sara thought fondly, taking hold of his hand. She read it out loud.

'Luke Hamsun.'

'That's me.' He beamed. Glad to be alive.

'Hamsun. Like handsome but back to front.'

'Norwegian.'

'Truly?'

He nodded.

Sara sat on the edge of the bed. 'So they think you've passed it?'

Luke looked pained. 'The stone? Yes. They said it must've been quite a small one. They usually disintegrate of their own accord.'

She held his hand and inspected his fingernails. Luke shifted.

'Don't be embarrassed,' she smiled, 'I'm a farmer. I'm perfectly accustomed to this kind of thing.'

'Gallstones?'

'My father suffered from them. This was way before they had lasers and all the technology they have now. He had his cut out and was given them after in a jar. One was as big as my fist. But I was only a child then, obviously.'

'A fist?'

Luke blanched.

'Yours was probably only the size of a seed.'

'A seed.'

He liked this idea. Seeds were invariably clean and perfectly inoffensive.

But Sara was not thinking of seeds. Her mind had turned back a reel. Back to what she'd said before, about being a farmer. Previously she'd always thought of herself as a farmer's wife. Previously? Previous to what? To fucking? Her insides curled.

Luke unlooped the camera from around Sara's neck and placed it against his eye. She was a real honey. She smiled but quickly turned her face away. Her fingers grasped the top of her towel and gave it a modest yank upwards.

Luke's own fingers moved automatically. As Sara turned, the camera clicked. A shot, taken. But he'd neglected to switch on the flash. He swore and stared at the camera, utterly bemused.

Jim walked slowly along the beach. He hadn't begun walking until he'd seen a wave touch the first of Connie's garments. He hadn't moved until her beige trousers had been lifted on to the swell, spat out, lifted again.

She was in quite deep now, a doughty swimmer. Over the final few yards he broke into a trot. The trousers were lost from view. Something else – turquoise – floated in the shallower waves, and something paler, a scrap, her knickers, floated alongside.

He pulled off his shoes, tossed Connie's sandals higher up the beach as a precaution and then waded into the water to retrieve the blue item. Shirt. His jeans got wet. He went in a few steps deeper for the scrap, then looked around for the trousers. No sign of them. He waded, hopelessly, and became so engrossed in his close inspection of the ocean bed that he didn't hear her come up behind him.

'Jesus,' she muttered, 'how stupid!'

Jim was soaked to his thighs. He didn't turn at first, but stared at her reflection in the water where it glistened whitely like a slither of coral. She was almost purple and exotically orange-speckled with the cold. Her arms were crossed over her chest, but she seemed uninhibited. He could tell that she came from another planet. A world where bodies weren't shameful things. Somewhere nice and kind and open. How would that be?

'Did I lose my trousers?'

Connie put out her hand for the shirt. He passed it to her and she tried to wring it out, then pulled it on, but with difficulty. The wet fabric clung to her and was tricky to manipulate.

'I can't see them,' Jim said. He was suprised by his own voice. 'I think they were washed away first.'

He took a step backwards, still holding her g-string. She reached out her hand for it. He looked down. 'Oh,' then passed it to her. She squeezed the water from it and then stuck it in her shirt's pocket before pulling down the hem and turning to wade for the shore.

'You're soaking,' she observed, kicking water out in front of her.

'It doesn't matter. I only live there.' Jim pointed to the prefab.

'You *only* live there?'

He thought she was mocking him and frowned. She hadn't meant to mock at all. She noticed his frown. He was serious. And odd-looking. Pale and hunched but with eyes like peanut brittle. 'You must be one of Lily's friends,' she said kindly. Jim paused, considered this statement, rebelled internally but still said, 'Yes.'

'Well, I'm Connie. A distant relative. Of hers, I mean.'

Connie held out her hand to Jim. For an instant he pretended that he hadn't seen it, but she continued to hold it there, out-stretched, up to her ankles in the swell. So he took it.

'Like a fish,' he muttered. It slipped out.

Connie smiled. 'What was that?'

'The water's cold.'

Jim walked on. Connie followed. 'A fish?'

She was grinning. He didn't answer. He had noticed how bruised her knees were. It seemed a particularly babyish injury.

'I don't suppose you'd have a towel I could borrow?'

Jim picked up his trainers. Connie picked up her sandals. He radiated indifference. She persisted. 'It's just that Lily will probably disown me if I have to walk all the way home like this.'

She glanced up the beach to where Lily was sitting. Jim glanced too, scowling.

'What are they doing?' Connie asked.

Jim shrugged. 'I wouldn't know.'

He began walking towards his prefab, hoping that she wouldn't follow, but she did.

'It must be amazing living here,' she said.

'Amazing.'

'Did you say what your name was before?'

He stopped walking, turned. 'I'm Jim.'

'And you have alopecia, Jim?'

He stared at her, stunned.

'I'm sorry,' she said, feeling awful, 'that sounded very rude.'

She regretted her own nauseating self-assurance.

'If you wait here for a moment I'll go and fetch you a towel.'

Jim withdrew into the prefab. She didn't dare follow. Instead she walked on further, to the front of Luke's prefab, where she peered in through the window. She couldn't see in beyond the nets. She walked back on herself and then, at a whim, down in between the two buildings. On her right side, above her head, was a small kitchen window, but too high to peek into. A few feet in front of her was another much lower one.

Connie took a couple of steps forward and then paused. This window was slightly ajar. Its nets billowed out. She had not considered that the prefab might be inhabited. It was definitely out of season.

She hesitated and would have turned back when the nets billowed again, higher this time and she saw right inside, into a bedroom, sparsely furnished. And two people. A man on a bed, laughing, and a woman nearby, facing Connie, almost, but holding a camera to her eye, taking a photo of the man and his large, erect penis which he held in his hand like a bunch of flowers.

The camera flashed. Connie blinked. The woman lowered the camera, and then the nets, on cue, billowed back in again, but not before the woman saw her. She was seen.

'Oh shit,' Connie turned on her heel. She ran out from between the two buildings.

Jim stood in front of his prefab clutching a towel. He looked at her. She put her hand to her mouth and spoke through her fingers.

'I've just done something so embarrassing . . .'

He was not particularly interested. He offered her the towel, saying nothing.

'The people next door . . .' She pointed.

'It's empty,' Jim said, still offering her the towel.

'No,' she took the towel from him, shaking her head, whispering almost, 'it isn't empty.'

Connie grabbed hold of Jim's arm and pulled him sideways, into his own prefab, shut the door behind her and then tied the towel around her waist. His arm had felt warm. She was freezing.

'There's a man next door. Fat, well tanned. And a woman. My aunt.'

Jim's eyes widened. He hadn't been aware of Luke's return.

Connie bit her lip. 'When I say my aunt I mean Lily's mother, Sara. I just met her for the first time this morning. She said she was going to get netting from a local farm . . . They were naked. I'm certain she saw me.'

'And so?' Jim was unshakeable. He did not care.

'But how will I face her? And Lily?'

Jim shrugged.

'Should I just pretend it didn't happen?'

He shrugged again. 'That's up to you.'

'Do you think Lily knows?'

He shook his head. 'That's none of my business.'

'Yes.'

Connie calmed down slightly. She looked around the room. 'Do you live here alone?'

'Why?'

'I don't know. I've got sand on your floor. Do you have a broom?'

'It doesn't matter.'

She paused. 'God!'

She stared at him.

'What?' Jim hated being stared at. He always felt ugly inside other people's eyes.

'Nothing,' Connie blinked, 'you just reminded me of someone.'

She turned and took hold of the door handle. She was suddenly tearful. 'I'm sorry. I don't know what's wrong with me. It's just that my dad . . .'

Her throat contracted. She coughed. Her cheeks were bright. She was burning. 'I'll return your towel as soon as I can.'

Her eyes were scorching.

'Keep it.'

She was gone, though, before he'd finished speaking.

29

Margery noticed the change.

'I phoned earlier,' she said, glancing at him over a glass of icy vodka, 'but you were out.'

'Really?'

Nathan wiped the foam off his top lip with the inside of his wrist. It was a disarming little movement, but she was not disarmed.

'So where were you?'

'I was at an art gallery.'

'Really?'

'Yes. The National.'

Margery stared at him. They were in a pub. It was quite empty.

'I didn't know you made a habit of going to art galleries.'

Nathan cleared his throat. 'I don't. It was just a fancy. I went straight from work.'

Margery continued to stare. There was a liveliness in Nathan's face which she had no recollection of ever noticing before. A glint. A fervour. He seemed less transparent, more *translucent*. She felt a vague moment's unease at her sudden inability to see straight through him. It had been a knack. A gift. Had she lost it? Was it gone? Was it merely mislaid?

Or was it him. Was it Nathan? She crossed her arms. Nathan idly watched the cleft at the top of her breasts deepen as her flesh blossomed out under the pressure of her wrists.

'So what did you see?'

She meant business.

'Uh . . .' he frowned slightly, as if it was difficult for him to recollect, 'the newest wing. Sainsbury's.'

'Modern pictures?'

'No. Quite old ones.'

Margery smiled, willing him to change his story. 'Were you really there?'

He smiled right back. 'Yes. Of course I was.'

But when he smiled his eyes were blank, were filmed. Because suddenly he did not see Margery at the other side of the table. Instead, in her place, he saw a delicious little angel, just glowing, just dangling.

Nathan took another sip of his drink, then tucked his hand into his trouser pocket and cleaned his thumbnail on the sharp edge of a business card. *Connie.* He was on the sweetest voyage. What he did not know, what he *could not consider*, was where he was heading. What he did know, though, what he was certain of, was that she, Connie, would be his very next port of call.

'Lily, let's go.'

Lily didn't want to. She was happy where she was. She glanced up at Connie. 'Couldn't you find your own way back? It's quite simple.'

Connie readjusted the towel around her waist. 'No.'

'Oh.'

Ronny lifted the peak of his hat and peered over his shoulder at her. 'Hello.'

'Hi.' She paused for a moment. 'You have no hair either?'

Ronny took off his hat. His skull was pale and strangely shaped, like a prune stone. 'Nope. No hair.'

She took a step closer. 'And what is it exactly that you're doing here?'

'A tableau,' Lily interjected.

Ronny nodded.

'He does everything with his left hand,' Lily said fondly, smiling at him. 'It's his . . . preoccupation.'

'Project,' Ronny said, and put his hat back on again.

'Ronny and I are in the middle of a great discussion,' Lily said, 'aren't we?'

Ronny just mumbled under his breath, somewhat evasively.

Connie stared at Ronny blankly for a moment, as though something terribly obvious had just occurred but she'd missed it.

Ronny.

The sun was sinking and her shirt was cold against her skin.

'Really? So what was it about, this discussion?'

'Ronny was telling me how certain kinds of letters make you feel cheerful.'

'Letters?'

Connie shoved her hair behind her ear, away from her face.

'In graphics . . .' Lily turned back to Ronny. 'How soon do you think before the sea comes right in?'

'I don't know.'

'Won't it wash away your tableau?'

'Probably.'

Ronny sounded unbothered. He stretched his spine as though it had grown uncomfortably stiff, then dusted some sand off his left hand by patting it on the front of his shirt. His right hand remained limp in his lap. Then very slowly, very gradually, he unwound, but without using his hands to push himself up, and keeping his feet close together so as not to disturb the circle of shells around him.

Once Ronny was standing he took in the circular sweep of his day's work. He smiled, then he frowned. 'Actually . . .' he scratched his leg, 'I think I'm stuck.'

Lily stood up herself and was immediately involved in Ronny's dilemma. 'Can't you jump over?'

He shook his head. 'Not from this position. No leverage.'

He looked around him, almost panicky. 'Where's Jim?'

Lily glanced up to the top of the nearby sand dunes as though she still expected Jim to be standing there. 'Jim? You mean the bald one?'

'The *other* bald one,' Connie murmured, studying Ronny's body language with some curiosity.

'Yes, 'Ronny nodded. 'I think I need Jim. I think I need him.'

Lily put out her hand. From the edge of the shell arrangement she could almost touch him. 'Why not grab hold of my fingers?'

'I can't balance.'

Ronny began to wobble.

'Jim's in his prefab,' Connie spoke, 'shall I go and call him?'

'Would you?'

Ronny peered at Connie over his shoulder, his expression chiselled with a sharp anxiety.

'No. Let me. I'll go.'

Lily would not be outdone. She would be indispensable. 'I said I'll go, Ronny.'

She rushed off, shoving past Connie in a slight demonstration of ill-grace. Connie stepped aside silently. She did not relish the notion of Lily stumbling across what she presumed to be Sara's secret dalliance with Jim's fat, tanned neighbour. But if Sara had any sense . . .

So they were left alone. Ronny was still wobbling slightly.

'Had you been sitting there long?' Connie walked around the shell circle so that he didn't have to turn his head to see her.

'Yes.'

'Maybe it's cramp.'

'No. I've always had problems with my balance.'

'Really?'

He nodded. 'Big toes.'

Connie stared at him. 'Pardon?'

'I have none.'

'No big toes?'

'It's the way I was born. I was imperfect.'

Imperfect. Connie disliked this choice of word, but her mind was temporarily distracted. 'You know,' she cleared her throat, 'there's a special kind of ape . . .'

'Yes,' Ronny frowned but he nodded, 'yes, I do know.'

He seemed unfazed, but slightly disgruntled.

'I mean, with no toes . . .' Connie continued, 'a pale giant.'

'Of course. I know all about that.'

Ronny glanced over his shoulder as though keen to curtail their conversation. In the distance, Jim had emerged from his prefab and was jogging across the beach, followed closely by Lily. Ronny returned his gaze to Connie. She was staring at him, thinking how thin he was. The sun was setting and it had bathed him in a strange, pinkish light which reflected from his pale face and hands. His wrists were facing outwards, limply, and were oddly pearly; striped, like the belly of a tiger fish. The sun was refracting off his scar tissue. Connie stared at his wrists, and then at his fingertips which also seemed to glow.

'Did you see any black rabbits yet?'

She was shaken. 'Pardon?'

She had almost to pinch herself.

'Black rabbits. They're a local peculiarity. Jim told me.'

'Uh . . . no,' Connie was confused, 'I've only just arrived here.'

'I see,' Ronny nodded but he seemed suspicious, 'me too.'

Jim finally reached them. He was short of breath. 'Ronny?' he panted.

He held out his hand, then stared at his outstretched arm with a look of genuine amazement. 'Jim!' Ronny exclaimed and began grinning. Without thinking he walked over the tableau, right through the middle of it, kicking the shells aside. Not noticing Connie any more, not noticing Lily. Like Jim was everything.

He took hold of Jim's arm. 'I didn't know where you'd got to.'

'I was in the prefab. We should eat something.'

'You're right.'

They walked off together. Totally engrossed in each other. Like two stringy, rheumy old men.

Connie rubbed her arms. Lily stared after the two of them, irritated. 'He's such a prick.'

'Who? Ronny?'

'No. Jim. He's such a prick.'

'We should go home. It's getting dark.'

'Yes.'

Lily set off along the beach at a great pace, taking extraordinarily lengthy strides with her skinny legs. Connie struggled to remain several paces behind her, but she was not in pursuit, she told herself, merely taking Lily's lead, quite submissively.

And anyway, her mind was elsewhere. It was fuddled and rosy and darkening over. Like the giant sky above her. No sun left, no moon up, no stars yet. Just shadow. A great, wide, hugely improbable inky blink.

30

Lily got up from the kitchen table half way through dinner, without uttering a word, and left them. Initially Connie thought she'd gone off to fetch something and anticipated her imminent return. But she didn't come back. They were eating a giant spinach omelette with boiled potatoes. Sara had been in the midst of preparing their meal – swathed in steam, beating eggs in a giant bowl – when they'd finally staggered home.

She'd turned the immersion heater on specially so that Connie could have a quick bath and change her clothes before dinner. She was being an exemplary hostess and gave every indication of feeling perfectly at her ease. During the meal they discussed a variety of subjects – Connie's work, Sara's chickens, local industry, sightings of hawks in the area – Lily, however, spoke very little.

'Apparently you have black rabbits,' Connie paused between forkfuls of omelette, 'I mean wild ones.'

'Yes,' Sara seemed indifferent, 'you see them a lot. They're very common. Down by the reserve especially.'

When Lily stood up and left the table, Sara kept on talking as if she hadn't noticed. 'I imagine a captive one was set free at some point and then the strain survived. We're all very accustomed to them.'

'I'd love to see one.'

Sara smiled, vaguely amused by Connie's enthusiasm. 'I'm sure you'll get a chance to if you stay in the area for any length of time.'

'Actually,' Connie put down her fork, 'I was wondering whether you might know of any holiday cottages up for rent locally. Or hotels.'

Before Sara had a chance to respond, Connie glanced uneasily over her shoulder and added, 'Is anything wrong? With Lily I mean.'

'No. She's probably just gone to her room.'

Connie pushed a potato around her plate with her knife. 'I thought I might have upset her, without realizing.'

Sara stood up to remove Lily's unfinished meal from the table. She placed the plate on to the draining board. When she next spoke it was with her back to Connie. Her voice was low. 'There's no question of your leaving us. You must stay here for as long as you like.'

Connie smiled. 'That's very kind of you.'

Sara turned around. Her face was bright. She seemed aroused, giddy almost. 'But you're wrong. I'm not being kind at all. It would be useful for me to have another person around. As a distraction. For Lily.'

Connie felt suddenly vulnerable, as though the net was billowing out again and she was seeing inside, into a place where she had no business trespassing.

'I want to show you something . . .' Sara took several steps forward, lifted the tablecloth and yanked open a small cutlery drawer which was hidden within the main body of the table. From inside the drawer she removed a camera. She held it in both hands like it was something infinitely delicate; some old china or a fledgling.

'I took it,' she said, her voice full of awe.

Connie stared at the camera.

'You took it?'

'Yes. Luke, the man you saw me with this afternoon, he's a photographer. This belongs to him. He thinks he's lost it. But I took it.'

She paused, then smiled. 'This is his favourite camera.'

Connie frowned. 'But didn't I see you using it earlier?'

'No. That was another one. This one was hidden in my bag all the while.'

Sara put the camera up to her eye. She stared at Connie through its lens, but she didn't see Connie; instead she saw

154

pink and white and yellow splashes. A dandelion. A marsh-mallow. She lowered the camera from her eye. 'I've never had one before.'

'Why not?'

Sara sat down. She continued to inspect the camera. She fiddled with the flash and the lens cap and the focus. 'Lily was born premature. Did you know that?'

Connie shook her head. 'I didn't.'

'There was some kind of problem with her bladder and her womb. Complications. Her blood doesn't clot too well. We thought we'd lose her. So we never took photos. We didn't do all those normal things that parents do with a new baby. Everything seemed so delicate, so fragile. We felt like we didn't want to tempt fate.' Sara looked up at Connie. 'And I never learned to drive, either, which was somehow another part of it. A kind of . . .' she coughed on the words, 'wishful thinking.'

Connie nodded, although she wasn't exactly sure what it was that she was agreeing to.

'When I first met Luke a couple of days ago, I saw all these photographs in his prefab. And I thought I'd felt some kind of strange connection with him, but the truth is, it was the photographs. The pictures. Time, crystallized. Life. All simple and clear and uninhibited.'

'What kinds of pictures?'

'Dirty.' Sara scratched her cheek. 'Pornography, mainly.'

'Right.'

'Are you shocked?'

'No,' Connie shook her head.

Sara rubbed at her nose with the back of her hand, inhaled deeply and then said, 'Actually I don't think Lily's father is coming home.'

Connie held her tongue. Sara seemed to appreciate it. 'It's only been two months but it feels like he's been gone forever. In fact,' she inspected her fingers, 'it's begining to feel like he was never even really here.'

Sara's nails were full of dirt and soil. Ingrained. She continued to inspect them. 'We used to farm pigs and grow crops too,

155

but after Lily was born he started farming boar. They're less time-consuming. I think he thought she'd need him more, because she wasn't too well. Or maybe that I'd need him more if we lost her. But we didn't lose her. So I didn't need him. And Lily's never really needed anyone. She's terribly independent . . .' Sara sighed. 'Anyhow, in the end I think he got to feel slightly . . . redundant. We argued quite a bit. He did a whole lot of campaigning about the nudist beach, which kept him busy for a while, but because of the boar he didn't really have a leg to stand on.'

Connie frowned. 'Why's that?'

'Local hostility. Lily's right though, the whole thing was ridiculous. I lost a lot of weight. I've a yeast allergy. We got on each other's nerves. And Lily's too, probably. Then his mother got sick. So he went to look after her for a while. I imagine she's better by now but he hasn't come home. He doesn't phone. It's all been . . .' she shrugged, 'well, empty, really. Blank. *Boring*. Sometimes I feel like my whole life has been a long, long wait for something horrible that never actually happened. Like I've been in water, up to my neck, fighting to stay afloat, year after year. But if only I'd felt for the bottom I'd have found it. It was there. The ocean bed, just below where I was treading. It was there.'

Sara pushed her chair back and pulled open the cutlery drawer again. She carefully placed the camera inside it.

'Coffee?' she said, smiling down at Connie, as if absolutely nothing of significance had just passed between them.

Lily inspected Connie's luggage. In the guest bedroom, open on the bed, lay a small suitcase. Next to it, a vanity case and a little bundle of papers tied up with a ribbon. Lily poked around in the case, lifting out and dropping several items. Then she turned her attention to the vanity case. She inspected a couple of Connie's lipsticks and pocketed a pink one.

Finally, the papers. She slipped a single letter out of the ribbon and opened it. She began reading.

Oh Ronny!
Where were you? I needed you but you were nowhere. I needed

you but you were everywhere. Why don't you write back to me, Ronny?

Where are you?

I cannot speak. My two lips and my tongue are so inflamed that my mouth hangs open and I drool on to my shirt-front. It's disgusting. And why? And how? Let me tell you. That demon. Louis. Him. Give me time and I'll draw breath. Give me a moment . . .

Louis. The smell of him! He's been drinking lately. In the dark, alone, cramped up inside that tiny shack. His pores ooze and ooze. He is relentlessly wet and hot and stinking. A foetid distillery. There is no escaping him. His eyes follow me. I can go no distance. He is behind me. And there is no private hidey-hole or secluded nook in this entire forest. In this whole giant hot green hell.

I hate him, Ronny. We are going crazy here together. Me with my radar and my fine-tuned hearing. Him with his pen, his finger, his flash and his eyes, all-seeing. Like one person, but fractured, each part pursuing the other. Hunting. Warring. He demands to know of all my movements. I am the enemy. He is under-cover. A spy. He is tracking me.

And somehow I feel like that great, white ape is watching us and laughing. We wanted to invade him but have only ended up invading each other. Sniffing and pawing and whittling.

It finally came to a head. It had to. Were you there, Ronny? Did you see it? I'll write you my side of things, anyhow, and then you can tell me if my account is the true account. Louis's is different. We keep lying to each other. We believe our own lies, religiously, but also each other's. Oh my brain is fizzing. It's curdling.

Here's how it went, Ronny. Here's the truth of it, honestly. Remember the bat cave? It all feels so long ago now; the clammy warmth of its darkness, its heady black blanket . . . Well, Louis got Monty and a couple of Monty's friends to stake it out. You wouldn't think it possible, but Louis made it so.

I arrived one morning, as usual, before dawn, and they were there by the mouth of the cave and they were building something out of leaves and twigs and straw. A giant bonfire. I asked them what they were doing. They were laughing at me. I said, 'If you light a fire in the entrance you'll kill the bats. They're just inside. Some of them are still returning home. See?'

I pointed skywards. In the air, above me, I could feel their radar.

Monty pulled a face like he didn't understand me. He was shaking a box of matches. He shook them and shook them, beating out his own sick little rhythm. Finally he spoke. 'We won't light it,' he said, 'until we absolutely have to.'

He cocked his head to one side. He grinned at me.

And I knew then that it was over. I'd been invaded. It was the end of the bat cave, Ronny. I could not enter. Instead, very quietly, so calmly and gently, I returned to the shacks. Louis was outside, sitting on an over-turned crate, cleaning his boots as though nothing at all was happening. I stood and I watched him. I said nothing.

He washed the mud off his boots. Then he dried them. He applied some polish with a cloth. He brushed them and brushed them. The sky was quite bright by the time that he'd finished. He was pleased with his job. He put the boots down in front of him and was about to pull them on when I tipped my head to one side. The slightest movement, but he caught it, Mr All-Eyes.

What? He glanced at me. What? I shrugged. What? 'You should buff,' I said quietly. Buff! Like this one word was the most delicious, the most seductive syllable ever spoken. He peered down at the boots. Buff? I have the softest cloth, I said, in a tin, under my bed.

Louis stood up and went into our shack. One of the boots fell over, as he passed it, on to its side. He was gone a while. I watched the boot. And I saw, at its lip, at its giant, dark entrance, a small congregation of insects; termites, leaf-cutter ants, who knows what else, just guarding, patrolling. And then I saw my sister, the scorpion, standing close by, just willing them to allow her to enter.

When Louis returned, he held the cloth, the buffing cloth, and he straightened the two boots and he buffed them with the stupid-

est, stuffiest military precision. Then, when it was done, he threw down the cloth and he pulled them on, one by one, so luxuriously.

But the second boot was already inhabited, and its inhabitant made a sudden, harsh acquaintance with Louis's big, boney ankle, his calf. She raised her tail – My sister! Just a warning, I tell you – but Louis doesn't understand warnings, only attack. So she stung him.

He screamed. He howled. I stood and watched him, doing nothing, not even smiling. He yanked the boot off. He was bleating. He ripped off his sock. He shook it, the boot too. He needed to find her, to see her, to identify. My sister was so tiny. But it's the tiny ones you have to watch.

Help me! He screamed. Slotted into my belt is my wide jungle knife. I unsheathed it. I took his sock, I shook it, I tied it above his calf, I tightened it. I touched the blade on the place that was red and now swelling. I sliced into him. Oh, the feeling!

Louis, meanwhile, was still gabbling, jabbering, hollering. He kept telling me that tourniquets were not proper medical practice any more. People get gangrene that way. Or clotting. He asked me what I was doing with the knife. And when I put my lips to the raw, new wound and sucked, his eyes widened as though I was draining out the very pith of him.

Then the storm abated. There was a strange quiet, a moment of respite, and Louis did something, Ronny. Something unthinkable. Before I could spit, he grabbed hold of my head, my chin, he placed his giant polish-smattered fingers over my mouth.

What would happen if I made you swallow? Monica? What would happen?

His blood and that tiny sting, discovering a new world inside my soft pink mouth. He held me and held me. I thought he would kill me. Then he let go. He watched me spitting and choking. He staggered back into the shack. I heard the mattress creaking as he lay down upon it.

God's truth.

M.

Connie was small and had a child's tread. So light she almost floated. When she entered her room, she was not heard. Lily was entirely engrossed, her eyes wide, her mouth ajar, her hand at her throat.

'What are you doing?'

Even as she spoke Connie knew that this was the silliest question. She could see perfectly well what Lily was doing. She was invading. She was knifing and filleting. Lily looked up, noticed Connie, was surprised that she'd materialized so silently but wasn't in the slightest bit ashamed at being apprehended. Connie saw it. Lily held out the paper. 'This is Ronny's letter,' she said, 'so why do you have it?'

Connie was laughing inside but also white with fury. 'Those are my letters,' she hissed, 'and nobody else's.'

My birthright, she was thinking, my deathright.

Lily reached out her hand for the rest of the bundle. Connie bounded forward and stopped her. She grabbed her wrist. Her hands were tiny but surprisingly powerful. Lily tried to free herself. Connie snatched the letters first, and then slapped her, so hard, with the back of her hand, that the neat little ring she wore snicked into Lily's cheek.

Lily gasped, amazed. She'd fallen back against the wall. But as soon as she'd exclaimed her lips snapped shut and her eyes tightened. Blood began trickling down her cheek. She did not try to stop it. Instead, she straightened up. She was tall. She towered. A skyscraper. A terrible, flat building. Ominously one-dimensional.

'Give me that!'

Connie put out her hand for the letter Lily still held.

'Why should I,' Lily smirked, 'when it's Ronny's?'

She folded the letter with a violent precision; once, twice, three times, then slipped it into her shirt pocket. In the same movement she withdrew Connie's lipstick, pulled off its cover, twirled it out, applied it to her lips, smacked them together, closed the lipstick and returned it to her pocket.

'Does it suit me?' she asked, primping hatefully. Connie was stunned by the spitefulness in Lily's small voice. But more stunned, really, by how protective she felt. The letters. The words. They were hers. *Hers*. Nobody else's.

She put her head to one side and stared at Lily's lips. 'It suits you perfectly,' she whispered, her eyes in slits.

'I know.'

Lily kissed the air and then left her.

31

Nathan returned the stolen book on Monday morning, but during his tea break he travelled to the Fine Art Bookshop – it was only a short trip on the bus – and attempted to buy a copy of his own. Unfortunately they didn't have another volume in stock, but the assistant found a different text – in Italian – which also contained a representation of Antonello's *Pietà*, as well as a further full-page colour illustration of another of his better known works: a painting of Saint Sebastian, who posed, quite exquisitely, the very epitome of youth and strength and gorgeousness. Almost naked, too, Nathan noted, vaguely unsettled, except for the briefest pair of tight, white, extremely modern-looking shorts.

Nathan paid up (a considerable sum) without a moment's hesitation and took his prize back to work with him. It was Laura's day off. Secure in this knowledge, Nathan kept his new book split open, its spine creaking, under his counter, and in between customers he glanced down at it, expecting, each time, that the sensation he felt – the charge – would be less powerful, watered down, weaker. But it was not.

During lunch he rang the number on Connie's business card. He received an answerphone message. The premises were now closed, any further inquiries etc. He jotted down a second number and rang it.

He found himself speaking to Connie's mother. As a ruse, he improvised a story about being one of Connie's old customers seeking out a prescription. It was all very simple. The deceit. Almost a treat. He rang on, to an aunt's house, and she, in turn, gave him the number of a distant relative in Sheppey where she thought Connie might be staying.

He smiled to himself as he copied the digits down on to the back of a lost property form. Then, on the spur of the moment, he turned the sheet over, and under the heading Item(s) Lost, he wrote: Inhibitions.

Then quickly scratched it out.

Jim had given Ronny his bed, because Ronny was so much taller than he was, and the sofa seemed a far more appropriate resting place for his own more compact torso. Ronny enjoyed lying on the bed. It was soft. He could smell Jim on the bed-clothes. On the sheet and the blankets. At night, if he couldn't sleep, he'd run his fingers along the scratches in the wall. Little sketches. Bats and leaves and tiny figures. Silly voodoo. Sometimes maps and sometimes doodles. On the windowsill he'd found an old compass. He chiselled his own name with it. The plaster disintegrated. It felt as soft as chalk.

In the morning, though, when Ronny awoke and tiptoed through to the living room, he couldn't help noticing that Jim was curled up completely, almost foetally, on the sofa, and even then seemed to experience almost as much difficulty finding space on it as he himself had.

'Jim.'

He stared down at him. Jim was deeply asleep. His eyes blinked rapidly under their swollen lids. And with each blink, a tear. Ronny watched the tears, gently lulled by their quiet regularity as they travelled from Jim's eyes and down on to his pillow. The pillow was stained with them. Little tidemarks, like splotches of lichen, white-edged. Ronny gazed at these marks, fascinated. How many nights of tears were resting here? How many years?

'Jim.'

The curtains were closed, but it was breezy outside. They moved intermittently, turning the grey ceiling and the walls into a kaleidoscope of rippling shadows.

'Jim.'

Jim did not seem like he was about to wake, so Ronny took a step away from the couch, intending to go into the kitchen to pour himself a glass of water. But it was this smallest and quietest of shuffling movements that generated something giant and raw and completely unforeseen: a scream, so shrill and wide and terrible that Ronny himself started violently and began screaming too, and Jim, who was hardly awake yet, opened his eyes to find himself standing, surrounded by a wild tornado of wailing – jolted, exposed, breathless.

'What? *What*?'

He blinked, dazed, seeing Ronny, not recognizing him at first, then recognizing. 'What?'

Ronny's heart was beating crazily.

'God,' he sat down on the sofa. His knees were weak.

'What am I doing?'

Jim looked down at himself, at where he was standing, completely disorientated, panting.

'I don't know. God,' Ronny repeated, feeling his new, smooth head with his left hand.

'Was I sleepwalking?' Jim said. 'Did I do anything?'

'Do anything? No. You jumped up and screamed, that's all.'

'Did you do anything?' Jim seemed suspicious. 'Did you?'

'Me? Nothing. I was going to get a glass of water. You scared me when you screamed so I screamed. It was . . .' he grinned shakily, 'very frightening.'

Jim finally stopped panting. He felt ludicrous.

'I'm sorry, then.'

'And you were crying,' Ronny said. He turned and touched the pillow where Jim's cheek had been. It was warm and damp. It made him think of the Mediterranean sea, although he'd never actually been anywhere near it.

'I don't cry.'

'Yes. While you were sleeping. And another thing . . .'

'What?' Jim was hunched over. His hands were linked tightly across his belly.

'We're the same size.'

Jim didn't know what he'd been expecting Ronny to say but it hadn't been that. Ronny stood up. He was wearing some pyjamas. Old ones that belonged to Jim. And his white shoes. He never took them off.

'Look. They fit. The pyjamas.'

He stood next to Jim. 'Up straight . . .'

'What?' Jim scowled.

'Up straight.'

Ronny placed his hand on to the small of Jim's back.

'Pull up.'

Jim jerked, reacting nervously to Ronny's touch.

'There,' Ronny pulled his own shoulders back, 'we are eye to eye. See?'

They were eye to eye.

'I am a firm believer,' Ronny continued, 'in good posture.'

Jim smiled. He couldn't help himself. It seemed like Ronny was a firm believer in only the silliest of things.

'Good posture.' He put his hand to his forehead. He felt ill. 'I don't feel too good.'

He went and sat down.

'Pills,' Ronny said. 'Your body's missing them.'

'I feel weak.'

'Then I'll get you something to eat.'

Ronny shuffled into the kitchen and opened the refrigerator. Inside were two eggs and a large bundle of small, foil-wrapped butter pats; the kind you might find in a café or at a service station. In the cupboard was tea, powdered milk and some tins of beans, meatballs, peas.

Ronny took hold of a couple of the butter pats and the two eggs. He walked back into the living room. 'Eggs all right?'

'Fine.' Jim was curled up at the end of the sofa. He had a blanket tight around him. He was shivering slightly. He looked anxious.

'I like these,' Ronny held the butter pats aloft, 'but the process involved in making tin foil is actually very harmful to the environment.'

'Really.' Jim seemed unstimulated.

'Someone told me that once while I was eating a Kit-Kat.'

Ronny returned to the kitchen. Here he opened the first of the butter pats, placed it into Jim's only saucepan, waited until the butter dissolved and then broke an egg on top. When it had cooked he placed it on to a plate and then repeated the process over.

After they'd eaten – Jim ate with his right hand, still determined to gratify Ronny, although the effort almost killed him; he was shaking too much for any real competence on either side – Ronny asked whether Jim would teach him to whistle. Jim's chest felt tight. He shook his head. 'I haven't much breath today.'

'Go on.'

Jim closed his eyes for a short interlude. 'Just give me a second . . .'

He spent some time considering how it was that he whistled. Eventually he decided on a good way of demonstrating it. 'If you pucker up your lips and then get your tongue and crush the tip of it down on to the back of your bottom row of teeth . . .'

Ronny looked confused.

'You do have a bottom row of teeth?'

Ronny bared his teeth. They were perfect.

'Perfect teeth,' he said proudly.

'Really?' Jim frowned, he felt a moment's unease and then suppressed it. 'No fillings?'

'None. How about you?'

'No, none either, but my teeth are a mess.'

'Why?'

'Because I won't allow anything inside my mouth.'

'How about food?'

Jim grimaced, then he tried to demonstrate the whistling again. Ronny copied. On his first go he trilled quite sweetly. He couldn't believe it. He slapped Jim on the shoulder. Jim was disconcerted and began hiccupping.

'Oh no,' he closed his eyes and held his breath.

Ronny gazed at him fixedly. 'When did you last see a white horse, Jim?'

Jim opened his eyes. He hiccupped. 'A white what?'

166

32

Lily arrived in the kitchen dressed and ready for college but with a pillowcase stuck to her left cheek. Sara was pouring Connie some coffee. 'Now what?'

'It won't come off.'

Lily picked up a piece of toast and ate a corner of it dry.

'Did you cut your cheek?'

'I suppose I must've.'

Lily smiled thinly as she chewed, avoiding Connie's eyes.

Sara went to inspect the pillowcase.

'There's a lot of blood, but it's very dry. Does it hurt at all?'

'Itches.'

'Let's put the case under the tap and wet it. Maybe it'll ease off more gently that way.'

Sara moved Lily over to the sink and ran the warm tap. Lily was forced to bend over and have her cheek fingered and manipulated. She did not complain, but she stared at Connie's bare knees and feet with an expression of intense smugness.

Very slowly and gently Sara eased the pillowcase off. The left side of Lily's face was stained brown with dry blood. Sara used a tissue to wipe it clean but avoided the small, still-moist-looking cut on Lily's cheek. Then she pulled down the bottom lid of Lily's eye and peered inside.

'Pale. Maybe you should skip college.'

'Nope.'

Lily took the tissue and slapped it on to her cheek.

'I'm off.'

She strolled out.

Connie inspected her small gold ring. Sara poured some washing liquid on to the pillowcase and began rubbing at it.

Connie drank her coffee and tried to stop herself from yawning. She hadn't slept well. Her brain had been buzzing. She rubbed her eyes and debated what to do next. What could she do?

'I want to show you something,' Sara had wrung out the pillowcase and was standing by the back door, 'outside.'

Connie stood up. She was wearing a short cotton nightdress. 'Can I come like this?'

'Uh . . . here . . .' Sara took a mackintosh from a hook and tossed it to her, then threw her a pair of large wellingtons. Connie yanked them both on. They went out and Sara walked over to the washing line with Connie clumping along behind her. Sara pointed.

'I gave this a rinse through before you got up.'

Connie stared at Jim's towel. It was a grey, breezy day. Quite nippy. She wrapped the mac closer around her. 'Well, thank you.'

'No, look,' Sara was smiling. She pointed. 'See?'

Connie peered more intently. 'Prison issue,' she read, out loud.

Sara hung up the pillowcase. The blood stain was still evident.

'Ruined,' she muttered grimly, and then turned resolutely back towards the house.

When Connie came downstairs again, properly dressed in some old jeans and a grey woollen sweater, she found Sara sitting at the kitchen table fiddling with Luke's camera. Her hair was unbrushed and she wore no make-up. Her cheeks and chin and nose all had the soft, dull shine of tan-coloured freshly laid eggs.

Connie pulled out a chair. 'So will you give it back?'

'The camera? Eventually. I'm trying to work out the timer.'

'Pass it over.' Connie took the camera and inspected it. 'Okay . . .'

She explained how she imagined it would work. Sara listened carefully. Then she took the camera back again.

'I'm going to take some pictures,' she said, 'do you want to watch?'

Connie checked the time. It was still early.

Her cheek was leaking when she found him. On the beach, naturally.

'Ronny.'

He glanced up. 'Lily.'

'So . . .' she looked at the shell piles, 'will you be making another uh . . .' she couldn't remember the word he'd used previously.

'No,' Ronny continued sorting, 'today I'm constructing something for Jim. It's a new project.'

'Right.' Lily's voice was plainly laced with a fine jealous thread.

'Jim's grief,' Ronny said, 'I'm making it solid.'

'Jim's *grief*?'

Lily didn't understand.

'Well, anyway,' she added, almost roughly, 'I have something for you.'

She pulled the letter from her school bag. 'It has your name on it. When I saw it I just knew that it was yours.'

She offered the letter to Ronny. He put out his left hand and took it. 'Thank you.'

He glanced at the handwriting. Horrible, jagged. He stuffed it into his pocket.

'Won't you read it?'

'What's it about?'

'Insects, blood and a cave. Somewhere foreign. A bat cave.'

'The bat cave.' Ronny nodded.

'Don't you want to know how I found it?'

'Yes.'

Ronny clearly did not want to know.

'Connie. The woman I was with yesterday. She had a whole pile of them. I tried to get hold of the rest but she hit me. See?'

Lily showed Ronny her cheek but he was not looking. She put her finger to the moist lip of the cut and felt tiny granules of sand nestling inside it.

'So . . .' she dawdled and then tightened her resolve, 'I suppose I've got a bus to catch.'

'Then I hope it's not a fast one.'

Lily frowned, smiled, then took off.

Her half-empty coffee cup. The washing line. The hen coop. A boar. Beetroots under tarpaulin. Her wedding ring. Her toothbrush. A paperback romance she'd been reading. A kitchen scale.

Connie watched mutely as Sara photographed all of these things. Each image took a long while to encapsulate – in the lens, in the black box – before it could be finally recorded.

The banisters, the toilet seat (down), her pillow – still featuring the indentation of her head – her favourite shoes, her hairbrush.

They were in Sara's bedroom. At long last she broke the silence between them.

'You look tired.'

Connie blinked. 'Do I?'

'Yes. Wasn't your bed comfortable?'

'It was fine. I haven't been sleeping well. Not since my dad. I got some tablets prescribed for it but I haven't taken them. I don't like forcing things.'

'It's unhealthy not to sleep.'

Connie shrugged.

'Actually . . .' Sara was concentrating on the camera's flash mechanism, 'would you mind doing something for me?'

Connie nodded. 'Anything.'

'Go downstairs, grab a kitchen stool and bring it back up here.'

Connie went and did as she was asked. Sara took the stool and stood it close to the foot of her bed, then placed the camera on top and peered through its lens. She adjusted the stool and looked once more.

'Climb on to the bed, will you?'

Connie climbed on to the bed. Sara stared through the lens at her.

'Right,' she said, 'that's all. You can go now.'

Connie clambered off the bed and tried not to feel pique at being personally excluded from Sara's burgeoning photographic montage.

'I'm just a shadow,' she thought wryly, yawning, heading downstairs again, feeling the banister smooth and cool and suddenly significant beneath her hand.

'Do you know how it was that I made my money?'

Luke was staring out to sea. He'd wandered down on to the beach to thank Ronny for what he'd believed at the time was saving his life. Now, of course, he knew that Ronny had not saved his life. His life had remained perfectly intact. Ronny had witnessed his pain, that was all.

Even so, he'd fully intended to thank him, but ended up staring out to sea instead and talking about something altogether different.

'I didn't realize that you had any money,' Ronny said, 'I never actually considered it.'

Ronny had three giant piles of shells around him, each of which he was now laboriously placing into three black dustbin liners.

'Dot-to-dot,' Luke said boldly.

Ronny scratched his nose. 'What's that?'

'Dot-to-dot books. That's how I made my money. Dirty ones. A photograph, only partially revealed, with the rest of the page numbered and dotted so that you can take a pen and fill in the pornographic segment yourself.'

'Really?' Ronny was vaguely incredulous. He'd never heard of such a thing.

'Yes. It wasn't entirely my idea. I just did the photos. Before that I'd done straight glamour work. Calendars, postcards, but I'd always found it frustrating. My tastes were generally more . . . eclectic.'

'Eclectic,' Ronny nodded.

'So I made some money on the dot-to-dots. I've done three books altogether. All quite successful. But what I couldn't help noticing – I mean at the time – was that I was basically taking pictures that no one would really get to see. So much of the picture was obscured. It was as though the picture's only . . . interest, *strength*, was in what was actually missing.'

'I like that.'

At last Ronny was fully engaged.

'What?'

'That the thing you are most interested in is the thing no one gets to see.'

'Really?' Luke's voice was cool. 'It's chilly.'

He rubbed his arms and decided that Ronny was either thoroughly insensitive, purposefully facetious or intensely, no, *incredibly* stupid.

Connie had worked out that all roads in this part of Sheppey were basically one road, and on this premiss, when her path divided into the route she'd taken the previous afternoon with Lily, to her right, and a rough walkway into what looked like a nature reserve to her left, she took the left-hand path and bargained that ultimately she'd end up exactly where she wanted.

In her arms she held the towel Jim had given her. When she'd taken it down from the line she'd sniffed at it, expecting to discover something. But the towel felt rough and smelled only of synthetic soap. She'd folded it and then kissed it. She often kissed inanimate objects and attached no significance to this practice. It was merely a foible.

In the reserve she saw a heron and a lark – a little brown bird which called so shrilly and then rose and rose up into the sky until it was almost invisible before diving down, dropping, plummeting, like a disappointed heart, a stone, a bullet.

She passed by the hides. She did not venture inside any of them. It was a bare day; huge and flat and empty and blowy and cheek-reddeningly cold. Her nose tingled.

Then she saw it. By chance. The rabbit. Far to her left, on a bushy little hillock. Running, no, chasing. Another rabbit. A brown one. But the first rabbit was jet black. An ink-spot. A small, tight pupil inside the pale green eye of the landscape.

It was so damn obvious! This sable bunny. This oddity. It was its own worst enemy. It was its own bellringer; a walking announcement. A misfit. She stopped and watched as it zipped along the horizon, like the tip of an etch-a-sketch, a nib, a shaving, a harsh jut of dark lead.

How did it survive? She laughed out loud. She didn't know why. How did it survive? Then she walked on, jauntily, fully secure that she merged in her blue jeans and her grey jumper, with her pale hair, her pale skin, confident, adapted, invisible, *disguised*.

On the beach Connie saw Ronny and Luke, deep in conversation. She skittered across the highest of the dunes, over and along, until she reached the prefabs. She raised her knuckles and knocked on Jim's door but the door was not shut, just pulled to, and it swung open under the weight of her fist.

'Oh. Sorry . . .'

She stood in the doorway. The room was grey, the curtains closed. She saw the tip of Jim's smooth head protruding over the arm of the sofa. Then it jerked. A hiccup.

'Hello,' she said, very quietly.

Jim sat up. He corkscrewed around. He rubbed at his eyes and then stared at her over the back of the sofa. 'What do you want?'

'I brought your towel back.'

He said nothing. Then he hiccupped.

'When was the last time you saw a white horse?'

'What?'

'A white horse.'

Jim hiccupped again.

'My dad used to say it. It's one of those things you always try when someone has the hiccups.'

'Right.'

'To distract them. If they think about something else then they forget that they have the hiccups and so get rid of them.'

Jim shook his head. 'That wouldn't work for me.'

'Why not?'

'It's not psychological. It's a physical thing. My stomach goes

173

into spasms. I can have them for whole days at a time.'

'You should visit a doctor.'

'Yes I should.'

Jim's voice was brutally dismissive. He hiccupped.

'It must be driving you crazy.'

He hiccupped. Connie grinned. 'It's driving me crazy.'

'So go away.'

Jim sniffed. His nose kept on running.

'I brought you back your towel,' Connie pointed to the towel.

He nodded. He did not think to thank her for returning it. He hiccupped.

'Prison Issue,' she said.

He jerked up. 'What?'

'Prison Issue.'

Jim was silent for a while. He stared at her. Eventually he said, 'So what's your problem?'

'My problem?'

'Yes.'

'I don't have a problem.'

Connie continued to stand in the doorway. There was something about this squib of a man that she found oddly compelling. When she asked herself why this should be, she decided that it was because he was the one thing she could not be interested in. He was not interesting. He was ungenial, self-contained, dull. And he was not Ronny. Ronny was sitting on the beach with his lacerated wrists and muck green eyes.

Jim had closed his own eyes for a moment, hoping that when he opened them Connie would be gone. But when he did finally open them she had drawn two steps closer.

'Gone,' she said.

'Pardon?'

'They've gone. Your hiccups.'

They had gone. Jim regretted their passing. Connie saw his expression. 'You're missing them.'

'What?'

'Are you deaf?'

'Deaf?'

'Every time I say something you repeat it.'

'I'm tired.'

He was still shivering. He struggled to stop himself.

'Are you ill?'

'No.' He sniffed.

'Can I ask you something?'

Jim's neck was hurting from staring over the back of the sofa. He turned around again so that he faced away from her. She took this as an invitation to walk around the sofa herself and to stand in front of him. He stared blankly at her grey sweater. The wool. The fibre. He hated wool. Why was that? He shuddered. Always a reason.

She thought he was looking at her breasts and actually didn't mind.

'I'm in a rather strange situation,' she said, and then cleared her throat. 'Uh . . .' she paused for a moment.'It's Ronny,' she said, 'there's a kind of . . . well, connection.'

For a moment Jim inspected Connie with what actually amounted to genuine interest. 'You *know* Ronny?'

'Well, not . . . kind of.' She nodded. 'Actually my father knew him. At least I think he did.'

'Your father?' Jim considered this for a second and then something astonishing struck him. 'Don't tell me you're his sister?'

'His sister?' Connie scowled. 'I didn't even know he had a sister.'

She thought about this for a moment and then burst out laughing. It was a ridiculous idea. His sister.

'You really think I could be his sister? Is that possible?'

Jim shrugged. He was confused. He stared into her small, bright face and tried to see some trace of Ronny in it. Connie was still reeling. 'His sister. God! His *half*-sister.'

She pushed a cushion and Jim's blanket aside and sat down on the sofa just along from him. She turned to face him. 'So you know Ronny well?'

Jim was trying to work out how he felt. He felt like a cat-owner who'd just discovered that his cat had been adopted as a stray. In short, he was jealous. Bereft. Here was someone to take Ronny away. To steal him. To rescue him. To save him.

'The point is . . .' Connie drew up her knees, 'I saw him yesterday on the beach and there was something . . .' she looked at Jim, almost apologetically, 'missing.'

'His hair,' Jim said quickly, 'he cut it off.'

'No.' Connie smiled. 'I don't mean that. I mean . . . more . . .' she paused, 'and then there's his wrists. All scarred and everything.'

Jim felt a sudden rush of dislike for this girl. She was a prig. She had no true understanding of anything. He said shortly, 'Ronny's had a difficult time of it. He's been very unhappy.'

While Jim spoke, though, he realized that he wasn't actually thinking of Ronny at all, but of himself. He was immediately appalled by this sudden, clean, harsh apprehension of his own self-pity. Was it transparent? He chewed on his lips to stop them from grimacing.

'The point is . . .' Connie inspected her hands, 'my dad died and he left Ronny some money in his will.'

Jim touched his cheek with his left hand, then remembered and snatched his fingers away. Connie watched him, intrigued.

'And in some respects he really looks like he could do with it.'

'No,' Jim shook his head, 'I don't think Ronny's very bothered about material things.'

He couldn't breathe properly. His nose was running again.

'I know,' Connie nodded at this. She looked very far away one moment and too, too close the next. 'Apparently when he was a child he used to break things.'

'Did he?'

Jim struggled to focus.

'Yes . . . you know . . . uh . . .'

Connie was staring at Jim and thinking something inexplicable. 'I saw a black rabbit on my way down here today.'

'A black rabbit?'

He tried to swallow. His mouth felt dry.

'Ronny asked me if I'd seen one and I said I hadn't but then I did see one. It was so strange. It really stood out. You'd think they'd be fair game, really, for all the bigger birds and the farmers.'

Connie's eyes were prickling. She rubbed them for a second and then found herself yawning. Jim was perspiring. And not just on his face, on his head too, the back of his neck.

'You look terrible, Jim.'

Connie had used his name. Jim glanced over his shoulder, as if someone else was in the room. Jim. Poor Jim. Things had been such a struggle for him. He suddenly felt so sorry for this Jim person. Poor Jim who felt so wretched.

He closed his eyes.

'Could I get you some water or anything?'

Connie stood up. Jim shook his head. He wanted her to go. But she went into the kitchen anyway and found a glass and filled it. When she returned to the living room Jim was curled up on the sofa, half-covered in the blanket, his pillow on the floor.

She picked up the pillow. 'Lift your head.'

He opened his eyes and lifted his head. His eyes were full of a kind of fury. He moved automatically. She pushed the pillow under him. It felt damp. She saw that it was marked by grey stains. It was an old pillow.

'You can relax now.'

Jim lowered his head, very slowly. She adjusted his blanket. He remained stiff.

'I've put some water on the floor next to the sofa,' Connie said. 'Can I do anything else for you?'

'No.'

His voice was hard. His eyes were closed. He was so strange-looking. Like a hedgehog, she told herself, without bristles. He was sweating. His nose was running. She put her hand into her pocket and pulled out a paper tissue. She unfolded it, sat down on the floor, leaned her shoulder against the sofa's arm, then tentatively reached out to dry his forehead. He did nothing. She dabbed the tissue under his nose. He didn't move, but his eyes were squeezed up tight, as if he couldn't bear her touching him.

177

'I'm an optician,' she said, eventually, like this would give him confidence, like it was something medical, some kind of sister qualification. She thought he was asleep, his breathing was so deep and so rhythmical. She was dazed by it. Stupefied.

But he was not asleep. 'I'm colour blind,' he said coldly, without opening his eyes. Colour blind, Connie thought, then her chin touched her breast-bone and she stopped thinking.

33

Her armpit, her nose, her knees, her in-grown toenail.

Her eyes, her nape, her arse, her knuckles.

Her breasts, her stretch-marks, her anus, her clitoris.

And each time the camera clicked she smiled and said to herself: This is me. It's true. It's real. I'm here. I'm it.

Her navel, her waist, her moles, her calluses.

Her fillings, her fumblings, her lapses, her laughter.

These things. Her life.

Telling, containing, revealing, relaying.

A click – a flash – a shutter.

Daughter – wife – mother – lover.

Yes.

And the rest.

Ronny staggered back to the prefab carrying the three bags. He supported two with his left hand, and the third he held gnashed between his teeth. It was heavy though. The weight of it snagged his bottom lip and splayed it out, purple-whitely, on to his chin.

It wasn't much of a distance, but by the time he'd arrived there he was struggling, he was puffed and spent and listing. He placed the bags down, very gently, and then stood in the prefab's open doorway, silently opening his mouth and stretching his jaw – like a child recovering from his first dental extraction – waggling his chin from left to right so as to return the feeling back to it.

Inside the prefab he saw something he had not expected. Connie, leaning against the sofa, her head tipped forward, her eyes closed. A stiff, blonde flower, its petals folded. And next to her, Jim, waxy pale, corpse-like, his eyes closed too, his breathing laboured.

Ronny paused in the doorway, gaping and smiling, but uneasy, as if faltering at the entrance to a hallowed place, an ancient tomb; somewhere sacred and complete and inaccessible. He took one step backwards, another, then a third, until he was out of the doorway's grey shade and back bathing in the light outside. He stared up into the bleary sun until he was dizzy, as if he wanted to burn the quiet scene he'd just witnessed clean out of his eyes.

Then he bent over and picked up the three bags. He used both hands. He carried them, blinking away a white-red spot in the centre of his vision, banging them clumsily up against his legs, to the back of the prefab, where he deposited them in a line along the back wall. He threw himself down next to them. His chest felt so empty but so heavy. He put his hands to his face.

'What's happening? Who am I?'

He spoke out loud, but not loudly.

He stared at his fingers as if they might tell him. But they didn't. He pursed his lips. He scowled. He pushed the tip of his tongue against his bottom row of teeth. He blew. He blew. No noise emerged, just a kind of panting. He tried harder. No sound. No sound.

He stopped trying. Instead, he plunged his hands into the closest black bag and pulled out some shells, put them down on to the ground, took off one of his shoes and banged at them with its heel. The shells shattered. He searched out the sharpest fragment, rolled up his trouser leg and applied the shell, forcefully, to his shin.

He made several deep indentations but the cuts didn't bleed. He became more frantic and slid the shell along his calf. Here the shell sliced wonderfully and the blood flowed freely. Thank God, he muttered. Thank God I'm alive. Thank God, thank God I'm alive. Thank God.

He threw the shell away and rolled down his trouser. He pulled his shoe back on. He sat for a while, breathing heavily.

Then something occurred to him. He shoved his hands into his pockets. He withdrew some tablets. Three types: little whites, little blues and some brighter, brasher capsules, all neat and curtailed in their foil and plastic. He chose randomly. The white ones. He took six, chewed, swallowed, without wincing.

When he returned the packets to his pocket Ronny discovered something else there. Monica's letter. He pulled it out. He felt so alone. He was alone. Jim had abandoned him. He opened it.

Dear Ronny, he read. *Dear Ronny*. He blinked a few times, gulped, then read on.

In a dream The Head had told her exactly what to do. Every detail. The Head was very interested in Ronny. He felt a *connection*, an empathy. The Head was convinced that Ronny had entered Lily's life for very specific reasons, although he didn't specify what these might be exactly. Specifications weren't really his strong point.

Lily sat on the bus trying to make sense of it, but not trying particularly hard. She didn't like making sense of things. It wasn't an especially helpful process, making sense. It wasn't one of her regular indulgences. But what she did decide, finally, was that a burial of some kind was necessary. A ceremony. Something formal. A gesture.

And tied up, linked, entwined in the burial process would be the death of something else (something raging, foetid, unspecific), or the birth, or the rebirth, an awakening. *Something*.

Sometimes Lily wished she'd been raised a Catholic. Then she wouldn't have needed to improvise so much. Things would've been so much more formal and lucid and constrained. In the well-worn form, the predictable angles of confession, forgiveness, catharsis.

Ronny had said . . . what was it? She couldn't remember. She stared out of the window. Was this an A road or a motorway? How big was London? Was it easily navigable?

What Ronny had in fact said was that devils and demons

were created simply as a means for primitive people to express their feelings – overwhelming feelings, engulfing feelings – of anger and guilt and panic. That was all. Easy.

Ronny had said these words but Lily hadn't understood what he'd meant by them exactly. Was it a denial? Was it ridicule? Was it all just lies? What she did understand, though, was that Ronny was more than just a pretty face. More. More. More. He was a missionary. He was an emissary. He was downright fucking edible.

A burial. That was it. What was needed. A burial followed by a wake a wake awake.

She licked her lips.

It was a long, straight road and they saw each other approaching from far, far away. Like two prize-fighters, all hips and holster and spur-twinkling stagger. Except that Ronny alone staggered – it was his habitual gait – and if Sara was ready to draw, to burst, to explode, it was merely an illusion, an aftertaste of the morning's fireworks.

She was finding herself. Even here, step after step on this long, straight road. Even here. But it was a curious journey. Hard on the feet. Tricky terrain.

They drew adjacent to one another. Ronny was in his own world. He seemed colourless. He barely noticed her.

'Ronny.'

'What?'

His voice was almost fractious. She could've been anybody.

'It's me. Sara. Remember?'

'Yes.'

He nodded but he hardly glanced at her. Then he walked on.

'Where are you going?'

She called after him.

'Nowhere.'

He kept on walking, hoping she'd forget about him if he held his breath. He held it. It worked.

Sara stood still and smiled to herself. She had the camera slung around her neck. It bumped against her breasts. Was she invisible? Was she truly invisible? Was everything too late now? She shook her head and walked onwards.

Ronny located the farm with ease. On the final leg of his walk he was accompanied by a strange group of companions. The boar. Each small pack trotted together in unison along the perimeter of their individual enclosures. They followed Ronny in relays. He was their skinny baton, and they all kept perfect time with him.

But Ronny didn't focus on the boar. He was focused else-where. Somewhere hot, somewhere scalding and dense and deep inside. The front door of the farmhouse was locked but the back door wasn't. He pushed it open. The kitchen smelled of coffee and of cabbage. He inspected the taps, the sink, the table, the crockery – a pale blue colour, standing jauntily on an old dresser, spotless.

He'd never had a proper home. Was this a proper home? He breathed it all in. The hallway. The stairway. He inspected the walls as he climbed the stairs, searching out residue from Lily's previous misadventure.

He drifted from room to room. First, Sara's bedroom. It was plain and powdery and vaguely mussed. The cupboard doors were open, and inside her clothes were hung on old metal hangers like a threadbare assemblage of frustrated sighs. He fingered the assorted fabrics. He looked down at the shoes. A hat-box on the top shelf, and, in the corner, under dense plastic, a long white dress. A wedding dress. He lifted the dress from the cupboard. He pulled off the plastic. Net and dust and old yellowy silk fell from his clumsy fingers and frothed on to the carpet.

He caught sight of himself in the dresser. He got a shock. He stared grimly, as though he almost didn't recognize his reflec-tion, but it was the actual possibility of recognition that both-ered him. He looked down at the dress again. He unfastened the zip. He used both hands. He pulled it wide, to its fullest extent, so that the dress lay open, like a fine cocoon, like a silk sleeping bag. He stepped into it, and pulled it on, over his clothes. He zipped it up again. It was big on him. He turned around slowly and then inspected himself in the mirror. He smiled, because now he was truly unrecognizable. He lifted his skirts with a swish and left the room.

Lily's bedroom. Books. Magazines. The bed unmade. A set of drawers. He yanked open the top one. Underwear. He closed it. The second one: T-shirts, jumpers, socks. The third. In the third drawer he discovered a selection of small animal pelts. Stiff. Some of them quite old. A vole. Two rabbits. A weasel. A bat – dried up – even a cat pelt. A small collection of pellets, deposited, he presumed, by an owl or something, containing, in crushed up perplexity, little bones and bits of skin and gristle and other stuff. He could've sworn he saw a jaw. A tiny jaw. A mouse's jaw. He marvelled then withdrew.

Also, some pieces of wire. Two knives. Both sharp. He tested them on his thumb, lovingly, kept hold of the sharpest, lifted his skirts and slipped it into his pocket, then put the other back. He continued inspecting. A lipstick (somewhat incongruous, he frowned) and feathers. Mainly pigeon and hen feathers but also some which were smaller and brighter.

Ronny pushed the drawer shut. He mopped at his face with his skirts. His face felt hot. Dust from the skirts made him feel like sneezing. He wheezed and then vacated. Connie's room. On the bed, a suitcase. He walked straight over to it, feeling like he was inside some kind of tunnel. With so much focus, so much magnification that it almost made him topple. This was the moment. He knew it. Something told him. The *moment*.

Ronny opened the suitcase. Clothes, cosmetics. An extra pair of sandals. But tucked into a corner, wrapped up in a ribbon, just as Lily had described them, the letters.

'Where have you been?' he asked, out loud, quite matter of factly. Then shoved in his hands – like a surgeon attending a routine caesarean – grasped hold of the letters and delivered them.

Jim couldn't tell the difference between waking and dreaming. There was no precise moment when he entered consciousness.

Just hotness. Confusion. He didn't even know that his eyes were open. But they were open. He was looking into the face of a girl. She was sleeping. It was all so calm. He was not thinking. Just staring, blankly.

A little face. Its brow puckered. He stared at the brow and the pucker. He wished the pucker would go. He imagined it gone. And no sooner had he imagined it than it went. His eyes slid down her nose and landed on her lips, which were neat and dry. He stared at her lips.

A thought entered his head. It said: You could do anything.

He considered the thought. Anything? What did that mean?

I know that I am evil, he told the thought, but I will do no harm here.

There. His heart lifted.

He circled his eyes around her face. Her chin, her cheeks, her brows, her crown. He circled. Time and time again. A mental massage. And as he circled – he was sure of it – her face relaxed, and relaxed, and all the sadness in it departed.

Her breathing grew deeper, then deeper still. The corners of her lips lifted. She was smiling, pretty much. Then she stopped breathing, just for a moment, and finally her eyes opened. She was staring into his face. He did not blink. He expected to see fear in her eyes, but there was nothing there but blue.

'I was dreaming of my father,' she said, her voice riddled with a dozy amazement, 'he was standing over me, touching my face. And all the hurt was drawn right out of me. Pulled out in one go, like a bee sting yanked free by tweezers.'

Jim continued to stare, without blinking, stifling everything in his chest, his face; deadening, ignoring what she'd said entirely, determined to feel nothing and, he told himself, succeeding.

'Hello? Are you awake?'

She leaned closer, frowning. 'Or are you sleeping?'

He felt her breath on his face.

'Are you sleeping?' she asked again, 'with your eyes wide open? Am I in your dreams? Do you see me?'

Connie imagined herself lost deep inside Jim's head. This

thought tickled her, somehow. She didn't dare wake him then, so she withdrew, very softly, a mere thought, a twinkle, a Tinkerbell, an Ariel; floating and golden and embossed. Beatific.

Ronny,

Whose fault is this? Is it my fault? Louis trapped me in a corner and started telling me about how animals had no fear of man before he made them fear him. In the Americas, he said, when people first landed on the Pacific islands, and in New Zealand too . . . In New Zealand. I don't know. Hang on. Let me get my facts straight. Should I brush up on my geography?

Screw the facts, anyway. Here's the gist: there were over sixty types of flightless bird at one time. In the world. Some were up to half a ton in weight. But because they lived in parts of the globe unexplored by man, they had never actually seen him before – this scrappy, fragile, two-legged creature – and so they had no reason to fear him.

They walked among the sweet, pink sailors when they landed, those sailors who were feeling the hard earth under their toes for the first time in so long, yes, they walked among them without apprehension, all peacefulness and openness. Welcoming. And the sailors, barely believing their luck, seeing these gentle creatures so real and trusting among them, raised their clubs and brought them down hard. Harder still. Killed them. Ate them. Extinguished them.

No scruples, Louis said. No bloody scruples.

And now there are no longer sixty types of flightless bird, some up to half a ton in weight. No. Now there are none. They are all gone.

You come from that place, Louis screamed, and there's no point in denying it. You can't arrive in these jungles and behave like nothing has happened. History. You can't come here and act like you aren't the thing you are. You exist on the back of all this slaughter. You are its product. You are its prize, its very reason.

So that was his basic point, Ronny. I am a success simply because I'm alive. I come from that stock, Louis said, the stock which survived all the wars and the plagues and the hardships. I am a success because I exist. My body is the product of all those previous equations. If life was a sum, my scrappy white torso – this sad, pale shell, this wracked thing – would be the answer to it.

Imagine!

That's such a responsibility, Ronny, don't you think?

But naturally I didn't take it all lying down. (Although I was in my bunk. He keeps waking me and making me talk. In the night. Late. In the morning, early.)

I didn't take it prone because it made no real sense. I said, 'It's really not like that, Louis. It's a fluke. You got your logic wrong. You got your sums wrong. You're doing it back to front. The fact that I exist doesn't mean anything. My existence is a question, not an answer. It's a joke, a mystery, a shot in the dark.'

'You can't be one of them,' Louis sneered, 'no matter how hard you try. You stick out. This whole environment is disgusted by you. By your white face and your thin arms, your long hair, your broken nails . . .

A jangling. Ronny looked up. He closed the letter, gathered all the others into a bundle, rose from the bed and walked towards it.

The phone was ringing in the hallway. It rang and rang.

'Hello?'

It was in his hand and he was speaking.

'Hello?' he repeated.

'James?'

A voice, surprised. Off-balance.

Ronny paused, then answered.

'No. Ronny. It's Ronny.'

Another pause.

'It's me. It's Nathan. Where are you?'

'Nathan? Oh . . .'

Ronny began smiling. 'Uh . . . Is it about the watch?'

'The watch?' Nathan echoed. Another pause.

'No. I'm sorry. I'm confused . . . In fact . . . in fact I was actually hoping to speak to Constance. To Connie.'

'Right.' Ronny's voice became hollow.

'Is she there?'

'No. She's with Jim.'

'But . . .'

Almost panic. Confusion. Ronny ignored it and pulled at the zip on the wedding dress with his free hand.

'I can't really speak right now,' he said softly. He was aching.

'Ronny?'

Then he smiled.

'You know . . .' his voice was so gentle . . . 'I somehow thought you'd rung for me.'

'Ronny?'

'But I was wrong to think that. I was wrong.'

He hung up.

34

'Tell me again how you found it.'

Luke was so pleased to have the camera back. Once it was gone he'd started to labour under the misapprehension that its absence symbolized something.

'I don't know. I just happened across it.'

Sara was a poor liar. And the excitement of what might yet occur was bubbling up within her.

'Inside the hide?'

'Underneath. But I'm certain it didn't come to any harm.'

He was inspecting it. 'It looks just fine.' He paused, frowning.

'What?'

'The film's been used. I didn't take any shots myself, at least I don't remember taking any . . .'

'Will you develop them?'

Sara was biting her lip.

'Uh. I don't know . . .'

'Maybe you should.'

Luke stared into Sara's face. It was so full of activity. It was burgeoning. It was beautiful.

'You want me to?'

'Yes. It's exciting, don't you think?'

'But it'll take a while.'

'Take as long as you want.'

Sara sat down on Luke's sofa and wrapped her arms around herself.

Lily felt like some kind of flimsy vapour walking among all these city folk, these brightly coloured, purposeful, brusque, shoving, thumping, pumping people. She became suddenly aware of her own slightness. She knew where she wanted to go but nothing seemed to want to take her there. She had ten pounds to spend. A ticket inspector told her to buy a One-Day Travelcard. Two zones. She did as he'd instructed, but suspiciously.

Finally, she found her way to Baker Street. Her cheek kept bleeding. Her blood was like water. No substance. No texture. She held her shirt cuff against her cheek. The cotton was already tight with plasma. Then she followed the signs to the Lost Property Office.

She'd arrived, finally. But it was late. Almost one. And the bus back left in only an hour. She pushed the door open and walked in. There were too many people. Two women and a man behind counters, and others, like herself, waiting for service. She nearly panicked but then she remembered how Ronny had specified that the person he'd dealt with was male, not female, so she avoided the queue and instead walked straight on over to the man in the payment cubicle.

Someone in the queue called out to her and then a woman on the counter told her that she needed to go around the other way if she wanted serving. But Lily, her one wrist jammed against her cheek, pushed her other hand flat down on to the counter and stared intently into the man's eyes.

'I've come for Ronny,' she said, above all the confusion and disgruntlement, 'about the beast.'

The man seemed confounded. 'This is a payment cubicle,' he said. 'To make a claim you'll have to fill in a form and then see one of my colleagues.'

He pointed and then paused. 'Are you hurt?'

'No. No. Like I said, I've come for Ronny.'

But his name seemed to spur no sense of recognition. None whatsoever.

Nathan had requested sick leave. He was feeling sick. It was almost a fever. Everything opening wide, inside him. That's what he'd said.

'Sounds like flu,' they'd responded, 'you'd better take a week.'

He'd collected his coat and was preparing to go. He was in

the toilet, staring at his reflection, straightening his collar, when a colleague entered.

'Don't come near me,' Nathan croaked, hoping to create an atmosphere of legitimacy, 'I might be infectious.'

The colleague smiled. 'No more infectious,' he said, 'than this crazy girl who was just at my counter, dripping blood and ranting on about The Beast.'

'What?'

Nathan chuckled.

'But The Beast wasn't actually hers, you understand. It belonged to her friend, Ronny. It was Ronny's beast. He'd wrapped it up in a cardboard box and then dropped it off here for safekeeping . . .'

Nathan stopped smiling.

'Is she still out there?'

'No. She just left . . .'

The man turned around as he spoke, but Nathan had already pushed on past him.

Lily was walking towards the escalator, thoroughly humiliated. The world was too big, she told herself. Someone should have warned her. Nathan actually nearly knocked her over. He backed into her. He'd been scanning faces, frantically, hoping to recognize someone, some*thing*. Lily staggered and then turned to face him. Her cheek was dripping.

'Is it you?' Nathan panted, seeing the blood. 'Did you come for Ronny?'

'It is me,' Lily mumbled, almost crying with relief, 'it is me. And I'm lost and I think I might be about to miss my bus.'

Nathan put his hand into his pocket and drew out a hankerchief.

'Here. Don't worry.'

Lily took it. He led her slowly towards the escalator.

'I'm Nathan,' he said gently, 'you're all right now. I'll look after you.'

He was developing in the bathroom. He had all the equipment. The red light, the washes, the paper, the dark blind for the window. Slowly, slowly, the images rose out of the whiteness; a wide smirk of black and grey shadows staining the paper's pale face.

First off, uh . . . he turned the picture up the other way . . . yes . . . a cup. An old mug. In full focus. That was all. Then a table. Some tarpaulin. A giant creature which almost made him squeal – with hair and horns, all tusky . . . Next, a piece of wood, polished. A banister?

Luke smiled to himself. Should he stop? Wasn't he wasting paper here? But he thought of Sara, sitting on his sofa, full of anticipation, and resolved to continue.

The next image made him tut. A toilet seat. Down. And then, a cloud? Something great and uninteresting and white . . . a pillow? And after. After? He squinted. Jesus *Christ*. His hands felt numb and heavy as he continued developing.

Ronny sat on a small hillock, surrounded by the letters. He was reading and reading. He'd been crying. 'It was me,' he kept saying, 'it was me. It was me. Hiding all the while, keeping myself safe and disguised until no one could possibly see who I was. But it was me.'

He'd pulled off his shoes. His long, pale feet were cushioned in the grass, grey with dirt, big toeless, like great dusty fins, or flippers. He inspected them as if they were some kind of irrefutable evidence.

He felt so sorry for Monica and the trouble she'd been through. He felt such a profound understanding. Her love of all the things she couldn't see. The desolation. The lack of belonging. The endless, pointless investing.

You feel very close at this moment. Is that stupid? Are you near me? Are you out there, hiding in the jungle, watching, waiting, but I just can't see you? Is it me who's dense or is it the forest? Is it me?

The letters weren't dated. But were they in some semblance of order? How did they unravel? Ronny rubbed at his eyes, which were red and sore, not from crying, he decided, but for some other reason. Maybe the sun. Maybe the pills he'd taken. He rubbed them again, harder, and then he hunted for the next letter in the pile. He craved a conclusion. He had to establish himself, within. Right now. Inside. He had to locate her. He stroked the letter. He drew a deep breath. He squinted. He opened it.

I had a dream.

Ronny? Am I writing? I think I am. Am I waking? Am I sleeping? Will this thing get through to you?

I had a dream about Louis and the white ape. Tell me if you think I'm going crazy. I had a dream. I was lying on a table. Or a camp bed, but high off the ground. And I was wearing an old nightshirt which kept shifting. It was too small. A child's shirt. And I was surrounded by people. All looking and staring.

I felt like Gulliver. As if my hands were tied, my legs, my ankles. But I couldn't feel any kind of rope or cord or string, even. Just a weight. And Louis was at the head of the table. And he was holding some kind of torch. And he had a Stanley knife in his other hand. And he was cutting my hair with it. And it wasn't just a brief interlude, it all took a long, long time. It went on and on for a long time. And sometimes I was crying. And sometimes I was silent. That's all.

It was only a dream.

But where was the white ape? I know that's what you're wondering. Where was it? Well in truth I think I was the white ape. That's my take on it. Lying on the table like some terrible experiment. Having my hair cut. Poked and prodded. Like I was the ape. Although that's just a take, Ronny, that's all it is.

I mentioned the dream to Louis and he was extremely tight-arsed about it. He said it sounded like an abduction dream. An alien abduction dream. He said that alien abduction dreams say a whole lot about the people who have them. He was very smug about it. As if it indicated something.

And suddenly it occurred to me that maybe Louis was trying to get me off track in some indefinable way. It felt as though he was trying to divert me. So when I went out into the forest, later on, and was certain that he was on my trail – he's always on my trail, that's the only thing I'm truly sure of – once I was convinced that he was following me, I doubled back on myself to con-

front him, but it was not Louis, it was Monty. And it wasn't even as if he was being all that subtle about it, either. He was slapdash and clumsy. He was sneering. Like this was something he'd long been in the habit of doing.

I began to wonder whether Louis had ever followed me (I mean since the bat cave) or whether, in fact, he was actually off elsewhere. But what was he doing in this other place? And where was it exactly? What was the allure? Did he know something? Had he discovered anything?

I went back to the shack. I waited. And that's just where you find me, Ronny.

Back here, dumb, dumb, dumb, and waiting.

M.

He finally came out. He was grim-faced. Sara peered up at him from the sofa. She didn't say anything though, just studied his expression for any small indication of understanding.

'So you took these?'

He held the thick sheath of photos fastidiously, between a prickly finger and thumb.

'Yes. Of course I did.'

She wasn't ashamed. Her voice was brash.

Luke scratched his belly and then shifted his weight from one foot to the other.

'I'm sorry . . .' he said eventually, 'but I've been rather taken by surprise here.'

'That's all right.' She was perfectly cool and calm. 'Would you like to go through them with me?'

'Uh . . .' he frowned, 'I've seen them all. I just developed them, obviously.'

'And what did you think?'

He shook his head.

'I don't know. What should I think?'

Sara put out her hand for the pictures.

'Were they clear enough?'

'Oh yes,' he almost smirked, 'they were clear enough. They were . . .' he struggled, 'they were *bald*.'

He passed the pictures over. Sara inspected the top print.

'This is my cup,' she said, 'it's the cup I always use. I have coffee in it, first thing. It's a plain cup, but I like it. I've grown accustomed to using it each day.

'And this . . .' The next picture. 'Well, this is my kitchen table. It was my mother's table. I think it's Victorian. Just clumsy and everything. Full of knots and little dips. When I was a kid I used to imagine all kinds of creatures in the knots. They were like eyes or tadpoles or something . . . and this . . .'

The next picture.

'This is the tarpaulin near the boar pens. I keep the beets under it so they don't rot too quickly or dry out or anything. I don't know why I've always liked it, but I have. I enjoy the *feel* of it. Kind of smooth. And it's thick and waterproof. It's hard to lift. I tack it down with tent pegs to keep it secure . . .'

The next picture. But Luke interrupted her.

'Details,' he said.

'Pardon?'

'These are just details . . .' It had been a concrete thought, initially, but then his voice petered out.

Sara considered it, anyhow. 'Yes,' she said slowly, 'but they are also what I am. You know? Sometimes I feel like I'm just an accumulation of objects. I mean, here's my pillow. It's made of goose feathers. It's a bit prickly, but I made it myself from a goose of mine. I was very proud of it at the time. I felt a great sense of achievement. And the dent in it is the dent from my head. See?'

Luke nodded. She shuffled the images forward a bit.

'That's my elbow. I think it's quite distinctive. The little knobbly bit at the side is bigger than on my other elbow because I cracked it when I was fifteen, skating. I used to skate a lot. I always longed to be a professional skater.'

She cleared her throat.

'Oh God. That's my arse. I mean my anus. I never saw it before. It's not quite like I expected. It's smaller.'

She turned the picture the other way up.

'I think I prefer it sideways. It seems more cheerful.'

Luke was rubbing his forehead. He was barely paying attention. He was ill at ease.

'You know what?' Sara asked.

'What?' He focused in on her again.

'I just wanted to be honest with you, and with myself. I wanted to show you who I was, but plainly and frankly. And actually, I wasn't even very sure that there would be anything to show.'

'But I already know who you are,' Luke was impatient.

'You do?' She didn't sound too certain.

'I don't need to see a picture of your mother's table to understand who you are.'

'But it helps to explain. It *enlarges* . . .'

'No.'

'It does.'

'No. I don't think so.'

Sara cleared her throat.

'You know what I'm truly looking for?' she asked, barely believing that she would actually dare to say it.

'Tell me,' Luke smiled.

She took a deep breath, then blurted it out. 'Total acceptance.'

Luke paused. 'Big words,' he said, continuing to smile but now clearly intimidated.

She looked down at her knees. 'And maybe I won't find that here.'

She gathered the pictures together. She'd had an inkling he'd be this way. But even so, she allowed herself to feel slightly hollow and vaguely forlorn. She stood up.

'We fucked,' she said, almost bitter now, 'but we were never intimate.'

'You've lost me.'

She'd lost him.

'No. You've lost me,' she said, 'because at heart – although you may not realize this – at heart you're a real . . .' she struggled, 'a true, a *complete* pornographer.'

Then she smiled, as though this had actually been a compliment, and the smile itself was merely the final blow in the gentlest of assassinations.

35

'I got some blood on the carpet. Sorry.'

Lily scuffed at the two drops with the toe of her trainer, worsening matters considerably.

'Don't worry,' Nathan returned from the bathroom clutching a wad of toilet paper. Lily took it and held it to her cheek, tossing Nathan's now-moist linen handkerchief into a nearby wastepaper bin.

She glanced around her. His flat was plain but comfortable. She was perfectly at her ease here. It felt safe.

'So where's the beast?'

Nathan pointed towards the sofa. 'It's there.'

Lily's eyes widened at the sight of the box, as though she couldn't quite believe that it actually existed.

'Did you open it yet?'

'No.'

'Why ever not?'

She seemed genuinely perturbed by his sense of restraint.

'I was asked to look after it. That was all.'

'So does Ronny make a habit of giving you stuff to keep for him?'

Nathan shook his head. 'No. Not really. Although he's always made a habit of losing things.'

His voice sounded wistful, but Lily didn't read anything into it. She put out her hands and touched the box's sharp corners, pressing her thumbs down on to them until they received little temporary indentations. She studied her thumbs and then looked up. 'Actually, Ronny just lost his hair. He set fire to it.'

Nathan looked uneasy. 'Why would he do that?'

'What?'

'Why would he set fire to himself?'

'I don't know. I imagine that it was an accident.'

Nathan smiled at this, but thinly.

'Why are you smiling?'

Nathan cleared his throat. 'Do you know . . .' he paused and then finally spoke the name, 'do you know Ronny well?'

Lily shrugged, slightly defensive now. 'I suppose so.'

He changed the subject. 'You look washed out.'

Lily was instantly all twinkles. 'I'm fine. Honest. That's just my natural colouring.'

For some reason she'd warmed to Nathan. There was something gentle, something vague, something almost spiritual about him. His eyes had a light shining out of them. After inspecting him for a while she said, 'You know, your face seems kind of familiar. Why should that be?'

'I have no idea.'

His jaw stiffened until her eyes returned to the box.

'You didn't even feel tempted to take a little peek?'

'No.'

Nathan sat himself down on the sofa. Lily stood up and then balanced her weight precariously on its arm.

'Did you ever see a beast before?' she asked, casually.

'A beast?' He paused then tried, with some difficulty, not to topple back into the obscene cavity of his past.

'I can't answer that,' he said softly.

'Why not?'

'Because I don't know what your definition of a beast is exactly.' He inhaled deeply. 'Maybe you should ring home and tell them that you might be late back.'

'Nah. They won't even notice I'm gone.'

Lily touched the box with her foot. To reassure herself. It was as though everything she'd ever feared – the horrors, the terrors, the mysteries – were right there, contained, shut up, within reach. It was all supremely energizing. Nathan shifted, clearly uncomfortable. 'You should ring them.'

He pointed to his phone. Lily clucked her tongue, but she

walked over and dialled anyhow. She waited. She didn't get connected.

Nathan stood up. 'What's wrong?'

'There's a voice saying how I don't have the correct code.'

Nathan joined her and took hold of the phone himself. 'Let me try. Tell me the number.'

Lily recited the digits. 'And the area?'

'Sheppey.'

He dialled immediately, seeming to know the code already without even looking it up. This impressed Lily. She thought he must be experienced, enlightened, thoroughly wise. He waited for the connection. Lily heard it ringing at the other end. She put out her hand for the receiver but he kept a tight hold of it until the phone was answered.

A woman's voice. Soft, firm, slightly piqued, determined. *Her* voice. Finally. Nathan's heart whooped inside his chest. But he said nothing, just passed the phone straight over.

Lily said, 'Hi. It's me. I'm going to be late back. Tell Mum, will you?'

Then she paused. She listened. She scowled.

'I don't know what you're talking about.'

Another pause.

'You're weird. Go fuck yourself.'

She hung up.

'Is there a problem?'

'Nope. Do you have a car?'

'I don't. But I can probably borrow one.'

'That's good. That's great.'

She wasn't concentrating. She was staring at the box again, chewing her lips. Nathan's lips were still stretched tight and smiling. There is a God, he was thinking. There is order, and reason, and meaning. There has to be. There has to be. There has to be . . .

The sharp letters cut into his tongue like little tin tacks.

S-A-L-V-A-T-I-O-N.

Ronny was dawdling in the swell. Jim saw him from his post in the doorway of the prefab. He called, but Ronny didn't look up, so he took some shaky steps down on to the sand, paused, took a few steps more. Eventually he reached him.

'Where did you get to? I was starting to worry.'

'Jim!' Ronny seemed so excitable, he kept blinking, his eyes were red. 'Jim I need some money.'

His face was enlivened. Animated, but ashen.

'Money?' Jim was baffled. He thought for a moment. 'You didn't just see Connie by any chance?'

Her name tasted like salt granules when he uttered it.

Ronny stood still. He received her name like he'd receive an unwanted gift; giving it a perfunctory shake and then discarding it.

'I didn't see anybody.' He kept on blinking.

'Are you upset about something?'

'No. No. No.' He paused, then added, 'Not upset, no.'

'Your shoes are getting wet.'

'So they are.'

'You seem agitated.'

'Do I? How about you?'

'Me?' Jim sniffed. 'I'm still a bit wobbly.'

Tucked into the waistband of Ronny's trousers were a batch of papers. His hands kept returning to them, like two anxious birds, shoring up a nest.

'What are those?' Jim pointed.

'Letters.'

Ronny inspected Jim's face, momentarily anxious. Jim's expression didn't alter.

'Letters? Are they yours?'

'I think so.'

'Who are they from?'

Ronny scratched his head.

'I can't focus,' he said, 'my eyes.'

'What's wrong with your eyes?'

'The sun. I was looking into it, earlier.'

'Why?'

'I don't know. I'm fine now. I'm great now. I'm very happy.'

'Good.'

Jim was not happy though. He said, 'I see you're using both hands.' He was worried, in part, and almost resentful.

'Am I?'

'Yes.'

Ronny looked down at his fingers, grinning. 'Jim,' he said, 'we should both eat something.'

'I'm not hungry.' Jim was petulant.

'Even so,' Ronny brushed this off, 'let's go indoors. Can I give you a hand?'

Before he could answer, Ronny had slung Jim's left arm over his shoulder, then put his own right arm around Jim's back, supporting him, firmly, under his armpit. Jim didn't resist. In fact he buckled. He gave way. He caved in. He felt like Jesus, brought down from the cross. Strung out. Aching. Woozy and all fuzzed up. It was a beautiful feeling.

Connie found herself thinking the most inappropriate thoughts, and she wanted to stop herself, but she seemed to have no control over what it was that entered her brain, what she could digest and what she could encompass. One second she was thinking *Fuck*! The next, *Father*! Then, and stupidest of all, *Cauliflower*!

Her hands smelled of cauliflower. There was a basket of them on the kitchen table. Yellow ones. She'd touched them on first entering the house and now her hands stank of them. Her fingers were covering both her nose and her mouth. Only this simple, fleshy restraint stopped her from screaming.

It was just panic. Panic. Her letters were gone. And suddenly, in the midst of all her breathlessness and shuddering and fury, she found herself thinking about a conversation she'd had the previous night with Sara, over dinner, concerning, of all subjects, the common hare. The common hare? Yes. Hares don't dig burrows, like rabbits do, Sara had said. No. They were altogether a different kind of creature.

Hares remained above ground, chiefly, and when they produced young, they dotted them, individually, over fairly wide sections of terrain, in little solo nests, so that if one baby hare was discovered by a predator and killed, the others would have a much greater chance of survival.

I should have learned from the hare, Connie kept thinking. I should have been cautious. I should have been canny. But I was spoiled and dumb. I left myself wide open.

And now it was too late to regret anything. The letters were gone. They were gone. They were gone. And nobody was home for Connie to take her rage out on. Not Lily, not Sara. So she walked around the house, befuddled. She kept returning to her room, unpacking her case on to the bed, then packing it up again and fastening the buckles, the clasps, like she was intending to leave, straight away, climb into her car and go.

On her third unpacking she noticed the cheque. And her purse, and her car keys. She was disgusted at herself. She'd been so fractured and irresponsible and *vague*. There really was no excusing it. She took a deep breath. Now what? And who? And why?

She barged into Lily's room. The bed, on top of it, under it. The dresser. The chest of drawers. Underwear, T-shirts, socks, a rabbit pelt, little skulls, feathers, a lipstick, a knife. Her bookshelf. On the shelf? Between the books? Inside them? Nothing, nothing, nothing.

She went downstairs and sat on a small milking stool stationed between the front door and the phone. She struggled to control her breathing. When the phone rang she pounced on it.

'Hello?'

'Hi. It's me. I'm going to be late back. Tell Mum, will you?'

Lily's voice. Utterly unrepentant.

Connie exploded.

'You stole my letters, didn't you? I want them back, Lily. I want them right back.'

'I don't know what you're talking about.' Lily sounded sincerely confounded.

'It's theft!' Connie was almost yelling, virtually hysterical. 'And they were my father's letters. They were his letters. They were *his*.'

'You're weird. Go fuck yourself.'

Dialling tone.

'Whose letters?'

Connie looked up, startled. Sara was standing in the door-way. She looked pale and her hair was scuffed up wildly, like two rooks fighting over her moon of a face. She turned and slammed the door behind her. There was grass stuck in the knit of her jumper.

Connie still held the receiver in her hand. For some reason she felt guilty. She placed it down, gently, as though it were a string of pearls she'd just considered stealing. 'Uh . . . ,' she cleared her throat, 'that was Lily. She said she'd be late home . . .'

'Good,' Sara smiled, somewhat lopsidedly, then she frowned, 'or is it good?'

Her speech was slurred. She looked around her, beetle-browed and scowling, then located the light switch on the wall and flicked it up. The hallway was suddenly brightly illuminated. She blinked. 'It wasn't dark yet, was it?' she asked bemusedly, then bent down and peered through the letterbox.

'It's probably just rain clouds,' Connie said, standing, 'making everything seem grey.'

Sara straightened up and then slouched against the wall, letting her one shoulder support her body weight. 'You smell of straw,' Connie muttered, trying vainly to establish herself again.

Sara nodded. 'Hops. Beer and teacakes. Yeast. I'm allergic so my body tries really hard at first to expel it. I break out in a sweat and then end up stinking like a bale of hay.'

'You've been drinking?' Connie asked.

'Stay there,' Sara mumbled, distractedly, not answering Connie's enquiry, 'and don't move.'

She pushed herself away from the wall and staggered off into the sitting room. She was gone for several minutes. Connie remained where she was, somewhat perplexed, until Sara re-emerged clutching a shotgun and a fistful of bullets. She propped herself up against the door frame while she laboriously loaded one into the other.

Connie watched, impassively. Sara kept the gun pointed at the floor.

'Safety precaution,' she muttered, half to herself.

Connie didn't like the gun. 'What's this all about?' she asked, and her voice sounded strangely little.

Sara looked up. 'Have you been out there lately?' she whispered, inclining her head towards the front door.

'Out where?'

'Out there.'

'Of course. Earlier.'

'And you didn't notice anything?'

'No. Nothing in particular.'

Sara rubbed her fist against her forehead. 'The thing is,' she said, her voice growing louder again, 'I was seeing stuff too clearly. I was all smug and contented and *hopeful*. I mean this morning. Last night. Then everything went downhill, slightly, and I suddenly felt like I didn't really *want* to see things clearly any more. So I went to the pub and had a few drinks. Self-pity. But it didn't work. It never does . . .'

She inspected the gun. 'Uh . . .' she sniffed.

'So what did you see,' Connie prompted, eventually, 'outside?'

She was hoping for clues to her own small mystery, but stupidly.

Sara closed her eyes and spoke slowly. 'On the road,' she said quietly, 'close to the electric fence. A thing in the road. A little, dark thing . . .' She shuddered. She opened her eyes again. 'Then I blinked and it was gone. But everything was so quiet, suddenly. No sounds. The hen coop was right close to where I was standing. And I'm so familiar with their chatter. But there was none. No chatter. So I went to the hens. I have hens . . .' she lost her drift and then found it again, 'in a pen. That rhymes. And they were all dead. Ten hens. All dead. None were missing. No sign of a forced entry or a struggle. No feathers. But blood. Dark. A little river of it. Like a strange . . . a very ugly . . . like a kind of silent *rebuke*.'

Sara shook her head, rapidly, as though she had water in her ears and longed to expel it. 'Afterwards I ran back towards the boar enclosures in a sort of panic. And the fence was down. And the electric wire too, inside it . . .'

She shuddered. 'Oh God! The fence was down. It was *down*!'

Connie struggled not to be infected by Sara's mood. 'But you knew that already,' she said gently, 'didn't you? You went out to get wire to fix it only yesterday.'

'Nope.' Sara shook her head. 'That's the whole point. I was with Luke yesterday. You saw me there. You did see me?'

'Yes.'

'And there was actually nothing wrong with the fence. I lied.'

Sara finished loading the gun. She took a deep breath. 'The big male's gone,' she said calmly. 'He'll probably be nearby, and he's dangerous. So we'll need this.' She held up the firearm.

'What will you do?'

'I'll find him. I'll shoot him. He couldn't get back into the enclosure now even if he wanted to. I've had to put the electric wire back up again to stop the rest of them from scarpering.'

'Shall I come with you?'

'Yes. Once we've rung the police.'

Connie felt a moment's unease. 'The police?'

'They'll need to contact the locals and warn them . . .'

Connie's mind turned to Jim and to Ronny.

'But he can't have gone all that far yet, can he?'

'No,' Sara hesitated, 'you're right. When they get out they just tend to panic. They're actually very homely. Unless . . .' she paused, 'unless he thinks he smells a female in the vicinity, or if he gets a whiff of what he takes to be a rival male . . .'

Sara walked to the front door and pulled it open. 'You've got a point though,' she ruminated, 'this whole mess does make me look like a total incompetent.'

'An hour,' Connie murmured, 'we could give it an hour.'

Sara rolled her shoulders back. 'But we'd have to prioritize. We'd need to take some positive action before dark.'

Connie peered over Sara's shoulder, bleakly. The sky was huge and it was already darkening.

'Was it him, then?' she asked softly.

'Who?'

'Was it him that killed the hens, him on the road?'

Sara smiled, rubbing the palm of her hand against the butt of her gun with a weirdly regretful luxuriousness.

'No,' she said finally. 'No. It wasn't him.'

36

Luke was pacing. He had a sheet of negatives in his hand which he kept holding up to the electric light on the living room ceiling and inspecting. He could see, uh, Sara's arse, her elbow, but small and blotchy and muted. Even so, quite well taken. *Encapsulated.* He threw himself down on to the sofa.

'A real pornographer.'

He spoke out loud, too loudly, like an old-fashioned head-master during school assembly. What did it mean? She'd said it like she approved of it. Well, almost. What did she mean? His fingers were twitching. He wanted a smoke. A drink. Old vices.

Total commitment? Fucked but not intimate? Lost?

Luke stared disconsolately, squinting slightly, at the small, dark negative of Sara's favourite cup and its saucer. Isn't this the same thing? he asked himself; exactly the same thing, in fact, as the dreaded dot-to-dots? Isn't the single most signifi-cant element in this image the very one which is absent?

In the first instance, sex, plain and simple. In the second – here, with the cup and its saucer – it was the lips that drank, the hand that held. It was Sara. Missing. The whole. And if she really did, truly consider this image to contain, in some crazy way, a significant part of herself, then she was simply deluded.

I long to see the lips, Luke thought, and the tongue and the mouth and the throat and the tits, in the same way that I long to see the people in the dot-to-dots just fucking. Not merely numbers on the page waiting to be joined in a rough approxi-mation. I want everything clear and clean and open. Not just bits and pieces. Is that wrong of me?

A real pornographer. What did it mean? All surface? Nothing under? Was that truly anything to be so ashamed of?

I have a big heart, Luke decided, and a small imagination. But women craved an imagination. They needed one. They wanted pretence and pseudo and phoney and rubbish. Women were after Polyfilla. They didn't want the real thing, the solid wall, non-porous. They didn't want your average fella. Not really.

I need a fag, Luke thought. I'm alive, for God's sake. I'm all here and all now and all ready and all able. I'm alive! He walked to the door and threw it open. The sea, the sea. Grey and brown. It would rain soon. It was bleak out, bleaker, if possible, than it had ever seemed before.

What a view. Luke grimaced. What a bloody landscape! And then, straight after, Screw the landscape, I want *more*. He needed a smoke.

Nathan tried to contact Margery at work, but she couldn't be located so he decided, on a spur, since this was practically an emergency, to write her a note, stick it through her door and then borrow her car without asking. He possessed his own set of keys. It would be fine. Even so, he dwelled carefully over the note's wording. But Lily was loitering. She was obtrusive. She kept butting in. She was dripping and mopping, in his small kitchen, while simultaneously preparing herself a sandwich. With endearing gusto she hunted down the various components in cupboard and drawer and fridge.

Margery,
I've borrowed the car. An old friend turned up . . .

'Where's the bin? Is it hidden?'
'Pardon?'
'I need the bin.'
'There's a kind of bag, in the cupboard, under the sink.'
'Oh. Right. Thanks.'

and I wanted . . .

He crossed this bit out.

and he needed to get to . . .

Lily peered over Nathan's shoulder while sipping on a glass of milk. He saw two dark drops of blood splash into its whiteness and then a brief, pale halo of strawberry appear in their wake.

'What are you doing?'

'I'm writing a note. I'm borrowing someone's car.'

'Well you'd better get a wriggle on or we'll hit the rush hour.'

A *wriggle*? Nathan tried not to smile.

New piece of paper.

Dear Margery,
I needed to borrow the car. It's not a real crisis or anything.
Nathan.

He folded the note in half. Lily was now devouring a honey sandwich.

'It was the runny stuff,' she said, 'but all crystallized. I had to chip away at it. You should've chucked it out already.'

'I will.'

He moved the junk off the top of the box, piling it on to the floor close by. Then he bent over to pick it up, but Lily interrupted him.

'Let me,' she said, passing him her sandwich and squatting down to grab it herself.

'You'll have to lug it a fair old distance,' Nathan observed, watching her strain at the unexpected weight of it.

'I'm great,' Lily managed, releasing a small milk and honey burp which sweetened the air in her immediate vicinity. Nathan carefully placed the rest of her sandwich into his shirt pocket and then felt around for his keys. He took nothing else with him except his art book, which he tucked under his right arm with as much gentle care as if it had been a precious but rather wriggly little pup.

'What's got into him?'

Luke spoke under his breath to Jim who was back at his old post on the sofa. He'd been sitting there for a while, all heavy and crushed up inside, struggling to remain upright.

'I don't know. I think he's just cheerful.'

But there was more to it than that. Jim knew. It wasn't real cheer, but an approximation. It was an intricate emotion composed out of equivalent substances.

'Cheerful?' Luke scratched his breast.

Ronny was whistling tunelessly in the kitchen and clattering. 'What a strange man.'

Jim smiled quietly. Luke stared. 'You look different.'

'Do I?'

'Bigger.'

Jim paused. 'Can I do anything for you?'

Luke seemed sheepish. 'I need a cigarette.'

Jim shook his head. 'Not a good idea.'

'Yes. I know. But I want one anyway.'

Luke slapped a rhythmical tattoo of expectant impatience out on to his wide belly. Jim watched, hypnotized by the sight of his brown skin juddering.

'Unfortunately,' Jim hesitated, feeling his smooth cheek with his right hand, 'I threw them away.'

Luke stopped his tattoo. 'You're kidding me.'

'No. I thought it would be the best way of stopping you if your will collapsed.'

Luke tried to digest this information, nodding slowly. Jim half-expected him to charge off, to leap into his car and make a dash for civilization. But no. Instead he threw himself down on to the sofa.

'Of all my vices,' Luke declaimed expansively, 'I consider women my worst. Cigarettes come second. Then food. Then booze.'

Jim said nothing. Luke shifted. He reached down and removed Ronny's cardigan from under him.

'My car's still over at Sara's farm, otherwise I'd be off in a flash to buy some. *Hey!*' He rubbed his thigh. 'Something just poked into me.'

Luke turned the cardigan around by its neck. Protruding from the left pocket was the silver tip of a knife.

'Dear Lordy.'

He plucked the knife from the pocket. As he removed it,

something else fell out too; a plastic sheet of tablets. The knife had a large non-retractable blade. It looked big, even inside his sizeable palm. Luke whistled. 'Is this thing yours?'

Jim bent down to retrieve the tablets. He slid the half-empty packet into his pocket. Luke was still inspecting the knife. He hadn't noticed.

'It's not mine. It must be Ronny's.' Jim's skin prickled at the sight of the blade. 'I don't like knives.'

'That's a proper hunting knife.'

'Yes.'

Luke continued to handle the knife. It seemed to be giving him pleasure. Eventually he said, 'So what shall I do with it?'

Jim held out his right hand. 'Give it here. I'll put it somewhere safe.'

He took the knife and placed it underneath the sofa. Luke was still holding the cardigan. He gave it a further shake.

'What's this?' He removed a letter from the other pocket.

'Oh. It's just a letter. '

He put it straight back again. The absolute soul of propriety.

Ronny had so much energy. So much that he didn't know quite where or how to direct it. It was flying out of him. The energy. It had been uncorked. Unplugged. It was everywhere. Reverberating off the floor, the walls, the ceiling, the windows.

On the cooker was a pan of spaghetti hoops, but the hot plate was still cold under it. Ronny was sitting on the lino, close by, his legs stretched out in front of him. In the palm of one hand he held a small, frozen butter pat. In his other hand he held the clutch of letters. He was trying to read them but he could not. Why? His eyes? No. Fear! That was it. He simply couldn't. He just *couldn't*. Because suddenly he had a bad feeling about everything.

Too much energy. When there was too much energy, where the hell did he direct the excess? And a portion of it was always bad energy. A small portion. A purple-black energy. Like a bruise. Spreading. Poisoning. Bleeding. Creeping. Deep down inside and under his skin.

If anything happens to Monica, he kept thinking, how could I stand it? He felt a moment of panic. What if I've found my home at last but the door is closed already? What if I've found my home, finally, and the door is locked and barred to me?

There were two more letters. He hadn't read them. Two more. The last one, very short. Just a few words. I need some money, he thought, I need some money. Then I won't have to read. I can go out and I can *find*.

The butter pat was melting. Ronny stared at his watch. How long had that taken? In his palm. From freezing to melting? He calculated.

Then he turned the watch over. 'To Big Ron, with love, your Elaine.'

For some unknown reason, he found himself shuddering.

37

Margery pushed the door open and walked inside.

'Nathan?'

She called out although she knew already that the flat would be empty. She shut the door behind her and leaned up against it. She held the note he'd written in her hand. It had not fooled her. Her eyes scanned the room. She breathed deeply. She could smell him. Hair oil. And another scent. Sandalwood.

She walked slowly around the room, touching things. The television. The back of the sofa, the bookshelf. It was a plain room. There was very little to feel in it. She noticed something on the carpet. A brown stain. Scuffed. Was that blood? She paused. She knelt down to inspect it more closely. Stop! she told herself. Stop looking for confirmation. Confirmation? Of *what*?

A paper clip and a little fragment of tissue were messing up the carpet near where she crouched. She picked them up, automatically, and threw them into the wastepaper bin.

She almost walked away and then . . . hang on . . . she peered inside the bin, reached out her hand –tentatively, fastidiously – and from its depths she withdrew a square of material: crisp and brown at its edges, moist and pink at its centre.

Like liver, she thought. Red and raw in the middle, brown-edged. Lamb's liver. Calf's liver. Liver. But of course this was simply Nathan's hanky. And this was blood. Probably his. Nosebleed. She dropped the hankerchief and walked through to the kitchen to rinse her fingers.

Here she found another trail of red-brown spots leading from the sink unit to the refrigerator. The honey was out. Left open on the worktop. And the milk.

She picked up the carton, instinctively, to return it back to the fridge. But as she yanked at its door and registered the suck of its rubber seal, her mind screamed CRIME SCENE.

She put the milk back in anyway. She forced herself. But the police are such sticklers for detail, she thought furtively, and my prints are everywhere . . .

She returned to the living room. She blinked back the tears. Was this a betrayal or was this just life? It was neither. It was the end of love. This is the end of love, she told herself. This is the end of love. Without trust there is suspicion. And suspicion's closest ally is contempt. And contempt? What relation could that ever bear to anything good?

Nathan's life was so full of spaces. Margery felt too small to fill them, too mean to overlook them. Spaces. And now she would leave yet another one.

38

'So did Luke get what he was after?'

They were sitting at the kitchen table. Ronny was speaking.

'No. He wanted his cigarettes.'

'But you'd thrown them away.'

Jim glanced up from his meal of tinned spaghetti, minted peas and meatballs. 'How did you know that?'

'I must've seen them. In the bin. Poor old Luke.' Ronny laughed. His mouth was half-full. It was like watching the interior of an inefficient Hotpoint struggling with its fast-coloureds programme.

He was eating at a quite remarkable speed and using both his hands. His fork, Jim observed, was held perfectly normally, but his knife was clutched in his clenched fist and was pointed, somewhat disconcertingly, directly towards his own chest.

While Ronny ate, he talked, intermittently, and he waved the knife, but not to emphasize anything of particular significance. He didn't seem able to maintain a single train of thought from one moment to the next.

Jim, by contrast, as a kind of forced reaction, ate slowly, using his right hand only. He consumed just a tiny portion of the meal Ronny had prepared for them and then pushed his bowl away. He was the very epitome of simplicity and restraint. If I try hard enough, he thought desperately, maybe I can transform Ronny into his better self again through my own positive example.

Under the table, inside his pocket, his left hand rested limply upon the half-empty pill packet. Ronny was speaking. He was saying, 'I collected three whole bags full of shells this afternoon. For the mural. You could come and help me with it after dinner if you wanted . . .'

Jim smiled, heartened. 'I'd love to help you,' he said, 'only first I promised Luke I'd go and fetch his car from the farm. For some reason he doesn't want to go over there and pick it up himself . . .'

'The farm?'

Ronny stopped chewing and focused in on Jim's smooth face. He was scowling. 'What's at the farm?'

For the briefest of moments, Jim's mind was inexplicably filled with a vision of Connie. She stood before him, pale, in the waves, her small white hands shielding her little nipples.

'What's at the farm?' Ronny reiterated, almost harshly. Jim blinked. 'His car's at the farm. Luke's car.'

Ronny laid his knife down on the table. He stared at it morosely. There was suddenly a great chasm between them. Jim couldn't fathom it. It was as if some kind of extraordinary betrayal had recently taken place. But on which side? And by whom?

'I've been considering what you said earlier,' he observed gently, 'about needing money. There might be a way of aquiring some . . .'

Ronny just winced. 'I can't think of that now,' he said quietly. His eyes were flitting, like two anxious greenfinches, around the room.

'There's some plaster in the cupboard under the sink,' Jim said, attempting to re-direct him again, 'and there should be a trowel . . .' He glanced over towards the window, 'but it's already getting dark out, and it looks like rain.'

Ronny stood up, abruptly. 'It's only right that I should finish things,' he said, turning and yanking the cupboard door wide, 'that I should complete the things I've started before moving on.'

With both hands he grabbed hold of the tub of plaster, the trowel and an old J-cloth. Jim remained seated, watching Ronny blankly, trying to figure out what he meant exactly. Moving on? Moving? *Where*?

Ronny headed outside, clutching his booty to his chest, his shoes squeaking and squelching as he walked through the lounge and then out into the grey.

Jim stared up at the ceiling and then down at the remains of his meal. He picked up the two bowls, the cutlery, with his right hand, piled them together and then took them over to the pedal bin to scrape them clean. He pushed the pedal with his foot and the lid sprang open. He leaned forward. But before he tipped, he paused. He peered.

Luke's cigarettes. Were they still there? He looked closer. Benson & Hedges. Gold box . . . Nope. No sign. He squinted. Glinting underneath a quantity of other refuse lay not the cigarette packet but another metallic, glimmering object. A watch. The gold watch. 'To Big Ron, with love, your Elaine.' Its face all crushed in and smashed.

Jim dumped the plates and pulled open the cutlery drawer. He inspected the selection of knives. One blunt bread knife, a smaller, sharper Kitchen Devil, one steak knife. He scooped them up. He also picked up the knife he'd not used for his own meal and Ronny's knife which was still on the table. He walked through to the living room, over to the sofa, bent down and retrieved the hunting knife from under it.

He walked to the open doorway and looked outside. The tide was lurching in. Its great, dirty tongue lapped and licked, foam-tipped, about ten foot away from where he stood. He walked down on to the sand, stared briefly at the knives in his hand, and then threw them, with as much force as he could muster, out, out, out into the rumbling belly of the sea.

Back inside the prefab, Jim hunted around for any other potentially hazardous objects. The tooth glass in the bathroom, a small mirror inside the bathroom cabinet and the razor. In the living room he picked up an old black and yellow screwdriver. In the kitchen, a ketchup bottle, half-full, and a glass jar of damson jam. The tin opener. Yes.

Back outside again, he tipped his head slightly and listened. Seagulls, the growl of the tide. He threw the second set of objects into the waves. He returned indoors. He stood next to the cold fire. He picked up the poker and appraised it, frowning, then he placed it back down again. He turned towards the sofa and noticed Ronny's cardigan. He walked over and grabbed it, plunged his hand into its pocket and withdrew the letter. He sat down and opened it.

Ronny darling,
We're still not speaking, Louis and me. He's slow to forgive. It takes him a while. Each new situation leaves him spinning. He has to dig in his heels hard, hard, take a deep breath and struggle to acclimatize.
So I'm back in the cave. The bat cave. You understand these places, don't you, Ronny?

Jim blinked.

So I'm back in the cave. The bat cave. You understand these places, don't you, Ronny?

He shook his head. He turned the letter over.

We both feel around blindly. Like deep water fish. Touching, whispering, bumping, retreating.

Jim screwed the letter up and threw it towards the fireplace. It hit the wall and landed. His shoulders were drawn up so high that they almost touched his ear-lobes. He struggled to stand. He was stiff. His body was stiff. It took a considerable effort to move himself. He was like a little tin robot; no neck, all shoulders.

He began to run. Had anyone seen him they would have laughed. He looked so silly. He looked so funny. He was hunted. His head, his chest, his legs looked as though they were prepared for some kind of extraordinary impact. Something huge. Something massive. No mere body could be big enough, could be tough enough for that kind of an assault. No mere body.

He ran out of the prefab. Stiff, stiff, stiff. Along the beach and then on and on and on and on.

39

'I never realized before,' Connie whispered, 'how terrible the outside could feel.'

Sara was walking several paces behind her. Connie had been perfectly calm at the outset, but then she'd heard the gun being cocked at her back and her entire torso had jolted. A small sound.

'You honestly never realized that?' Sara's voice was hushed.

They both paused for a moment before shuffling onwards. The giant grey sky seemed to draw everything up into its muffling clouds. Voices, sniffs, footfalls. Sara had been right about the quiet.

They reached the Volvo. The plan was for Sara to walk, in an ever-expanding circle, from the boar enclosures outwards, until she'd reached the furthest boundaries of the farm. She would go alone. She would take the gun. Connie would take Luke's car. 'It's a Volvo,' Sara reasoned, 'it's got to be tougher than your little city runabout. If you make any sightings you'll have to come back and fetch me. Everything's really muddy. The tracks especially. You won't leave the vehicle, not even for a moment. Promise?'

'Promise.'

Connie had begun feeling like the whole world was threatening. Even the air. Even the mud. Everything. Sara had pulled on her waterproofs.

'Report back every half hour or so.'

'Fine.'

She climbed in. She adjusted the seat and the mirror. Sara handed her the keys. 'And hurry,' she said, 'the sun's almost setting. When it gets dark here it's like pitch. It's like swimming in black treacle.'

Connie started up the engine. She pulled off. This was a big car. The wide bumpers reassured her.

Sara began walking. She was still skittery. Her eyes were peeled but she could barely concentrate. I must evaluate what this means, she kept thinking. This escape. I must calculate its significance. But she couldn't. She was moist-eyed and full of wonder. Her lips kept forming the shapes of words. She had no voice left though, no breath. But her lips worked anyway. I'm alone, they said. I'm alone. I am finally alone.

Connie drove slowly, her headlights on already. Twice she pulled up, befuddled by stiles and by hay bales. She drove past a field head-high with maize. And she noticed that there had been some kind of a disturbance among a portion of the stalks which were crushed and broken and pressed down flat. She braked. She peered. It could have been the wind. It could have been a big dog. Or a small cow. Even a tractor. She touched the accelerator for one moment and then lifted her foot again.

No.

Everything seemed so glowy, outside. Like the whole earth was covered in a sweet pink candy. The sun was setting. It had started to rain.

But inside, *inside*, everything inside seemed so bloody noisy: the engine, the tyres turning, the loose stones hitting the car's hard underbelly.

She turned off the engine.

Quiet. She glanced down at herself. Pink! I am glowing! I am all-glowing! Her voice sounded strange. Was she thinking? Was she speaking? She tried to focus and to listen but the voice she heard was too distant. Like a memory. Like a muffled sneeze behind somebody's hand. A seductive whisper through a pane of glass, or a curtain, or a flimsy hardboard partition. There was no *air*.

She opened the car door and stepped outside. Yes. She could

breathe again. It was cool. And the voice was clearer here, too. Something called her. Was it the sea? Or the wind in the top of the maize? Was it the rain? Was it her heart? Her bladder? It could have been anything. She was transgressing. She was outside again and she suddenly felt fearless.

You know when you think that death will come quickly, Ronny, but it doesn't come quickly? You know? You think death will come quickly but it doesn't come. It goads you. It strings you along. It presses down on you. It steals the fucking breath from you. It glares at you. It takes the piss out of you. But it won't come. It won't come.

You know when you think that death will come quickly, Ronny, but it just won't come?

Let me die! Let me die! Please God let me die! Release me! Free me! Consume me! Kill me!

But it won't come.

I waited and I waited for Louis. But like death he would not come. I watched the sun setting and the sun rising. I missed you. I remembered those conversations we'd had. Remember? Those whispered conversations. And that time when you squeezed my hand? Remember?

I dreamed that I was lying on a table and I couldn't move my body. But you were there in the dream and you squeezed my hand. Did I mention that before?

At dawn I left the shack. It was all aglow outside. And the mist. The vapour seemed to coalesce. It formed such tantalizing shapes only a few yards in front of me. I saw a thin, pale creature and he beckoned to me. I followed him, mutely.

The ground was swampy. Then we reached some fields. And the crop? Was it coffee? There was a path that was established and then the path merged with the jungle again. The sun was rising and I saw the vapour disappearing. Into nothing. Evaporating.

I almost panicked. I was surrounded by trees. They were tall and it was too dark and the sun poked through their branches only very occasionally. It was damp. I was shivering. I tried to find glimpses of light so that I could warm myself in them. I stood in one particular patch for a long, long while. My bones were aching. I looked up into the sun's eye, squinting.

The sun winked at me. For one second. It really winked at me. And in that second I saw that in the tree directly above, swinging from its canopy, like a giant bat, a black sloth, something, was a man. All I could see from below were his big, dark boots. Like a soldier's, or a policeman's. Giant boots.

The branch was creaking. But it was a good, strong branch. A proper, powerful branch. It had been carefully selected. The sun stopped her winking, began her shining, and then he was all fuzzed out and gone again.

I was not sad, Ronny. No, not at all. In fact I felt like singing. I skipped and I ran and I grabbed hold of that tree's wide waist like she was my dancing partner. I found knots and juts and bits of bark. I held on. I waltzed and I rumba'd. My knees began bleeding. My palms. But I scaled her.

Soon I was above him. I looked down. He was balding. You know I never even noticed that before? He was balding. On top. And he still wore his camera. I took out my knife and I cut it free from his neck (how else to remove it?).

There was something poking whitely from his front pocket. Money? I reached down. It was so far! I stretched and I stretched. My arm touched his face and his nose and his cheek. All cold. Finally I reached it. A piece of paper, neatly folded. I opened it. On one side, the receipt from a magazine for an article he'd written. On the other? Three words. Three little words, in capitals, Ronny.

I FOUND HIM.

Found.

Found?

I would have cut Louis down, but those three little words almost finished me. So instead I left him hanging there in his big, bad boots for the whole hungry jungle to feed upon.

I found him.

Where were you, Ronny? Why did you bring me to this dark place? I called your name. I called it all the way back to that little black shack. Where were you? Why won't you let me go? Let *me go! Stop squeezing! The touch of your hand in mine almost saved me.*

Your touch almost saved me.

But I didn't want saving. It was the last thing I wanted.

Oh why oh why won't you just LISTEN, Ronny?

M.

All was silent. Connie looked around her. She was tiny. The maize was thick and it surrounded her. It was wet and everything felt much darker than it should have been. Like coal, but without the glittering. At first there had been a path but now the path was nowhere. Her hands were hurting. Something was cutting. She looked down. The keys.

She tried to walk but horrible stalks blocked her way at each turn. She began crying. I'm such a girl! I'm such a fucking girl! I don't believe this. I'm such a stupid fucking girl!

She heard a noise and struggled to avoid it. But the maize blocked her. She ran into it wildly, imagining all kinds of horrors. The teeth, the tusks, the fiery eyes. All that hide, all those ridges, all that roughness! She was soaking and howling. She was hysterical. She'd gone and left the car after all her promises! Her face was whipped and her hair was full of bits of stalk and husk and cob.

'Stop that. Keep still. What's wrong with you?'

She could barely hear his voice over her own gurgling.

'I won't hurt you. Stop crying.'

She put out her hands. 'I can't see anything. I can't feel. I think I'm dead!'

'No. It's dark. You have hair in your eyes. You're soaking.'

She felt someone touching her fringe.

'Stop cringing.' He sounded angry.

'It's still too dark,' she said.

'There are no stars tonight. No moon. Only clouds.'

Connie blinked a few times.

'Show me your hands,' she demanded.

Something flapped whitely in front of her. She reached out her own hands and touched him. His skin was so soft. His hands were warm.

'How did you find me here?'

'I was passing. I saw the car. I heard you crying.'

'What's wrong with me?'

'I don't know.'

She held on to his hand. 'You're out of breath.'

'I've been running.'

He was still struggling to breathe.

'You seem taller than before.'

He said nothing. She smiled. 'Your hand's all warm.'

'Let's get back to the car.'

Jim turned and led her through the maize. It was actually no distance at all. Five or six measly steps and they were standing on the road again. She could almost see him properly now. She sniffed, slightly abashed. 'One of the boars escaped from the farm. Sara was going to contact the police but I persuaded her not to . . .' She stared into his face. He was trying not to look at her. He was wheezing.

'Perhaps she should have called them,' he managed finally.

'I was thinking about you,' Connie said softly, then grimaced at how this sounded before adding, 'and I was thinking about Ronny.'

She squeezed his hand.

'And I was thinking about my father and his money and the connection . . .' She paused. 'I felt as though I needed to understand something about his connection with Ronny. And I swear I didn't ever want to know what it was that Ronny did. I wouldn't judge him. I just needed to understand my father's . . .' she didn't want to utter that same word again, so she chose another word. 'My father's death. His death.'

Jim remained silent. He was breathing through his nose again. His mouth was closed tightly. She stared at him. 'What's the matter?'

He frowned. 'Don't squeeze my hand like that.'

She squeezed his hand again.

'I don't know why it is,' she said, 'but I keep doing all the wrong things around you.'

'You're *hurting*.'

From the intense tone of his voice she knew that he didn't mean his fingers. She was bemused.

'I'm not hurting anyone. I only want to clear things up. I only want to help. I want . . .'

The weight Jim had felt before, on the beach, on the road, had almost lifted, but it was not gone. Now it simply hovered above him like two great disembodied black wings.

'We don't want helping. We don't need saving. Just *leave* us.'

He tried to pull his hand away, but she held on fast. He watched, fascinated, as the yank of his arm transmitted through to her arm, jerked into her shoulder socket and then pulled her one step closer to him. She was so small. He shuddered.

'I won't hurt you.'

She was whispering. Staring up at him and looking so open. She was a mess. Her face was scratched and streaming. He stared at her, like he couldn't understand what it was that she wanted.

'The moon's shining again,' she said, 'and I can see everything.'

She put out her free hand, looped it around his neck and pulled his head down towards her. His face was bright. She kissed his lips. They were soft. She pressed hard and felt his teeth, all firm, just under them. His skin was so smooth she could have rubbed her wet nose all over it. But he pulled away.

'It's a car,' he said, wiping his mouth. His face was fully illuminated and then it went dark again.

'I didn't hear it,' Connie whispered, 'I didn't see it.'

She let go of his hand and touched her lips with her fingertips.

Jim was free again. He backed off, slowly, but he did not break Connie's gaze. He held it with infinite care, like it was a fragile egg balanced between his forefinger and his thumb. He held it and held it, then something untoward and terrible seemed to strike him and he let go, his eyes dropped, he turned and strode away, in the direction of the beach and the prefabs, his shoulders hunching up again and his head balancing between them like a pale field mushroom.

40

Lily refused to put the box into the boot or to rest it upon the back seat. 'Nothing's as safe as my own two arms,' she'd observed, and to prove as much had placed the box on to her scraggy lap, had slung her arms around it and then perched her small but pointy chin on top. Her shoulders were soon aching, but she didn't care.

Her sense of direction was pitiable. Even after crossing the Kingsferry bridge she gave every appearance of being completely adrift when by rights she should have been plumb back in her own zone.

Nathan found her astonishing. As a child he'd developed an affection for American comics. There he'd discovered all kinds of exotica, not least, the Twinkie and the Oreo cookie, neither of which had he ever tasted, only dreamed of. And also, among the small ads with a tiny illustration, he'd encountered the Sea Monkey. A kind of underwater creature, a leggy mermaid; wispy and pale and lean. A female gargoyle, all loose-limbed and translucent. All fish-lipped and long-lashed, and with witchy nails that dragged and snagged. It was a real entity, for sale (just add water) but Nathan thought it must be like a unicorn or a dragon. It was pure, crazy, comic-book folly.

Yet in Lily he thought he'd found this aquatic organism made flesh. She was every inch a Sea Monkey. She was fish and chimp in one being. Pale and alien and underwatery.

She didn't speak much, only when he requested directions. Then she'd say, 'Uh, left, maybe?' and peer off anxiously to the right. So this was how they'd proceeded, tentatively. They didn't say much otherwise. Nathan turned on the radio and doodled along quietly to the gentle tunes that filtered out at random.

'Ah! The prison.'

Lily perked up.

'I finally know where I am.' She pointed. 'See?'

Through his side window Nathan saw a distant crust of mismatching eczema perched on the crest of a preponderantly flat landscape. It was dusk. Lights hatched out like angry zits.

'Right. Yes.'

He shuddered.

'I saw that.'

'What?'

'You shivered.'

'Cold.'

He put his hand to the heater.

'Brake.'

Lily spoke so gently that Nathan didn't initially register the nature of her request.

'I said *stop!*' This time she spoke louder.

He pulled over. They were on a small, winding country road. Lily wound down her window.

'Oi!'

The engine idled. Behind him Nathan saw a fat man, trundling in the verge.

'Oi!'

The fat man paused and then looked over his shoulder. He faltered. He didn't seem especially pleased to see them.

'Where are you going?' Lily yelled.

The fat man scowled. 'Why?'

'I just wondered.'

'I'm going to the pub to buy cigarettes.'

'But you're way past it.'

'Pardon?'

'You're way past it. You should've turned off to the left a mile or so back.'

The flat man looked deflated. 'Shit.'

'So I suppose you'll be after a lift, then?'

The fat man took a few steps towards them. 'Actually, yes. If that isn't too much trouble.'

'But it is too much trouble.' Lily wound up her window. 'Let's go.'

Nathan didn't move. He kept checking his rear-view mirror. Luke looked a mixture of angry and disconsolate. It was a pitiable combination.

'We can't just leave him, surely?'

'Of course we can. Do it!'

Nathan pulled off and accelerated away.

'Anyhow,' Lily grinned, 'he smells of fish. He'd stink out the car.'

'Of fish?'

'Yep. Revolting.'

A loose stone hit their flanks. Nathan braked slightly. It was almost dark now. He turned his headlights on. To the right of his peripheral vision he saw something temporarily illuminated in the sudden blaze. It appeared solid but mobile and fairly prodigious. It bucked once and then skittered from view.

'Did you see that thing?'

His foot touched the brake again. Lily was clutching the parcel and staring straight ahead of her.

'Keep driving.'

'But did you see it?' he repeated.

'I saw it.'

She seemed slightly unnerved but grimly unflappable. 'We need to get home. Quickly.'

Her directions became minutely precise, her voice, curter, gruffer. 'Faster,' she said, when he'd changed down a gear to negotiate a corner, 'keep going.'

'Was it a pig or a pony?'

'A boar. A wild boar. We farm them.'

'Should it be out on the road like that?'

Lily rolled her eyes.

'Is it dangerous?'

She cleared her throat but neglected to answer.

They were heading along a rough road next to a large field of maize. Up in front of them a car was parked with its lights off and driving door wide open. There were two people, standing alongside it.

Nathan slowed down.

'Don't slow down.'

'I'm not sure if there's room on this road for two cars.'

'There's room.'

She was such a bully. A little tyrant. Even so, Nathan slowed down an iota and dipped his lights. They passed – just enough space – and he glanced over at the couple. Lily looked too. She inhaled sharply. She saw Connie and she thought she saw Ronny.

Nathan could only see the man clearly. A tall man. Hairless. The light bounced off his bald head and formed a glossy halo. He was sharp and thin and badly dressed. The woman – much smaller – was almost entirely obscured by his bony shoulders. But the man . . .

Nathan's brain didn't react, or his head, or his tongue or his chest – unlike Lily's – even his belly failed to respond. Only his heart reacted. It swooped, it tapped, it buckled.

'Are you listening to me?'

His head swivelled. 'What?'

'I said next left. Sharp left.'

He turned the car. 'Stop!' Lily squealed. 'That's my mother!'

Nathan slammed on the brakes.

There, next to a large, open, wrought-iron fence stood a dark-haired woman holding a torch and a shotgun. Lily carefully placed the box on to the back seat then clambered out and marched up to her. 'I saw something at the turn-off,' she said, 'we both did.'

Sara was blinking in the glare of the headlights. 'The turn-off? Are you certain?'

'Yep.'

'I sent Connie out in the Volvo . . .'

Lily clucked. 'We just passed her, parked up next to the maize.'

Sara switched off her torch. 'What was she doing?'

'How should I know?'

'The turn-off . . .' Sara was perplexed, 'that's some distance.'

She indicated towards Nathan with the gun. Nathan didn't observe this. He was looking at his own face in the side mirror. Inspecting every niche and nook and cranny of it. Trying to recognize something.

'Who is that? Will he be OK to drive me back there?'

Lily nodded. 'He's Nathan. He's very obliging.'

'Hi. I'm Sara,' she said, sliding into the front passenger seat.

'Hello,' Nathan nodded, bemusedly.

Lily clambered into the back, settling the box on to her lap again. 'She's my mother,' Lily observed darkly, 'and her gun's loaded.'

Nathan merely smiled.

'She wants you to drive us back to where we saw the fat man before.'

Sara's head turned. 'Which fat man?'

Nathan set the car into reverse.

'Which fat man, Lily?'

Lily groaned. 'That fat slug from the prefabs. Mr Fish.'

'Luke?'

'He was after some cigarettes. We offered him a lift but he said he'd just as soon walk.'

'And this was before or after you saw the boar?'

'Uh . . .' Lily focused on the ceiling, 'I forget which.'

Nathan glanced nervously at Sara and then at Lily in the rear-view mirror. She didn't make eye contact. He put the car into first gear and moved off. After a few seconds he said, 'I'll need directions.'

'Of course,' Sara reached out her hand and turned down the radio, 'head straight on.'

Before long the car's lights picked out the Volvo and Connie, crouched on all fours next to it, searching the ground for something.

'Stop for a second.'

Sara wound down her window. As they approached Connie straightened up, like a weasel. But she didn't stand. She remained on her knees.

'What's going on?' Sara asked, as they drew level. 'Did something happen here?'

Connie was soaked and her face looked scratched and haggard. 'No,' she said, 'nothing happened.'

She seemed dazed. She was holding the car keys. They were covered in mud. She inspected her hands with a slight look of distaste.

'Then get back into the Volvo and return to the farm. Lily saw the boar near the main road. We're just going back there.'

Connie's expression remained vague. Her eyes slid past Sara and glanced deeper into the car. In the darkness she saw Nathan. Her eyes widened. 'Nathan?'

Before anything else could be said, Nathan pulled off with a small skid. The car kangarooed. Sara jerked forward. Lily grunted, enraged, from the back seat. He quickly readjusted his foot over the clutch and then drove on.

Sara wound up her window. 'Do take care,' she said tersely, 'I'm holding a firearm.'

'Yes. Of course. Sorry. It's just that . . . it's just . . .' Nathan took a deep breath. 'I'm Ronny's brother,' he said softly, all in a rush, feeling like this was a truly incredible admission. 'I'm his brother.'

'Really?' Sara spoke. She was simply filling in conversational spaces. Her eyes were ransacking the darkness.

Nathan switched the windscreen wipers from slow to fast. He checked his rear-view mirror. Lily's eyes met his in the glass. And they were tight eyes. They were mean old monkey eyes.

41

Jim approached the prefabs on numb, heavily sodden feet, wearing the dark like a big, black wrap around him. Everything here conspired to keep him a secret. The weather – it was windy and raining harder again – the sound of the waves, the sheets of heavy grey cloud in the sky which expunged the moon and all but the most steely and persistent of the stars.

The other buildings were, without exception, in total darkness. Only his prefab's sharp angles were defined by the bleak glow of an electric bulb. Jim saw that Ronny had constructed a system of lighting to accompany his creative project by pulling an anglepoise lamp through the bedroom window and dangling it upside down from the sill. Its weight was supported only by its wire and the plug, which, by every indication, seemed to be pulling loose, because the light generated was of such a feeble quality; like a bad stutter or a fast blink.

But nothing deterred Ronny. He worked instinctively, slapping on the plaster with his small, silver-handled trowel, thinning it out, smoothing it down, dipping his hands, first into one bag, then another. He was applying the shells in tightly choreographed circles. On the wall in front of him, a crazy lichen was growing and adhering and enveloping.

Jim drew gradually closer until eventually he was sheltered from the worst of the elements in the lee of the building. He was so near to Ronny now that he could hear the rattle and pant of his breathing.

Every so often, Ronny would pause, stop what he was doing and rub at his eyes. But his fingers were coated in plaster, in sand and in salt from the shells. After a while he yanked up his T-shirt and rubbed hard at his whole face with it.

Jim saw Ronny's ribs, all clearly articulated and distinct, protruding like half a dozen slim book spines. He struggled against the impulse to reach out his fingers to grasp and withdraw one of these small pale volumes. Ronny released the fabric of his T-shirt, bent down to pick up the trowel and then paused. 'So where did you get to?'

He didn't turn as he spoke.

Jim was taken aback. He'd supposed himself invisible.

'A walk.'

'What's wrong?'

'Wrong?'

'You sounded . . . uh . . .' Ronny couldn't summon up the word.

'Nothing's wrong. I just didn't want to disturb you.'

'The trowel. See the tip? I saw your head reflected in it. At first I thought you were the moon.'

Ronny chuckled at this idea, and the light punctuated his amusement by turning off and then on again.

Jim frowned. 'I think the light's . . .'

It went.

'Even in the dark,' Ronny muttered, 'I still have this red glow in the centre of my eyes.'

Jim saw the grey outline of Ronny's head and arm. He was vigorously rubbing his eyes again.

'A red glow?'

Jim grabbed hold of the lamp and yanked at its wire. The plug came free and he felt the fitment's full weight in his hand.

'I was staring into the sun this afternoon and now I have this red glow.'

'In both eyes?'

'I don't know. How would I tell?'

'Close one eye at a time.'

'But the light's still there when I close them.'

While Ronny spoke, Jim turned and peered out into the darkness.

'Did you hear something?' he asked softly. 'Can you see anything?'

Ronny turned. 'I see splotches. Red ones.'

'For quite a while now I've just had this feeling . . .' Jim was almost whispering, 'my hackles . . .'

Ronny dusted the sand off his hands on to the front of his trousers.

'I thought only dogs had those. And wolves.'

'Yes . . .' Jim was vague and prickly.

'And cats . . .'

Before Ronny could complete what he was saying, a distant rumble of thunder precipitated a wild, honking squeal, higher in pitch than the thunder's low grumble, but much closer by and infinitely more affecting.

Jim swore, threw the lamp randomly out into the darkness – another grunt followed, more confused, less alarmed – then yanked Ronny up and dragged him at full pelt down between the prefabs. They turned sharply and rushed straight in through the front door. Jim slammed it shut behind them and reached out his hand for the light switch, but Ronny stopped him, panting. 'Leave it off . . .'

As he spoke, he felt his way to the window, pulled back the nets and peered out. Jim stayed where he was. 'Did something follow us?'

'I don't know.'

'You didn't see it then?'

'No. But . . .'

Ronny's voice was suddenly hushed and awestruck. Jim could see his hand waving in the darkness, beckoning him over. Jim pulled off his wet shoes and then joined him by the window. It was a small window, dirtied by salt and ocean spray. The tide had gone out a little but the wind played with the waves like a rough hand tousling a child's curls. Just their white tips were visible; rushing, mounting, toppling, crashing.

'To the left.'

Ronny rubbed at the pane where his breath had steamed it up, then pointed. 'See? Far left. Next to Luke's prefab.'

Jim stared. He could distinguish a small, sloping expanse of beach and the pale waves devouring it, that was all. He felt

Ronny next to him. His arm. His shoulder. And then he remembered Connie's ears. Her *ears*. So small. Like tiny conches.

The moon came out. Not properly. It didn't beam or radiate. It peeked quickly from behind the clouds like a commuter glancing up briefly from his newspaper. But that was long enough. 'Oh shit,' Jim's heart was struck wide, 'what's he doing?'

Ronny's fingers gripped a hold of his arm. They were damp and cold from their previous contact with the windowpane. Jim felt them, just above his elbow.

'You know what?' Ronny whispered. 'I think he's looking at the sea.'

A giant, shaggy beast, perfectly still, his four feet firmly planted in the sand and the shells and the shingle, *staring*, mesmerized, at the sea.

'He's wondering whether he might challenge it,' Jim said.

'He isn't.'

'Yes. He's a wild beast. He longs to dominate everything.'

'No. He's just staring. He's probably never seen the sea before. He's struggling to understand it.'

The boar lifted its head and sniffed.

'Pigs have poor eyesight,' Jim said.

'What does he make of it?' Ronny wondered. 'What do you think he makes of it?'

Jim couldn't answer immediately. He felt Ronny's fingers.

'He's probably thinking that today's been worthwhile after all,' he said, finally.

Ronny's eyes shifted from the boar and focused in on Jim for a second. 'You really think so?'

Jim had been joking, but the instant Ronny reacted with such sweet credulity he swallowed the joke down like a headache tablet. 'Yes. The escape, the stress, the risk, everything. Today was worth it. Just to get to see the sea.'

Ronny's eyes returned to the beast. 'He isn't moving.'

'He's in a trance.' Jim paused and then he found himself saying, with perfect calmness, 'Perhaps we should leave this place.'

Ronny didn't react. Jim repeated himself.

'Let's leave this place. Soon. Tonight.'

He didn't really know what he meant or what he wanted.

Ronny continued to stare at the boar. 'Why?' he asked softly.

'Everything's closing in,' Jim said.

'No.' Ronny's mouth was smiling. 'It's opening up,' he murmured gently, 'don't you see? It's *opening*.'

He squeezed Jim's arm, one more time, and then let go.

42

'This was the spot,' Lily said, interrupting the kind of silence all but the most vocally assertive might think twice before violating.

'Here?' Sara's head rotated fiercely, like a hawk's. 'You're sure?'

'Yep.'

Nathan stopped the car. It was raining heavily. It was horribly dark. He didn't like the dark. It was always too deep, too inpenetrable.

'And this is where you think you saw Luke?'

'Luke?' Lily fingered her chin. 'Is that his name?'

Sara didn't weaken. 'That's his name.'

'No. He was down the road a way.'

'Then we should drive on. He must've walked further.'

'But he was intending to turn back, wasn't he?' Nathan interjected, he thought, quite helpfully.

Sara looked confused. 'Why?'

'Because he was walking in the wrong direction. For the pub. He was after cigarettes.'

Sara continued to stare at him. 'But that isn't logical. The pub's a half mile further on up this road.'

'Oh,' Nathan withdrew, 'I must've got my wires crossed.'

'Yes,' Lily said tightly, choosing, however, not to elucidate.

Sara wound down her window and the rain hit her in the face.

'It's bucketing. There's no visibility.'

Nathan felt a moment's concern about the car's upholstery. 'Perhaps he left the road and walked over the fields or something.'

Sara shook her head. 'He wouldn't risk it. Especially in the dark. He's new to the area.'

'He's probably home and dry by now.'

This was Lily's deeply unperturbed contribution from the back seat.

'Don't be stupid,' Sara's jaw was stiff. 'We should drive on.'

Nathan did exactly as he was instructed. He drove slowly. But even squinting, he could see only a few feet in front of the car's bonnet. After a couple of minutes, when he was beginning to lose all faith in the existence of anything beyond the dull glare of the headlights, he suddenly noticed something vague and ghostly reflecting in their shine. A shirt, a pale face, two white hands. Like a scarecrow, cowering close to the dark hedgerow.

'Look,' he pointed, 'is that anything?'

Luke. Drenched, depressed, desperately seeking shelter next to a stunted hawthorn. Lily chuckled at the sight of him. They pulled up adjacent and Sara opened her door a fraction. 'Luke!' she yelled. 'Climb in.'

Luke looked towards the car, his expression awash with suspicious antipathy. It took him a moment to recognize Sara. Once he had, his frown deepened. 'No. I'm fine.'

'What?' Sara could barely hear him over the engine and the wind.

'I'm fine. I don't need a lift.'

He waved her away like she was a dirty pigeon eyeing up a slice of pizza.

Lily began sniggering again. Sara ignored her and clambered out of the car, leaving the door wide behind her. 'You're drenched,' she said, 'get in.'

Luke was shivering. Improperly dressed in Farahs, a cotton shirt and a cardigan. Sara noted that he still wore his hospital bangle.

She lowered her voice. 'Come on,' she said, 'get in the car. One of my boars has escaped. It's risky walking.'

Luke glanced over at the car. The light was on. He saw Lily gurning at him from the back seat.

'I don't want a lift,' he said coolly, 'I'm fine walking.'

Sara felt rain water slithering past her collar and down her neck. She shuddered. 'This is silly . . .'

He resented her quick selection of such a nursery-style word to describe his distinctly tragic predicament. 'It's not silly at all,' he said, brimming with righteousness, 'I simply want to be left.'

Sara lowered her voice even further. 'I *can't* leave you here. It's much too risky. You might get hurt and then I'd be held responsible.'

Lily was leaning forward in her seat, listening intently.

'I'm not getting into that car.'

'Why?'

He said nothing.

'Why? You're soaking wet. You're being ridiculous.'

'That's enough.'

Luke stepped off the grassy verge and on to the rough tarmac of the road. He began walking. Sara followed. 'I *won't* leave you here. Are you listening? It wouldn't be professional.'

'Oh yes,' Luke sniped, 'I understand all about professionalism . . .' he spat out water as he spoke, 'after all, I'm a *real* pornographer.'

Sara was nonplussed. 'What does that mean?'

'You should know,' Luke glared forward resentfully, 'you said it.'

'I said what?'

He was walking at a good speed. 'A *real* pornographer.'

Sara slowed down for a moment – as if thinking posed an obstacle to concerted motion – then speeded up and stuck at his shoulder, easily keeping his pace again.

Nathan trailed along behind them in first gear. From the rear, the car's lights were disorientating. It felt like being on stage in the world's most inhospitable theatre.

'Stop following me!' Luke bellowed.

'But I don't even remember saying that pornography thing.'

'Of course you don't.'

'No, truly.'

Sara felt a slight glow inside her. That she might have said something so impulsive and profound and deeply affecting, all in the heat of the moment, without even thinking! But what had she meant? A real pornographer? And how could she wriggle her way out of it now?

'I was talking rubbish,' she said, 'just off the top of my head. What the hell do I know about pornography?'

'It's a cold thing,' Luke said, almost to himself, 'but your pictures were cold too. They were colder.'

Sara stiffened. She remained sensitive. His rejection was still new and raw.

Luke sniffed. His face was streaming. The rain hurt his skin. It felt like he was being trampled by a swarm of damp ants in army boots.

'I don't think I like it here,' he announced soulfully.

'What?'

Sara had heard him, but she couldn't take him seriously. She was out of breath and had begun to worry that the rain might get into the gun and jam its mechanism.

'It isn't like the moon after all,' Luke continued, 'it's like hell. Or purgatory.'

'It's beautiful here in the summer,' she said, lifting the gun up and inspecting its barrel, 'with the clear light and everything. But you missed the summer.'

'The sea's freezing cold, and it isn't even the sea.'

'Of course it is. What else could you call it?'

Luke didn't respond.

'What else could you call it, Luke?'

Again. No response.

'Fine,' Sara muttered, 'if that's the way you want to play it.' She stopped walking, waited for the car to catch up with her and climbed back inside.

'Right,' she said, carefully supporting the gun between her knees, 'just follow him.'

'And I'll pay for the petrol,' she added, registering Nathan's expression of mute disgruntlement as she slicked back her wet hair until it stuck to her skull and glistened like it was oiled.

43

To see Nathan like that, completely out of context. *Nathan*. It had shaken her. Because at some basic level she'd found his previous performance convincing. He'd been gentle. He'd had this quality . . . a naïvety, an innocence. A detachment. And she'd believed in him, somehow, when he'd said that Ronny was no longer any part of his life. Even after discovering the lost property form with the Sheppey connection. Even then.

She was sitting, slumped at the kitchen table, exhausted, cradling one of the cauliflowers in her hands and waiting. How long before they returned? And would Nathan be with them? What did he want? From her? From Ronny?

Just an hour ago she'd been lost in the maize and Jim had saved her. Jim. She touched the head of the cauliflower with her fingertips, then absentmindedly pulled back the green fronds which sheltered its heart, pushed her fingers underneath its neck, yanked a small floret free and inspected it. She sniffed. The smell reminded her of the letters. That first extraordinary moment when she'd discovered them gone.

She tried to spur herself on, mentally, to investigate her position, her needs, her options, but it was too difficult. She was too tired. She glanced down at herself. She wore only an old robe which she'd found hung on the back of the bathroom door. Green, made of towelling. It swamped her and draped on the floor around her ankles. Her feet were uncovered though, and her toes tingled against the kitchen flags.

Jim. She touched the small cauliflower floret to her lips then popped it into her mouth. The belt of the robe was slack and the front section fell open as she moved her arm to her mouth.

She looked down at herself as she chewed, at her chest and her belly. Corpse-white. And the green of the robe? She felt hard and cold like a vegetable, with her soft towelling leaves pulling loose. She watched blankly as her skin tightened up into goosebumps. She swallowed, closed her eyes and saw Jim's face. His skin looked so bright. It glowed like a light bulb. Or was the brightness she imagined, in fact, just the fluorescent kitchen strip peeking in through her lashes?

For three seconds she contemplated this possibility, too exhausted to consider opening her eyes to find out conclusively. She felt her jaw loosening, her mouth falling open. Her brain was all flashes and crackles. I am asleep, she told herself, I am finally asleep, but then a chill began creeping, up her fingers, through her toes. Death is sudden, she found herself thinking. Sudden. It was not always as gradual as Monica had described it.

Her father; he was there and then he was gone. One door opened, another closed. She tried to picture him in her mind's eye but she couldn't. Every time she thought she'd got him cornered, turned him around to face her, tried to focus, to identify, he was sucked down and out from the space behind her eyes like a slick of oily water being dragged through a plughole.

Connie opened her eyes. My father was a good man, she told herself, tearfully, a good man. Ronny knew. Jim knew. Maybe even Nathan knew. Soon they would confirm everything. Soon. Soon they would confirm.

Yes. Yes. She kept repeating.

The lights were still off. Ronny remained by the window, obscured by the nets, cocooned, like a giant pallid chrysalis. Jim's eyes had grown accustomed to the darkness. He was crouching next to the fireplace, debating whether he could risk burning something. His clothes were damp. He was beginning to feel the cold.

'He's back again,' Ronny whispered, 'that's his seventh circuit.'

'Where does he go?' Jim asked idly.

'Luke's prefab. Something's attracting him to it. Do you think Luke's inside there? The lights are all off.'

'I don't know. Perhaps not.'

'So where is he?'

'Luke? The pub. He was planning to walk there if he grew desperate enough.'

'It's the smell,' Ronny intoned softly, 'don't you think?'

'The smell?'

'That fishy smell. It's like his calling card.'

Jim half-smiled. 'You really think that's why the boar's here?'

'Why not? He senses a rival.'

'I thought we'd decided he'd come to see the sea.'

'He came to find Luke and then ended up seeing the sea. The sea was an added bonus.'

Jim stretched out his hand and tentatively ran it along the wall next to the fireplace. He was feeling for the ball of paper he'd thrown there earlier.

'I have the letter,' Ronny said quietly, 'if that's what you're after.'

Jim paused.

'I've been watching you,' Ronny smiled, 'through the nets.'

He moved away from the window, towards the sofa, felt his way around it and then sat down. Jim remained crouched where he was.

'Can you see me?' Ronny asked.

'Yes. I can see your hands and your face.'

'Good.'

Ronny bent over and took hold of one of his white shoes. Jim could see that his hands were shaking.

'Remember on the bridge, when you asked me about my shoes?'

Jim nodded. Ronny pulled off his shoe.

'Look.'

Jim squinted in the darkness. He saw the pale outline of Ronny's foot. It was a long foot and delicately boned, but it was not like other feet he'd seen. It tapered.

'No big toe,' Ronny said, his voice expressionless, 'on either foot.'

Jim's mouth went dry.

'What happened?' he managed.

Ronny smiled. 'Nothing. I never had any.'

Jim continued to stare at Ronny's foot. 'It must be difficult to balance,' he said eventually.

'You have no face, Jim,' Ronny observed fondly, 'not this close up. Just a red glow.'

'Maybe you damaged your cornea.'

'Tell me she isn't dead.'

'What?' Jim's throat tightened and his shoulders rose defensively.

'I had this strong feeling, all along, that she was dead. Tell me she isn't.'

Jim stood up, but with difficulty. 'I think I hear something outside,' he said.

'Tell me nothing terrible happened.' Ronny dropped his shoe. He tried to pick it up again but his hand wouldn't seem to work properly.

'Nothing terrible happened,' Jim whispered, but he couldn't breathe. Everything was closing in.

'I was looking for a knife before,' Ronny mused, 'to smooth the putty on the back wall. I couldn't find one. Not in the drawer. Not in the sink. I thought that must mean something.'

Jim cleared his throat. 'But you were doing a great job with the trowel.'

He went to the window. 'I think a car's pulled up outside. Everything's brighter. That must be the headlights.'

'It's the moon.'

'Don't you hear voices? I hear them.'

Jim pushed the nets aside and peered out. Ronny stood up too. He began to walk over.

'No,' Jim said suddenly, 'don't come any closer.'

But Ronny kept walking. 'Keep away from the window!' Jim cried, turning, and throwing out his arms to ward Ronny off, to try and shield him, but Ronny would not be directed and he would not be protected. He stopped, stood firm and stared blankly over Jim's shoulder as one, two, three, four shots rang out.

All in the chest. She was a great shot. Luke was crushed up against the wall of his prefab. Lily was out of the car and prancing. Nathan was standing on the driver's side, his ears still reverberating from the sound of gunfire.

'Is it dead?' Luke asked, finally starting to inhale again. Lily walked over.

'Be careful!' Sara yelled. Her voice was higher than usual.

'It's still breathing,' Lily observed, 'big slow breaths.'

Luke moved forward. He brushed past Sara. 'I didn't even see it, but the noise it made! That squeal! And it kept on running once you'd shot at it. I thought it would never stop.'

'They always do that,' Sara said softly. 'They're almost too tough. They fight so hard for every inch of ground.'

'If we hadn't turned the car, I'd never have spotted him,' Lily said, squatting down.

Luke drew closer to the boar.

'I haven't ever seen one before,' he murmured, 'not in the flesh. It's a giant. Is it really still alive?'

'All four bullets hit the chest,' Lily said. 'I see the fucker stewed, I see it minced, I see it roasted . . .'

Her initial euphoria began to wane though at the sight of this huge, dismantled, panting creature.

'Come on, die,' she mumbled, almost furtively.

'I'm glad we followed you now,' Sara said, carefully putting the gun's safety catch back on. Luke crouched over the beast, still gazing in wonder at the size of it. Nathan, too, had finally strolled over.

'And I'm very grateful that you drove us,' Sara added, turning to him.

'It was nothing.' Nathan remained cautious. 'So is it dead yet?'

'Its chest is still heaving,' Nathan said, taking a tentative step back just as the prefab door flew open and Ronny rushed out.

He clattered towards them unsteadily. He wore only one shoe.

'I don't understand . . .' his voice was soft but ragged, 'he was just staring out at the sea. He was so peaceful. He meant no harm to anyone . . .'

'If he was just staring out to sea,' Luke interjected, 'how come all the shots are in his chest?'

'He turned around, that's all. He didn't understand the commotion . . .'

Jim stood in the open doorway, watching but saying nothing.

'It would've ended this way eventually,' Lily said gently, her original triumphalism now almost completely abandoned.

Ronny fell to his knees alongside the boar. 'His eyes are open. And his mouth. Why won't he die? Shoot him again,' he looked up at Sara, imploringly, 'just finish him.'

Sara didn't move.

'He's in pain. He's in *pain*! I can't stand it!'

Nathan took another step back. He didn't want to be noticed or involved or implicated. But Ronny saw something moving, in the mesh of shadows between the prefabs. He glanced over at Nathan for a second, then his sore eyes returned inexorably to the boar.

Jim turned too. His eyes were fine. And with his two fine eyes he saw his only brother.

Nathan. Smaller than he remembered him. Older now. With less hair, and looking so much like their father . . . But gentle. Nathan stared back, his expression anything but brotherly. It was hard, angry, distant. His face expressed his gut's instinct; his every familiar feature studiously riveted into hard lines of disdain. His mouth curled, instinctively, as if he'd just taken a slug of stale milk. Nothing was forgotten. Nothing had diminished. Jim saw his whole sad, grim, paltry life in the sudden, tiny, bolshy lift of Nathan's jaw.

The boar, meanwhile, took one, deep, shuddering breath and then all its breathing ended.

'It's over, Ronny,' Lily said, and put out her hand to touch his arm. Ronny yanked his arm away.

'We'll need to move the carcass somehow,' Sara said, trying

to be practical in the face of Ronny's emotional intervention, 'and he'll weigh a ton.'

Ronny clambered to his feet, turned, staggered back past Jim and into the prefab, slamming the door behind him.

'Jim?' Luke spoke. 'Will you give us a hand?'

Jim remained where he was, apparently bewildered, saying nothing.

'I have something back at the farm which'll make the whole thing easier,' Sara said. 'It's a kind of manual forklift. We should head on back and fetch it.'

Luke put out a tentative hand to feel the texture of the boar's pelt. It was rough, like shredded bark. The flesh underneath was still warm to the touch. He had forgotten how cold he was, and how wet. But it was still cold and it was still raining.

Jim put his own hand behind him and felt for the door handle. His fingers gripped it. He pressed it down, pushed it back and then manoeuvred himself slowly into the prefab, shutting the door gently, very gently, in front of him.

Ronny stood in the middle of the living room struggling to remove the letters from his belt.

'Turn on the light,' he said, his voice all torn.

'Not yet,' Jim whispered.

'Yes. Right now. Turn it on.'

Jim switched on the light. It was a cruel light. Everything was suddenly sharp and hideous and multi-dimensional. Even Ronny, who pulled open letter after letter, identified each one as best he could and then cast them into a heap on the floor at his feet. Eventually he reached the shortest of them all. The last letter. He held it out to Jim.

'Read it to me,' he said, 'my eyes are ruined.'

'Not now,' Jim said weakly.

Everything appeared too bright but too bleary. His eyes were salt-sodden. His smooth cheeks were a clear ski-run of tears.

Ronny didn't move. He didn't give in. He continued to hold out the letter defiantly, while Jim shuffled past, head bowed, shoulders hunched, looking as though every inch of his own battered will had finally upped and died inside him.

44

They faced each other like two spiteful, glimmering starlings across the length of the kitchen. Lily's arms were stretched around a large, slightly battered cardboard box, which she rested on the table but refused to release. Connie stood next to the Aga, glad to have the table between them.

Sara ran in – with the gun, which she carefully unloaded and locked away – then picked up some keys and headed straight out again.

'We killed it,' Lily announced brashly, 'on the beach.'

Connie gave her a thin smile.

'And I saw you in the road with Ronny before . . .'

'With Ronny?' Connie shook her head. 'I don't think so.'

Lily's eyes tightened. 'I'm not stupid. I saw you.'

'But I wasn't with Ronny,' Connie stuck her two hands defiantly into the pockets of her robe, 'which means that, yes, Lily, you must be pretty stupid.'

'That's my father's bathrobe,' Lily said thickly, 'take it off.'

'Gladly.' Connie pulled off the bathrobe and dropped it on to the floor. She wore nothing under it.

'Happy now?'

Lily was not happy. Connie was so neat, so little. She hated her for it. Her *completeness*. 'Why won't you leave Ronny alone?' she snarled. 'He doesn't like you. He doesn't trust you. None of us do.'

'You're breaking my heart,' Connie grinned. 'You're snapping it in two. You stole my letters and now you feel the need to lecture *me* on issues of trust?'

Lily growled, grabbed the box and headed upstairs with it.

Once she had gone, Connie's grin disintegrated. She pulled

the robe back on again. She was shivering. She walked to the doorway. Outside she could see Sara unlocking one of the larger outhouses and Nathan, sitting inside his car with the door wide and the light on. He was staring straight ahead of him, through the windscreen. Into the rain and the darkness beyond it.

Connie wrapped the robe tight around her and then jogged out to the car, still barefoot. She climbed in on the passenger side. 'I can't pretend to understand any of this, Nathan,' she said calmly, slamming the door shut behind her. 'How about you?'

Nathan did not look quite himself. He seemed ravaged. He didn't make eye contact. 'You probably won't believe me,' he said, reaching out and closing his own door, 'but I didn't know Ronny would be here.'

'Did you see him?'

'Yes.'

'Did you speak to him?'

'No. We didn't speak.'

'Then why did you come if not for Ronny?'

Nathan had a book on his lap. His hands were stretched across it.

'I came for you. I needed to show you something.'

'Me?'

He passed Connie the book. She took it, handled it briefly, closed her eyes and sniffed it.

'Italian,' she said, exhaling.

'Why do people always do that?'

Nathan thought of Laura for a split second. Poor Laura.

'It's a hardback,' Connie fingered the book's spine. 'I love the aroma of hardbacks. Especially art books. They smell like wax and hamsters. My dad used to buy books like this. Our house is still full of them.'

Nathan reached out his hand and pulled the book open at a place marked by the jacket flap. Then he glanced up and admired Connie's fine little face in profile. She seemed exhausted. He felt a strong urge to stroke her cheek. But instead, to compensate, he stroked his one hand with his other.

Connie's eyes gradually ingested the glossy illustration. 'That's Jesus,' she said finally, 'and he's *gorgeous*.'

Nathan opened his mouth to say something but was pipped at the post by Sara, who suddenly materialized at Connie's window, rapped on it and tried the door handle. The door opened.

'You'll catch your death wearing only that thing,' she muttered tartly. 'Where's Lily?'

Connie closed the book. 'Inside. Upstairs.'

'I'll need her to give me a hand with the carcass. And you . . .' she leaned forward, 'you too, Nathan, if you're sure you don't mind.'

'No,' Nathan said, automatically, 'I don't mind.'

Connie peered over at him. He looked like he minded.

Lily placed the box on her bed and sat down next to it, her expression staunch, but cautious, as if she and the box were on a first date together and she wasn't exactly sure what its intentions might be. She stared at it for a long while, quite gravely, and then stood up, walked over to her chest of drawers, opened the third drawer down and inspected its contents. She picked up a penknife – but she was frowning as she handled it – then rifled with great care through the rest of the drawer's jumble. For all her carefulness, she failed to locate what she wanted and finally, abandoning her search, huffed frustratedly.

She went and sat down on the bed again, repositioned the penknife in her hand, pulled it open, but instead of applying it to the box, applied it lightly to the very tip of her own tongue.

'Ow!'

The blade was sharp. She blotted her tongue on to her hand and studied her damp skin to see if any trace of blood remained. None. She smiled, then took the knife and applied it with a grand flourish to the brown tape on the box. She cut with a light, measured stroke; one side, two sides, three sides. She snapped the knife back into its shell and dropped it carelessly on to the counterpane.

She stared at the box again, took a deep, preparatory breath and then reached out a tentative hand to pull the flap open.

'Lily!'

Connie's voice, in the hall.

She frowned.

'Lily!'

Connie's voice again, on the stair.

'What?' she barked.

'Your mother wants you. She's outside.'

'Tell her I'm busy.'

'Tell her yourself. They're heading back down to the beach again to fetch the carcass.'

Lily said nothing.

'If you don't want to help them then I'll go.'

'No!' Lily stood up. 'Tell her I'm coming.'

She yanked on her shoes, picked up her rain mac, slung it over her shoulder, and was just about to leave her room when something struck her. She turned and stared at the box on her bed. She grimaced. She took the key from the small lock on the inside of her bedroom door, reached around and pushed it into the outside lock. She turned off her light, closed the door behind her, twisted the key and pocketed it.

Connie sat at the kitchen table with Nathan's book closed in front of her. She heard Lily cantering down the stairs, the front door slamming and a short while after the sound of a car's engine firing. Her nose was running. She sniffed. She went upstairs to the bathroom for a tissue, but instead of finding herself at the bathroom door, she found herself turning the handle to Lily's room. Jammed. She twisted the handle and pushed a little harder. Not jammed, locked. She kicked the door.

'Damn her!'

She went into her bedroom, took off the robe and pulled on some jeans and a jumper. She sneezed. Her eyes began watering. She cleared her throat but it would not clear completely. She went into the bathroom and lapped at some water from the cold tap.

On her way back downstairs she thought she heard something. A knock. A clatter. In the kitchen? Perhaps it was Sara, home again, having forgotten something? She tried to recollect whether she'd left the back door open. It's a cold night, she thought, a wet night. Her nose was still running. She blotted at it with a fistful of toilet paper, then slowly made her way down the last of the stairs. She paused for a moment in the hallway and listened. Everything was still.

The door through to the kitchen was slightly ajar. She pushed it with her foot and walked inside. The light was on. The Aga grumbled. It was still warm, but the back door was swinging on its hinges. She walked over and closed it, then returned to the table.

Nathan's book. She put out her hand and pulled it open. The beautiful Jesus. She looked more closely. His eyes were closed. His mouth was open. Why should that one particular combination prove so fiendishly sexy? She smiled to herself, slightly perplexed. The wound under his right nipple . . . wasn't it too artificial-looking? Too gaudily ornate? And the sparse cloth barely covering his groin? Creased with the precision of a concertina. A red-head. Jesus? And the angel. His small face so tragic, his arm so protective, and the delicate tracing of a single tear . . .

A slight sound. So slight a sound that it was barely anything. A panting, perhaps. The sound of fur touching something. A boot? A broom? Connie turned from the book, very slowly, and glanced around her. She saw the wall, the door, the refrigerator, the dresser, the old kitchen clock. Nothing else. Nothing.

Her eyes returned to the book. The sky was blue. No sun was visible in the painting, but even so she could almost feel the warmth of it. She'd never imagined the crucifixion as a sultry, sensual, balmy affair before. Never. But here it was, and it was all of these things.

A clanking. This time Connie's eyes flew straight to it. A small weeding fork leaning up against a wicker basket containing potatoes and carrot tops. It had fallen over. The fork. She was afraid, and fear made her move towards it. She bent over and picked it up. It was old and muddy with three small prongs.

She detected an even softer bumping, directly to her left. The kitchen table. The chairs. Their legs. They shifted, once, with a little clatter. Connie sprang backwards. Whatever this creature was it was surely a tiny thing. It was a little thing. It was nothing. But it was strange. She felt as if her whole heart had lifted. It felt higher than usual. And it was beating away inside her like a wooden spoon against an empty dish. In fact it was all she could do not to reverberate with it. Her hands were shaking as she held the fork up high in front of her.

And then . . . she blinked. She blinked again. Her eyes focused between the smooth forest of chair and table legs. Was it? Could it really be? She grinned, almost hysterically. A *bunny*?

Its ears. That's principally what identified it. Classic bunny ears. Beatrix Potter ears. Bugs Bunny ears. One up and jaunty, the other curved and half-cocked. A plain brown bunny. Tiny. In the kitchen. Connie bent down slightly. It was facing away from her, but she could still make out its white cotton-ball tail and the gentle sprigs of paler fur on the back of its brown heels. It held its head to one side. It must have crept in, she reasoned, a short while ago when the kitchen was empty.

Her nose kept on running. She put her hand to it and gave a small sniff. The rabbit reacted. It lurched. It wheeled around to face her. Its head all lopsided. Its eyes almost bursting. Connie straightened up a fraction. This could not be right. There was something wrong. Its eyes were all weird-angled, and its head . . . It moved slightly and hit the table leg. Its head swivelled again, aimlessly. It looked upwards but at nothing. She saw its chest palpitating.

Who was the more frightened between them? Connie took a step backwards, away from this sick creature, this cornball perversion, this diseased thing, towards the back door. She reached out her hand and opened it. 'Go on. Get out. Go on. Shoo!'

But it moved away from her voice, towards the Aga, horribly

tentative, as if every second it might risk a bump or a crash or a jolt. Its eyes rolled uselessly. Its ears, so sweet before, so funny, now looked forlorn and broken and ruined and faulty. It hit the wall. Its head sank, then rose. It was lost. It no longer knew or cared about the difference between night and light.

Connie remembered her father breaking the neck of an abandoned fledgling. She remembered an old boyfriend stamping on an injured frog. To kill it. That would be the brave thing. She clenched the fork in her hand. 'But I can't. I can't!'

She dropped the fork, hating herself, and grabbed hold of a kitchen broom. She held just the end of it. Slowly, she edged her way around the table. She swept the bristles along, hoping that their approaching swish would comfort the rabbit and not seem too cruelly random when they eventually made contact with it. The rabbit didn't move. It remained close to the Aga, its nose twitching, its eyes bulging. The broom was soon merely a few feet distant, and then simply inches. Connie's hands began shaking. To prod it! And what if it ran towards her instead of away?

But it did not run. It did not jump. The broom touched it. Connie barely felt the weight of the rabbit before it was moving, and not voluntarily, it was swept along, all stiff and still lolling.

She felt ashamed. Past the table she swept it, past the chairs, the wicker basket, the lines of boots, the galoshes, up to the doorway. But she couldn't push it off the step and out into the darkness. No. There was a small metal rim at the lip of the doorway. The broom, the rabbit, came to a halt here.

'Get out,' she said. 'Get out.'

She gave the broom a harder push. But the rabbit was stiff. It was lost in terror and in blackness. It would not move. All its places were terrible places.

Connie dropped the end of the broom, hoping that the clatter might frighten the rabbit backwards, over the doorstep, away from her. But the broom clattered and still it did not move.

'Oh no.' She fell to her knees. She waved ineffectually at it. 'Go on. Just go.'

She inched closer.

'Go on.'

Closer. And then her hands were only centimetres away from it. Her fingers felt stiff and unwieldy in this close a proximity. She bit her lip. 'Out,' she said, and then she touched it. It was a thing so full of horrors and yet so *soft*. And she felt its heart beating under her palms. It was terrified, but its head rolled, uselessly. She lifted it slightly. It was so light. Its ribs. She felt them. It was so *thin*.

'Go on boy. Out.'

Over the rim of the door and into the dark she lifted it. She gently touched it down. It was wet out and raining. She saw the rain hitting the rabbit. Its head swerved up to meet the rain, as if the rain could have been tin-tacks or little fists or anything.

Connie looked down at her two hands. Her mouth curled. She jumped up and ran to the sink. She turned on the tap and shoved her hands under it. She was crying. Her nose was running. She picked up a bottle of washing-up liquid to apply to her fingers.

The phone started ringing. She put the bottle down. She ran to the doorway, her hands still dripping, and stared out into the darkness. Was it gone? She wasn't certain. She saw something pale near the woodpile. She slammed the door shut. She leaned up against it, shuddering. She tried to move the broom but a wave of revulsion prevented her. She sprang over it and sprinted into the hallway.

'Hello?'

The phone was in her hand.

'Constance?'

Not a voice she recognized. A rough voice, but gentle.

'Yes?'

'Hello. My name's John Arnold. I'm ringing from the prison.'

'Yes?' She was almost gasping.

'Is this a bad time?'

'Uh . . .'

Connie felt a supreme urge to answer his question literally. Was this a bad time? Was it?

'I have a cold,' she said, and sniffed, 'that's all.'

She tried to stop her hands from shaking.

'I've been away on a transfer,' he said, 'in Durham. My daughter's been in hospital there.'

'Yes,' Connie nodded.

'It's all been a bit . . . well, nerve-racking, but she's fine now.'

'Good. Yes . . .'

Connie was staring down at her feet. They were covered in mud. She hadn't noticed before. The man took a deep breath. 'I heard that your father died.'

'Um . . .' she frowned. 'Yes . . .' she blinked, 'yes, he did die.'

'I'm very sorry.'

She sniffed. 'That's OK.'

'I only met him a couple of times but I liked him. He took people on face value and that's a rare quality.'

'So . . .'

Connie could not think of her father.

'You shared a cell with Ronny, then?' she asked tiredly.

'No.'

She paused. 'Pardon?'

'No.'

'You *didn't* share a cell with Ronny?'

'No.'

'So . . .' She was confounded.

'I wrote down his letters,' the man said casually, 'that's all.'

Connie couldn't understand him at first. 'I'm sorry . . .? *You* wrote Ronny's letters?'

'No. I copied them. For your father. From the walls.'

Connie was stunned, then wobbly. She sat down with a bump on the carpet. 'You're saying that Ronny wrote those letters himself, and that he wrote them all on the *walls*?'

'Yes,' the man sounded unperturbed, 'he scratched them into the plaster. It was a strange habit. But when I moved into the cell I really wanted to redecorate. I made a request for paint. Then your father turned up at a good moment and sorted it all out for me.'

'But you copied the letters?'

256

'For your father. Yes. Before we painted. He found them interesting.'

'Interesting.'

Connie's mind was spinning. 'And your daughter? You said she was sick?'

'She's on the mend now. For a while we thought we'd have to take her to America for special treatment. Private treatment. She has a problem with her ears. But they sorted it out here after all.'

'Good.'

'Your father was a kind man,' he said, 'and extremely generous.'

'Yes,' Connie sniffed, 'he was a kind man. He was a generous man. Thank you.'

They said good night and hung up.

Connie pressed her hands to her diaphragm and took a deep breath. She felt her own ribs with her fingers. She was dizzy.

'I'm relieved,' she muttered softly, 'and that's why my chest feels this way. It's only relief.'

She looked around her. Oh Jesus, she so much wanted to leave this place!

But she remained where she was. She rocked back down on to her heels. She listened to the house creaking around her and to the vague tick of the kitchen clock, and to the rain.

45

Ronny was no longer interested in what was happening outside. He was sitting on the sofa, his hands folded on his lap,
saying nothing, staring straight ahead of him. This time it was
Jim's turn to take heed, to stand at the window and scrutinize.
He turned the light back off to facilitate his observations.

Eventually the players returned to the boar and Jim saw
plenty. He saw Nathan and Sara and Lily struggling with the
carcass. He heard cursing and hearty expostulations. He saw
Luke rolling up his sleeves and lending a hand. Luke was
stronger than the others.

The forklift was difficult to utilize on the beach. It kept sinking
into the sand or lurching over sideways. Eventually they abandoned it and opted to drag the carcass manually to the harder
dirt road behind the prefabs, with Nathan and Luke to the fore,
a trotter each between them, and Sara and Lily to the rear.

Jim kept up a running commentary in a thin, bleak voice,
even though Ronny gave not the slightest indication of com-
prehending him. But Jim kept it up just the same, feeling that it
was the least he could do in the circumstances, to try and distract Ronny and to buoy him.

'Sara seems to be having problems with her back . . .' he observed gamely, and then, 'Lily isn't helping much. I think she's
feeling the cold . . . Luke's tougher than you might think . . .'

At no point did Jim mention Nathan's involvement in the
proceedings, but his eyes strayed more to Nathan's hard
endeavours than to anybody else's. Yet at no point did Nathan
direct his gaze towards Jim's prefab. Not even for the shortest
or meanest of glances.

Lily came and knocked at the door three times. Each time Jim imagined that she would turn the handle and walk straight in. But she did not. Each time she knocked, waited, knocked again, but she didn't try to force things. She exhibited an admirable restraint.

'It's Lily,' Jim muttered, each time she knocked. 'It's Lily at the door.'

He almost wished Lily would rush on in and snap Ronny out of it. But she didn't, and Ronny remained on the sofa, studiously dumb and numb and motionless.

Sara played a leading role in all of the manoeuvrings, but her back started to niggle her half way through so eventually she abandoned the lifting and the humping and decided that it was preferable to oversee the entire operation instead, with her hands placed firmly on to her hips and with an eye to maintaining the ultimate good condition of the carcass. This was business, after all. This was lunch and dinner. This was a full freezer. And now that the main drama was over she felt no pity for the dead creature, no spark of sentiment. She couldn't afford any.

Once they'd moved the boar to the dirt road they loaded it on to the forklift without too much difficulty and Sara prepared to haul it to the farm on foot.

Lily had climbed into the back of Nathan's car to shelter from the rain, and was sitting there expectantly, hoping shortly to be driven home again.

'I'll need you to give me a hand, Lily,' Sara said, beckoning her out with a peremptory finger, 'I can't manage this thing myself. The road's getting really muddy.'

'What?' Lily tried to look disparaging.

Luke stood nearby. He touched Sara's arm to attract her attention. 'I'm happy to help out,' he said quietly, 'my car's parked over at the farm anyway.'

Lily observed Luke's hand on Sara's elbow, and expected it to be removed at any second. But the hand remained there, and Sara did not shrug it off.

'It's fine, I'll do it,' Lily said determinedly, yanking up the hood on her mac and preparing to clamber out of the car again.

'Luke's stronger,' Sara said, and then smiled at him.

Finally he removed his hand, then busied himself turning the forklift around in the road, grunting as he shifted it. Nathan started up the engine. Lily didn't move.

'Will you close your door?' Nathan asked.

Still Lily did not move. Sara stepped forward and slammed the door shut, seemingly oblivious to Lily's pique. 'Do we turn,' Nathan asked, 'or can we head back this way?'

'Did you notice the fish?' Lily answered.

'What?'

'The fish. He stinks of fish.'

Nathan shook his head. 'No,' he said, 'I didn't notice.'

'Fuck him.'

Lily delivered the back of the passenger seat a ferocious jab with her boot. Nathan turned on the ventilation and fervently hoped that her shoes were clean.

They were no such thing.

'So, will you eat this thing?' Luke puffed, a full five minutes after they'd begun pushing.

'Of course. I can't sell it.'

'Why not?'

'Regulations and stuff.'

After a short pause Sara added, 'I appreciate your help.' She removed some hair from her eyes. 'And I am truly sorry about the pornography mix up.'

'I know you are,' Luke smiled, 'and your photos were great too. I was just a little intimidated initially.'

'Watch out for the pothole . . .'

Luke steered sideways.

'You saved my life back there,' he grunted, 'this thing could have killed me.'

Sara shook her head. 'He would never have escaped in the first place if I'd been doing my job properly. It was poor husbandry.'

'I'd love a picture of you with the boar and a gun,' Luke

grinned, 'like a hunter. Foot on the body, hands on your hips . . .'

'With the carcass?'

'Yes.'

Sara visualized what he'd described. After a while she said slowly, 'And would I be wearing any clothes in this photo?'

'Uh . . .' Luke thought for a moment, 'probably not, no.'

Sara smiled to herself.

'I could do a series of them,' Luke said, quite delighted with the idea.

Sara took her hands off the forklift and shoved them into her pockets. Luke positioned himself more centrally at the handle.

'I could do a spread,' he said thoughtfully, 'in the *Sunday Telegraph Magazine*. Very wild, very rural.'

Sara glanced at him sideways to see if he was joking. He didn't seem to be. But he was frowning and concentrating principally on the load.

That I could have shagged this man and enjoyed it, she thought amazedly. Then silently congratulated herself on her sharp use of the modern sexual idiom.

Shagged. Now that was surely progress.

'What can I say?' Jim stood in front of Ronny, but Ronny stared straight through him. 'Is there anything I can do to make things easier?'

Ronny felt an impulse to respond to Jim's question, but failed to summon up the energy. He was elsewhere. Miles away. Somewhere grey.

'I'll even read you the letter,' Jim said finally, 'if you really want me to.'

Ronny struggled to focus. 'You will?'

His hands rested passively upon the bundle of letters on his lap. The final letter was on top of the pile.

'It's very short,' he said, brightening visibly, 'it won't take you long.'

He passed the letter over. 'Will you need more light?'

'No.'

Jim took the letter. It was too dark to read it properly but he knew what it said. He didn't consider altering the content or varying the words. He saw no reason to employ cunning. Anyway, he believed that everything in the world had its own kind of truth. Its own integrity. Even lies.

Ronny, he began, then he cleared his throat and his voice grew softer, *Ronny*,

I dreamed I saw you dead in a place by the water. A ravaged place. All flat and empty and wide open. Not like here at all. Not full and moist and dense. Not like here: all blocked up and hot and savage. But on a moon's surface. And you were covered in some kind of binding. Like a mummy. Cotton. Or plastic? Something white and reflective. From head to toe.

And the light shone on you. Oh, how it shone on you! It glanced off you and it was like a pure bright silver. The wind was singing. It sang: you have suffered enough. You have suffered enough.

Then Death came and he kissed you. Lightly. Gently. Upon the lips. There is nothing beyond, he whispered, only me, only me.

There is nothing beyond. Only me.

Jim finished speaking. When he next spoke his voice was louder.

'It's cold,' he said, 'don't you think?'

Ronny said nothing.

'Ronny?'

'I can't talk,' he whispered, 'I feel so happy.'

'Happy?'

'Yes. Happy.'

'May I tell you something about Monica?' Jim asked.

'No more words.'

Ronny closed his eyes. 'It's too beautiful in here,' he said, touching his hands to his temples, 'my head's all golden inside.'

Jim watched Ronny, silently. The need to unburden, he reasoned, was a selfish need. Words were cruel things. So he held his tongue and savoured the discomfort it afforded him, continuing to savour it, quietly, passively, as the night gradually

262

dragged its heavy black belly the length and breadth of the patient heavens. Was Ronny sleeping? Bolt upright with such a wide smile on his face? Was he waking? Was he dreaming?

It didn't matter. Nothing mattered. Jim guarded him with every inch of his attention, every shred of concentration, perched on the sofa next to him, all eye, like a loyal, gentle, wordless cyclops.

46

They pulled up outside the farmhouse. Nathan killed the engine and switched off the lights.

'It's late,' he said.

'Will you drive home now?' Lily seemed unconcerned by this prospect.

'I think I may need a map or something.'

'A map? You've spent half the night trawling up and down these roads.'

Nathan glanced over towards the farmhouse. The kitchen light was burning.

'Do you have one inside?'

'A map?' Lily scratched at her head with all the uncultured abandon of a flea-ridden tom. 'I don't know.'

She clambered over the gearstick and into the front passenger seat. 'But I want to stay out here for a while yet,' she confided, settling herself down.

'Why?' Nathan frowned. 'You must be chilly.'

'Not really.'

Lily stared at Nathan evenly for a duration. He took her scrutiny without a flinch.

'You didn't speak to Ronny earlier,' she said, 'and you had plenty of opportunities.'

'I know. Bad timing.'

Lily digested this, but not fully. She changed tack. 'So how did you come to meet Connie before?'

Nathan cleared his throat. 'Lost Property.'

'Really?'

'Yes. She'd found some letters and she needed to trace Ronny.'

'So you sent her here?'

'In a manner of speaking.'

'And now *you're* here.'

'Yes.'

'In a manner of speaking.'

Nathan smiled weakly. Lily smiled back. 'Do you like her?'

Nathan looked surprised. 'I don't know her terribly well.'

Lily nodded. 'Even so. I think she likes you.'

Nathan shook his head.

'Honestly,' Lily was wide-eyed and emphatic, 'you should both drive home together. It's the same route.'

Nathan inspected his car keys. They were silent for a while.

'So are you going inside now or what?' Lily spoke.

'You want me to?'

'Yes. Get yourself a cup of tea or something.'

Nathan nodded. 'Fine. I might just do that.'

He climbed out of the car and slammed the door behind him.

Lily sank down in her seat, shoved her cold hands under opposite armpits, then watched through hooded eyes as Nathan tramped over towards the farmhouse.

Connie was drying her feet on a towel next to the Aga when Nathan walked in. She looked up, guiltily. 'I hope this isn't a tea towel,' she said, 'because my feet were filthy.'

Nathan noticed his book still lying open on the table. He walked over to it. 'You've been looking at this?' he asked, touching the glossy page with a tentative finger.

'Yes.'

'And did you reach any conclusions about it?'

'Conclusions?'

Connie threw down the towel and went over to stand by him. 'What kinds of conclusions?'

'About the picture.'

She pulled out a chair and sat on it.

'It's beautiful,' she said, 'and it's very sexy . . .'

'And the angel?'

Connie looked up at him. He was utterly engrossed. 'You

don't think this is a little strange, Nathan?' she asked softly. 'You come all the way down here with a picture of Jesus and then ask me what I think of it?'

'I didn't really consider it that way.'

Nathan pulled out a chair and sat down himself.

'Are you finding religion or something?'

'Me?' He looked amused. 'I don't think so.'

'Then what is it?'

'I don't know.'

Connie picked up the book. 'I suppose that in a quite poor light the angel looks a tiny bit like I do, and Jesus, if I screw up my eyes, he looks a little bit like you do . . .'

'It's odd that you should put it that way,' Nathan said, slightly unsettled by her bluntness.

'You asked what I thought,' Connie smiled, 'and so I'm telling you. The truth is,' she continued, 'that I don't think this picture is about me at all. Or you for that matter. I think it's about Ronny.'

Nathan inspected his fingers. He didn't like what he was hearing.

'It's about forgiveness,' Connie said, putting the book down, 'and it's about sex.'

She pointed. 'I was looking at Jesus's hand earlier. Do you see it? His left hand. It's curled up on his thigh as if he'd just finished masturbating with it. And his mouth is open. His eyes are closed. He looks kind of . . . ecstatic.'

Nathan shook his head.

'No,' he said.

'And the angel,' Connie continued, 'he seems very upset. He's been crying. Perhaps he's just sad or perhaps he's feeling guilty about something.'

Nathan's eyes were suddenly fully focused upon the angel.

'He?'

'Angels are always boys,' Connie said, 'aren't they?'

Nathan stood up. His face was red.

'What's wrong?' Connie didn't understand this dramatic mood change.

266

'I thought it was a girl,' Nathan muttered, and then began rubbing his hand across his chest as if trying to wipe something from it.

'I think it's one of the weirdest, crudest, rudest paintings I've ever seen,' Connie said, 'and I'm glad you brought it to show me. But I also think you've come here to forgive Ronny. This was just your roundabout way of doing so.'

She sat back and watched as a whole herd of expressions trampled over Nathan's face. For a second he was full of an inexpressible agony, and then fear kicked it out and took up a cold residency in his lips and in his eyes.

And for some reason – although she gave no outward sign of it – Connie found herself enjoying the sight of Nathan's misery, she celebrated it, quietly, deeply, inside herself. Because on some strange level, it all felt so neat, so complete, so *necessary*.

'Can I do anything else for you?'

Luke had pushed the boar's carcass into an outhouse and then had helped to secure the door with a padlock.

'I don't think so,' Sara put the key back into her pocket, 'but thanks anyway.'

They were standing close together in the darkness, facing each other.

'Feel my hands,' Luke said, and touched the back of his fin-gers to Sara's cheek.

'Cold,' she smiled.

'Extremely.'

'I'd invite you in,' she said, 'but I don't think it's a good idea under the circumstances.'

'No.'

'Your car's over there.'

Sara pointed. Luke took this opportunity to kiss her on the nose, and then on the lips. She was moderately responsive, but her face was wet with rain and her skin was slightly red and numb. The waterproof fabric of their coats made a little scrap-ing noise as they clashed.

'Friction,' Sara said, once he'd finally withdrawn.

'Will I see you again?' Luke asked.

'If you must know,' Sara said, 'I've actually been thinking a good deal about your dot-to-dots.'

Luke found her timing inappropriate. He straightened up a fraction. 'Really?'

The dot-to-dots were absolutely the last thing on his mind.

'Yes. I decided that it was very interesting how the thing you found most fascinating about the dot-to-dots was actually the part which was missing . . .'

He frowned. He was confused.

'Because when I really thought about it,' Sara continued, 'I actually found the *least* fascinating part the bit which was missing.'

Luke smiled, Sara felt, somewhat patronizingly. 'Men and women, huh?' he intoned carelessly.

'One day,' Sara said, 'and hopefully it'll be one day soon, somebody will come along who'll manage to make the other bits seem fascinating to you. But she isn't me. She just isn't,' she smiled kindly, 'and that's really all I wanted to say on the subject.'

Luke nodded. 'Good,' he took several steps back, 'you said my car was where?'

Sara pointed again.

'Thank you.'

He smiled back at her, but his cheeks were clenched.

That's probably the cold, Sara reasoned, then put her hands up to her own cheeks, feeling vaguely corny but as smug as hell.

'What's going on?'

Connie walked over to the window and tried to peer out through it, but the glass was steamy. She tried to wipe clear a peep-hole with her hand. Outside she saw the tail-lights of the Volvo disappearing, and, closer by, Sara and Lily in the midst of an extremely heated confrontation.

'Oh dear,' she moved back a fraction, 'I think all hell just broke loose.'

Nathan had closed his book. He looked up.

'There were four of them,' he said, 'our father, Little Ronny and two others. They kept her in the flat for almost a week. She was sedated to keep the noise down.'

Connie turned away from the window. 'They kept who?'

'The girl. She came from a local estate. She was two years younger than Ronny. He might have seen her at school sometimes. At first nobody missed her.'

Connie put her hand up to her throat. 'Monica?'

'No,' Nathan shook his head, frowning, 'she had a different name. One of the others was a lab assistant at the school. That's how the connection was made. My father preferred boys, actually,' Nathan said, and as he said it, his tongue stuck to the roof of his mouth.

Connie's heart twisted for him. 'So where were you while all this was happening?' she asked softly.

'I had a flat. I'd left by then. I escaped.'

'And Ronny?'

'Seventeen. But he seemed much younger.'

'He could have escaped too.'

'I begged him. He wouldn't leave. He wanted me to force him.'

Connie considered this for a while. 'To force him? Why?'

'Because he was frightened. Because that's what he was used to. That was all he understood.'

'But you didn't force him.'

'No,' Nathan shook his head, 'I couldn't.'

'So they killed her.'

'Yes. Eventually.'

Connie pulled out a chair. 'I didn't ever want to know what he'd done,' she said, 'and now that I do know . . .'

But she couldn't complete what she'd wanted to say. She sat down. 'Poor Monica,' she muttered eventually, 'now I realize what she meant. Death came so slowly.'

She looked up at Nathan. He seemed perfectly composed again. Her eye slipped down to his shirt pocket. It was full of something white and had a kind of sticky-looking stain on it

269

which had spread down from the pocket and into a couple of square inches of the fabric below.

'There's a leak or something . . .' Connie indicated. Nathan glanced down at himself. 'Oh. It's just honey,' he said, and drew out Lily's sandwich. Connie went to the sink and picked up a cloth, squeezed it firmly and then ran it under the warm tap.

'I saw you!' Lily screamed. 'I saw him with his hands all over you!'

She'd sprung from the car with all the momentum of a jackrabbit as soon as Luke had driven out and on to the road. She'd bided her time, this time.

Sara hadn't bargained on a witness, or, for that matter, a confrontation.

'It was nothing,' she said airily, 'and it was none of your business. Where's Nathan? Why were you sitting out here all alone in the dark?'

'He's a monster!' Lily bellowed. 'He stinks of fish! How could you let him touch you? You're disgusting!'

'No.' Sara shook her head. 'No, I am not disgusting.'

'And what about Dad?'

'Dad?' Sara's eyes widened. 'Don't pretend you give a damn about his feelings. You haven't mentioned him once since he left this house. Not one word in two whole months. Your dad doesn't even enter into it.'

'You don't know what I'm thinking!' Lily screamed. 'You've never known what I was thinking!'

Sara stared bemusedly at Lily's rage-torn face. 'No. Sometimes I don't know what you're thinking. You never tell me what you're thinking. I'm not a mind-reader, Lily. I'm your mother. That's all.'

'You're not my mother,' Lily snarled. 'You wanted me dead. You always wanted me dead. You both did.'

Sara choked down a laugh. 'You're being stupid. You're just hysterical. Luke and I had a brief . . .' she struggled to find an inoffensive, unincriminating word, 'a brief understanding.'

'Understanding? *Understanding*! Is that what you call it? You never had an understanding with me. Never! You never wanted an understanding with me!'

'You're my daughter,' Sara said evenly, 'of course I have an understanding with you.'

'You never liked me. Do you think I couldn't tell? Every time I was ill you wished I'd die. But I'm not dead. I'm here. I'm *here* and you can't ignore me. And I'm not going to die.'

'But I don't want you to die.' Sara was confused. 'I don't understand where all this is coming from. I'm not even seeing Luke any more. It was *nothing*.'

'I don't care about Luke!'

'But you obviously do care. Why would you hide in the dark spying on us both if you didn't care about it?'

'You don't know what I care about. You don't understand anything about me!'

Sara began to lose her temper. 'What is this? Of course I care about you. What do you expect to gain by telling me that I don't care about you?'

'Waiting for me to die!' Lily screamed, flecks of foam spilling down her chin. 'Like I was some sick animal. You never liked me. You never took any interest in me. You didn't love me. But you love that fishy pig. That stinking man. You love him but you never loved me . . .' Lily's hands were clawing at her chest, 'and I'm your *daughter*!'

'You know what?' Sara was angry now, she took a step backwards to give herself room. 'I do love you, but sometimes I don't *like* you very much.'

Lily exploded. 'You hate me! I know you hate me!'

'No. But I don't like the way you treat me and I don't like the way you kill my hens and I don't like the way you sneak around the place as if I'm some kind of fool who doesn't have a clue about what you're up to.'

'*I didn't kill your fucking hens. I never killed your fucking hens!*'

Lily smashed her fist into the roof of Nathan's car.

'*Never! Never! Never! Never!*'

Sara stepped forward and tried to stop Lily from denting

Nathan's roof. She attempted to grab her flailing arms. Lily was powerful though and knocked her away.

'Let go of me, you fucking bitch!'

Sara decided that the moment had come to raise her voice. 'Don't you *dare* call me a bitch! And don't you *dare* swear like that in front of me again!'

Lily clenched her fists and then swung out her right arm with all her might. Her knuckle made a temporary connection with Sara's jaw. Sara's jaw gave a brief little clicking sound and then she discovered herself down on the floor, on her back like some kind of bug, legs up, arms everywhere, sliding around in the mud. Lily stood over her, almost unnerved by the success of her assault. 'You won't kill me,' she whispered, 'not you, not Dad.'

Sara lay at Lily's feet, looking up at her. This is it, she thought, this is really it. With as much force as she could muster, she kicked out her leg towards Lily's ankles. Before Lily knew what was happening, her feet had slipped out from under her and her head had smashed into the passenger door of Nathan's car with a resounding *crack*!

Sara scrambled to her feet.

'No,' she growled through her stiff, throbbing jaw. 'I have no intention of killing you, Lily, not even if sometimes I feel pretty sorely bloody tempted.'

She turned away, then turned back again. 'And if you touch another one of my hens I'll turf you out and let you live in the barn with the rest of the animals. Is that understood?'

Lily didn't speak. Not at first. But as Sara slammed her way into the house she could have sworn she heard a selection of words which sounded suspiciously like 'I love you'.

She stopped in her tracks, blinked. Her mind went into a kind of reverse. Then she played that strange audiotape over again in her head. She realized that what had in fact been uttered was 'Fuck you'. But without much emphasis. Well that, she told herself firmly, has got to be better than nothing.

'Are you bleeding?'

Connie was bent over Lily, trying to discover which was the

top end of her and which the bottom. Lily didn't answer her question, but she grunted, thereby indicating that her head was obscured by the car's undercarriage.

'Are you hurt? We heard the bang from the kitchen as your head hit the door.'

'Congratulations,' Lily croaked.

Connie fastened her hands around Lily's midriff and yanked her out from under the car. Then she straightened herself up again. 'I think Sara hurt her jaw. She was cradling it when she ran upstairs.'

Lily didn't react.

'That was quite some disagreement.'

'I hate her.'

'I get the impression that the feeling's pretty mutual at the moment.'

Lily tried to pull herself up into a sitting position. 'She was screwing that fish-farm.'

'Luke?'

'Yes.' Lily shook her head experimentally. 'Ow!'

'I bet you'll have a big bump,' Connie observed, watching her.

'I hope I broke her fucking jaw,' Lily said thickly.

'Can I help you inside?' Connie put out her hand.

'I'm never stepping into that house again. I'll sleep in the barn first.'

'Did you ever sleep in the barn before?'

'No.'

'Then I don't think it's a great idea to start now. You might be concussed.'

'Fuck off, anyway.'

'You know,' Connie squatted down, 'my mother had an affair when I was your age.'

'So what?'

'I know how bad it feels at first, that's all. But when you get older it doesn't seem to matter so much. You realize that your parents are only human and it's actually quite a relief.'

'I *am* older.'

'Even older then.'

While they spoke, Nathan gradually picked his way over towards the car. He was buttoning up his coat. He had his book tucked under his arm.

'Are you going somewhere?' she asked.

'I'm heading off,' he said, 'it's very late.'

He stood next to the car and ran his hand over the roof. 'Why didn't you just punch your mother to start off with and leave my car out of it?' he said tersely.

'Don't piss around with me,' Lily said coldly, 'if you haven't already noticed, I don't have much of a sense of humour.'

'But I had noticed,' Nathan said gently, 'because it seems such a pity.'

'I'm going in,' Lily announced, pushing herself up and then staggering over towards the house.

Connie tried to inspect the roof for damage. 'Did she dent it?'

'No.'

'Will you drive home now?'

'Probably.'

Nathan walked around to the driver's side of the car and opened the door. 'I really didn't mean to upset you before, Nathan,' Connie said suddenly.

'But you did,' Nathan replied cheerfully, 'and people always do.'

He climbed inside the car, slammed his door shut and started up the engine.

What had he meant, Connie wondered, that I did hurt him or that I did *mean* to hurt him? Which was it? And what was the difference between the two?

Nathan put the car into reverse. Connie frowned, then took a few steps back to allow him space to manoeuvre.

47

Jim awoke to the sound of the fridge door closing. It seemed that he'd fallen asleep after all, against the entire sum of his good intentions, curled up in a ball at the end of the sofa. He unwound himself slightly, feeling stiff. His neck hurt. He moved his arm and realized that he'd been covered in a blanket. He felt warm. When he opened his eyes a fraction he saw that it was light outside, light inside. And he could no longer hear the rain falling. Only seagulls and the sea. He closed his eyes again. He heard Ronny moving around in the kitchen. He imagined him making breakfast for the two of them. This image was so sweet, so conjugal, so incongruous, that he smiled and for a brief moment allowed himself to dwell on it.

Shuffling. How much later? Hours? Minutes? Seconds? Jim's eyes shot open and he yanked himself up. The prefab was silent. But he'd detected . . . what? The door closing? He looked over towards the window and his heart began hammering. He threw off the blanket and walked to the door. He opened it. He peered out into the bright morning. It was brisk. There was a sharp wind. What time was it? Still early.

The beach was empty. But when he looked out and along, sharply, to his right, he thought he saw something white . . . just fluttering. In the distance. A sail? A gull? A plastic bag? No. No. Bigger. Far away. Something bright and light and strangely reflective. Then it struck him like a giant breaker. The white suit. It was the white suit! Bleached. Plastic. Lily-pale. Alabaster. The spacesuit. It was the white suit. And the light was glancing off it. And the wind was blowing. And it was Ronny wearing it. It was Ronny.

Jim gave a low, wounded gasp, then started running.

I was lost, Nathan told himself, but now I am found. He climbed out of the car to stretch his legs and glanced around him. His feet were numb. He had yet to work out whether he'd stayed because he'd wanted to or because, finally, he hadn't known where the hell he was heading.

He was parked up in a dead-end, close to a desolate-looking fenced-off cluster of holiday chalets. The prefabs were a short distance behind him. The nature reserve lay ahead. The road just stopped. It was a true dead ending.

And it had been the longest of nights. The car had been cold. He'd run the engine, intermittently, but then he'd noticed the petrol gauge leaning eerily towards the empty mark. After that he'd just shivered, his coat spread ineffectually across his knees.

A short while after five the sun came up. Over the sea. And Nathan had stared at it. He'd thought about himself. He'd thought about Ronny. He'd thought about Connie. She was right, he reasoned, about angels usually being boys. She was right about the masturbating Jesus. He tried to understand what it meant, this rightness. In the end he resolved that it meant only two things, and even they weren't mutually exclusive.

The first? Well, at some level, some *subtle* level, it seemed as if maybe he'd always known that the angel was a boy. Perhaps, he thought, the evil really is inside me. Deep inside me like I always feared it would be. That unexplored dread was a real dread. That unbidden terror, a true terror. Yet when he faced this possibility, head on, a wall rose up inside him, same as always, and his thoughts turned away.

The second thing. The other option? He tried to focus again. The second possibility was that this whole mess was not about love or infatuation or art or anything, but about God. *God.* Perhaps he had finally found his own true salvation in the strange, tarnished image of this masturbating Christ? This idiosyncratic Jesus, this human Jesus, this sensual, unashamed, uninhibited Jesus could surely understand and encompass all those black, unthinkable feelings which tormented and dogged and plagued him. This worldly Jesus would not turn away from sin. No. He would *embrace* it. Here, in this dark saviour, Nathan told himself, lay a final, complete and absolute understanding.

This was a bold Jesus, after all. This was the fearless Jesus who would, without thinking, have forced Little Ronny to leave his father's wicked house. This Jesus would have damned the consequences. This was the Jesus who could forgive himself anything, and in so doing, forgive others all of their sinning.

I cannot get over what has happened, Nathan told himself, but I can let go of it. I can simply let go of it. I can forgive. I can forgive myself. I can forgive Little Ronny. I can forgive Big Ronny. Yes. Even him.

And as the sun rose, Nathan felt something corresponding within him. Something hot. A nugget. Something rising. It burned inside of him. This is Jesus, Nathan told himself, this is God. And God was an enormous, infinite, all-consuming blankness.

Nathan closed his eyes and felt himself transformed into a state of total rapture as the sheer, clean, white spirit of the good father filled him. At last, he sighed, at long last, I am truly *lifted*.

She hadn't opened the box. If I open it, she thought furtively, then I'm merely replacing one bad thing with another. I have to hold back, like Ronny said, just this once. I have to turn away. She wondered, idly, as she fell to sleeping, whether growing up was simply about relinquishing everything of value. Dreams, fears, expectations. This cynical concept appealed to her. But she didn't relinquish the box, just the same. She closed her eyes and slept with her arms still curled like small, pale stamens, tightly and firmly around it.

Another interminable night of not-quite-sleeping. Connie half-dreamed that she saw her father sobbing, elbows up, head down, at the kitchen table. She was a little girl again, at home, and had accidentally walked in on him. *Daddy?* He'd lifted his head as she approached, and pretended that he'd not been cry-

ing after all. I'll never forgive you! She found herself screaming. But she was screaming not at her father but at Lily, outside,
by Nathan's car, and Lily was Sara, only younger. *I'll never forgive you your awful betrayal! Never!* Then she turned back to face
her father again , picked up a dirty dishcloth and tried to blot
his tears with it. But his tears were blood, not water. His eyes
were red and they were bleeding.

Shit!

Connie sat up and scrabbled around in the sleeve of her
jumper for a tissue. Her nostrils were burning. Her throat was
dry. She blew her nose, swung her feet out of bed, then pulled
on her trousers and her shoes. It was morning. At last. She crept
through the house and out into the world. She began walking.

Ronny was not thinking. He was counting. All the way along
the beach, a sharp left turn, then up over a dune, past the
chalets and into the reserve. To his right, the river and the
fields, to his left, the extensive, desolate swampy yellow of the
salt flats. He picked up pace when he saw them.

It was difficult walking in the white suit. It was difficult
inhaling. It was difficult hearing anything except his own
breaths and the thoughts he was thinking. The counting. He
had only so much time. He did not notice Nathan standing by
his car. He did not hear Jim calling. Everything was slow and
calm and self-contained. He walked on, along the flats and out
towards the sea.

Outside, in the world, Jim was running and shouting and
waving his arms. 'Stop him!' he yelled, 'just stop him!'

He wanted to pick up pace, he wanted to, but his feet kept
sinking in the sand like they were lead weighted. He couldn't
move.

Nathan turned and saw his brother, far away, in the distance.
He curved his hands around his lips to form a fleshy mega-
phone. 'It's nothing,' he shouted, 'he can't possibly sink in that
suit. It's plastic. It'll simply fill with air.'

But Jim kept running, onwards and then upwards, not even
seeing Nathan, not even hearing him.

Ronny found the proper place. He felt a dampness around his ankles. It was wetter here than he'd anticipated. But that didn't matter, did it? No. He shook his head. He opened his right hand and stared at what it contained through the clear plastic visor of his face mask. Nestled inside his palm was a butter pat. A small square. Innoffensive. Hard. Cold. Gold-wrapped.

He lifted his visor to render his mouth accessible. He placed the butter pat on to his tongue, then shoved it down into his throat with a white-gloved finger until it lodged hard and deep and fast inside there. He didn't gag.

I really want to die, he thought. Then he lay down on the grass, feeling the wind blowing against his clothing, hearing it like a giant, imaginary audience roaring along to this, his final act; laughing and cheering and whooping and jeering. All in equal measure.

Connie had seen him, in the distance, white-suited like an astronaut. She'd kept on walking, vaguely perplexed, but her mind was full of other things. Then she heard something. But it was so faint and far away. Like the sad cry of a curlew. A kind of wailing. Finally she saw Jim, and behind him she saw Nathan. Jim was running. But not Nathan. He walked. Connie stopped. She turned towards the salt flats. Then who . . .?

The white figure lay down. He rested his hands across his chest. He relaxed. Then his head, with a terrible gradualness, turned slowly, gently sideways. How many seconds passed before Jim reached him? Thirty? Forty? More? And when Jim did reach him, Connie took it as a signal to start walking again. Fast and then faster.

On her way down towards the shore she met Nathan.

'Is it Ronny?' she panted. Nathan nodded, but he didn't pick up pace. Connie ran on and down towards the others. Jim was screaming. He'd ripped off Ronny's white helmet and his visor. He was yanking at his head.

'What did you do? What did you do? Where are you? What did you do?'

Ronny's eyes were closed as though he was sleeping. He did not respond to Jim's violent admonishments. Connie fell to her knees. 'Leave him!' she shouted. 'Let him go!'

She pulled Ronny's eyelids open. She saw only whites.

'What's happened? Tell me!'

Jim was howling. 'I don't know. I don't know. He put his hand to his mouth. I saw him put his hand to his mouth and then he lay down.'

Connie prised Ronny's jaw open. She tried to look past his tongue. Then she placed both her hands on the outside of his neck and squeezed gently.

'I think I feel something . . . I think he swallowed something.'

She plunged her hand into his mouth and attempted to force her fingers down his throat.

Nathan finally reached them. He said nothing. He crouched down and took hold of Ronny's arm but couldn't gain access to his wrist, so he pulled the plastic suit open at the front and then ripped it across and over his shoulder, yanking up Ronny's hand to feel for a pulse. He couldn't locate one. He kept on trying.

'No pulse,' he said eventually, and dropped Ronny's arm. 'He's gone,' he said.

'No!' Jim shouted. 'No, he isn't dead! No, he isn't dead! No, he isn't, he isn't . . .'

He started shaking uncontrollably. He jumped forward and began banging his full weight on to Ronny's diaphragm.

'He is dead,' Connie whispered, withdrawing her hand. In it she held a small, gold butter pat, still frozen. She started to cry. 'Oh fuck. He is dead.'

When she'd removed her hand from his mouth, Ronny's jaw sagged open. She tried to close it. It wouldn't close.

'He isn't dead,' Jim yelled again, and continued pummelling. Nathan leaned forward and calmly back-handed his face, very hard. Once, twice.

Jim gasped. He put his hands to his cheeks. He stared at his brother, dumbfounded.

'Pull the suit off,' Nathan said. 'Help me.'

He yanked the suit away from Ronny's skinny torso while

the two of them watched him. The suit was already muddy. Ronny's legs were steeped in it.

'The gold watch I gave him,' Nathan said, 'is it on him anywhere?'

'The gold watch?' Jim repeated blankly.

'Is it on him?' Nathan yelled.

Jim blinked. 'I don't know. I don't. I think he broke it.'

He began rocking.

Nathan pulled the remainder of the suit off, then placed his hands under Ronny's armpits and yanked him out several feet further towards the sea. As he yanked, Ronny's shoes came loose.

'What are you doing?' Jim sprang back to life again. 'Leave him alone! Not his shoes! Leave him, Nathan! *Leave* him!'

He scrambled forwards, into the mud, grabbing one of the shoes and trying vainly to fit it back on to Ronny's foot again. 'Not his shoes! He never took off his shoes!'

'I'm saving you,' Nathan yelled, his face puce with both his rage and his exertions. 'I'm saving you. Don't you *understand*? Get away from here! Go *away*!'

Connie saw Nathan sinking up to his thighs in mud and then Ronny's pale, limp body sliding gently into it. Jim was deep in mud himself and flailing around helplessly.

'Don't do this,' he screamed, 'just leave him. Just leave him alone. Just leave him!'

But Ronny's body sank anyway until eventually Connie stared vainly at where it once had been because it was as if she'd only ever dreamed it there. Pieces of the suit began shifting in the wind across the flats.

'Get those, Connie,' Nathan pointed.

She found herself doing as he'd instructed. She gathered up the helmet and visor, the suit, one of the shoes. Jim still held the other.

The two brothers faced each other. No words were exchanged between them. Then Nathan turned and began wading back towards drier land. Back to his car. Back to his life. Everything is finally over, he thought thankfully, everything is dead, everything is finished. He took a long, slow, deep breath, and even as he began to exhale it, he was well on his way to forgiving himself.

First she carried the cardboard box outside and placed it down gently, then she returned to her room and began piling armloads of stuff on to the counterpane of her bed. All the clothes from her cupboards and her drawers, all the crazy mementoes she'd accumulated, all her schoolbooks and folders, all her toys and her knick-knacks. Even the few posters on her walls. Then she pulled each of the four corners of the counterpane together and dragged the whole giant bundle out of the house and into the farmyard.

With a touch of disarming level-headedness, Lily positioned herself a sensible distance away from the outbuildings, the farmhouse itself and the animals. She went and grabbed a selection of logs from under the woodpile. The drier, she reasoned, the better. In the kitchen she found meths and matches.

Sara awoke still clutching her aching jaw. It hurt when she moved it. She gently ground her teeth together, relishing the dart of discomfort this generated, then lay back limply, listening. All was quiet. She checked her bedside clock. She checked it again. She climbed out of bed, rather creakily and walked down the corridor. Connie's bedroom door was ajar, her bed was unmade and empty. Lily's door was wide open. All her things were gone.

Is there something about me? Sara wondered quietly, which makes people keep on disappearing? Then she turned, clumped downstairs at full tilt and bellowed out Lily's name into the downy silence.

Lily yanked off the clothes she wore, layer by layer, until she stood naked next to the smoke and the flames.

'Look at me!' she screamed, up into the sky, straight into the heavens. 'LOOK AT ME! I AM ABSOLUTELY BLOODY GORGEOUS!'

She started laughing, clutching at her ribs, then bent over

and picked up the cardboard box. The fire was burning fiercely. The wind was blustering and changing direction. One moment the smoke flew one way, the next, the other. Lily inhaled some of it and began coughing. Through her tears she saw the farm-house door opening. Through the flames she espied her mother. She whooped with glee, sprang into the air, threw the box on to the blistering fire and then with a final spectacularly unholy yodel, she turned on her dirty heels and ran.

Nathan had gone. Neither Connie nor Jim had moved an inch. They each clutched one of Ronny's shoes. Eventually Connie held out her hand to him. 'Come back,' she said, 'get out of that mud.'

'Death is my gift,' Jim whispered hoarsely, not moving. 'Don't you see? Death is all I ever bring.'

'He swallowed a butter pat,' Connie said, refusing to acknowledge Jim's declaration, opening her hand to show him the little gold packet. 'Isn't that funny?'

Jim stared at her, but it was as if he couldn't quite see her.

'Do you know how badly someone must want to die to kill themselves that way,' she asked gently, 'with a butter pat?'

Jim said nothing.

'Please come out of there,' she said kindly. 'Look. I have his other shoe.'

When Connie mentioned the other shoe, Jim focused in on it and then immediately began wading back again. She offered him the shoe. He took it.

'Perhaps you'd better leave this place,' she said.

'No, 'Jim held the two shoes to his chest, 'I'm not going any-where.'

'Ronny's dead,' she said, 'and now you're free.'

Jim stared at her as if for the very first time, his face taut with incredulity. 'But I *am* Ronny,' he said.

Connie stared back at him for a while. 'Yes,' she replied even-tually, 'I know perfectly well who you are.'

Jim's eyes returned to the muddy ground again. He slowly began walking towards the beach.

'I realized the very first day I ever met you,' Connie called after him, 'I always *knew* it was you.'

He walked on. Connie glared after him, blinking angrily, clenching her fingers tightly around the little foil-wrapped square.

Luke told himself that he had been injured irreparably by Sara's comments about the dot-to-dots. He found it hard to believe that anybody, least of all Sara, could seriously imagine that another person might be so dramatically altered by love. Love? What could be more ridiculous than that? Or more insulting?

Even so, on the drive back to his prefab the night before, something extraordinary had occurred to him. Something momentous. And it was actually connected to the dot-to-dots. It tied in.

You see, in some ways, he conceded, Sara had been right, and Ronny too, when they'd said that he should not reject the dot-to-dots so absolutely. He had come to this godforsaken hole to try and discover something complete and absolute and significant in his work, in himself even, something total and real and true. Something *more*.

It had been a mistake. Now it seemed so clear to him. He should never have left what he knew, he should merely have *explored* it a little better. He should have exploited it. All he'd ever needed was a stronger nerve and a new angle.

Suddenly, now, out of the blue, he had one. An exhibition, he told himself, a real exhibition of the dot-to-dots. But proper pictures this time, giant prints, all bold and brassy and blown up. And some would be his way around (all sex, no love) and some would be Sara's way, the silly way. Now that was an *idea*. Photography was only about images, after all, but ideas? Well! Those were about *art*.

Yes. He chuckled. *Art*.

All the way along the beach, just below the high tideline, Lily found a strange collection of knives. The sea had spewed them out on to the low dunes. It seemed to have had no use for them. Lily picked them up, one after the other and clutched them against her bare chest. One of the knives, she noted, actually belonged to her. But while she was tickled by its reappearance, she had no intention of keeping it. Instead she took the knives to Jim's prefab and knocked on the door.

'Ronny?'

She waited then knocked again. 'Ronny!'

After a while, Jim pulled the door open. He was partially covered in mud.

'Where's Ronny?' she asked.

Jim paused. 'Sleeping,' he said softly. He seemed calm but preoccupied.

'Look what I found . . .' Lily showed him the knives.

Jim nodded.

'On the beach!'

He smiled weakly and nodded again.

'Do you want them?'

She offered him the bundle.

Jim hesitated and considered her offer. He decided that it would be churlish to reject a gift so freely given. He took the knives from her. All of them.

'Thank you,' he said.

'I'm going swimming,' Lily confided, 'will you join me?'

Jim shook his head.

'Suit yourself.'

She grinned and then ran off down the beach, yelping like a pup at the feel of broken shells against the bare fleshy soles of her feet.

Jim took the knives inside with him and closed the door. He inspected his muddy trousers. He walked into his bedroom in search of clean clothes. He put the bundle of knives down on his bed and began to undress. He pulled off his trousers, then his T-shirt. As he pulled off his T-shirt he noticed something unexpected on the inside of his arm. A series of white marks. Neat plaster fingerprints. He stared at them, then swallowed hard.

He looked around for some clean clothes. He quickly located a shirt and some jeans. He pulled them on. He inspected the clutch of knives on the bed again. Among them he saw his father's razor. He picked it up and took it into the kitchen. Under the sink he found a plastic carrier bag. He took it back through to the living room and laid it out flat on the floor. He sat down. He rested his two feet on top of it. He inspected the blade. It was sharp as an angry word in a gentle ear.

Connie saw the fire burning from halfway down the drive. Sara was running backwards and forwards with buckets of water.

'What happened?'

'I have a bad feeling,' Sara said grimly, 'that Lily is intent on re-inventing herself.'

'Oh.'

'What smoulders before you is the former Lily.'

'Right.'

'The new Lily is running naked through the fields.'

Connie didn't smile, although Sara had intended her to. She was still holding Ronny's white spacesuit and visor. She bundled it all together in her hands and threw it down on to the flames, happy, at last, to be rid of it.

'Thanks,' Sara muttered.

'What?' Connie glanced at her.

'I'm trying to put it out,' Sara said drily, 'not feeding it.'

She returned to a tap by one of the outhouses, filled the bucket and brought it back again. She tossed it on to the flames. The fire hissed.

Close to the smouldering edge of it, Connie noticed something domed and smoke-stained. It cracked as the water made contact with it, and the dome split in two. There was a little brief spurt of steam but it quickly evaporated. Connie stared impassively into the fire. She could have sworn she saw a tiny, brown-furred puppy-like creature, but many limbed. Standing on its hind legs, with eyes as sweet as cane sugar. She leaned forward. The wind changed direction. Smoke billowed out and the little beast was gone.

'You're too close,' Sara said.

'What?'

'Step back a bit. You're too close. You're dripping.'

'Dripping?'

Connie took a step backwards. She looked down at herself. Oil slid from her fist and on to the gravel driveway. When she opened her hand, all it contained was a small, thin strip of gold foil.

'I have to go now, Sara,' she said quietly, only pausing to rub the oil from her fingers deep and hard into the surrounding skin.

Lily was leaping about in the waves. Connie parked her car, climbed out of it and walked around to the front of the prefab. She knocked. There was no answer. She knocked again and walked in. The living room was empty, the kitchen. She went into the bedroom. Jim lay on the bed, sleeping, covered in a sheet and a blanket.

'Jim?'

Connie walked over to the edge of the bed.

'Are you sleeping?'

His face was so pale. There were tears still wet on his cheeks. She knelt down and kissed them. 'Your face feels so cold,' she said, 'Jim?'

She leaned over to adjust his blanket which was slithering off the end of the bed. As she lifted it, she saw that the bottom of his sheet was drenched with blood. She dropped the blanket.

'Jim?'

She lifted the sheet and saw his two mutilated feet.

'Jim!'

He opened his eyes.

'Look,' he mumbled, 'my arm.' He pointed to his arm. 'Those white marks are where he touched me.'

'What have you done?'

Connie did not look at the white marks.

'I said what have you done?'

'I'm wide open,' Jim said, smiling, 'like a stinking can of worms.'

'Sit up,' Connie spoke calmly.

He considered her request for a moment but then obliged her clumsily.

'I know a doctor,' she said, 'I'll take you there.'

'No doctors.' Jim shook his head.

'It's all right,' Connie said firmly, 'can you walk?'

'I don't know.'

Connie went into the bathroom and returned with a roll of toilet paper. She began to unwind it, then crouched down and rewound it around the ends of each of Jim's feet.

'You were never even in a rain forest, were you?' she asked, almost conversationally.

'Never.'

Jim inspected his wadded-up feet bemusedly. Connie gathered the bloody sheets and stuck them into the fireplace. She found the carrier bag and its grizzly contents. She swallowed hard, picked them up, and added them to the sheets. She put some logs on to the fire and lit them. Her hands were shaking. On the sofa she saw the letters. She took them and burned them, one by one. Then she picked up the razor from the place where it lay on the carpet, ran it under a tap and put it back into the bathroom cabinet.

Through the front window she saw Lily, still swimming about in the sea. She walked back to the bedroom again. Jim sat where she'd left him. He was rubbing his eyes.

'Lily's outside,' she said, 'but she's in the sea. Do you need anything?'

'My hat,' he said. She found a woollen cap and threw it over to him. He pulled it on. 'My shoes,' he said, and pointed. Connie went and picked up Ronny's white shoes. She stared at them, scowling, then handed them over. Jim put them down on to the floor and slowly pushed his two feet into them. Even with the tissues, the shoes almost fitted. He winced, then frowned.

'These aren't my shoes,' he said. And his mind turned back to the bridge and the wasp and the sting. Connie put out her arm to help him up. He let her. His balance was all gone. 'Do you need anything else?' she asked, as they staggered, with difficulty, towards the door. He shook his head. 'No. Nothing.'

She pulled the door open. The wind hit them. Jim grabbed her arm even harder for support. They stepped outside. Lily was swimming far out in the waves. At first she didn't see them. They made their way back, quietly, towards the road and the car.

'Ronny!'

A distant voice, but insistent.

'Ronny!'

Connie let go of Jim's arm. He was suddenly on his own. He looked down at himself for a moment. He wobbled slightly. But he kept his balance. He turned. He saw Lily, waving at him, jumping around in the surf.

'Wave at her, Ronny,' Constance said, her eyes steady and calm on him. Ronny paused, he thought for a moment, then he slowly raised his right hand and waved at Lily with it. Lily waved back at him. Then he smiled, turned, and they both staggered on again.

'Don't you think it's beautiful?' Lily said, inspecting the half-completed back wall of shells. Luke frowned. He was loading stuff into the boot of his car. 'It's just shells,' he said, 'isn't it?'

'I suppose so,' Lily shivered. 'Do you have a shirt I could borrow?'

'You need one,' Luke said drily, 'you're way out of the nudist section. I should call the police. I should have you arrested.'

'Good,' Lily said, 'you'd be doing me a favour.'

Her moon-face split into a grin.

'You have strong teeth,' Luke said, 'but very gappy.'

'You stink like a kipper,' Lily said.

'That's only sex you smell on me,' Luke said, undaunted, 'and it frightens the hell out of you.'

'If that's sex I smell,' Lily said sweetly, 'then take me to a fucking nunnery.'

Luke noticed that she was slowly turning purple. He headed back towards his prefab.

There was a nip in the air. Lily wrapped her arms around

herself. When Luke re-emerged with a spare shirt and saw her, she reminded him of her mother. Of Sara. There was an icy wind blowing. A winter wind. She was facing right into it.

'Do you need anything else?' he asked. 'Because I'm actually very busy . . .'

'Ssshhhhhh!'

Lily pressed her finger to her lips, and turned into the wind again, her eyes glowing.

'What?' he scowled at her. She shook her head and kept her finger where it was.

'What?' he repeated.

I dreamed I saw you dead in a place by the water. A ravaged place. All flat and empty and wide open. And you were covered in some kind of binding. Like a mummy. Something white and reflective, from head to toe.

And the light shone on you. Oh, how it shone on you! It glanced off you, and it was like a pure, bright silver.

The wind was singing. It sang: you have suffered enough. You have suffered enough.

Then death came and he kissed you. Lightly. Gently. Upon the lips. There is nothing beyond, he whispered, only me, only me.

There is nothing beyond.

Only me.

About the Author

Nicola Barker, born in 1966, has written five books, including the short story collection *Love Your Enemies* (winner of the David Higham Prize for Fiction and joint winner of the Macmillan Silver Pen Award for Fiction). She lives and works in Hackney, London.